SHADOWS OF GOLD

SHADOWS OF GOLD

DRAKA BOOK THREE

AvaritiaBona

Podium

Podium

SHADOWS
OF GOLD

CHAPTER ONE

Property

That morning I'd been having a lovely breakfast with all my favorite humans. Tam and Val were back. Their ship had anchored the previous night, and they'd brought an absolute fortune in gold, gems, and silver with them. After a minor detour to the local guardhouse, after I very publicly tore a shipload of harbor pirates to pieces, we had all returned to Her Grace's Favor, my friends' favorite inn. They'd snuck me in through a window, and after a nice, long nap we'd all been in the mood to celebrate our new riches. Rib and Pot, being bona fide aristocrats, had a suite, and we'd filled it with all kinds of delicacies. It had been absolutely goddamn delightful.

Then a guard captain, who may or may not have been in the pocket of our worst enemy, showed up and escorted them all to the authorities.

They hadn't actually been gone long—less than two hours—but in that time I had cooked up all kinds of scenarios in my head, which ended with them dead or detained in some dank cell. By the time I could feel them moving again, I was just about ready to ignore their pleas that I not get involved, and go look for them. After all, I didn't actually know if Mak needed to be alive for me to sense her, and they had been practically still for quite a while. Thus, when I felt Mak coming closer again, and at a pretty relaxed pace, I relaxed properly for the first time since they'd left.

It was pretty telling that when I thought their deaths would mean I got to keep the whole treasure, I *didn't care*. They—or at least Herald, for sure, and probably Mak—were worth more than the contents of that magic box. The reason I had stayed wasn't because I was hesitant to leave the box unguarded, but because I'd promised that I would, to give them a chance to solve things peacefully. If they'd delayed another hour, though, with no word . . .

I traced Mak's path all the way back, and when the door to Rib and Pot's suite opened, I had a ridiculous impulse to throw myself at the door like an overly excited dog. But I maintained my dignity, sitting calm and composed on the floor. Rib and Pot came in, of course, as did Garal and Lalia and Ardek, all of whom immediately started picking over whatever leftovers remained after I'd ravaged the table in my worry and boredom. Of the other four, though, there were plenty of greetings as they passed the door, but only Mak stepped inside. She walked straight up to me, a confused jumble of emotions on her face, and put her hand on my shoulder.

"*Thank you,*" she said in Tekereteki. "*Thank you for your patience. I could feel your anxiety growing. I worried you might do something . . . brave.*"

"*Something foolish, you mean?*" I said.

She smiled. "*Shall we settle on rash?*"

I snorted, and couldn't help but smile. "Rash" would do.

"*We will change out of these stifling outfits and then join you. It will only be a moment,*" she said and left the room.

I could still feel the touch of her hand lingering on my shoulder. Metaphorically, at least; I was literally covered in armor, and any soft touch was a light pressure at best. It took a while for any warmth to seep through. But Mak had been getting more comfortable around me lately, and it was . . . nice. The novelty of having her terrified of me had worn off quickly, and then the quasi-worship to which she'd swung over had been a little disturbing. Over the last week, though, she had been stabilizing somewhere between those extremes. Still deferential, respectful, and possibly a little bit awestruck, but also familiar. Not like Herald, of course. I didn't know if Mak actually liked me, but I was pretty sure that she loved me, in a way, and I cherished that.

"Can you tell me anything?" I turned to the humans remaining in the room.

"They didn't say much," Lalia said, tearing a piece of bread apart with her hands. "Just told us to wait until we got back. Seemed kind of . . . thoughtful, though. All of them."

"They're not in jail, and there weren't any guards going back with us, so aren't they in the clear?" Ardek asked.

"They have the personal attention of one of the justices," Garal said, frowning. "That can't be good."

At that point the door opened and Tam walked in, followed shortly by Val. I tried to get something out of them, but they asked me to wait until the sisters joined us, which didn't take long.

"Great! The whole family's together! Now, can I get some answers?" I said, looking around and trying to make my impatience clear.

Mak didn't need to see or hear me to pick up on it. "All right, Draka," she said. "Sorry that we kept you waiting. Those clothes are as comfortable as a tailor can make them, but that isn't saying much. Yes, you can all get some answers. Here's the summary: the lady justice, while she does not speak for the entire council, does not intend to do anything. Yet. We have not broken any laws, after all, that she knows of or can prove. But that does not mean that you, Draka, are safe to move around openly in the city. As she put it, and I'm sorry for how awful this is going to sound, the law sees you as a dangerous animal."

Well fuck you, too, lady justice. I felt the anger in my toes as my claws dug into the floorboards.

"Easy now," Tam said. His voice was jovial, but his eyes were worried as he looked at me. "We're thinking about buying that floor, you know?"

"*But*," Mak said, continuing quickly, "she made it pretty clear that if a big, dangerous animal were to kill the Night Blossom, no one could really be blamed."

I swung my head back to Mak. "Really don't like you using that word," I growled. Being called an animal bothered me. Their laws didn't concern me much, unless those laws threatened my humans. But to be disrespected like that by one of the rulers of the city, and then have Mak repeat those insulting words back to me—that stung my pride far more than it should have.

"Sorry." She looked honestly apologetic. Not afraid, but upset that she'd hurt me. "I didn't mean—"

"I know. You wanted me to see the silver lining. But I don't need any reminders that this society despises me. I'd prefer to be called a monster, however much I've whinged about that. At least a monster gets some fear and respect." I laid down. Just thinking about it was exhausting. "I'm a person, damnit!"

"You are," Mak agreed as she came and sat on the floor next to me. I could see my own frustration and sadness reflected in her. Herald soon joined her, and then so did Ardek, though he looked a little uncertain and awkward about it. "We all know that," Mak continued, "but the city at large . . . There is too much history, too many half-remembered stories. Maybe we can do something about it? It would take time, but—" she looked around the room. I don't know what she saw, but she didn't look reassured. "Some kind of legal status, perhaps?"

"At the very least, you will always have us," Herald said, scratching the bump where my horn might be growing in.

"I don't need much if I have you guys," I muttered, leaning into the scratches. "But some recognition that I'm as smart as any human would be nice."

"There was a great focus on the letter of the law," Val said. "The lady justice is known for her strict adherence to it. I do not believe that any disrespect was intended, only to emphasize your position. The law makes no mention at all of dragons in this city, so it defaults to the fact that you are not human. A grave oversight, perhaps."

"Yeah, yeah," I muttered. I was a little annoyed at how reasonable his argument was, but it did make me feel a little better. "But you're all in the clear?"

"We . . . are," Mak said. "The lady justice made it very clear that she does not want us connected to anything you might do, so we shouldn't be seen together again if we can avoid it, and you should go on as you have, staying hidden as much as you can. And, while there's no way to tell how fast word will get around, we have to expect some would-be dragon slayers to show up."

I thought about that. Anyone who came after me would do whatever it took to find me, and if people knew that there was a connection between me and my humans, they might go after them for information. No matter how that worked out, it would be bad.

"I want you to deny knowing anything about me," I said. "If anyone asks you, that is. Consider that an order, if it helps," I added, looking at Mak, which got us both some questioning looks from Tam and Val.

"Mak?" Tam asked simply.

She waved him off. "Later. I promise."

I continued, ignoring the interruption. "You don't know where I might be found, and you don't know anything about me. You have no idea why I attacked those harbor pirates. It was pure luck on your part, as far as you're concerned." I looked at Tam, who gave me a careful smile. He did not look at all satisfied with Mak's promise of an explanation 'later', but neither did he argue. "Now, what are your next steps? I'm dying to get my cut of the treasure back to my hoard, so I'd really like to fulfill that promise I made."

"Well," Tam said, still looking at me curiously, "we need to bring the temple of the Three their share, and the sooner, the better. Not everybody loves them"— Val and Herald snorted in weird harmony—"but it'll help our reputation. And it's the right thing to do. A bunch of the money's going to the dead expedition's families, anyway. And then . . ." Tam looked to the others, then settled on Mak. "We all agree, right? We're accepting Reben's offer?"

"We are," Mak said, as Herald and Val nodded. "It's a steal. Crazy not to."

"So you're buying this place?" I asked. I felt a tentative excitement at the idea, and it rid me of the last of my sulking. Them owning the place should make it a lot easier for me to meet people, if I could have a room to myself. Something in the cellar would do nicely.

"Reben's even offered to stay and run it for us!" Tam said. "We looked at his accounts, and he's making money, just not enough. Debts and all, you know? The interest is eating all his profit, and he keeps getting in deeper." He paused. "Ah . . . do you know how loans work?"

I rolled my eyes. It was a reasonable question, since he had no idea that I used to be human, but still. "Yes," I told him. "I know about loans and interest."

"Right. Well, with what we're paying he'll be rid of his debts and have enough for a very comfortable retirement, if he wanted to. But since he's offered to stay, I think he'll put it toward his grandkids. This inn is his life. I doubt he'll ever retire, if he has his way."

"How much are you paying?"

"Two hundred."

Ardek and Lalia's eyes bugged. "Wait, *dragons*?" Lalia asked incredulously.

"This place makes about a dragon in profit on a good month," Mak said. "He could have asked for three hundred and it would've still been reasonable, but with his debt getting bigger, and the fact that we've been so merciful, he decided to accept our offer."

"Still," Lalia said. "Two hundred dragons . . . I doubt I'll see that much money in my life!"

"Hang around this one long enough and you might," Herald said, jerking her head in my direction with a grin.

"That'll still take you, what, seventeen years to make your money back?" I pointed out, and they all stopped for a moment to consider my calculations. Well, except Ardek, who didn't even try and just nodded sagely.

"Without a damned counting frame," Herald muttered.

"Perhaps," Mak said. "But that's only half the point. It's profitable, meaning it's steady money. It's not a bunch of loose coins that need to be kept safe. And, most importantly, it's valuable enough to establish us. Officially, I mean."

"We can get a name!" Herald blurted happily. "We can be a real family! A House!"

I'd heard them talk about that before, when they discussed what to do with their money, but I didn't understand it. "Care to explain to the dragon?" I asked. "You look like a family to me already."

"We're a family, yes," Mak said slowly, looking a little baffled by my confusion. "But if we own enough property we can be a Family."

And then I heard it. I was so used to just understanding that I rarely thought about the words, but what I had thought were two different words for the same thing were actually quite different. There were families, sure, with parents, children, cousins, and all that. And then there were Families, and the word itself had connotations of nobility and rulership, of simply being a better class of people.

"And only *real* families—Houses—have names?" I asked, wanting to make things clear for myself.

"Yes!" Herald said, full of excitement. "We would not just be the family of Makanna anymore; we would be . . . Well, I do not know. We have not discussed it properly yet. It seemed like such a dream that I, at least, have not wanted to bring bad luck upon it."

The others just nodded their agreement.

"And if you buy this place, you'll own enough property?"

"More than enough," Tam said. "Even with Val holding a fourth share of the inn we, the family that Mak is the head of, will own enough." He turned to Val. "And, of course, once we get married, and you become part of the family officially . . ."

"Patience," Val replied, but the smile he gave Tam was so warm that I wondered why they hadn't just done it already. That was their business, though, and I figured they must have their reasons.

"And what does it actually mean?" I asked. "I mean, what's the difference? You clearly care about this very much. Why?"

"Why?" Mak said, still seemingly confused, as though this should be self-evident. "There's the respect, for one. But also, when we have children they could join the high clergy, or become officers in the army or the navy. They could work in the high offices of the city. They could . . . *We* could even, and dear Mercies, I swear I'm not trying to tempt fate, but we could get a seat on the council!"

"And legal charges can be brought, if we find who the Night Blossom is, with a hope of winning," Val added.

There was a snort from Herald. "Val, if we find her, she is dead. If Draka does not get her first, Mak or I will do it. I do not care if she is the richest woman in Karakan, or the head of the council. I will see her die, and I will not risk the law getting in the way."

Her voice was entirely conversational. There was no anger or any other emotion, just a matter-of-fact tone that left no doubt she was entirely serious.

"Kitten . . ." Tam said, his face full of concern. "Surely—"

"She's right," Mak said, silencing her brother. "You don't know what she did. Not in detail. I did not and I will not tell you because I want to spare you. But believe me when I say that we will not be whole again until that woman has suffered for what she's done to us."

No one spoke after Mak's declaration. I didn't actually know if they'd told anyone except me the details of what happened, and I certainly wasn't going to. But I approved of their resolve. I was never going to forgive the Night Blossom or her creatures, and I didn't expect the sisters to do so, either. And as much as I wanted to do the deed myself, I was determined to let them do it, if at all possible.

"Well," Tam said, breaking the silence. "In any case our legal position will be stronger. And we will be able to extend that to our friends, as necessary. And since the investment will make us enough money to live off comfortably, it's an easy decision."

"Makes sense," I said agreeably. "I'm happy for you, but can you take care of it quickly? I *really* want to get back to my hoard for a while."

"I don't see any reason not to talk to Reben today. Right now even," Mak said. "We will need to go with him to draw up the contract and to pay off whoever owns his debt, I suppose, but if you all have time . . ." She looked around the room.

"Neither of us is on duty until tomorrow," Lalia said, volunteering herself and Garal. "We'd be happy to escort you."

"Yeah, no worries, right, Pot?" Rib said.

"Nah. Whenever you're ready," her cousin agreed.

"Then," Mak said, rising from her chair, "I'll go talk to the old man and see if he's still agreeable."

Things moved quickly after that. Reben was apparently surprisingly agreeable, eager to salve his conscience and get out from under whatever crushing debt he had; he was paying more than a dragon in interest every month. They grabbed the red lacquered box with the treasure, after counting out my share and leaving it with me in a small sack, then left. I chose not to follow them. They were going to some kind of government office, then to a money lender in one of the nicer parts of the city. Finally, they were going to the temple of the Three, and then they'd come right back, so I saw no need to worry. Instead I stayed. I felt for Mak's movement, napped, and enjoyed the scent of the rather massive amount of gold and silver I was curled up around. I let it soothe and intoxicate me, thinking about what I would pick when I returned to my nest and inevitably gained an advancement.

Charisma, perhaps? While my existence wasn't common knowledge, exactly, I had shown myself. The authorities knew about me, and being able to talk someone down instead of tearing them apart might come in handy. I might even be able to turn them to my side, which could be incredibly useful. Cunning was interesting, too, since we needed to find our enemy and get at her. And, not to forget, whatever I took would affect Mak, too. Both of those seemed like they'd be more important for her than for me, since she'd be dealing with humans outside of our circle a lot more than I would.

There would also be a replacement of some kind for command, which was impossible to prepare for. I was very curious about what I might be offered next. Knowing me, if it sounded good, I might just grab it on impulse.

And, of course, there was a certain draw to physical greatness, which I did my best to ignore. Knowing that it would strengthen instinct, my draconic side, had slowly gone from a downside to something tentatively attractive, and that was why I needed to *not* take it. The more dragon I became, the more dragon I would want to become. I was sure of it, and I was having enough trouble staying in touch with Conscience, my human side, as it was.

Besides, Herald had made her feelings clear about her little big sister suddenly getting taller. Perhaps not the best way to decide on something this important, but I'd rather not upset her if there were good alternatives.

It was well after dark when they returned, the lockbox rattling and noticeably lighter than when they'd left. "It's done," Mak said, sounding slightly awestruck. "We own Her Grace's Favor."

"Mak and Val do, technically," Herald added. "And the Three-ers have received their share."

"I know we just came back," Garal said to me, then grinned, "but we were hoping to have a drink downstairs with our new hosts."

"Oh, no problem," I said, turning to Mak. "You have somewhere to stash the rest of the money, right?"

"There's a strongroom which . . . It's ours. So, yes!" She smiled brightly. "We can stash *our gold* in *our strongroom* in *our cellar!*"

I grinned back at her, and at the rest of them. "So I've fulfilled my promise, right? I can leave with a clear conscience?"

"You have, and you can," Val said cheerfully.

"In that case, congratulations! You all do whatever you want, have a great time, and I'll be back . . . tomorrow evening, I guess." I grabbed my bag of money and looked toward the window.

"Wait!" Herald said, getting to her feet. "Would you take me with you?"

"Sure," I said, pleasantly surprised. "Shouldn't you celebrate with your family, though? This is a big moment."

"Yes, but . . ." She looked apologetically at the others and switched to Tekereteki. *"I hope to be there when you get your advancement, as I am sure that you will. If that is acceptable, of course."*

I laughed. That was sweet, it really was. And she was concerned enough about keeping my secrets that she'd openly conceal things in front of the others.

I didn't deserve her.

"And here I thought that I had full clearance," Garal said with mock sadness, shaking his head.

I grinned at him, then told Herald, "I'd love to have you along. Meet me in the yard?"

She smacked her hands together in excitement. "Yes!"

"And . . ." I turned to the others. "You all can know. I get my advancements by growing my hoard. I think all dragons do. Not a huge secret, I guess. And this," I said, hefting the bag, "should get me *something.*"

"So that's why you've been so anxious!" Mak said slowly. She had a smile on her face, and there was something hungry in her eyes. She knew. Oh, yeah. She knew. "Come on then," she said to the others. "Let's not keep them."

When Mak started ushering people out of the room she seemed almost as eager as I felt, and once everyone had left the room she turned back to me, key in hand. *"See you tomorrow,"* she told me with a grin and shut the door.

CHAPTER TWO

Power

Flying back to the mountain, my share of the treasure in my grip and Herald's arms wrapped around my shoulders, I was almost giddy with excitement. I flew as fast as I could without freaking Herald out. The faster I flew, the more excited she got, pushing me to add in swoops and climbs and far more turns than necessary just to hear her whoop and cheer.

I set us down on the ledge before my cave, and when Herald climbed off she couldn't stop grinning at me. As I led her into the deep she was giggling and spinning as she walked, talking excitedly about her favorite parts of the flight.

"Promise me that I will never grow tired of that," she begged after she'd calmed down a little, and I turned my head to grin at her.

"If you feel like you might," I said, *"just let me know and I will see what I can do. For now, we should get you some good cold weather gear so I can take you really high."*

"We have the money!" she laughed. *"I would love that. The view is already amazing but . . . could you take me above the clouds? Can you go that high?"*

I had to think about that one. I wasn't sure about air pressure and everything, and how that might mess with her breathing. I was pretty sure that most people who climbed to the top of Mount Everest carried oxygen with them, but the lowest clouds were nowhere near that high, right?

"Let us take it step by step, yeah?" I said. *"Things get difficult up there."*

"You are the expert," she agreed cheerfully.

"What about that unbreakable bow you've talked about? You spent most of your money on the inn."

"I know," she agreed, sighing, then laughed. *"I spent most of my money, and I still have more than fifteen dragons to my name. Fifteen dragons! I could comfortably live for years on that! An impossible dream before I met you. So I am not worried. I have no doubt that my future is golden. I can wait."*

After a pause she added, *"I just might get the bow, unenchanted, though."*

"Or the enchanted arrows," I suggested, remembering the first time we talked about this.

"*Or the arrows,*" she agreed.

And then we were there. The nest was just as I'd left it; I only paused to charge the lightstone before lying down. I stretched myself out with a little mewling sound that would have embarrassed me terribly in front of anyone else, and which fell into a luxuriating, rumbling purr as I rubbed my face in my hoard. Herald just smiled and sat on a pillow, running her hand over some silver coins.

"*So . . .*" she said after a while, looking at me with great expectation and more than a little amusement.

"*Right,*" I said, sitting up and lifting the bag of coins and precious stones that I'd been carrying. "*There is no time like now, is there?*"

"*No,*" she whispered, grinning, waiting with bated breath as I grabbed the bag by the bottom and tipped it over, dumping the contents unceremoniously onto the existing carpet of coins.

The familiar, welcome pressure came, and it built, and built, and built. I couldn't breathe. I was vaguely aware of Herald gasping, a look of awe on her face as knowledge burned itself into me. I had the same choices as before, as I'd known that I would, as well as a new one. Grace—peerless ease of movement in any element. But there was no room in my mind to consider my choices. I went with charisma, which I had already been leaning toward, because that took the least amount of thinking.

I was overcome. Entirely. I had not only reached a minor advancement, I had blown right past it, leaving it far behind and crossing the threshold to the next. And that was my second major advancement. With it came the knowledge that what I could already do—manipulate and shift into the shadows—was only the beginning. I had amassed a hoard worthy of an adolescent dragon. I was no longer a whelp; I was coming into the power that was my birthright.

"*We are shadow, and the shadows are our allies to command, no matter where they lie,*" Instinct's long absent voice whispered in my head. "*We are fear, and fear is our tool to use.*"

Not our only tool, countered the other little voice, the human one that I thought of as Conscience. The same, yet distinct, and which I felt more than heard. *We have reason, and we have mercy, and kindness.*

"*Those who oppose us will fear, and they will suffer, and they will die. Not even sleep will give them respite from our wrath!*"

They will understand their mistakes, and they will regret them. We will show them mercy and give them a chance to seek our forgiveness, Conscience insisted.

There was something like the idea of a snort when Instinct said "*We shall see,*" and I collapsed onto my hoard, sucking air into my lungs as though I had never breathed before.

"Draka!" Herald cried, throwing herself forward and taking my head in her hands. "Draka, are you all right? That was terrifying. Amazing! What happened?"

"Oh, *fuuuck,*" I groaned. "Everything hurts!"

There was a bone-deep ache throughout my entire body, like nothing I'd ever felt before, like I'd been stretched and squeezed and twisted all at once. Skin, muscle, and bone. Head and eyes and teeth and guts, from my snout to the tip of my tail, everything hurt. Even my horn and my claws were in pain.

And why the hell had I been hearing both voices at once?

"You . . . I do not know if there is a word for it, Draka. The opposite of shone? You gloomed. You shaded. Darkled? You did not even shift; it was as though you ate the light!"

"Wow," I whined. "Ace. Absolutely."

"And Draka . . . you grew. I had suspected, from before, but I saw it! Before my eyes, you grew!" Then she chuckled softly. "That might explain the pain. I went through something similar when I . . ." She waved one hand at her own tall body. "Six months of hell, off and on."

"Yeah, so I'm not dying," I muttered. "Wait . . . how much?"

"Hush," she said, laying my head on the bed of coins beneath me. "We can figure that out tomorrow. Sleep, for now. Recover."

I didn't argue with her. I was too tired to pretend that I didn't want to do exactly what she suggested, and the way she stroked my head was so very soothing. "I hit a second major threshold," I mumbled as my eyes grew heavy.

"Of course you did." No one I knew was quite as good at verbally demonstrating an eye roll as she was. "Have I told you how unfair it is that you grow so quickly?"

"Repeatedly. But I don't think . . ." I said, slowly fading out. ". . . don't think people are supposed to just gimme stuff . . ."

And I was gone.

I was dreaming. It was odd, because I knew that I was dreaming the moment it started. There was none of the confusion where most of the dream goes on normally before you realize that, hey, this isn't real! Instead I found myself just hanging in the night sky, watching Herald fly.

She was straddling something immense and black and infinitely powerful. The thing hurtled through the air with her on its back, and she whooped and cheered for it to go faster, higher, and it did! With every stroke of its immense wings, it—I—carried her higher into the starry sky, bringing her to speeds that took us across forests and seas in an instant. I could *feel* her wild excitement, the unbridled joy that she wanted to never end, and I couldn't help but share it, a dumb grin on my face as I just watched her dream.

Because this *was* her dream. I knew it in my bones, a knowledge born of instinct that felt so absolutely true that I didn't even question it.

Is that how she sees us? a voice asked tenderly in my ear, and I didn't know if I should feel proud or flattered or embarrassed at just how superlative Herald's impression of me was.

The other voice was immensely pleased with what it saw. *"The Herald is perceptive,"* it purred, *"and no human knows us like she."*

I felt that, if I only pushed a little, I could have spoken to her. I chose not to. I didn't want to spoil or interrupt her joy with confusion, so I watched her for a little while until the dream seemed to end naturally, and I moved on.

What I saw next was much less clear, and less orderly, but I recognized Jekrie. His dream was a mess of flashing images of hunger, monsters, and fear, of running, always running, never being able to stop anywhere and truly be safe. Which was wrong, of course. He was mine now, though it looked like I needed to make him understand what that meant.

I wasn't sure exactly how I might speak into his dream, but I tried to let instinct guide me.

"You can stop now," I told him, or said to him, at least. "You can rest. Rebuild. Make a life again. You don't need to run. So long as you stay with me, you are safe. I take care of what is mine."

I couldn't tell if I'd been successful, but I'd done what I could.

After I left Jekrie, there was a flash of something. A dimly lit library perhaps, or somewhere else with a lot of books. I saw a tall man who looked familiar, but I couldn't see his face properly. He was sort of blurry, his features shifting subtly. He sat at a desk, trying to read, but his head kept drifting away from the scroll in front of him, looking in the shadows. The whole dream was slippery, and after only a few moments it drifted away from me.

Last, and to my surprise, I found Barro. What I saw was a complete mess at first, so I had to work a little to see what he was dreaming about. When I did, his dreams were . . . interesting. Instinct huffed with amusement, while embarrassment, curiosity, and embarrassment at that curiosity poured from Conscience. "Come to Her Grace's Favor," I told Barro, and then forced myself out of there.

I didn't recognize any of the women in his dream, if they were even real, but there was nothing I needed to see. At least he seemed to be very considerate, even while dreaming.

I wondered why these were the people I'd . . . connected to. Herald made sense. Knowing her, she'd be asleep snuggled up close to me, literally as close as could be. And Jekrie was just down the mountain. But Barro? I didn't even know where he laid his head. Why not Kira, or Mak? I wondered if I could somehow cast about and find someone, and was about to try—

—and I jolted awake as Herald turned next to me. She was lying with her head on my arm, covered by my wing, but she was jerking almost spasmodically, her breath coming in gasps and leaving in whines and moans. Her new dream clearly was nowhere near as pleasant as the one I'd seen.

"Hush, girl," I said soothingly, holding her closer as she continued to kick. "Hush. It's all right, Herald. It's all right. You're safe. I'm here."

Only Herald would be comforted by soft words from a dragon, but it worked. Her movements slowly became smaller, her breathing less harsh, and after a minute or so she had finally passed back into peaceful sleep.

When I joined her I did not return to the dreamscape.

I woke with a strange . . . not quite a hunger. A need that I couldn't name. But I quickly pushed that to the back of my mind when I realized that I was alone. I felt an instant spike of loss, anger, and a sense of something precious missing. I forced it down. Herald, I reminded myself again, was not a thing. She could not steal herself.

I still ached a little, but it was much better than the night before, and I got to my feet. Worriedly, I sniffed the air. The slow, constant draft from deeper into the mountain carried Herald's scent to me, and I followed it, finding her sitting in near absolute darkness where the passage dropped sharply into the deepest part of the system.

And . . . I could feel her, I realized as I approached. Just like Mak. I could still feel Mak in the distance, though faintly. The sisters each had a different feel to them, as distinct as their voices or their scents.

"*It happened.*" Herald didn't turn as I approached, her voice echoing off the walls. "*It finally happened. I am only seventeen, and it happened!*"

She turned halfway around to face me, one leg still dangling, and I could see tears on her face as she beamed at me.

Her eyes shone gold, and she gasped when she saw me.

"*You are so bright! So bright. Like molten gold! You are . . . Gods, Draka, you are so beautiful!*"

"*So . . .*" I began, feeling a little awkward at her words, and with the way she was admiring me. I felt like I should be blushing. Her voice was so full of awe, her face so utterly open and honest, that there was no possible way to doubt that she meant what she said. Together with what I'd seen in the night I swelled with pride and appreciation and just . . . love for my friend. And it had been a long time since anyone called me beautiful, so her words brought up all kinds of emotions. But, looking at her, the morning should clearly not be about me, not with the magic glowing in her eyes.

"*So,*" I tried again, "*you got your major advancement?*"

"*I did,*" she said, her voice high and tight behind her smile. "*Thanks to you. I got it thanks to you!*"

"*No,*" I said. "*I do not believe that. Not after everything you have been through. You are so strong, so resilient. You would have it whether you ever met me or not.*"

"*Not this,*" she insisted. "*Perhaps something else, some other time, but not this. Not now.*"

"*What did you get?*" I asked, but I already knew. Or I thought I did, but my suspicion was strong.

"*Oh! Come, come!*" she said, getting to her feet, full of excitement. She practically skipped to my side, gave me a quick hug—which made me realize that I was now looking *down* on her by half a foot—then just grabbed my wing and pulled me along. Part of me wanted to protest the rough treatment, but her enthusiasm was so infectious that I would have allowed her anything in that moment.

"*I have been up for . . . oh, hours, I think, trying things! Come on, we need light!*"

I picked up the pace, and soon I saw the glow of the lightstone in the distance. The lightstone, which should have burned out by the time I woke up. And I hadn't been the one to charge it.

I smiled sheepishly to myself. I should have noticed that, but I'd been so focused on finding Herald that I hadn't been paying attention. Meanwhile, Herald was speaking rapidly, so excited to tell me what she'd awakened to that she could barely contain herself.

"*It took a little while to figure out the lightstone,*" she said. "*I mean, I knew that I needed to push magic into it, but how do you do that? You cannot learn that from someone else, it is like telling someone to use a sense or to move a muscle that they do not have. So it took almost an hour to figure that out, but I knew that I could do it! I had a dream, oh, gods, what a dream it was. I was with you, and we were flying, and I felt invincible, invulnerable, and you told me that if I followed you into the shadows we would never be apart, and I would have everything I could possibly desire. And it was you, so how could I refuse? And you enveloped me in your shadows, but it did not make me afraid, not like with Jekrie. It made me feel strong, and . . . and loved. And . . . I think that was my advancement! It was not like before, not at all, but I think that was it. And when I awoke, I just knew, and it was dark, and all I had to do was to think about it, and everything . . . inverted? Do you know what I mean? The dark became light! Is that what you see? So I—*"

"*Slow down!*" I laughed. "*Yes, that is what I see, when I use my shadowsight. Now show me!*"

"*Right, yes! Look!*"

And with that, Herald stepped into one of the deep shadows cast by the stone pillars that separated my nest chamber from the passage, and she disappeared.

It was so sudden, so unexpected, that I actually jumped just the tiniest bit. I blinked over to shadowsight, and I still couldn't see her, neither in the light of the shadows or in the darkness cast by the lightstone. I could feel her there, in front of me, and I could smell her, but I couldn't see her at all!

As I watched, the shadow she had entered bent and lengthened before my eyes, until it connected with another, and I felt her move. There was the barest scratch of her feet on the stone as she snuck around behind me, and if I hadn't been able to feel her, I doubt that I would have noticed.

I decided to play along, jumping and whirling around in a way that should be very convincing as she popped out and yanked on my tail.

"*Whoa!*" I cried. She grinned at me, though she looked a little woozy and had to sit down after her display. "*Did you just shift?*"

"*Yes! I mean, not quite, not like you, but it is like . . . When I am shifted it feels as though the shadows hold me, if that makes any sense? I feel safe, almost invisible. Could you see me at all?*"

I shook my head. "*No, not with either my normal sight or with shadowsight. Like you said, as far as I was concerned, you were invisible. There was not even a glow of magic! You just disappeared!*"

"*But you felt me, did you not?*" she said, smiling shrewdly. "*Like you feel Mak. Like I feel you. You are not the best actress.*"

"*Yes.*" I snorted, smiling at being caught. "*I felt you. And I feel you now, just like Mak. But I did not see you.*"

That gave me an idea. "*Speaking of seeing . . .*" I said, and went to fetch the lightstone. Holding it, I said, "*Look closely at my hand,*" then pushed some magic into the stone. I could see it, of course, but when I looked at Herald she didn't act like she'd seen anything.

"*Nothing?*" I asked, and she shook her head. Then I saw her eyes shift, taking on the golden glow that I'd seen before.

"*Try again,*" she said, and this time, when I pushed, she gasped softly. "*Like shadow, flecked with gold,*" she said in a hushed tone. "*Does this mean that I can see magic?*"

"*I do not know for sure,*" I said. "*How about this?*"

I put the lightstone back on the other side of the pillar, then pushed the shadow before me to join with the ones further down the passage, and there was an excited squeal from Herald.

"*Yes! Yes! I saw it! Your shadows moved like a cloud, with a golden lining at the front of them! I can see magic! Draka, I can see magic!*"

Her voice rose to a squeak as she threw her arms around my neck, squeezing so hard that I could barely breathe. If I hadn't known better, I would have thought that she had a strength advancement or two, but in her case it was all hard work and archery practice.

"*Thank you, Draka,*" she whispered. "*Thank you.*"

CHAPTER THREE

Cult

"I *saw you, when you were dreaming,*" I told Herald as we walked up the passages toward the opening in the mountainside. I'd been a little wary of telling her, thinking she might not appreciate my kind-of-but-not-really accidental voyeurism. To my relief she only gave me a curious look. "*As in, I saw your dreams. In my own, I mean. I think that is what my major advancement does. I can see the dreams of those I have touched. Maybe even speak to them.*"

"*You keep surprising me with impossible things.*" There was no condemnation in Herald's voice, and not a hint that she might doubt me. "*Only those you have touched? Like . . . me? Or Mak?*"

"*That is my guess, but I only saw you, Jekrie, and Barro. Although, perhaps it will be possible to see others, with time and practice. It took months to learn that I could project fear with my shadows.*"

"*Then practice,*" Herald encouraged me. "*I have nothing to hide. Not from you.*"

"*It means a lot to me that I know you mean that,*" I said. My worries were gone, and I felt better for having told her.

She smiled and continued. "*I certainly intend to practice. And I hope that you can help me. There is surely no one else alive who knows more about the gift that I have received than you.*"

"*Eh . . . probably?*" I hedged. I might have a mother out there. Or distant family, more likely, considering the centuries that I had been asleep. "*It gets easier with more practice, I know that much,*" I told her. "*If your shadows are like mine, I mean.*"

"*That is good to hear. Moving in the shadows is tiring, but moving them around . . . I thought my head might split.*"

I nodded. "*It was the same for me. It gets better.*"

"*I still can hardly believe that it is real. I have wanted this for so long. Magic, I mean. And now I have it, and it is . . . perhaps not unique, but I have never heard of it before meeting you. I cannot change into shadow like you—*"

"*We do not know that,*" I interjected. "*You may just not know how. I learned by accident.*"

"Perhaps," she conceded, *"but I would say that being invisible within shadows which I can move at will? It is not much worse."*

"And your things go with you," I pointed out. *"Clothes and such. Not much of a problem in my case, but I imagine you would find it a little embarrassing."*

In the inverted light of my shadow vision, Herald's face grew brighter as she blushed. *"Yes,"* she agreed after a short pause, her voice a little squeaky. *"That would have been a problem."*

When we reached the entrance and stepped out into the light, Herald didn't change back to normal sight for a long time. I could still see the gold shine in her eyes as she marveled at how different the world looked, even in sunlight. She didn't speak, just looked around at the forest, the clouds, the shadows cast by the walls of the crack in the mountain that we stood in.

I waited patiently.

"It is so strange," she said after a long while, and smiled at me. *"Like the world ends where the sunlight falls. But I can still see you, do you know that? Even in full sunlight, where I can see nothing else, there you are. As beautiful as ever."* Then she closed her eyes. When she opened them, there was no glow. But something about them was different than I remembered, and I moved in to look closer. As I got close Herald laughed, not at all concerned at having a predator the size of a small horse stick its face in hers. *"Draka, what are you doing?"*

I looked into her eyes in the light, and I gasped. Or rather, I took a short, strong breath through my nose, which was apparently the equivalent reflex for dragons.

"Herald," I said, slipping back into Karakani, "your eyes are gold!"

Because they were. Bright and beautiful. And not just in color. There was a sheen to them, as though her irises had been replaced by rings of burnished metal, glimmering in the sun.

Her face went slack with surprise and confusion, and she slowly brought her hand up to touch the cheek under her left eye, as though that would let her feel the truth of what I'd told her.

"My eyes?" she asked, her voice trembling. "They've changed? My eyes are gold?"

I saw tears forming, and at first I thought that she was horrified. But then . . .

"Like yours?" she asked, and sniffed as the tears spilled over, her mouth drawing into a wide smile. "I have golden eyes, like yours?"

"You do, yeah," I said. "Wait, *I* have golden eyes?"

"Yes, you silly lizard!" she laughed, taking my head in both of her hands. "For as long as I've known you! And your eyes glow when you use the other sight."

"Like yours," I grinned.

"Like mine!" she agreed, nodding enthusiastically. "Thank the Mercies and bless the gods that they crossed our paths in that mine!"

"Thank Tam for losing his shit on some guy who was harassing Mak," I countered, and she laughed. She stroked my face almost randomly, like she wasn't sure what to do with her hands. I probably would have been offended if it were anyone else. It was similar to how I'd sometimes treated my brother's dog in my previous life. Finally, her right hand settled on scratching the bump where my horn had been.

"Speaking of the mine," she said, and giggled softly, "I think your fears are coming true. That horn you lost is definitely growing in again."

"Aw, damn it!" I groaned. "It's going to look so dumb!"

"And who is going to dare make fun of you?" she said, scratching the area where I could now, after she pointed it out, feel a large bump. And, to drive the point home, she tapped something that definitely was neither scale nor hide.

"Yeah, fair," I sulked, resigning myself. "But I'll know."

We spent a few more minutes on the ledge, enjoying the sun, and then I brought her up to the plateau where my stream was for a drink and to take care of other necessities. She was noticeably more comfortable on my back as we flew; I was a little longer now, and the space between my wings had broadened. The growth hadn't come for free, though, and I felt a rumble in my belly, which was strong enough that Herald must have felt it through my back.

"*Do you need to hunt?*" she asked.

"*I will be fine,*" I answered, though the idea was tempting. I had other things to do, and I had gone a little hard on the nearby goats over the past few months. It was better to leave them alone, and I'd rather not go any farther afield. "*I will see if Jekrie has anything to spare, or we will figure something out. I want to see him anyway.*"

I brought us down, landing near the nascent hamlet. I had only shown myself to Jekrie, and a small child who had seen my tail and thought that I was a snake. I asked Herald to go and bring Jekrie and Kira, and she jogged off with a spring in her step that I couldn't help but smile at.

I did not smile when she returned alone, rubbing her neck awkwardly. "*Ah . . . you had best come down,*" she said, looking back the way she'd come. "*You will want to see this.*"

Her whole vibe made me wary. "*What is going on?*" I asked, and she just smiled wryly and shook her head.

"*No, really. You will want to see this.*"

That didn't exactly make me any more comfortable, but this was Herald, so I went with her. We rounded the spit of rock that had screened us from the camp-site by the gate, where a few simple huts had now sprung up as more permanent homes were being built. I stayed hidden as we approached, but I soon realized it was pointless.

Everybody was waiting. Not that there were many of them, but all twelve adults were standing around nervously, plus Kira, who stood apart, looking awkward. Jekrie stepped forward as Herald approached them, asking, "Is she here? Did she come?"

"Yes," Herald sighed, "she came."

Jekrie turned to the trees and the rock, calling out, "Please, Great Lady! Come out! Show yourself!"

Great Lady. I liked the sound of that. But I didn't like how openly he called for me. Not at all.

"*You may as well,*" Herald added. "*He has told them about you. There is no point in hiding from them.*"

That . . . to say that it annoyed me did not do the emotion justice. Who and what I was, was not Jekrie's secret to share. I had chosen to speak to only him specifically because I didn't want the rest of them to know about me. Now he'd gone and run his mouth, and I had a mighty urge to show him just how displeased I was, an urge that I had to fight to control. With only the slightest hesitation I stepped out from the bushes where I lurked. I stalked toward him, my claws tearing into the soil, and as he spotted me I saw his face go from surprise to delight to the realization that I was not at all happy with him.

I heard gasps from the others, but ignored them, and a fearful silence filled the air. I wasn't sure what I was going to do. Something terrible, possibly. But then I remembered his little baby daughter, and his wife, who worried so much, and I forcibly reined myself in.

Instead of doing whatever Instinct would have had me do, I gave Jekrie a piece of my mind. "When I wanted to talk to you," I growled, "I brought you away from the others. Why do you think I did that?"

"Great Lady," he said, holding his hands up defensively, "I—"

I cut him off. "That was a rhetorical question. That means I expect you to keep your mouth shut! The answer is, I did that because I didn't want everyone to know about me. Because I didn't want people either freaking out or doing something stupid. And now you've told everybody?"

Jekrie's mouth moved, but he didn't say anything. He learned quickly.

"Speak!" I hissed.

"Great Lady, I had to!"

"Why?"

"They were afraid!" he blurted, finding his spine somewhere and slowly meeting my eyes. "There were twenty-five of us setting out, and only fifteen now. We are plagued by nightmares and fears that the monsters will find us! I have tried to keep spirits up, but it's been hard, and then last night I had a dream, and I woke knowing, knowing sure, that if we only trusted in you, we would be safe." His back straightened, and his face grew just the slightest bit defiant. "So I gathered all, before the sun rose, and I told them. Please, Great Lady, I meant no disrespect. I only hoped that, in knowing that we have such a great protector, my kin might finally know peace."

I stood stock still, studying him for a long moment. His face radiated honesty and openness. There was fear, yes. He stank of it, as he should. But he meant what he said. And his crime was, in the greater scheme of things, minor. He'd told the people closest to him about me because he believed in me and respected me. I had shown myself to hundreds already. What harm could a dozen more do? I also had to accept that he'd only done it because of something I'd done—either I'd spoken to him, dream to dream, or this was a huge coincidence. And I'd never actually told him not to talk about me.

But it wasn't about that. The problem was that I'd thought that I knew where I had him. Now he'd gone and surprised me by doing something unexpected, and I didn't know Jekrie well enough to trust him.

I sighed and walked past him. "Come on," I told him quietly as I passed. "Let's meet your people."

The other adults were all right there. They'd been listening in awed silence as we spoke. They had seen my displeasure, and now they waited in fear as I approached. But they didn't cower, and they didn't run, and that pleased me. It felt nice. For all that I enjoyed their fear, I didn't actually want it. I didn't want people to flee from me. I would much rather have their respect.

Above all, I wanted their adoration.

One woman stepped forward. I recognized her as Jekrie's wife, and the fear in her eyes was tempered by a silent strength, the strength of a wife and mother who was determined to do what she must to protect her family. She approached within a few feet, her eyes locked on mine. It wasn't a challenge. Not quite. Then she slowly got to her knees, and bowed her head for a moment before raising her face to me again.

"Great Lady," she said, and I liked it just as much coming from her as from her husband. "When my husband said this morning that our protector was a dragon, a mighty creature of legend, I feared him mad. I feared that our flight and the loss of his brother had gotten to him, finally. At best, I thought that he was telling tales, but he has never been one to do so. Now, I see you before me, and it is as he claimed. You are as real and as mighty as he said. Please, Great Lady. I cannot speak for my kin, but I swear that if you keep my child safe, and my husband, I will do all that you ask. I will live or die as you please, if I can rely on you for this."

The wind in the trees, the cawing of crows, the nervous shuffling of feet, and the muted crying of a baby were the only sounds I heard as I looked down at the human kneeling before me. Pride and greed warred with a sudden desire to flee, to abandon this responsibility that I had already accepted, whether the woman in front of me knew it or not. Then, silently, first one, then two, then all of the refugees joined her, Jekrie coming around from behind me and kneeling by her side.

Herald stood beside me, her hand almost possessive on my back. To the side, Kira was a silent observer, her eyes uncertain and her mouth a tight line. Looking from her to the humans arrayed before me I remembered what she had said about dragon worship being outlawed in her homeland, and all that I had heard about dragons and their cults. It was pretty obvious what the scene must look like to her. The question was how she'd react.

"Stand," I said. I tried to sound . . . perhaps not gentle, but at least not intimidating. Looking at them I doubted there was any tone I could take that would set them at ease, but I didn't want them any more frightened than they already were.

They stood. They did it slowly and with a great deal of nervous glances. Most of them waited until Jekrie and his wife were on their feet and unharmed before following suit. But they stood.

"You," I said to Jekrie's wife. "What is your name?"

"Tinir, Great Lady," she answered. "Once of Piter's Clearing. Now of . . . here, I suppose, though it's yet to be named."

"We never did name it, yeah," I mused. "Well, Tinir, I have already promised your husband to do what I can to keep you safe. And I'll repeat that promise to any of you who will swear yourself to me. I don't ask much. Follow my commands if I give any. Live in peace. Keep my secrets, and do what you can to keep what is mine safe. That's about it. I can't guarantee your safety absolutely, and I won't always be here, but the hunting's good and there's far fewer monsters than in the north. Can you agree to that? All of you," I added, sweeping my gaze across the small group.

"I swear it," Tinir said, quickly and with complete confidence.

"As do I," said Jekrie a moment later.

"And I."

"And I."

"And I!"

They all swore. Some hesitated, others seemed eager, and when it was over my small flock of followers had grown by twelve souls.

"Well, then," I said cheerfully, "as you were. Don't let me keep you."

They shuffled their feet and gave each other questioning looks, but no one moved.

I snorted. "You all have things to do, yeah? Houses to build, food to prepare? That's all I ask of you for now. Settle in and survive. Maybe keep an eye to the north when you're out hunting? Go on, now! And don't think I can't hear that baby crying, Tinir. Get on with it!" I snapped the last part, and that got them moving. With respectful nods or touches to the chest, the group broke up and cautiously moved off, and I turned to Kira.

She was trying to sneak away.

"*Kira!*" I called, and she stopped, turning to watch me guiltily as I approached with Herald in tow. "*Let's talk.*"

"*How have you been these past few days?*" I asked her as we walked among the trees.

"*Fine,*" she replied meekly. She was trying to keep her back straight, to come across as sure of herself, but there was something fragile about her.

"*Have you not been lonely with no one to talk to?*" Herald wondered.

"*The people have been kind. And the children do not care so much that we cannot understand each other. I have learned some few words.*"

"*Oh, good,*" I said. "*That is good. So what is wrong?*"

"*Nothing is wrong,*" she lied, with a tremble in her voice.

"*Kira*," Herald said, a warning in her voice as she flanked the woman and hemmed her in between the two of us. "*Please. You look ready to run. What is wrong?*"

Kira looked at me to her right, then Herald to her left. Her eyes flicked to Herald's, and she stopped.

"*What is wrong?*" she said desperately. "*What is* right? *I am far from my people and my friends, by no fault that I can admit of my own! The children have been lovely and the people kind, but I cannot talk to anyone! And now they . . .*" Her voice hitched, and she swallowed thickly before she managed to continue. "*They fell on their knees before you. You spoke to them like a queen! And you!*" She turned to Herald. "*Your eyes . . . your eyes are like hers. Like Draka's. What am I supposed to think?*"

Herald bristled at the accusation in Kira's voice, and I quickly spoke up. "*What are you afraid of, Kira? Tell me! Let me put your mind at ease!*"

"That is *what I am afraid of!*" she exclaimed, wrapping her arms around herself. "*I have seen how they act around you. Herald. Makanna. Jekrie and others. And I can feel—*"

Her voice broke, and tears streaked her face as she closed her eyes.

"*I can feel that my thoughts are not my own anymore. Not entirely. Even this, now! I should not be telling you my fears so openly, but I cannot help myself! When I was bonded, at least I had my mind! I could think whatever I wished about the one who held my bond! Now even my thoughts are held captive. Do you understand? I am not myself, and yet I am myself enough to know that!*"

I stood there, like an asshole, as Kira broke down into dull, despairing tears. Herald wrapped her arms around the much smaller woman after a moment's hesitation, and Kira barely reacted, but I just stood there, paralyzed. I was torn between smug satisfaction, disgust, pity, confusion, searing shame, and guilt, with competing desires to comfort her and promise her that everything would be all right, or to command her to get out of my sight.

I didn't know what to do, and so I did nothing.

CHAPTER FOUR

Archer

'm sorry," I heard myself say in Kira's vulgar dialect of Tekereteki. *"I never meant for that to happen, but I knew that it might. And I don't know if I can do anything about it."*

It had been a few minutes. Kira had gone from standing stiffly, merely allowing Herald to hold her as she cried, to returning the embrace and full-on burying her face in Herald's chest as her body was wracked by sobs. She'd finally cried herself out, and Herald stroked her hair as she breathed shakily.

"That's all right," Kira whispered, then looked close to tears again. *"No. I take it back. It's not all right. I know that it's not all right. That's how I feel, but it's not how I should feel. Don't get me wrong. I'm grateful that you spared my life, and for giving me what limited freedom I have. But my mind . . . It's terrifying. I can't feel anything toward you except gratitude and forgiveness, and it's terrifying!"*

"Do you want to hate me?" I asked.

"No."

"Do you want to be angry with me, or disappointed?"

"No, I don't."

"Do you want to feel anything bad about me, at all?"

"You killed almost everyone I could tolerate in that company," she whispered. *"And whenever I think of it I tell myself that I shouldn't judge you. That you were justified. That's not right."*

"They were mercenaries, who killed indiscriminately to cover up the fact that they were enslaving innocent people. Was I not justified in killing them?"

Kira closed her eyes, and a few stray tears escaped. *"They were still the closest thing I had to friends."*

I sighed. *"Yeah, I can see how that makes a difference. For what it's worth, I'm sorry for what you've been through. Not for my part in it, but you didn't deserve all this shit."*

"Can you just . . . take the rest of my mind?" she asked, opening her eyes and looking at me with a heartbreaking glimmer of hope. *"Make me content to serve*

you? If I must know that part of my mind is not my own, I would rather not care about it."

I shook my head. *"I don't think it works that way, Kira. This isn't anything I do consciously, yeah. It just happens. I mean, there's something I could try, but . . ."*

"Please. Whatever it is, please try it. If you can't undo whatever this half-domination is . . . I know that I should fight you. That I should try to break free. But I'm tired, and I'm not brave enough. Please, try it."

"I think I understood some of those words," Herald said, still calmly stroking Kira's hair. *"Care to fill me in?"*

"Whatever she has done to you," Kira said, looking up at Herald, *"I want it. I do not want to care that I cannot hate her."*

"Oh, Kira," Herald sighed. *"You do not understand. I do not care that I cannot hate Draka, but it is not because of anything she has done to me. It is because she has been my friend since the day we met, and I love her. I would not wish to hate her, even if I could."*

"But she said that there was something she could try! I . . . Please!"

Herald looked at me and said, *"The shadows?"*

"Yeah," I answered. *"It might work."*

"I would not," Herald said, shaking her head gently. *"Kira, that would not make you happy. It would make you too terrified to dare hate her. That is not what you want."*

"Then there is no hope for me," Kira said, looking somehow even smaller.

"Sure, there is," Herald said brightly. *"You only need to get to know her. You have mostly seen her wrath. You have not seen how caring she can be, and how generous, and kind. Yes, really! She can be unbelievably selfless! And you should spend more time with those who call her 'friend', those of us that you can speak with."* She turned to me. *"We could take her with us to the city, could we not, Draka?"*

"I could fly carefully," I said, considering. If Kira wanted to return to Karakan with us, I didn't mind. We could leave her at the inn, and she could go out with the siblings. Nobody there knew who she was besides Lalia, Rib, and Pot, and I doubted that any of them would say anything.

"You would have Mak and myself to talk to," Herald said before Kira had a chance to reply, *"and Tamor, our brother! His Tekereteki is . . . well, it is terrible, to be honest, but it would be good for him to practice."*

"What if I were to run?" Kira asked, but it sounded more like she said it out of some sense of duty than actual desire.

"Where would you go?" Herald countered. *"There are only a handful of people in the city who speak Tekereteki, unless you count the visiting merchants. But would you approach them? I do not think so. Because you could be free, Kira. This 'being bonded' that you speak of, it does not exist here. You would be a foreigner, yes, but you would be our guest, and I doubt that anyone would bother you. If they did, you could claim to be a refugee, like my parents. What do you say?"*

"*I would still be a captive,*" Kira objected, but there wasn't much conviction in her voice.

"*No more than you were with the mercenaries. And your companions would be much kinder, and the food much better. And if it does not work out, I am sure that Draka would be happy to bring you back here.*"

"You don't think that she'd run?" I asked, switching to Karakani.

Herald snorted softly. "No, I do not. If she feels what I have felt, and what Mak and Ardek feel, she cannot. She is only talking about flight because she feels that she should. And possibly because she is miserable out here. Have you noticed how much she loves to talk? It must be torture for her. Besides, how much damage could she do, if she managed to go through with it?"

"She could tell someone about us," I pointed out. "It's one thing for one person on the council to know, yeah? And whoever Sempralia chooses to tell, I guess. It's something completely different if it becomes common knowledge that you're friends with a dragon."

"No one would ever believe that we were friends on the word of one foreigner, but it makes no difference. I do not believe that Kira could betray us. Not now. She cannot run away, I am sure of that, and she cannot speak ill of you. I would be amazed if she could do anything to harm you, and that includes harming people close to you."

I thought about it for about half a second. "In that case . . ." I said, and switched back to Tekereteki, "*Kira, if you want to come, take whatever you have that you would like to bring. We will leave as soon as you are ready.*"

"*Will we fly?*" Kira asked.

"*Until the edge of the forest, we will,*" I said. "*Is that a problem?*"

"*I suppose not,*" she said, sighing. "*It was not so bad once I knew that you would not drop me.*"

"*Allow yourself to enjoy it,*" Herald said, smiling wide just thinking about it. "*If you only trust her, flying is marvelous! How many can say that they have seen the world from so high? Do you understand how privileged that makes you?*"

"*Perhaps you are right,*" Kira said, though she didn't sound convinced. "*I admit I did not look much, and it was quite dark much of the time. I can try, I suppose.*"

"*We are in no hurry,*" I said. "*I will try to go slow, so that you can look around and will not get too cold. Now, get your things. Say goodbye to the children, maybe? We will be here.*"

It took Kira only minutes to gather what little she had. It was a little bag holding some simple gifts, she told me. A pair of fur-lined moccasins, a carved bone comb, practical things like that, gifts given in exchange for looking after the children, for helping with simple tasks, and for healing the many small scrapes and injuries that the refugees had either brought with them or accrued while building their simple shelters. She had clearly made no secret of her talents, and it seemed to be in her nature to help. My followers looked genuinely sad to see her go, and it was easy to see why.

If only they could speak with each other, she might have been happier, I told myself, and decided that I should bring her back once she learned some Karakani. Any idea of handing her over to the Wolves or the authorities was long gone. As I'd told the humans, I was keeping her. Anyone who wanted her would have to fight me. I just had to remember that she was a person with her own feelings and dreams and desires, and that was hard sometimes. It was the same with Ardek, although I had spent more time with him and had seen that he could be useful. It probably wasn't fair, but that made him a little more important to me, let him take up a little more space in my mind. The simple solution was to do the same with Kira—keep her around me, and let her be useful.

And if that made her feel better, I certainly wouldn't complain. She didn't deserve what had happened to her. It wasn't like she could have stopped her companions from doing what they did, capturing magic users and killing entire villages to cover that up. It wasn't even really like she could have helped the captives escape, not with a company of horsemen following them. She'd done what she could to help and to comfort, and I'd put her through hell simply because she'd been the only one to surrender. I could tell myself that I hadn't known at the time; that I hadn't had the full picture, and was doing what I felt was right based on what I knew. But that wasn't much of an excuse. Being an asshole due to faulty assumptions was still being an asshole.

I didn't blame myself for what had happened to her, but as I got to know her I wished that I'd acted differently from the start. Kira deserved to be happy. The least I could do was give her a chance.

I had Herald and Kira follow me to the top of the cliff overlooking the gate. The village below stopped to watch and point as Herald climbed on my back. Kira stood before me. I wrapped my arms around her chest, and she locked her hands under mine, keeping her securely in place—we'd figured that out once when I braked too hard and she'd slipped forward—and then I leapt from the cliff.

We fell forward in a long glide, my locked wings taking us over the small settlement before I began beating, taking us slowly higher until we were a dozen feet above the tallest trees. As I felt the wind under my wings I had an impulse to go north, but shook it off. We needed to get back to the city.

It was the middle of the day, and I wanted to stay low to minimize the chance of being spotted. Kira was less stiff in my arms than she had been on previous flights, and as slow as I was going I thought I heard her saying something. I strained to hear, and I realized that she was repeating, over and over, slowly and calmly like a mantra "She won't drop me. I can fly. I am not afraid. She won't drop me . . ."

Herald, of course, was laughing and cheering. Not as much as usual, since I was trying to make this particular flight as unexciting as I could for Kira's sake, but I doubted that I could ever take Herald into the air without making her half delirious with joy. After a while she contented herself with relaxing into my back. I felt her chin resting on my neck as she looked ahead.

"How are you doing, Kira?" Herald shouted down to my other passenger when we were about halfway to our destination.

"Not bad!" Kira shouted back. *"You were right! It is more enjoyable when I relax!"*

*"See? I thought—*Draka, ahead!"

Herald suddenly cried a warning, and I saw what she meant just in time. There was a figure clinging to a tall tree before us, and I only spotted it by the glint of gold as it released an arrow from the large bow it was holding, which shone as it streaked right for us. I dove and rolled to the side, but I wasn't fast enough. Pain shot up my leg as the arrow lodged in my thigh, and I bit down on a scream.

A mix of rage and relief washed over me. A magic damned archer! At the speed the damned arrow was going it went right through my scales, but I could take it. If it had hit Herald . . . Hell, it nearly did hit Kira!

I wasn't sure what to do. I wanted to fight. All of me—Instinct, Conscience, and whatever in-between part that was uniquely *me*—wanted, oh so badly, to fight, to tear this arrogant fool to pieces and feast on their innards, but I couldn't. I had Kira in my arms and Herald on my back, and I couldn't fight our attacker without risking both of their lives. So, as much as I hated it, I decided to flee.

I passed the tree with the archer as they were readying another arrow. I caught a glance of a wiry build, a wildly swirling sphere of light in their chest, and an androgynous face surrounded by long, curly, brown hair as I tore past. Then I flew as fast as I could, staying low and juking repeatedly. I was rewarded by the next arrow missing, a streak of light vanishing ahead of us, passing within inches of me despite my evasive flying. Even when I was sure that we must be out of range of even the most advanced archer, I kept my speed up, heedless of the pain, the burn in my muscles, and the way Kira tensed in my arms.

"Fucking tree-humping piece of shit! Magic-slinging bag of dicks! Are you two all right?" I growled, looking between my two passengers, frantically searching for any sign of injury I might have missed.

"No!" Kira screamed. *"I am not all right! Someone tried to kill us! You're hurt! How could I be all right?"*

"Fine, but are you hurt? Injured?"

"No!" she replied, but even while shouting she managed to sound fragile and terrified. I tightened my grip on her. It was the only thing I could do to try and reassure her at the moment.

"What about you, Herald? Tell me that you are not hurt!"

"I am fine," she replied tersely. She'd been silent since the first arrow flew. It took a moment, but then she blurted, *"How fucking dare he! How dare that bastard ruin such a lovely flight for us!"*

"Did you get a good look at him?"

"No one I recognized," she answered bitterly. *"Tall and thin, narrow face, full lips, bushy eyebrows. Long hair. Think I saw some stubble, but it could have been the shade. I was too busy staying on as you dodged to look much closer."*

"Yeah, sorry about that!"

"*Better than an arrow in the gut! And I might recognize him if I saw him again!*"

I flew on. I could handle the pain. What scared me was when the pain started to fade.

"*Kira!*" I called down. "*You're going to need to hold on tight! My leg's going numb!*"

"*Numb?*" she called back. When I looked down I saw her hand on my leg by the arrow, and though I felt nothing it was wreathed in light.

"*You're poisoned! A curse on their filthy fucking soul, that bastard poisoned you! But I can't do anything until the arrow comes out! You have to land!*"

Against Kira's protests I kept going, putting a dozen or more miles between us and the archer before I landed in a meadow near the southern edge of the forest. Kira had to steel herself before I dropped her the last few feet, rolling in the grass as I carefully made the most graceful landing I could manage. Herald still had to bail as my numb leg buckled beneath me.

"That needs to come out, now," Kira pronounced as I lay on the grass, going fully into her role as a healer. I was numb to the hip at that point and felt nothing as she pulled gently on the arrow. "Stuck firm. We'll need to cut it out."

Getting the arrow out was deeply unpleasant. It wasn't too deep, but it was barbed, and neither Herald nor Kira could cut it out due to how tough my scales and hide were. So, it fell to me to dig it out with my claws. The damned Mercies be blessed that it was a numbing poison.

Finally I had made enough of a mess of the wound that Herald, with one foot braced against my leg, could pull the arrow out. It was accompanied by a gout of blood that stopped almost instantly when Kira pumped magical healing into me, and she was going all out from the look of it. There was only a moment of pain between the poison being neutralized and the magic numbing the pain.

"*Great job, Kira,*" I told her after she broke off, panting and slightly unsteady where she sat next to me. I truly meant it. She hadn't hesitated, and she'd done everything she could. "*Thank you. Truly.*"

"*My . . . my pleasure,*" she panted, smiling weakly. "*Love to help.*" Then she passed out.

I believed her.

CHAPTER FIVE

Barleans

We rested for a while, but once Kira looked strong enough for the walk to the city I got up, careful not to put too much weight on the healing leg.

"All right," I said to them both once I had their attention. *"I will make my way in on my own. Do not ask me how. Trust me, you do not want to know. Keep to the main streets, and I will try to find you."*

"You need to rest!" Kira protested. A plea, not an order.

"I need you two in the city, and I need to go with you and keep you safe," I countered, and she just gave me a pleading look before looking away, shaking her head.

"Do not worry, Draka," Herald said. *"There is no need for you to take a risk like that. We will make it safely back to the inn without you hovering over us."*

"But the—" I began, but Herald cut me off.

"The Night Blossom does not even know that any of us are out of the city, nor is she stupid enough to try to abduct us or have us killed in the middle of a busy street. If you were so worried, you should have waited until night, but you did not, because we both know that it is not necessary. And the archer was after you. Be careful, take it slow, and we will see you at the inn. Go! We will be fine!"

I wanted to protest, but I couldn't. I knew that she was right. I was the danger magnet, not them. I still snorted and pawed the ground, my claws digging frustrated furrows in the loamy soil as Herald watched me patiently, Kira with worry, until I realized what I was doing and stopped out of sheer embarrassment.

"Are you done?" Herald asked, looking entirely unimpressed with my little tantrum. When I didn't answer she continued, in a much gentler tone, *"I know that you worry about me, Draka, about all of us, but you can be overly protective and you have just been hurt. If you are seen near me . . . Think about that. We may be safer in the long run if you do not follow us on the street. And you can always find me, now, right?"*

"I suppose I can, but what if—"

"I have my sword and my dagger, and Kira, if anything goes wrong. But nothing will. Again, whoever shot at us today was after you; we all know that." She sighed.

"Think instead about what to do if he got a good look at me and returns to the city telling tales of a dragon carrying a Tekereteki woman on its back."

Damn. I hadn't even thought about it that way. They'd hurt me, and they might be a danger to my humans simply by running their mouth! *"I'm going to tear that bastard's lungs out,"* I growled.

"We need to figure out who it was first, and who he is here with. I doubt that he is alone. Luckily, we just happen to own a popular adventurers' inn! Which is where we will meet, if you would just stop worrying about us and get going."

"You know," I grumbled, *"sometimes I wish that you were a little more obsequious, like Ardek and Mak and . . ."*

"And me," Kira filled in awkwardly.

"Yeah."

"No, that would make you miserable," Herald said happily. *"Mak is nearly back to her old self, and you love it; we both know that. You would hate it if no one challenged you. Which is something you should learn, Kira! She does not mind, as long as you are being thoughtful and reasonable."*

Kira looked at the two of us in doubtful silence, then said, hesitantly, *"You really should rest that leg."*

I looked at Herald, the traitor, my closest friend. Helping Kira find her backbone? How could she do this to me?

"Now, it is time for us to go. Draka, please, do not follow us around. I will know, and I will be disappointed with you. Come on, Kira."

With that Herald gave me a fond pat on the neck, then put a hand on Kira's shoulder and led her off in the direction of the road, talking softly about what the other woman should expect.

I hated how right she was. When I forced myself to be reasonable I agreed with almost everything she had said. But in many ways she was still my greatest treasure, my most prized possession, and the urge to watch her, to guard her jealously, to keep her safe from those who might harm or, well, *steal* her, was strong. Not too strong to overcome, but always there, like a persistent intrusive thought or a song stuck in my head.

With that on my mind I took to the air. I briefly toyed with the idea of letting Instinct take the wheel, of flying back toward the northwest to hunt the pathetic creature that had dared challenge me, to attack me, to threaten the well-being of *my* Herald and of an invaluable follower. Oh, such terrible things I would do to them, and anyone unfortunate enough to have been so stupid as to associate with them. I would—

I would wait. I forced myself to believe that. I would be careful, and patient. There was almost no chance of me finding them, except in the form of an arrow or three fired from the forest floor as I flew over. No, I would return to the city, as I had said. I would focus on the Night Blossom, and on keeping my humans safe, and on trying to make Kira feel like her life was at least tolerable.

And *then* I could do terrible things to the archer. It was important to have something to look forward to, after all.

I flew straight for the coast, keeping my eyes open for sails. Again I felt that pull north, and again I ignored it.

I was heading for the sewer entrance, and I didn't want anyone to see me go in there if I could help it. There were a few ships going up and down the coast. I knew that the waters near the city were well trafficked, and it was full daylight, so I had expected that. It still annoyed me, since it forced a delay.

I landed before I reached the cliffs and crept up to the edge, finding a good place where I could shift and drop over the edge without too much effort. Sneaking around felt like a step backward, but I knew, rationally, that it was the right approach. To my delight I found it far less difficult to shift than I'd expected. The shadows responded almost eagerly, a dark pillar from one of the few trees along the cliff reaching out and wrapping around me easily, despite the afternoon sun, letting me glide smoothly down to the waterline. Not only had my second major advancement let me mess around in some kind of dreamworld, but it had made my old, familiar abilities easier to use, and I absolutely loved it! No more headaches!

Of course, knowing me I'd just find a new, painful limit to push. But, fewer headaches!

I remained shifted as I moved down the coast, and not only was it less tiring, but I was moving noticeably faster than I was used to, as well. It still took over half an hour to cover the two miles or so to the sea cave, but a brisk walking pace or slow jog was much better than anything I had managed before. Hell, along the stones and water of the rough shore I would have never been able to go even that fast by foot, so as far as I was concerned, my second major advancement was a great improvement, with or without the dream stuff.

The sewer drain was just as horrible as ever, and I shifted back briefly well away from it to rest for a short while before entering. With my wound I definitely wouldn't have tried this a few days ago, but with some experience I felt confident in my ability to get through the sewer without shifting back halfway. And I did it! I vaguely remembered the way to enter into the storm water system and got there a lot more easily than the first time. By then it felt like Herald was somewhere in the city, so with a need to assert myself, I headed for her. I followed along as best I could; the tunnels were mostly straight, but the roads weren't, and I had to move in a kind of zig-zag pattern to keep up, occasionally squeezing through narrow connecting tunnels. Again, I noticed how an aspect of my shadow magic had become a little easier to use, and a little more effective. It took much less effort now to squeeze through the narrowest pipes I'd managed before, despite my body being physically larger than it had been.

I did stay in the tunnels. I had promised, after all. I took it easy, and I kept my weight off the leg as best I could. It wasn't at all that I was worried about making Herald mad or disappointed; I was just serious about keeping my promises. That and nothing else.

I followed along until I felt that Herald and Mak were close to each other. At that point she and Kira were as safe as they could be away from me, and I decided to give them some space. As nice as it might have been to hang out in the cellar, they'd just bought the place, and I was sure that they had plenty of things to sort out.

Besides, I was nowhere near done exploring the tunnels under the city. I'd found a couple of access points to the surface, presumably secret ones, and I wanted to know where they led and who used them, and if there were more. There was also the sea cave I'd found connected to the tunnels, and presumably whoever used that also used at least one of the entrances.

I checked the entrances I'd found, trying to look closely for signs that someone had been through recently, but had no luck. Although they didn't look abandoned, there was no sign that anyone had been through in the last few days or longer.

I briefly considered breaking open the hatch of the first entrance I'd found but decided against it. If anyone was there, it would definitely alert them, and then they might abandon the place. Until I had a pressing reason to risk that, I'd rather wait and see. Instead, I systematically scoured the tunnels for more entrances. I already knew that would take more than one day, with all the miles and miles of tunnels I had to cover—I could do maybe three miles an hour, stopping to check every intersection and connecting pipe. But it stirred my curiosity, and it might be useful in the future, both for myself and my humans. Being able to get around covertly might be a lifesaver one day. Sure, it wouldn't be a fun experience for someone tall, like Herald, but Mak might be able to walk upright, or at least not need to bend so much as to be uncomfortable.

So that was how I spent the rest of my day. Walking up one tunnel, then down another, carefully checking every turn and every nook and cranny in case there was something interesting or useful there. All the while I did my best to keep track of Herald and Mak, trusting that they and the others were keeping each other safe. They didn't always stay put, going out twice for short excursions of some kind, but they stayed together in both cases, going to wherever it was, not staying for too long, and then returning to the inn. I kept fighting an urge to turn back, to return to the inn to check on them, but I fought it down pretty admirably, if I do say so myself.

I was happy with my day's work—even though I'd only found one new entrance in the hours I'd spent—and was returning to the inn when I heard voices echo through the tunnels. I had meant to return to the humans, but here was an opportunity I couldn't very well miss.

"Come on, come on, quickly now," said a hushed voice ahead of me. It sounded like a woman. Her voice was low and a little scratchy, and she was speaking in Barlean.

"Are you sure you know where you're going, Auntie?" said a younger-sounding male voice, as soft footsteps echoed down the tunnel. I slowly crept closer to the source of the sound. Up ahead was an intersection, and it sounded like they were coming from the left, which would be . . . southwest, I thought.

I saw a weak flickering light in the intersection, growing brighter as the steps grew louder. "Do I know . . . Of course I . . . I am sure, boy, I am sure! Now come on, it's . . ."

I crouched the best I could in the cramped tunnel, about fifty feet away from the intersection. Crouching didn't actually do much since I practically filled the tunnel, but it felt easier to stay still and quiet that way. I could have shifted, of course, but that distorted my senses too much, and I wanted to be able to clearly hear what they said.

Of course, they had to go and make things difficult for me. Two people, crouching under the low ceiling, crept into the intersection. The first was a woman, perhaps in her forties, with the wrinkles of someone who squinted and smiled a lot. She held a torch which she swung left and right, looking nervously in my direction but obviously not seeing me, judging by the lack of screaming. After her came a teenaged boy carrying a large sack. He looked tired and frightened.

"It should be this way, it should be," the woman said, half to herself, and I barely had time to shift as she moved my way. I tried to back up and realized, for the first time because I had never *tried*, that I couldn't move backward. As long as I was shifted it was forward or nothing, and I did the only thing I could think of. I called up the thickest shadow I could, to beat out the light of the woman's torch, stretched myself to touch them as little as possible, and I surged forward and past them.

The woman yelped and dropped her torch, its flame nearly smothered as I moved. The boy took a single, sharp breath and stood paralyzed. I made it to the intersection and turned around to watch them. It took several seconds before the woman snatched the torch up with a shaky hand and stood, speechless and turning, looking up and down the tunnel.

"Auntie," the boy moaned, his voice shaking, "did you feel that? What *was* that?"

"I don't know, boy," she whispered, her eyes wide as she stared into the darkness, almost straight at me. "I don't know. Nothing. An ill wind. It must have been nothing. But we have to keep on moving. Come, quickly now."

"Yeah," the boy agreed. "Let's get out of here. Let's get out!"

Now that I had a second, and something to look at and listen to, I realized that things were much less distorted than they had been before when I was shifted. There was still no smell, and thank the Mercies for that, because I would have discovered that very quickly as I moved through the sewer. But while everything was still slightly out of focus, and sound was still distorted, it was nothing like I was used to. I could actually see some small level of detail and hear a little of the nuance in their voices, which was fortunate considering how important tone and cadence were in Barlean.

The two were scrambling up the tunnel as fast as they could go, though Auntie stopped at every side tunnel, looking for something. I had no idea what. Meanwhile, I quietly glided along behind them, wondering what the hurry was. Well, not now. Now they were terrified and wanted to get out, but before. I was pretty sure that they were smugglers. They were coming from the harbor, carrying a sack of . . . something, and while they were decently dressed, that didn't mean much. So why the rush?

After half a mile Auntie found what she was looking for. "Here, here!" she said hurriedly and turned into a connecting tunnel, the boy close behind. "Help me, now!"

I followed and saw the two removing loose stones from the wall, revealing an opening like those leading to the small chambers I'd found. This one was new, though, and I gave silent thanks to the two Barleans for the help.

"In here. Quickly now, boy, quickly. Then climb the ladder, and open the hatch in the ceiling."

There wasn't even a chamber here, just a break in the wall, a narrow tunnel, and then a shaft with a ladder fixed to the wall. I followed only a few feet behind them, close enough to see the fear and confusion in Auntie's eyes when she briefly turned around and couldn't see the end of the short passage she was in. The boy scurried up the ladder easily, still holding onto the bag, and pushed on the hatch. It moved an inch at most, then stopped, and he tried harder but nothing happened.

"It's stuck, Auntie! It's stuck!" he hissed, looking down at the woman.

"Slide it, boy! Slide!" she hissed back. He tried again, and there was a soft scraping noise as the hatch moved aside.

"Depths swallow this . . ." he grumbled, and there came another scraping sound. "There was another one. And a rug!" Then he disappeared up through the hole.

His auntie followed, climbing as easily as the boy had, even with the torch in one hand. I didn't even hesitate. I followed them up into a small room containing only a simple bed and a nightstand, slipping through the opening behind her while she blocked the boy's view of me. I still saw her shudder and look back, but there was nothing to see. She closed both hatches with a jerk, then turned around in the small room, a nostalgic look coming over her.

"This is right, yes, this is right," she whispered. "The door, gently, now!"

The door had a simple wooden latch. It stuck when the boy lifted it, but he gave it a couple of careful strikes upward with the heel of his hand. On the third the latch jerked into the up position, and the door swung open, smoothly and without even a creak.

The boy crept out, disappearing around the corner, and for about fifteen seconds there was no sound but his soft steps. Then he said, softly but not quite whispering, "There's no one here, Auntie. There's no one."

Auntie exhaled heavily and walked out of the small room, relaxing a little for the first time since I'd seen the two.

"Oh, it's just as I remember it, it is," she said, her voice thick with the memory of days long gone.

"You really lived here, Auntie?" the boy asked, looking around skeptically. "On land?"

"I did, I did," she said with a soft, bright laughter that made her sound twenty years younger. "For three years I was lost, I was, never setting foot on ship or boat, only feeling the breeze and the salt from the shore. Unimaginable to you, I know. But I was in love, and that was how long it took to make a sailor of your uncle, it was. But he never sold the house." She sighed, that brittle mirth in her voice replaced by sadness. "It's mine now, I suppose."

She sniffed once and wiped quickly at her eyes, then took a key out from a small pouch at her belt. "But that is enough of an old woman's nostalgia, it is. Come. We have a delivery to make, and a debt to settle, we do!"

CHAPTER SIX

I Am the Night

The boy looked around the small, dusty room some more while Auntie unlocked the door. So did I. There wasn't much. A fireplace that doubled as a stove, with a metal plate on top, and some racks for pots and pans around it. A table with two chairs. Some empty shelves. Besides the small bedroom, there was a tiny toilet, the door hanging open, and another door which was closed, and which I couldn't open without shifting back. The main room had a single, empty window, shuttered and barred from the inside.

"Come now, come," Auntie said, having opened the door, and the boy walked past her out the door. She quickly followed, closing the door behind her and leaving me alone, but I wasn't done with them. I intended to see where they went. I had no pressing reason to do so; I wanted to know where in the city I was, sure, now that I knew that this particular entrance to the tunnels was in a mostly abandoned house, but the two Barleans were nothing to me. But I was curious, so I decided to follow.

I shifted back into my body only long enough to lift the bar on the window and let it swing open. I looked around, then slipped out and quickly closed the window the best I could, then shifted back into the shadows and out into the street. It wasn't completely dark yet, but it was getting there, and there were few people out. I looked up and down the street, catching sight of the two just before they turned a bend and disappeared.

I set after them, keeping to the low roofs of what must have been the western part of the city, and caught up to them before they turned onto a larger street running north toward the main boulevard. They walked casually, probably trying to not draw any more attention than they already would as two Barleans this far from the harbor.

Before they reached the boulevard, Auntie stopped the boy, taking the bag and pointing across the way. "There, in the tavern, is where you will find our buyer, you will," she said. "Torem. He is a tall, fat man with a large, braided beard, he is. He has a notch in one ear, he does, and he is Karakani, but he speaks

Barlean well enough, he does. Go inside, and bring him here. He is a good and honest man, so far as one in his line of work can be, he is, but I have not met him for many years, and the people he surrounds himself with have fighting advancements, they do. Do not be ashamed to run if you feel threatened. Understand, do you? Return to the ship, and do not worry about me, do not!"

"But, Auntie—"

She silenced him with a gesture. "I will be in no danger, I will not, but I am already ashamed to bring you into this, I am. Do not risk yourself for this. Do not! Run if you must! Run!"

The boy hung his head. "Yes, Auntie," he said, though I, personally, did not feel at all convinced.

Watching from a roof as the boy set out across the boulevard, and Auntie waited in an alley and watched his progress around the corner, I was pleased with my decision to follow the two Barleans. Smugglers, meeting with their contact for a drop off? A woman, perhaps recently bereaved, with a scandalous past? I may not have movies anymore, but this would do!

The boy vanished through the door that Auntie had pointed out as a tavern, and after many long, tense minutes he came back out, followed by a large—a *very* large—man. The guy must have been closing in on seven feet tall and was built like a well-fed bear. He towered over the boy, following him with long, easy strides across the boulevard, and Auntie stiffened when she saw him.

As she was focused on the two men approaching her, I saw another few men stepping out of the tavern. They looked after the two, then all but one took off down a side street. They looked like trouble, and I settled in to see what might happen, staying wrapped in my shadows with only minimal effort.

"Haalemetellee! It is so good to see you, it is!" the large man—Torem, she'd called him—said in heavily accented Barlean. "How many years it has been, how many?"

Faster than she could react he swept the woman up in a hug, her feet leaving the ground and kicking feebly as she gave off a little squeak of surprise. Her voice, when she answered, was choked from the pressure of his hug. "It is good to see you, too, Torem, it is!"

"Can I still call you Tellee, can I? Oh, it was good to get your letter, so good. We never saw enough of you and Varen. You made your mark on him in just a few years, you did!"

He put her down, letting her catch her breath, and she gestured to the boy, saying, "You've met Semteellaa, you have. My son-in-law-to-be."

If I hadn't been shifted, I might have laughed at how the boy shied back when Torem whirled to face him, his long, braided beard whipping around, almost catching the boy on the cheek. "Marrying little Ganny, are you, boy? Gonna be my nephew, are you?" Torem said in Karakani. "Let me get a look at you!"

"I . . . marry. Yes," the boy stuttered back in the same language, as the large man grabbed him by the shoulders, turning him around, then lifting his arms and poking him seemingly at random, every movement quick and precise.

"You'll do, you will, I think," Torem said with a grin. "Depths take me if I know, so may they! But Tellee would have stabbed you and fed you to the fishes if not, she would have, so I'm sure that you'll do, hah!"

"Thank you, Uncle?" the boy said with hesitation, looking to Tellee, his auntie, who nodded with an amused smile.

"You haven't changed at all, you have not," she said to Torem. "Do you want to come to the ship, do you, when we have finished this? Ganny would love—"

As I listened to this little reunion take place, I'd been watching half a dozen people converge on them from two directions. Now, as they got close, one of them spoke up, interrupting Tellee. "Torem!" he drawled with mock friendliness, and all three turned to look at him. "I was wondering where you'd gone! Didn't think I'd find you in a gutter with some Barlean snipe, but here we are. And what a bulging bag she has! Is that the silver you owe me, Torem?"

"Stub," Torem said, with the kind of tone that most people would save for a dead mouse they found under the sink, or something equally unpleasant. "I know the best part of you dribbled down your mother's leg, but I thought even you'd understand that you'll never collect on this imagined debt of yours. Go choke!"

This just kept getting better, I thought from my perch. *It's not just a mugging. There's history here!*

"You fucking scrum-cudgler," Stub hissed. "I'm out thirty-five eagles because of you, and I'm here to collect, with interest. I don't care if I take it out of you, the boy, or the snipe. Whatever you have on you, and what's in that bag—that'll be a start. Boys!"

Three men stepped up from the street, blocking off the entrance to the alley. As they took out small blades and cudgels, Tellee lifted one side of her skirt and produced something between a bowie knife and a short sword. Torem pushed the boy behind himself, taking a position back to back with Tellee and the boy between them. The boy had grabbed the sack from Tellee, holding onto it like his life depended on it and looking ready to bite. But he was just a kid, and there was no telling if he had any advancements to help him fight. This looked like a six-on-two, to me. Hardly fair.

The thugs closed in. They looked almost professional. There was no stupid banter, no overconfident smiles, just the calculating looks of people who intended to hurt someone because that was their job. And with that, I decided, the fun was over.

I was kind of invested in Tellee and the kid. They weren't mine, but I didn't want to see them hurt, robbed, or anything else. So I decided to even the odds a little.

The shadow I was in snaked down into the alley, and I went with it. As Stub and the two thugs with him moved in they were suddenly swaddled in absolute darkness. I wrapped them in shadow and then, for lack of a better description, *squeezed*. I made the shadows around them deeper than deep, darker than dark, and it worked wonderfully. A dull pain throbbed in my head, but I was rewarded by shouts of surprise from both inside and outside of my shadows, and then a groan, a moan, and a strangled wail of terror from the three who stood rooted in the darkness I'd called up.

I could have simply killed them, of course. I'd considered it. They didn't seem like even halfway decent people. It would have been quicker and more effective than putting some nameless terror in them and, considering what had happened with Jekrie and Barro, using my magic on them might end up with a couple of mind-whammied thugs down the line. I'd prefer to avoid that. I really should be trying to choose who I affected, if at all possible. But I didn't see much choice if I wanted to help the Barleans, since killing the thugs would reflect badly on my humans. The justice lady that they'd met with would probably put two and two together pretty quickly if she heard about six people being torn to shreds in an alley. While she couldn't blame my humans directly for anything I did, she had apparently made it clear that she didn't want me to be seen in the city, and there was no way to guarantee that she wouldn't make their lives difficult if I was. Or if fairly obvious evidence of me was, anyway.

So, good old terror it was. "Fear is a tool" and all that.

I turned from them to see how the Barleans and their friend were faring, and saw that Torem, at least, had not been idle. One thug lay limp in the dirt, and Torem, with a nasty cut on one arm, was holding the remaining two at bay with wide swings of the cudgel he must have taken off him. Tellee, meanwhile, was holding her blade like she knew how to use it. She looked fearful but determined, mostly staring my way but throwing frequent looks Torem's way. The two remaining thugs both had smaller knives, and if it were two on two, then Tellee and Torem would probably win, but she couldn't very well turn her back on my three and the mysterious darkness that had swallowed them. Torem, meanwhile, was already bleeding badly, and while he was holding the two back, they both gave me the impression of fighters, and there were two of them. Sooner or later, Torem would tire or slip up, and then he'd get another cut. Maybe that would be the end of it, or maybe it would take another two or three rounds, but I didn't see him winning, not against the two he was facing. So, I shifted my attention.

I withdrew my shadows from Stub and his two wingmen. Stub was on his knees, weeping, and one of the two thugs he had with him turned tail and ran, screaming, the moment she had her legs back. The other was made of sterner stuff, gritting his teeth and reaching down with one hand to haul Stub to his feet while still menacing Tellee with his cudgel. Meanwhile, I had moved on and wrapped up one of the two knife-wielders, his blade thumping softly to the ground and his breath catching as I made sure that he'd never again sleep without a lamp lit.

Tellee proved herself to be nothing if not adaptable. She gestured to the man that my shadows had just swallowed, her face twisting in a sneer. Then she said, in Karakani with a clear Barlean accent, "Run away, or I give you another dose. I do this!"

She raised her free hand toward Stub and his remaining thug, and that was it. The thug broke, yanking on Stub's arm as he turned and ran down the alley. Stub took a stumbling step backward. "Sea witch," he moaned. "A fucking sea witch!" Then he, too, turned and fled.

The one thug, who was still kind of fighting, looked wide-eyed at his downed partner, the inexplicable darkness where another should be, and finally at Tellee, who turned and regarded him coldly, quirking an eyebrow. I withdrew from the man that I'd taken, sliding back up to the roof, and I could have sworn that Tellee watched me go. The thug I'd just released stood, arms wrapped around himself and shivering as he looked around wildly.

"I'll take my guys and go, yeah?" the remaining thug said.

I was impressed. I'd expected him to just run.

Tellee looked at him silently, then rolled her eyes. "Fine."

His eyes locked on Tellee and Torem, the thug sidled over to his conscious companion. "Bord," he said coolly, "Help me with Roven."

"W-what?" Bord stuttered, looking at his partner with a complete lack of comprehension.

"Help me with Roven," the thug said carefully, kneeling down and putting his arms under the unconscious man's shoulders, barely taking his eyes off Tellee.

"R-right. Right. Yeah. Right," Bord said, grabbing Roven's ankles.

Neither of the thugs turned their backs to Tellee as they first shuffled, then walked, and finally jogged off down the street, taking their limp friend with them.

As soon as the three were alone in the alley, Tellee dropped her knife and slumped against a stone wall. There she sat, breathing heavily, until the boy spoke up.

"Auntie!" the boy said, looking around quickly with his eyes full of fear and worry. He put down the bag and grabbed Tellee's hands, not quite pulling her to her feet. "Get up, Auntie! We can't stay here!"

She looked at him and blinked once, slowly. "Yes. Right. You are right, you are," she said, letting him help her up and collecting her blade, making it disappear into her skirt again. "Torem, we must—Your arm! You're bleeding, you are!"

"This is nothing, it is not," the big man answered, though he was grimacing against the pain. "A quarter potion, and I will be fine, I will. But what by the stars and the waves was that? What did you do?"

"Nothing. I did nothing," Tellee said, searching the alley. "The darkness, we . . . We felt something in the drains, we did. Something in the dark. I just . . . I used it. Played along. But I don't know, I don't. We should finish our business and go, we should, and pray it is satisfied!"

"I understand. Quick, then, quick! I have the gold. Show me the goods, boy, show me!"

The boy obediently took out a simple, round, wooden box from the bag, opening it toward Torem.

"Beautiful," Torem said, reaching out and gently touching the . . . whatever. I couldn't see. "Just as you said. But Tellee, are you sure you would not have me broker it instead, are you? I can get you more in a month than I can pay myself tonight, I can."

Tellee shook her head hurriedly. "We need the money now, we do. Take it and sell it, and enjoy the profit with our blessing. Enjoy it!"

"Well, here." Torem handed over a pouch, though he didn't seem happy about it. "All I could get, it is, more than we agreed on *and do not argue, do not*!" He raised his voice over Tellee's protests, closing her hands around the bag. "You are family, you are. The wife of the man who could have been my brother shall not be short-changed, she shall not!"

There was a little more arguing back and forth until Tellee finally took the money, and at the boulevard they hugged and went their own ways. Torem had to hide whatever it was he'd bought somewhere, but Tellee insisted that he was welcome on their ship if he had time before they left.

Telle and the boy, Sem-something, looked anxiously over their shoulders as they set off in the direction of the harbor, staying in the best lit areas. I followed them, of course. I wanted to see this through, see where they ended up. There was also the fact that they had a small pouch of gold, and I toyed with the idea of stopping them and demanding a reward. But in the end I decided against it. I was not a thug, and my conscience would not allow it. Tellee had sounded serious when she said that they needed the money now, for whatever purpose.

At the harbor I watched them get into a small boat with a single set of oars, manned by one man, and row out to a middling ship anchored in the harbor. I wished them well.

I saw that the *Laughing Gull* was gone, and I wondered if they'd ever come back to Karakan. I'd probably scared the piss out of the poor crew on the launch, and thinking of it made me . . . well, not grin, because I was shifted and didn't have a mouth, but the equivalent feeling.

I hung around, watching the harbor for a while. It was much calmer than it had been two days earlier, though whether that had anything to do with me, who could tell? It was still nice. I shifted back for a while just to smell the sea, and sat there, watching the ships and the sea with my regular eyes until I'd had my fill and the sun was well and truly set. It was a dark, cloudy night, and rather than making my way back to the inn the hard way I took to the skies, trusting my stealth to keep me hidden from watchful eyes. I took a lap around the city, marveling at how it sprawled, miles wide in any direction, then headed for my humans. I'd been good, and I'd kept my promise to Herald. I hadn't hovered over them. Now I deserved to quiet that nagging little worry at the back of my mind and make sure that they were all safe and where they were supposed to be.

I passed over the inn, which was right where I'd left it, thank the Mercies. I hadn't been entirely sure that no one would try to burn it down the moment the deed was transferred, or however property ownership worked here. I didn't land on the roof, both because I didn't want to be spotted and associated with them, and because I didn't want to accidentally break any of the roof tiles. Instead I set down in the small, overgrown garden that Garal had shown me. Being both secluded and apparently forgotten made it an excellent place for take-offs and landings, and from there I made my way, shifted, to the inn.

There was a lively celebration going on, the sounds of cheer and music—a brassy wind instrument and some kind of plucked strings—spilling out through the open windows, and it both relaxed me and warmed my heart. Nothing bad could have happened in my absence if there was a party going!

Once I set up on the roof it didn't take long for the cellar door to open. Ardek stepped out, turning around a little unsteadily and looking around the small yard. It apparently didn't occur to him to look up, but he was having trouble staying on his feet, so I wasn't surprised.

I dropped behind him, making my way inside the cellar and making sure that it was clear before shifting back. "Hey, Ardek," I said, repeating myself when he didn't immediately react.

He turned around, looking at me with that relaxed contentment on his face that you can get when you're just the right side of passing out. "Oh, hey, boss. You jus' come outta nowhere, don't you?" he said, stumbling to the side and steadying himself against the slanted frame of the door. "Sorry, I'm s'pose to let . . . oh, yeah, yeah, right!"

He grabbed the door, closing it behind him as he stepped in, and nearly tumbled when it fell closed the last bit on its own. He was saved by his grip on the handle and looked at the door angrily for a moment. Then, with exaggerated care, he put the bar in place and picked up the lantern he'd left on the floor.

"Wann . . . wanna come upstairs, boss?" he asked. "Lots of guests, bunch of musicians, real good night!"

"I'd love to," I told him drily as I lay down on the floor, "but I'll stay here. Send down Herald and Mak and anyone else who wants to join, though."

"Yes, boss!" Moments later I heard him stumbling up the stairs. He took the lantern with him, leaving me comfortable in the dark.

CHAPTER SEVEN

Celebration

The muted sounds of music, of celebration and the thumping of feet on the thick wooden boards separating me from the inn's common room, confirmed what Ardek had told me. The music was all right, different than I was used to but cheerful and lively, and I relaxed as best I could, content to listen to the party upstairs. There was a crowd, which made me all kinds of pleased for my friends. It was good to see them doing well right off. Herald had mentioned buying something like an inn several times over the past few months, initially as a long-term dream and then as a way to invest the money they expected to gain from our adventure in the north, and now, here we were. They didn't even have to give up adventuring to run it, since it came with staff, including a contrite, thankful, and experienced innkeeper. Which was fortunate because, out of the four, Mak was the only one I could possibly see being content running the place. Tam and Val may stick around for a while, but Herald? I would give her a month tops before she'd be bored out of her mind.

I could feel Herald move to the door at the top of the stairs, and I shifted, just in case she had someone with her. It wouldn't do to scare the life out of some poor barmaid coming down to help her fetch something. But the rapid, excited steps were enough to tell me that she was alone as she rushed down, eyes glowing, and stopped on the last step. She struck an unsteady pose, pointing at me dramatically.

"I can *see* you!" she declared, a big, smug smile on her face. "Righ'there!"

She rushed forward the rest of the way and tried to hug me, which felt like death trying to grab me as her arm passed through me. I shuddered internally and pulled back, and she looked highly offended as she followed me with her eyes.

"Come on, shift back!" she demanded. I complied, and her smile returned with a squeal as I took form in front of her.

She choked me lovingly for a few seconds while Mak descended the stairs. She had Tam and Val with her, and Tam was almost as drunk as Ardek, while Mak and Val looked completely sober.

"Hope you don't mind," Mak said, raising a large lantern, which she hung on a hook in the ceiling with the help of a pole. "Let me get a look at your leg, please. I . . ." She approached me and switched to a whisper. "Mercies, Draka, when I felt you get afraid . . . I was so relieved when Herald and Kira came and told me that you were all safe. They told me about the archer. Must have an archery major at least."

"Yeah, whoever that was, they have magic. They can channel it into their arrows. Don't know what it does for sure, but safe to say it's strong."

"If they can get an arrow through your scales, then yes. Definitely strong. We'll see if we can figure out who it might be." She fussed a little over my leg, then made a little surprised noise when she pushed some healing into it.

"What was that?" I asked, getting worried. It's rarely a good thing when your doctor sounds surprised.

"No resistance," she replied with a satisfied smile. "I could just heal you, easy as anything."

I grinned back at her. That made sense. She was mine, after all.

Meanwhile, Tam stumbled forward, almost as enthusiastic as Herald had been. "Draka!" he exclaimed, with an almost childish exuberance. "I've got my tavern, Draka! Own tavern! Inn, whatever!"

Val steadied him with a firm hand on his shoulder, smiling patiently. "Apologies, Draka. Most of the month's profits have been drunk, I believe, by these two." He indicated Tam and Herald.

"Not Mak?" I asked, looking at her.

"I tried some wine," Mak said, frowning. "It somehow doesn't agree with me anymore."

There was a crash from upstairs, followed by a chaotic mix of laughter and angry voices.

Val looked up, then rolled his eyes at me. "My intervention may be needed. Word got out of our fortune. You understand. A celebration was in order, and we know many lively and energetic people. Thank you again, Draka, for your part in this." With that, he turned and bounded up the stairs, and a moment later I heard his voice, stern yet cheerful, loud but impossible to understand.

"Right, yeah!" Tam said as Val was leaving, grinning my way and slurring slightly. "Thank you, you beautiful, wonderful dragon! I've always been lucky, but since you . . . Mercies, you're my luck, you know that? Just heaps and heaps of it!"

"She is!" Herald agreed, turning to her brother. "Gettin' you outta jail, gettin' you outta the tunnels, the villa . . ." She ticked each item off as she said it.

"Getting us out," Mak said, looking at Herald and smiling sadly.

"Yeah." Herald hesitated, then rallied. "An' your a'va'cement! And *my* a'va'cement! Hah!"

With that she did a little twirl, stumbled, recovered so that she'd put me between herself and the lantern, and disappeared.

Tam blinked. "You fall?" he asked, moving to look behind me. Mak gasped and covered her mouth with both hands, her eyes locked on the shadow where Herald had been a moment ago.

Herald had been keeping secrets.

I could still feel her there, of course. Not that I needed to. She laughed, an oddly distant sound full of drunken mischief. My shadow flickered and waved, bent and stretched until it touched the darkness behind a stack of barrels, and my sense of where she was moved, the sound of her laughter moving with it. When my shadow snapped back she was already moving again, the shadows near her dancing as she moved through them.

Either her shadow magic took a lot less effort to use than mine, or she was improving unfairly quickly. It had taken me months to move as smoothly as she was. Or it was her being drunk and just *doing* it, instead of worrying about strain or how to do it the right way or anything like that. I'd done stuff drunk before that I could never have done sober.

Whatever it was, I was impressed, and more than a little envious that she made it look so easy. And that she could see me when I was shifted, but I couldn't see her when she was invisible. That hardly seemed fair to me. I was the magic shadow dragon, damn it! But it wasn't like I could stay mad at her. It was Herald, and she was so happy!

When Herald finally popped out of the shadows she, of course, scared the crap out of Mak. Tam, though, being severely pissed, took it in stride. There were a lot of questions. Herald had apparently told the others *that* she'd received her major advancement. They'd had a private celebration before whatever was happening upstairs. And she'd told them that it was a magical one—which made the siblings three for three, remarkable in itself—but she hadn't told them anything about it. She'd wanted to show them. And now she had, and they were appropriately impressed, and they wanted to know *everything.*

Herald still insisted they wait until Val came back downstairs, which took a little while. "Apologies," he said. "Baran and Yana were fighting again."

"So's they . . . ?" Tam asked, with a knowing grin.

"A room was hurriedly paid for, yes," Val confirmed with a long-suffering sigh. "I would prefer if their foreplay was less disruptive, but it works for them, I suppose."

"Baran . . ." I mused. I recognize that name. "He's an adventurer, right? Runs with a woman with great hair, a big, bearded guy with a bow, and a short guy built like a brick barbecue, yeah?"

"That's them!" Tam confirmed gleefully. "Baran an' Yana, they're married, an' Jor an' Gelven, they're brothers. Good bunch! We compete for a lotta the same jobs, but, eh, yeah? Herald! Show Val the thing!"

Herald, who'd been waiting impatiently for the spotlight, grinned and practically fell backward into the shadows, where she promptly disappeared again as the darkness seemed to reach up and swallow her.

"This . . ." Val gasped, trailing off as he walked up and looked behind the barrels where Herald had disappeared. I felt Herald move, saw the shadows stretch out to join my own, and this time I *thought* that I saw a shadow flit across the narrow bridge that Herald had created.

I also saw Val perk up, going stock still and turning his head slowly. Tracking her by the sound of her steps, perhaps? If he could hear her steps, muffled and distant, over the sound of Tam's laughter, I would be very impressed.

I felt a hand stroke my back, warm and reassuring, as Herald passed behind me. Then, in a sudden burst, my shadow stretched out until it touched Tam, who didn't even notice. He was still laughing, looking at Val who was listening with an expression of complete focus.

Mak wasn't breathing, her eyes locked on where my shadow touched Tam. Then I had that same sense of something insubstantial flitting through my vision as I felt Herald round me and shoot toward her brother, who suddenly leapt back with a yell.

"Hells and Sorrows! Herald, wassat you?!" he asked, wide-eyed as he brushed at the front of his tunic. "Something just poked me!"

My shadow snapped back, and it was as though a black blanket had been pulled back to reveal Herald, kneeling on the floor, gasping for air from a combination of debilitating laughter and exhaustion.

"I—I—!" she laughed, then went completely silent, looking up with a panicked expression and scrambling for the barred door.

"I'm gon' . . . gonna hurl!" she groaned, struggling with the bar, and then Val was at her side, lifting it and opening the door for her. She gave him a pitifully grateful look, her hand clenched over her mouth, as she vanished into the yard, Val close behind her.

Mak took an abortive step toward the door, but stayed. "Well," she said over the sounds of Herald retching outside, and Val's soothing words, "aftermath aside, I think we all agree—that's amazing. I'd guess you knew already, Draka?"

"I did, yeah," I said, looking out the door. Herald sounded like she was having a rough time. "But I didn't know that she could touch things. And did you see her eyes?"

"Gold," Mak said, nodding. "Like yours."

"'s pretty," Tam said, sitting down on the lowest step of the stairs. He was looking pretty crook, too. "Should getter some nice earrings to match, or something."

"That's a nice idea," I told him. Gold earrings. I liked that. And the right ones *would* look great on her. I'd only ever seen her with studs, but some nice threaders, maybe? Or a bajoran if she had her ears pierced for it?

But that wasn't what I'd wanted to talk to them about and, frankly, Herald and Tam didn't seem like they'd be able to contribute much.

"Mak," I said, leaning in, "would you get Val and help your siblings to bed? Then bring Val back down here. I want to talk."

Mak looked at her brother, who was now sitting elbows on knees and face in hands, breathing heavily, then out the door. "I'll do that," she said, getting up and leaving through the cellar door. I heard soft voices from outside, and some pitiful groans from Herald, and then all three came in, Val closing and barring the door behind them.

Herald was a mess, stumbling and mumbling as she looked at Mak and asked, "Did you like it? My magic, did—Did you like it?"

"It was fantastic," Mak reassured her as she led her toward the stairs. "Like nothing I've ever seen before. I'm so proud of you."

"Really?" Herald sounded almost desperate, pulling loose from Val and wrapping Mak in a sloppy hug. "I love you so much," she squeaked into the top of Mak's head. "So much!"

"I love you, too," Mak said, patiently supporting and guiding Herald up the stairs as Val simply picked Tam up in a princess carry and followed them.

Ten minutes later, with the drunk half of the family safely tucked into bed, Mak and Val came back down into the cellar.

Mak sat down on a barrel. "I asked Kira to look after Herald," she said. "Her new advancement is amazing. Is it . . . ?" She gestured between the two of us, then broke into a smile when I answered.

"Yeah. And I can feel her, just like you."

"It is still a strange thing, difficult to believe," Val said from where he sat on the stairs. "I must believe it, since it was you who told me, Mak, but it is like nothing I have heard of before. Advancements directly connecting you to someone else."

"Yes, well . . ." Mak said, her tone making it clear that she was gathering her thoughts. "Herald should have been here, really. She's more well-read than I am. But, we may have let her celebrate a little too freely, so you get my thoughts on it.

"If people normally got advancements binding them together, we should know about it. If nothing else, Val, you and Tam should have at least one between the two of you. But me and Herald have talked about it and, well, the obvious difference here is that we are all human, but Draka is not. She is a dragon. Her advancements are those of a dragon, and so is her magic. I have never heard of any first-hand accounts of what it is like to be in a dragon cult, or to have any other kind of connection to a dragon, and neither has Herald, and you know how obsessed she's been. So, for all we know, this might be completely normal, just . . . hidden, I guess. Suppressed, maybe. It's not like there's a lot of reliable information on dragons out there."

Val rubbed his smooth head thoughtfully, looking at me, then Mak, and back. "It is said, in the north, that dragons would surround themselves not only with worshipers and sycophants, but with mighty warriors and demagogues, the backbone of their cults. It is assumed that these people were already powerful, and were drawn into the service of a dragon by fear or greed or the promise of more power. But there is new evidence here, in you, Mak, and in Herald. There is the possibility that they were made mighty by their connection to the dragon."

"As interesting as that is," I said, breaking into the conversation, "that's not what I wanted to talk about. Mak, Val. You own this place now. You have an enemy here in the city, who's wealthy and ruthless. What are you doing to defend what is yours?"

Mak grimaced. "Not much, yet. We haven't had the time. We've got an agreement with some street kids to feed them if they keep their eyes open for us. And this is an adventurers' inn, and we've got a good reputation among them. The inn will lose some business since we took over—"

"What?" I interrupted. "Why?"

"Because we're *Tekereteki*." Mak said it as though it was the most obvious thing in the world. "Most of the adventurers won't mind, which is one of the reasons we've been staying here, but—"

"Fucking bullshit," I mumbled. "Racist pricks . . ."

Mak sighed. "Yes. But as much as we hate it, that's how it is. We're all used to it. What I was saying was that we don't expect monthly profits to be affected too much. As long as the inn makes *any* profit, or just breaks even, we're fine. But the point is that it's an inn full of brave fighting men and women who mostly like us, and we hope that they'll help defend us and the inn if the Night Blossom tries anything. At least until we can arrange something, or deal with her."

"What about arson?" I asked. "The Wolves' warehouse got burned down."

"The Wolves' warehouse didn't have the protections that this place does. There is an enchantment against fire around the foundation. Old, from when the place was built, but Reben swears that he had it checked by an enchanter only a few years ago, and it should be effective. It would take effort, real effort, to cause any significant damage."

I looked at her skeptically. That didn't sound like a sure thing at all.

"I know," she said, no doubt feeling my skepticism through our bond. "It's not much. For now, we're leaning heavily on Tam to see trouble coming, and on his luck to help deal with it."

"The same guy who's passed out drunk upstairs?"

Val chuckled. "The plan is not perfect; this is clear. We will need to guard in shifts, just like when we camp. This has already been decided. The woman Kira, who Herald brought, will help, or so I have been told, as I cannot speak with her. I . . . She's unknown to me, nor can I get to know her. I will not pretend to be comfortable with this. But if the two of you and Herald trust her, then so will I."

"Unless she's a fantastic actress, we don't need to worry." I was completely sure of that. There was just something about Kira. I didn't like to describe anyone as "pitiful," but . . . sincerely sad, maybe? "She doesn't want to see anyone get hurt. If she says she'll stand guard, I trust that she will. Just don't expect her to fight."

Val nodded. "As I said, I will trust your judgment on this."

"Besides," I added, "she knows what I'll do to her if she allows anyone close to me to come to harm. She won't risk angering me; you can be sure of that."

Val looked about to speak, but hesitated for some reason. He looked at Mak, who nodded, confirming my words, and he finally said, "I see."

I thought about what I had just said. Yeah, that didn't sound great.

"To be clear, I didn't hurt her. Much. Recently."

That wasn't much better.

"What I mean is that she's seen the worst of me, and that should be enough to keep her from doing anything stupid. And she's not violent. All she wants is to help people. And some friends, I guess."

"What Draka's saying," Mak said, looking at me, asking if I wanted her to stop, "is that she feels a little guilty about how she treated the woman. Kira, while she can be annoying, is pretty much a victim here, but one that we can't let go. Even bringing her here is a risk, but Herald seemed to think that she was miserable in the forest. If we can let her feel included and useful, it might make her feel better about her situation. Is that about right, Draka?"

I wanted to scoff and act aloof about the whole thing, but what she said was true. I did feel guilty. Of course I did. It wasn't the visceral guilt that I'd felt as a mere human, that sick feeling of having done something terribly unjust to someone who didn't deserve it. It was an intellectual thing, knowing, not feeling that I should be better than that, and a calculating part of me told me that it might make Kira less loyal to me, and that it might damage my image in the eyes of others, but it was guilt all the same.

I sighed. "That's about right, yeah."

"And, Val," Mak continued, "I agree with Draka. I've spent more time with Kira than she has. I've talked to her a lot. I know that she won't let anyone get hurt, and I doubt that she'll run. She's rather disillusioned about serving her country, no matter what lip-service she pays to it."

"Being enslaved and forced to work for murderers will do that," I muttered.

"She was a slave?" Val asked. "I was told that she was bonded, but I confess I don't fully understand what that means."

"It means, if I have it right," Mak said, "that they tell you where to live, what to do, and who to serve. You get paid some small amount, but since you're never expected to live an independent life, it's not enough for . . . anything, really. It's worse than our indentured servitude. The only thing they can't do to a bonded person is to harm them or force them to . . . ah . . . breed."

"Whoever owns them is not allowed to rape them. How kind," Val said drily.

"And if a magic user does not report for bonding voluntarily, they lose even that protection," Mak continued, her lip curling with disgust. "Talking to Kira has made it clear to me why my mother and father left Tekeretek. She went willingly, of course. She thought they'd put her in a sick house somewhere, or with the army. Perhaps on some rich House's staff. Instead she got sold to a mercenary company that makes the Cranes look like saints. She didn't say it, but from talking to her she hasn't been happy in years."

"And she still mourned the ones I killed," I said.

Val raised his hands as though to ward us off. "Please," he said, "I do not mean to say that I mistrust her, only that I don't know her. There's no need to tell me more. My heart already breaks for her. I will show her kindness, and ask Tam to do the same. He, at least, can speak a few words with her."

I nodded gratefully. "I think she'd appreciate that. Do you think we could arrange something where she can heal people, for a fee? I think she'd feel good about that."

"Oh, easily. As long as she is comfortable with making her ability to heal public, there's good money to be made, though she'll need a license, so we'll need to figure that out."

"Great. Look into that. Now, did anything happen today that I should know about?"

"Yes!" Mak said. "I've been waiting to tell you. That Barro guy is upstairs. He's been waiting for you all day."

"It's been good to see him again," Val agreed, a contented smile creeping onto his face. "We haven't met much since Tam and Mak and I became a team. Would you like me to bring him down?"

"Yes, please do!" I said, perking up at the mention of Barro. The man was supposed to have something for me, and I'd been curious ever since Lalia told me, several days earlier. "I'd asked Lalia and Garal to arrange a meeting, but this is even better."

"I will only be a moment, then," Val said, rising from the step and heading upstairs.

CHAPTER EIGHT

Consideration

After Val left to get Barro I turned to Mak. "Barro's been waiting all day? Really?"

She shrugged where she sat, her elbows on her knees. "Reben says that he came early in the morning. Said that he needed to speak to me or Herald urgently, but Reben told him that he could damn well wait until we woke up, so we found him in the common room when we came for breakfast. He was pretty disappointed when I told him that you weren't here."

"Did he say what he wanted to tell me?"

She scoffed. "No, says he has to talk to you in person. He had breakfast, stayed for lunch, got disappointed when Herald and Kira arrived without you and stayed for dinner, and now he's been upstairs, finally relaxing a little after an ale or two. Val's been keeping him company. They've been talking for hours." She glanced toward the door. "While we're alone, if it's all right that I ask, you got something yourself, didn't you? Something that affects me? I felt something odd last night. My whole head tingled suddenly, like when your foot has gone to sleep and is waking up."

"I did," I said smugly. "Charisma. And I have high hopes for what it'll do for you."

Moments later the door upstairs opened again. "Go on," Val's voice said, and I heard heavy, hesitant footfalls on the steps. A tall figure came down the stairs, and I recognized Barro's long, messy hair, then his rugged face as he reached the bottom stair.

"It's you!" His voice was almost drowned out by the crowd upstairs. It was hushed, almost reverential, and he took two long strides forward, kneeling before me under the lantern hanging from the ceiling.

"You called me," he said, looking up at me with unashamed adoration. "Like before. You called me, and I've come."

I had expected Barro to have something to tell me. I had expected him to be nervous, anxious, perhaps a little afraid and perhaps a little excited. I didn't know

the guy that well, but those would all be entirely reasonable reactions to having a
dragon talk to you in your dreams, telling you to come meet her at a tavern.

I did not expect him to worship me. I was a tiny bit embarrassed, deep inside,
but every part of me liked it. I'd had my pride as a woman, and Instinct had ten
times more, and the way Barro knelt before me, the look in his eye and the tone
of his voice, they all came together to make me very, very pleased. It was like Jekrie,
without the fear. Like Mak, but without the guilt.

Val had come down behind Barro and was looking confused and uncomfortable, so I raised my hand magnanimously. "On your feet, Barro. There's no need
for that. Thank you for coming. Lalia tells me that you've found something that
should interest me?"

"I have," Barro said, slowly standing up and taking a marginally more relaxed
stance, moving a little to the side so that the four of us, with Val standing in front
of the stairs and Mak sitting on her barrel, formed a rough diamond. "You asked
me about Miss Tavia and Mister Ramban, if they'd be willing to share their knowledge with you. And about the house on Cloud Street that was attacked. I think
that Mister Ramban might be willing to talk to someone who knows more about
the gate and the one in the dark, and I've found who owns the house. Two of
three isn't bad, is it?"

"Two out of three is twice as good as I'd hoped for," I said. Ramban! Of course!
That was who I'd seen when I was dreaming, the one I couldn't pin down. This
was great! He and Tavia, the scholars who'd invaded my mountain, had seemed
to be sitting on a trove of historical information that might tell me more about
who I was and what had happened to my father. My dragon father, that was. And
finding who owned the house where Herald, Mak, and myself had been imprisoned would get us, or at least get us closer to, the Night Blossom.

One thing bothered me, though. "What did you tell the scholars?" I asked.

"Well," he said, combing his hand through his long hair, "I told them some
of the truth. Nothing about you," he added hastily. "I told them that I'd returned
to their dig site and that I'd met someone there who knew things about the tunnels that they might be willing to share. Miss Tavia wants nothing more to do
with it, but Mister Ramban seemed willing enough to meet."

"So he knows nothing about me?" I asked. That was good. I'd probably have
to do something to him to keep him quiet if I talked to him directly, but a better
idea might be to have Herald meet with him. I could wait in the wings.

"Nothing from me, at least, I can promise you that much."

"Is it possible that I might be told what's going on?" Val asked, looking
around the small group. "Some of these things sound familiar, but I am fairly
lost."

Right. Tam and Val had been away for the end of the whole scholar situation.
I considered how much to tell him, and decided he might as well know everything. "Do you remember the scholars I told you all about? The ones camping at
the foot of my mountain, digging out one of the gates? That's them, Tavia and

Ramban. Your friend Barro, here, was the head of their guard while they were working. To make a long story short, I left the gate open for them, they decided to explore, and I scared them half to death. But they know a lot about the mountain, more than I do, at least, so when Barro came back—"

"Of course *you'd* go back," Val muttered, rolling his eyes at Barro who shrugged helplessly.

"—the girls"—I nodded to Mak—"and I made sure that he could be trusted, and I asked him to look into some things for me. One was if he could learn anything from the scholars, or if he could arrange some kind of meeting or exchange of information. The other was to see if he could find who owns the house where the girls and I were imprisoned. And from what he's telling me, he's done a great job!"

"And what is the meaning, Barro, when you say that she has called you?"

Ah. That. I wasn't sure how comfortable I was with Val knowing about the whole dream-walking thing, and I hurried to preempt Barro before he said something well-meaning. *Charisma, don't fail me now*, I thought.

The lie, or half-truth, came surprisingly smoothly. "Like I said," I told Val while shooting Barro a pointed look, "I asked Lalia and Garal to set up a meeting with Barro for me. They must have asked him to come here. Isn't that right, Barro?"

"Ah, well," Barro answered evasively, catching my meaning but looking uncomfortable. He probably didn't like deceiving Val. "I did meet them here, and they told me that Miss Makanna and Miss Herald were staying here, yeah."

"Oh," was all Val said. His face was utterly unreadable.

"So, what did you learn about the house?" I asked, wanting to move the conversation along. "You said that you have an owner for me."

"Right, I do!" Barro said, fishing out a folded piece of paper from his vest. "A friend in the censor's office got it for me. The house used to belong to a wealthy family, the Reverrions, but they sold it about three years ago when the patriarch was appointed to a magisterial position in the south, and they relocated the entire household. It was bought by one Parvion Sardin, to be held by Parvion Tarkarran."

"That little shit," I growled.

"Oh, you know him?" Barro asked.

I was about to reply, but Mak beat me to it. "Tarkarran. Tark. He tortured me," she said. Her voice was low and dangerous, tight with the same suppressed rage that I felt. She'd been sitting on her barrel off to the side and away from the meager light of the lantern, easy to miss, and Barro jumped a little when she spoke. And no wonder, since she was now advancing on him seemingly from nowhere as she continued. "Then he tortured my sister in front of me. Again, and again, and again. Tell me, Mister Barro, do you know anything else about this man? We know where we might be able to find him, but do you know anything about his friends? His family? His habits? What can you find for us regarding Parvion Tarkarran?"

"Mercies and Sorrows," he whispered, and I saw a flash of honest, sympathetic pain on his face. "I remember you told me . . ." he said to me before turning back to Mak. "I didn't realize that it was you and Miss Herald she meant."

"Your sympathy is appreciated." Mak's voice was flat. "What do you know about him?"

"Nothing. He's not a public figure. His family, though, they're merchants. Not very prominent, but a good reputation. High-value goods, like spices and dyes. They own . . . three ships, I think. Not sure about the names, but those should be easy enough to find. Trade mostly in the east and south. Tavvanar, Tekeretek, Falthi, places like that."

"Are you currently employed, Barro?" Mak asked, and he shook his head.

"I've been living off what the scholars paid me. Which was quite generous, all credit to them. Why—"

His hand came out reflexively, mid-sentence, as Mak threw him a gold coin.

"Consider yourself on retainer." Despite being a foot shorter than Barro, Mak somehow filled the place. Her tone left no room for negotiation or refusal, and Barro just stood silently, looking between her and the coin in his hand.

I hadn't been surprised to see Mak speak up, but the way she was stepping in to take charge, that was interesting. I backed up a little and lay down on the floor again, deciding to see how this played out. And honestly, I found the whole situation pretty funny. Val seemed to agree. He rolled his eyes at his friend, and we shared a grin before Mak continued.

"I'll take your silence as agreement. That should cover services rendered and the next two months, don't you agree?"

"Ah, yes!" Barro found his voice, the coin disappearing into his vest. "Certainly! Very generous, Miss—"

"I think we can drop the formalities," Mak said. "Makanna will do."

"As you say, then, Makanna. What do you want from me?"

"Anything you can find out about Tarkarran, the Night Blossom, or anyone associated with them. You know why. And if your conscience has begun to pain you since the first time we met, you should know that they tried to murder Val a few days ago, as he and my brother came ashore from their ship."

"Ah," he answered simply, as his nostrils flared and his eyes narrowed. He looked at Val.

"We were fortunate," Val said, nodding to me. "Draka took care of the attackers quite . . . effectively."

Brutally and with extreme prejudice, I thought with great satisfaction.

"I'd heard about that," Barro said. "There was talk about the mysterious wyvern, surely some advanced specimen, attacking a boat in the harbor. Only, some people insist that it had both wings and four legs. I thought of you, of course. But few people dare use the word *dragon*."

"Some people must be taking it seriously," I told him. "I took a damn arrow to the leg when I flew in." Barro's eyes widened at that. "Almost hit Kira. They weren't your average adventurer, I'm sure of that. Those arrows flew way too fast. I mean, it *could* be a coincidence, yeah? But my bet would be that someone who'd never stoop to hunting a wyvern has decided to join the game."

"Did you get a good look at whoever shot you?" Barro asked. "Anyone who could hurt *you* must be powerful, and should be well known."

I huffed. "Androgynous, wiry build, curly brown hair . . . They had lighter hair than most Karakani, but they didn't look Barlean. Herald didn't recognize them, either, though she's sure we're dealing with a man."

"I can ask around about any big-name hunters, either new to the city or someone who might have become more active recently. Would that help?"

"Do it," Mak said before I could reply. "Do you have anything else for us now?"

Barro thought about it. "No, I don't think so," he concluded.

"Then feel free to return upstairs. There should be a few rooms free if you'd rather not leave tonight," Mak said, then turned to Val. "I'd like to talk to Draka alone, if that's all right?"

"I have no problem with that," Val said. "Draka, do you have anything else?"

I shook my head. "There's always tomorrow. You two go back to the fun upstairs."

"In that case, good night," Val said. "Come on, Barro! The night is yet young!"

Barro looked chagrined at his sudden dismissal but left with Val, touching his chest and giving me a respectful nod on the way out.

Mak deflated as soon as the door upstairs closed, and she looked at me anxiously.

"Was that all right?" she asked. "I didn't mean to step on your authority, but when Barro was talking I just . . . It felt right. I'm sorry if I overstepped. I didn't, did I?"

Had she? I hadn't told her to speak for me, or to handle anyone for me. But she'd done well. And it was nice to know that I could rely on her to deal with people, and to see her getting back some of that authoritative air that she'd had before I broke her. She was slowly returning to her old self, and not just that, but better, backed by command and charisma, the minor advancements that she had through me.

So, no. She hadn't overstepped. And frankly she looked so nervous and vulnerable that I might have let it slide even if she had.

"You did great," I told her, trying to really feel it, so that she would as well. "You handled that perfectly. But, a whole dragon? Really? Isn't that a little much? It's not like I can pay you back."

Mak's relief was clear in her relaxed shoulders, in her smile, and in the way she approached me. "It's a lot, yes," she said, "but not unreasonable. He's an experienced adventurer, and he knows a lot of people in a lot of places. And let's not pretend like there's any difference between my money and yours, yeah? I owe you more than I can ever repay, and I would never have this money in the first place if not for you."

"Perhaps. But even if that's how you feel, don't go spending like crazy just because it's for me. I'd rather see you all prosper."

"All right, I'll keep that in mind," she said, nodding seriously. Then she remained silent for a little while, except for her fingers drumming on the support she stood by. She was getting fidgety overall, with a nervous energy about her that got stronger as the seconds passed. And then she broke. "Oh, hells! The others should have been here for this, but I can't wait to show you."

"Hmm? What?"

"Would you come with me? It's just down here," she said, backing up slowly toward a door leading to a short corridor.

I got to my feet, following her curiously. It was a testament to how much my trust in her had grown in the last several weeks that I didn't hesitate even for a moment. She led me through the door into the darkness, down the corridor, past the room where we had interrogated Simdal, and to the heavy door at the end. Casting her darksight spell on herself, she took out a keyring and selected a large key, using it to unlock a solid-looking lock. When she pulled the door open it went slowly; she lacked the weight, not the strength, to quickly open the thick door reinforced with metal bands.

"This is the inn's strongroom," she said. I looked inside a small room, ten feet or so on a side, with walls of large stone bricks. It contained two things—a small nest of pillows and blankets, and a table carrying the red lacquered box that had until recently contained our fortune.

"The room doubles as a safe room. See? The door can be barred from the inside," Mak said, stepping inside and pointing out the heavy wooden beam and the brackets on the frame and the door. "We thought you might like to have somewhere comfortable to rest in the city. Somewhere safe, where no one can bother you."

"You thought of . . ." I started, then found myself speechless. I couldn't for the life of me figure out why. Of course they should think of my comfort, and it made perfect sense, then, to put me in the strongroom that no one but them should be entering anyway. But a significant part of me only saw that they had prepared this place for me here, in their home, in a very real way telling me that I was as welcome in their daily life as I wished, and that part of me wanted to cry.

I didn't finish the sentence. Instead I just wrapped my neck around Mak, and when that wasn't enough, I added one of my arms, crushing her into my chest.

She laughed, high and delighted. It was a beautiful sound. "Me and Herald thought of it," she said, putting her arms around me and running her fingers down my scales, "but everyone was involved. Even Ardek and Kira, though Kira mostly came out with us to see the market and such. Val chose the fabrics, of course. You can't see it, but they're all silver-gray and golden yellow." She hesitated. "Ah . . . we chose hard-wearing fabrics rather than soft. We figured—"

"Yeah, good choice," I said, my throat thick. "I can't feel the difference anyway. It's perfect."

We stayed like that for a little while, then released each other. I curled up on the nest, the chest behind me, and relaxed happily. "This is an excellent gift," I told her, and I could see on her face that she felt just how sincerely I meant that.

"We have another surprise for you, too," she said, barely able to hide her excitement now that I'd been so grateful for this first one. "But we all promised Herald that she could be the one to tell you, so it will have to wait for the morning."

"What?" I asked, disappointed, but I forced myself to be patient. If they'd promised Herald . . .

"You'll have to wait," Mak repeated. "Sorry."

"Nah, yeah. It's all right. But don't let Herald oversleep, okay? I don't care what it takes to make her and Tam into people again tomorrow. I don't want to wait until noon to find out what you're keeping from me." I hesitated, then added, "Please?"

"Don't worry," Mak said. "We all need to be at the censor's office before noon tomorrow, anyway, and we all want to tell you the surprise before that. We'll be down here early tomorrow, even if I have to pour one of Rib's energy potions down each of their throats."

"Promise accepted, then," I told her, and she smiled at me.

"I'll go upstairs now. There's plenty to take care of before the night is over. I'd love to bring you up there, but . . . well. Maybe one day? Now, I'll keep one of the keys to this door. The other is on a hook on the wall, there."

I looked and confirmed that, yes, there was a key on the wall.

"I don't see any way that you'd get locked in here by accident, but please don't close the door unless you have the key in here, yeah? A door like this is expensive, and I'd rather not test if you could break it down."

I snorted at that, though I did consider it. Could I break the door down? Maybe. "I'll make sure," I told her. "Good night, Mak."

"Good night, Draka," she said, then left, closing the door behind her.

I got up and dropped the bar. For the first time in a long time I felt completely safe and alone, an unfamiliar and welcome feeling. A few tears trickled down my cheeks before I wiped them away. Was this the kindness of my dear friends, or the dutifulness of my loyal servants? It didn't matter. My gratitude, and my appreciation for them, was the same either way.

There was no banging on the ceiling here. It was dark, quiet, and comfortable. I lacked my hoard, but the box smelled of gold and silver. I curled up on the nest, my little home away from home, and fell fast asleep.

CHAPTER NINE

In the Rolls

I awoke to knocking on the door, followed by a groan that I only belatedly recognized as my name. The unnamed need that I'd felt last time I woke was still there. No stronger, no weaker, but still there, and I had no idea what to do about it. I got up, stretched, and lifted the bar, then gently pushed the door open.

Outside Herald stood, supporting herself with one hand on the doorframe and a perfect picture of well-deserved misery. She scowled at me, her hands clenching and unclenching, and I raised my eyebrows at her and backed up, lying down again in my warm, comfy nest.

Narrowing her eyes, Herald seemed to come to a decision. She drew in a long, sharp breath through her nose, then half stomped, half stumbled into the small room and draped herself on top of me.

"Mak woke me at the ass crack of dawn," she complained into my back, "and I want to die."

"Did you eat anything?" I asked.

"Kill me," she demanded.

"Did you drink anything? A big mug of water?"

"I will never drink anything ever again. Please just spray venom directly into my lungs and end this."

"Herald. Go back upstairs, to the kitchen. Drink plenty of water, and eat something. Preferably something greasy. And if you have anything you usually drink for pain, like for cramps or something, drink some of that. Or, you know what? Ask Mak. She should know a thing or two about hangovers."

"She laughed at me!" Herald moaned miserably. "She thinks this is funny!"

"She also loves you, and will help you if you ask her. Now go!" I said, putting all the gentle force I could muster behind my words.

Herald growled, but she got to her feet. With a look of incredulous betrayal, she turned and left. I closed the door behind her, and shortly thereafter I could feel her and Mak close together, walking around the inn.

I hadn't gone to the dream-place this night, I thought as I drifted off again. Odd. I wondered if there was something that triggered it, and if I could control it somehow. I'd have to figure it out at some point.

The next time I was awoken I could feel both of the sisters outside my door. And when I opened it I saw not only them, but Tam and Val as well.

Herald looked marginally better, even managing a weak smile. Tam was . . . keeping himself together. He was hanging off of Val and raised his hand weakly in salute, but that was it.

"Good morning!" Mak said, oddly cheerful. She patted her sister on the arm. "And thank you for getting this one to come to me for some help with her hangover."

"Yeah, well, I figured you'd know better than me. Not like you have electrolyte drinks or aspirin here." That got an odd look from the men, but I just ignored it. Herald and Mak, who knew where I'd come from, just took anything odd I said in stride at this point. "Are you all heading out to the, what? Censor's office, was it?"

"That's right!" Mak said, her mouth curling into a wide smile. "We need to be registered in the tax rolls!"

First I blinked. Then I thought about what she'd said, trying to decide if there was any way I could have possibly misheard her. But, no, she had definitely said that she was going to get them signed up to pay taxes. Which, yeah, sure, perhaps you needed to do that to avoid getting in trouble later, but why the hell was she so happy about it?

"And that's a good thing?" I asked. "Very exciting?"

"It is! Because only families who own at least one hundred twenty dragons' worth of property more than their debts are required to register in the rolls. And we do. And it's the family that's registered, not members. I mean, each member is on the census rolls, to keep track of the population, but a family only truly exists if it's in the tax rolls!"

Then it dawned on me. "And if you're going to register, that means that your family will have a name?"

"That's exactly what it means!" Mak said. They were all smiling now, even Tam, and Mak's was wide enough that it threatened to split her head in half. "From refugees to a real Karakani family in one generation, it's . . ."

Her voice broke, and suddenly she was crying, still smiling wildly as Herald wrapped one arm around her and pulled her into a tight side hug. "Thank you, Draka. If you hadn't been with us in the north . . . Thank you! Herald, do you want to . . . ?" She looked at her sister while waving one hand at me.

Herald looked at her sister with a perfect lack of comprehension, then her eyes went wide and she turned to me. "Yes! Of course, yes! Ah, um, so . . . Draka. We need to register a family name. In the rolls! And we have been talking it through, and we were wondering . . . could we use yours?"

Time stopped.

What did she mean, use my name? They couldn't register me. Sure, I probably had enough money in my hoard, but I wasn't a citizen. I wasn't even a person as far as most of the city was concerned. And I sure as shit wasn't paying any tax!

Then things fell into place piece by beautiful piece. What Mak had told me the night before, about having another surprise. How they'd all promised Herald that she could be the one to tell me, which must mean that it was something Herald was excited about. And now this, asking if they could use my name for the rolls. They wanted to put my name in the rolls when they registered themselves.

They wanted to name their family after me. An achievement that most citizens didn't even bother dreaming about, and they wanted to use it to honor me. Sure, Mak was right—I had been instrumental in finding the treasure, but we'd all been there, clearing out the trolls, and Tam and Val did all the legwork afterward.

They'd made this little place for me, inviting me into their home. But with what they were asking, they were inviting me into their family.

Still standing silent in front of them, I, the mighty dragon, began to cry. My pride flared and so did my anger, directed at myself for showing them this, or any, weakness. I shoved it aside. There was no place for it. Not here, not now.

"Yeah, nah, yeah, that's . . ." I said, trying to sound dismissive and turning my head away in embarrassment. "That's fine. Yeah. You go ahead and—"

At that point I was cut off as Herald wrapped her arms around me, squealing with delight. Then Mak joined her, and then Tam and even Val crowded into the small room and turned it into a big, awkward group hug.

"Thank you, Draka," Herald whispered.

"Yeah. Of course! Just, if my name gets out there, maybe something like "Drakona" or "Drakonus" is better? Or "Drakonum?" I don't know if it's grammatically correct but "Drakonum Draka" sounds better, anyway, and it gives you some plausible deniability and—"

"Sure, we can do that," Mak laughed, no doubt feeling every shred of how moved and overwhelmed I was at that moment. "We'll all know where it came from either way."

I wanted so badly to go with them. And perhaps I could have, staying in the shadows and playing my little game of mobile hide-and-go-seek with the entire population of Karakan. But while I didn't care much about getting spotted anymore, getting spotted near them would be risky. They were already pushing it by taking a name that could, without much imagination, be connected to me. So I stayed. I asked them to take Ardek with them again, with instructions for him to run back and let me know immediately if anything happened, and asked them to send Kira down on their way out. Then, when I was alone in the cellar, I let myself cry properly for a little while.

In a fairly messed up way, I had a family again. I had already begun to think of Herald and Mak in that way, but for all of them to recognize it in such a permanent way, it was more than I could handle. And while I knew exactly why I was reacting this way, part of me was still confused and annoyed at my reaction; though the fact that I was alone at least kept the anger at bay.

I wiped my face furiously on my pillows when there came a knock on the door. I'd retreated back to the strongroom; this was still a working inn with guests, and there were staff who needed to get things from the cellar now and then. We might have to let them know the situation at some point, at least Reben, who still handled the day-to-day operation, but it was still too early for that.

I lifted the bar and gave the door a light shove, and a narrow sliver of pale light came in through the crack, growing wider and brighter as Kira struggled to open the door enough to enter.

"You asked for me," she said, looking around the small room nervously. She was carrying one of the lightstones, clutching it in both hands between us like a talisman to ward me off. I wondered what I looked like, lit from below by that single, cold light as I towered above her, seated on my throne of pillows and blankets.

"*You can change the color of those, you know.*" I reached out to tap the stone lightly. "*Want me to show you?*"

She stared at the stone for a moment. "*Please. This cold light is depressing.*"

So I took the time to show her what I'd figured out about the things, and my experience translated pretty well. She listened seriously and understood my explanations quickly, and soon she was adjusting the hue and brightness of the light to her liking, spending some time getting it just right. I watched, proud and satisfied that I'd actually taught her something useful.

She settled on an orange tone that reminded me of a sunset, though much brighter. "*There,*" she said, satisfaction tugging at the corners of her mouth. "*That's it.*"

"*What is it?*"

"Home," she sighed. "*It's the light through the window of the big room of our house, right before the sun dipped below the hills in the evening. Something in the air there does something to the light. I didn't think I'd ever see it again after I was bonded.*"

"*Stick with us and you can have it anytime you feel homesick.*"

Or if she stole one of the lightstones and took off, I thought, but that was neither likely nor something she needed to hear.

"*I'd like that,*" she whispered. Then, in a more normal tone, she said, "*So, what did you want with me?*"

What did I want? I hadn't had a plan when I asked the others to send Kira down. I suspected that I just didn't want to be alone, though it could also be that I wanted to keep an eye on her.

Or it could be that I was alone and, in most ways that mattered, so was she.

I settled on asking her, "*Have you been learning any Karakani?*"

She concentrated and said, "Little I learning." She messed up the word order and missed a prefix, but her pronunciation was solid. "Stone, frog, play . . ." She smiled fondly and switched back to her own language. *"The kids back at the moun-tain taught me some 'important' words, but your servants have been trying to teach me to actually speak the language."*

I snorted at that. "Servants." I still had some complicated feelings about that description, even if I couldn't deny that it fit Mak, to some degree at least. She'd be the first to agree, whatever I'd told her about my feelings on the subject. But Herald? She was mine, there was no doubt about that, but calling her my servant felt . . . It wasn't enough. She was so far above that. Ardek was a servant. Kira might be, though that was a whole situation in itself. But Herald?

My dearest friend couldn't be my servant. Companion, perhaps? Partner in crime?

As I pondered I realized that I'd been quiet for quite some time. Kira was getting fidgety and otherwise looking anxious, probably worrying that she'd some-how offended me.

"That's good," I said, breaking the tension and allowing Kira to relax. *"I'm happy to hear that. What have you been practicing?"*

We spent the next hour working on her Karakani, practicing simple sentences. I let her choose what she wanted to learn, and wasn't surprised when she had me teach her things like, "Are you hurt? Where does it hurt? I can help. Sit still. Hold him. Hold her," and similar short phrases. That led into me asking her about how she'd gotten her healing advancement, and what other advancements she had.

Kira was almost entirely open. She didn't hesitate to tell me about her advance-ments, except for one, which I had to drag out of her. Her first two advancements were about helping the sick and injured, figuring out exactly what was wrong and what to do about it. The last one, though, the third minor that she'd gotten before her major, her healing magic . . .

"Fine," she said, surrendering to my badgering before I felt it necessary to resort to commands or threats. Her face was flushed with embarrassment. *"Healthy pregnancies and easy childbirth, all right? I always wanted a herd of kids, but I assisted a midwife for years and . . . well, I don't know what it's like for a dragon to lay an egg, but I've seen too many complications."* She sighed, her mood steadily dropping. *"I was scared. Then when I hit my threshold, it was that or being much more resistant to disease. But it was never a good time, and then I got my major and I was bonded, and it wasn't like I was going to bring a child into that kind of life . . ."*

Her voice croaked at the end, but she sniffed once and kept herself together. *"When I got my first high minor I got the disease resistance. I can't heal disease, and there's a lot of bad water in the field, so I had to protect myself. And that's where I'm at."*

"How do you not hate them?" The words just fell out of my mouth, with no conscious thought connected to them. An anger had grown inside me as she spoke, and I couldn't keep it inside anymore. *"They took your dreams! They forced you into what is just a word away from slavery! How can you defend that place?"*

"It's home," she said helplessly.

"They took your life away!" Some of my anger was turning against her now. For her weakness, for the way she didn't stand up for herself. She could have run. She could have made a new life for herself somewhere else, like Herald and Mak and Tam's parents had done. I felt a disgust rise inside me, wondering why she hadn't fought, when even death would have been better than what she'd submitted to.

Then just as quickly I was filled with anger and disgust at myself. She wasn't a warrior. That was the first thing she had told me. All she wanted was to help people and to have a bunch of kids, and I was angry at her for not fighting? No. I stomped that part of myself down into a corner of my mind. I didn't need Instinct right then. Kira didn't need her. She needed some goddamn sympathy. And I understood, or at least I thought I did. I had been so happy about being included in Herald's little family, and that was all that Kira wanted. A family. People who loved her.

She cowered at my outburst, unable to look at me. I didn't know if she was too afraid to move or if she was literally unable to run from me, but I felt so fucking ashamed. How could I blame her for what others had done to her?

"Kira," I said gently. *"Kira, look at me."*

I could see her trembling, and her gaze stayed fixed on the lightstone in her hands.

"Kira. Please."

She slowly, with little jerks, raised her head and met my eyes.

"I'm sorry. I'm sorry for everything that's happened to you, and I'm sorry for what I said just now. But it's not too late, is it? You're young. You could make a life here, as a healer. Learn the language. Meet someone. Have a whole bunch of kids. I wouldn't stop you."

"How could I?" she whispered. *"I'm still not free."*

"Perhaps not. But you're freer than you were, and I think you could still be happy. Here in the city, or with the refugees back at the mountain, or in some village . . . Anywhere you go, there will be people who need help. And . . . What would you do if I let you go?"

"What do you mean?"

"If I told you, right now, that you're free to go. Even asked the others to give you some money to help you on your way. What would you do?"

"I . . . I'd go back, I guess."

"Would you? Could you go back to the people who forced you to travel with a band of murderers and kidnappers? What would they do with you? Do you think they would let you live out your life in peace?"

She slumped at that. When she answered, her voice was barely a whisper, only audible in the silence of the small room. *"No."*

"They'd probably send you right back, wouldn't they?"

"Yes."

"*To the death and the cruelty and the suffering.*"

She squeezed her eyes shut, fighting tears. "*Yes.*"

"*I would never ask that of you, Bekiratag,*" I told her, and I meant it. "*I've told you before, and I'll tell you again, I will never ask you to be part of anything that involves harming anyone else. I might ask you to heal someone afterward, but that's as far as it would go. Doesn't that sound better?*"

"*Yes.*"

"*Look at me, Kira,*" I said, and she opened her red-rimmed eyes. "*Believe it or not, but I want everyone who belongs to me to be happy. I want them to be safe and healthy and prosperous. One big happy family. Doesn't that sound good?*"

"*Yes!*" she sobbed, her face twisting for a second as she fought to control herself.

"*You could be a part of that, Kira. I want you to be a part of that. I could make you, but I don't want to see any more fear in your eyes than I already do. I want it to come from you. I want you to accept that you belong to me. That you belong here, with us.*"

"*I . . .*"

"*You don't need to say anything now. But I want you to think about it. Really look inside yourself. And if you truly believe that there is no place for you here, that you have to return to your people, to Tekeretek, that you will be better off there, then I promise you that I'll make it happen. I'll let you go, with enough money to get you there. No matter what the council thinks. I swear it, on . . . on my hoard.*"

She looked at me, silently, with a desperate hope in her eyes, and I knew that I had her. She knew as well as I did that there was no chance for her to be happy in Tekeretek. They'd sold her to the highest bidder, and they'd either return her there or do it again. And I meant every word that I'd said to her.

"*Think about it.*"

CHAPTER TEN

Family

Kira didn't leave. Nor did she answer me. I made some room for her among the pillows and blankets, and she sat with me as we continued our lessons in Karakani. I'd been keeping track of Herald and Mak, of course, making sure that they stayed together and didn't seem like they were in any trouble, but I didn't let that interrupt my time with Kira. This was the first time we'd actually done something normal together, and I didn't want her to feel like I wasn't giving her my undivided attention.

I only rounded off when I felt my friends returning to the inn, but I asked her to stay. When they piled into the strongroom they were far less boisterously cheerful than I'd expected, but their smiles were as bright as any I'd ever seen.

"It is done," Herald said. "We're a real family. The House Drakonum!"

"The taxes are ridiculous," Mak said, grinning. "Three dragons per year, but we should be fine. We may need to go out on another adventure or two every so often, though."

No one seemed upset about that.

"Anyway, we've talked a lot these last few days. And, now that it's all official—and I want you to know that this isn't Herald and me! Tam agrees, and Val likes the idea." She turned to look at the others, who just smiled and nodded.

I felt a warm, wonderful pressure in my chest. I knew what was happening. It wasn't hard to guess, but I needed to hear her say it. "Go on."

She gathered herself, looking straight at me. "Draka, I can't officially adopt you, unfortunately, but as matriarch of House Drakonum, I would like to formally extend to you an invitation to join our House. There would usually be a ceremony, and there's a whole ritual where you'd accept my authority over you in all things"—she grinned and shook her head—"but, we all know *that's* not happening. And legally anything you own would be mine to dispose of as I see fit, but . . . yeah. We can skip that, too. Really, I'll have to improvise. So, Draka, of parts unknown, will you join our family, House Drakonum, the House named for you, that you made possible? Will you defend us as we defend you, be it a question of life, happiness, or prosperity?"

Herald had leaned in close to Kira, whose eyes grew wide as she heard Herald's translated words.

"Will you be our sister in all ways but blood? Before the gods, if not the law? Will you do us this honor?"

It was completely unnecessary, of course. We were already bound to each other in a way that I knew no way of breaking. I would already defend their lives, their happiness, and their prosperity, because I take care of what is mine. But at the same time, they were offering to give me the only thing they had that I could not simply take.

A traitorous thought tried to make me doubt their sincerity. To make me believe that they were only acting out of obligation, or compulsion, or even cynical selfishness. But the outpouring of sincerity and open love and kindness that I felt crushed that voice utterly.

"Yes!" I looked at them each in turn, sitting up to my full height and spreading my wings so that they filled the room, their tips curled around Kira and Val on the edges of the group. "Yes. Happily, and without a shred of doubt."

I nearly had the wind knocked out of me as Herald laughed with unbridled joy and threw herself at me, and I choked just a bit as she wrapped her arms around my neck.

Mak laughed and continued in Tekereteki. "*Kira. Bekiratag. You understand that I do not know you well enough to extend the same invitation to you. But, as long as you stay with us, you are a guest of House Drakonum and under our protection, such as it is.*"

Mak held out her hand. Kira looked at her, then me, taking in the entirety of the House with one long, slow sweep of her eyes before settling on Mak again.

"*Thank you,*" she said without a trace of sarcasm as she clasped Mak's wrist. "*If nothing else, I have no doubts about my safety.*"

We had a private celebration that evening, just the five of us. The family. Well, Val wasn't legally part of the family, for whatever reason, but neither was I. It didn't make it any less real.

We sat in the cellar, the bar upstairs well stocked and the door barred from the inside to prevent any interruptions. A table and four chairs had been brought down, with me sitting on a pile of pillows at the short end, opposite Mak. We talked, we sang, and we laughed. We ate ridiculous amounts of roasted meat. They drank—too much in the case of Tam and Val. They decided to try and get some wine in me, and it wasn't like I wasn't curious. I'd barely thought about alcohol since coming to Mallin, being too busy surviving and making a life for myself, but I'd always liked splitting a bottle or two, or much, much more. But I had no idea what it might do to me, and the idea of losing my inhibitions in the body I had now, with Instinct always lurking in the back of my mind . . . no. I politely declined, and when Mak felt my unease she stepped in as well. But that didn't diminish my enjoyment of the night one bit. It reminded me of our evenings around the fire as we returned triumphant from the north, but better, and it was a wonderful time.

As close as I felt to everyone present that night, I still couldn't bring myself to tell Tam and Val my secrets. They were my allies, they were my brothers, but they weren't mine. They didn't belong to me. I cared about them, and I would defend them and do what I could for them. But a deep-seated part of me still couldn't trust them completely.

I didn't control them. It was as simple as that.

But I didn't let that dampen my mood, either. We continued well into the night, until the time came when Tam and Val were simply too drunk, almost passing out where they sat, and needed to be put to bed. Mak decided to be the responsible one, coaxing them out of their chairs and up the stairs, and we all said our good nights.

Herald, though, clever girl that she was, had snuck a nice, long nap in the afternoon. She was barely tipsy and had no interest in sleeping, and we both agreed that there was only one thing to do. She let me out the cellar door, went out the front door herself, and then we were flitting through the shadows of the street, sometimes together and sometimes racing each other, reveling in this incredible thing that we shared only with each other.

I discovered something then. I'd always thought that my shadowsight was the same no matter what, so it came as a surprise that when we were shifted I could both see and hear her perfectly. There was none of the distortion that I experienced with everything else, or the odd distance that I'd heard in her voice when she was shifted and I was not. And she was breathtaking, a shining, ethereal spirit dancing and leaping and laughing through the light of our inverted landscape.

I let her win, just so I could watch her revel in her newly claimed power. I could have watched her all night. My magnificent little sister.

We finished at the abandoned garden. We shifted back, she leaped onto my back, and I took off, climbing hard. Soon we were high above the city, Herald whooping and cheering and just barely hanging on as I dove and whirled and cruised, and climbed and climbed and climbed and climbed! Herald kept shouting, "*Higher, big sister! Higher!*" How could I deny her anything when she asked like that? I went higher and higher until the whole city was visible in a single glance, and I only turned the climb into a long, lazy descent when I heard her voice shudder with the cold—not that it stopped her howls of joy.

I settled on the roof of the towering lighthouse, which sat at the end of the spit of land embracing the city's harbor. I did so lightly, and if the lighthouse keepers heard and wondered about the thump on the roof, they didn't make a fuss. With a bright light below me and the darkness behind I should have been impossible to spot, but I chose the side facing the sea on the off chance that someone with the right advancement and the right interest just happened to be looking our way. There, with me lying down on the lightly sloping roof and holding onto the spire at its peak, and Herald relaxed on my back in something like a full-body hug, we looked at the city across the water.

"*It is beautiful,*" I whispered.

Herald hummed in agreement. "*I pity anyone with regular night vision. To not be able to see how the city glows in the light of lanterns and torches . . .*"

"*Yeah.*"

"*What are the cities like where you are from? At night, I mean.*"

"*There are so many lights that you often cannot even see the stars. Buildings and signs lit up in every color you can imagine. Towers a thousand feet high, with tens of thousands of people living and working in them, shining in the dark, visible from a hundred miles away on a clear night. The roads and streets are ribbons of light, just miles and miles and miles of them, with carriages moving on their own, visible as little dots sliding along them. I . . . did not like it much. It can be beautiful, but for me it was usually just too much. This . . .*" I looked across the harbor at the muted lights of Karakan. "*This is just right.*"

"*Do you miss it?*"

"*Honestly, I barely think about it anymore. I know it has not been long, but . . . it is only relevant to part of me. How can I be nostalgic for something that one half of me never knew? So, yeah, I will remember family sometimes, or Andrea, my best friend, and I will wonder how they are doing. But it does not hurt. I still love them, but not like I love you, little sister. You are important to all of me.*"

She giggled happily at that, and only held me tighter. She had no problem with being called "little," as long as it was me doing it.

After looking at the city in silence for a while I felt Herald shift her weight upward along my body. "*Is this all right?*" she asked.

I turned my head to see what she was doing. "*Yeah.*"

She finished maneuvering herself so that she sat with her legs slung over my shoulders, giving her a better view of the harbor and the city. "*So, what have you figured out about your advancement? Your second major advancement. In . . . Gods, in four months, you horribly spoiled lizard!*"

I bumped her on the arm with my horn for that, and she rubbed it in mock outrage, which was somewhat spoiled by her laughter. "*Well, I need to figure out how to do the dream thing. It has not happened again, so it is not something that just happens whenever I sleep.*"

"*Is that it?*"

"*Yeah? Oh, and I can see you when we are both shifted.*"

"*Yeah, you said.*" She pouted, then looked at me sternly. "*Draka, have you been trying at all?*"

"*What? I have been using my magic like I always do. It is easier, all right?*"

"*Fine, yes, but have you been pushing your boundaries? Listening to your instincts? Are you sure that there is nothing else you can do?*"

"*I mean . . .*" It had taken me three months or more to figure out the fear thing with my shadows. "*Aw, shit. No. I guess I have not really been trying.*"

"Well, I guess we know what we are doing tomorrow, while we wait for Ardek and Barro to bring back news about the Night Blossom."

"Ardek?" He was never around much, come to think of it. I'd been wondering if he was avoiding me, but hadn't cared enough to be annoyed as long as the others kept track of him.

"Yeah. Mak has him helping Barro. It keeps him mostly safe while also keeping him out of the inn. You know. Away from her."

"Oh." I was surprised that Mak was ordering *my* servant around, but found that I didn't mind. And I had told her outright that I appreciated her handling stuff like that. *"I do not suppose that Mak offered him the protection of our House? Like with Kira?"*

Herald laughed at that. *"Ardek? Mak? No."*

It was no surprise that Mak hadn't offered Ardek the same formal hospitality as she had Kira. She'd apologized for how she'd treated him. For beating the shit out of him in a fit of pent-up rage, really. Since then they'd been getting along politely enough, at least around me, but there was still some clear lingering resentment on her part, which might never go away completely. And I didn't blame her. If Ardek wanted her forgiveness, or Herald's, he would have to earn it. To his credit, he had been trying to do just that, and doing a good job helping Barro should go a long way.

"He is doing a good job," she continued. *"He recruited some old friends of his from the street to help him out, so we have some less recognizable people to keep an eye on the streets for us now. We are mostly paying them in meals and peacocks. He has not told them a word about us, of course. As far as they know, they are working for him, and we're just the new proprietors of the inn where he feeds them."*

I made some appreciative noises. I liked his initiative. The kid was clearly serious about making himself useful.

Herald stilled where she sat on my shoulders, and her face became serious. *"He mostly has them watching Tark. Parvion Tarkarran. The little shit who . . . you know."*

"I know."

"Draka, when we kill him, it needs to be me who does it. If at all possible, it needs to be me. I know he hurt Mak, too, but . . . I still have nightmares, Draka. I do not know if they will ever go away." She shuddered. *"It needs to be me. Please."*

"I would not have it any other way," I promised. *"If at all possible. But if it is a choice between me killing him or letting him get away—"*

"Yeah. I understand. And I agree. But if you can—"

"I will leave him for you, little sister."

"Thank you." She stroked my head and scratched the dumb little bump where my left horn was growing back. The right one was four inches long now, curving slightly back over my neck, and then on the left there was that little . . . thing. *"We should be getting back, I guess."*

She was right. My internal clock was pretty good, and it told me that it was well into the small hours. Dawn couldn't be far off. "*Yeah. Lie back down, and let us get going.*"

"*Tomorrow we will do some serious practice.*" Herald's tone left no room for discussion. "*We are going to figure out what you can do.*"

I sighed. "*Yeah, all right. What about you?*"

"*I figured out my abilities before you even woke up that morning in the cave. But I should probably try to push my limits. Just getting to the garden before was exhausting.*"

I didn't tell her that staying shifted for as long as she had, only days after I got my powers, would have been unimaginable to me. I loved the girl, but she was getting a big head about it as it was.

"*Have you tried using your shadows on people, like I do? Can you cause fear? It took me months to figure that one out.*"

"*I . . . well, no,*" she admitted. "*I should probably try that. But it is not like I have anyone I would like to try it on, in case it works. I do not want to terrify someone I like, you know? And some poor innocent person would be even worse!*"

"*Just ask first! I am sure that Ardek would let you, if you asked nicely.*"

"*Yeah,*" she said dismissively. "*Maybe.*"

That whole line of thinking seemed to bother her, so I changed subjects. "*Will you get a license? The whole reason we met was that Tam tried to save twenty eagles on a magic-in-the-city license and slipped up, remember?*"

"*I have thought about it. But what I can do—invisibility, manipulating shadows, perhaps more? They are so remarkable that I am worried about drawing the wrong kind of attention. Perhaps I am being romantic or paranoid, but I do not want to be pressured into acting as a spy or assassin or something like that.*"

That hadn't even occurred to me, but I remembered vaguely when Rib and Pot had told me that despite all the magic in this world, invisibility was considered in the realm of fantasy. Herald might be right to be worried.

"*Well, be careful, then,*" I told her. "*Your powers are too strong to not use them.*"

"*You say that as though I could stop myself,*" she scoffed with a little laugh.

That night I dreamed of shadows and blood. Not another lucid dream, though I tried to will that to happen as I went to sleep. In a completely normal dream I followed the scent of jasmine through dark streets, biting and tearing at the poor fools my prey threw in my way, never seeing more of her than a flutter of silk as she ran from me. But I was relentless, and after an eternity I had her cornered in my strongroom. She turned, her face covered by a veil, and I rushed forward and ripped the damn thing from her face so that I could look her in the eye when I—

An impassive, androgynous face stared back at me, and I felt a sharp pain as an arrow slammed into my chest. In spite and fury I tried to tear my killer's throat out, but my whole body was going numb. They simply pushed me to the side, took the red lacquered box under one arm, and stepped past me out the door.

When Herald woke me by banging on the heavy strongroom door the next day, my internal clock told me that it was nearly noon. The need was still there, and I still ignored it.

When I unbarred the door and opened it for her I was met by a big, eager grin. *"Come on, great lazy one,"* Herald said. *"We have work to do!"*

"It is the middle of the day!" I complained. *"I will not be able to fly you out without risking being seen together!"*

"Why would we need that?" She waved me out and through the short corridor that connected the strongroom to the main cellar. *"We have the whole cellar to practice in!"*

The table and chairs from the night before had been cleared. Someone, presumably Herald, had placed lanterns here and there, and the columns, barrels, and shelves cast numerous overlapping shadows around the space.

"What about the staff? Will they not need to come down?"

"Maybe. I told them that I would be doing some training and exercises here, so they should at least knock first. Why? Are you afraid of being seen? Do you doubt that you could hide in time?"

I snorted at her in irritation. *"I do not care about being seen. I care about making you all targets, worse than you already are. Every time I wake up, I am surprised that the Night Blossom's goons have not tried to torch this place yet."*

She sighed. *"There is that, I suppose. Though my theory is that she is simply afraid of you."*

"Afraid?" I liked the sound of that.

"You killed her guards, and then you killed her pirates. Quite publicly, I should add. Perhaps some of her people are rethinking their loyalties. Perhaps she hopes that you will leave her alone if she does not provoke you anymore."

"That would be nice. It would buy us a lot of time. But I doubt it. She did not strike me as the careful type."

"Yeah, me neither. So we are waiting for her next move and taking precautions, while planning our own. You can feel that Mak is out, can you not?"

I checked, and yeah, she was definitely out. In the direction of the center of the city. *"What is she doing?"*

"Attending an open council session with Val. She hopes that the Night Blossom will be there. She might be able to get her real name that way."

"Sounds like a boring way to go about it when we can just tear it out of Tark. Which is what we should be doing instead of—"

"Draka, please." Herald looked at me patiently. *"Calm. Careful. Barro and Ardek are gathering more information on where and how we can move against him, remember? We do not know nearly enough. We know where we might find him, yes, but we

do not know who he surrounds himself with, or if there is a better place to strike where he will be more vulnerable. And when we do strike, we need to know if there are any tools you have at your disposal that you have overlooked. Besides, we need to be more careful, now that we know he is not just some connected nobody. His family may not be powerful, but they are rich enough to be in the rolls. We need to know if and how they may retaliate against us, if it became known that we were the ones to kill him. We need to take our time."

I huffed and clenched my jaw at that, but she was right. I had asked her and Mak to help me when I became too eager, and that would only do any good if I forced myself to listen and accept their judgment.

It still rankled, though. I wanted to take Herald on my back and fly out to the upscale tavern that Simdal had pointed out as his most common haunt. Grab the little bastard, break his limbs until he told us everything we wanted to know, and then let Herald slit his throat, or turn him into a bloody sculpture, or whatever she needed to do to put her nightmares to rest. And then I wanted to dump whatever was left of him on the Forum and let anyone cowering nearby know that the Night Blossom was next, whoever she was.

Yeah. I definitely needed to listen to Herald.

CHAPTER ELEVEN

Training Day

So, how do you want to do this?"

I walked into the middle of the room and sat down under the lantern, hanging from the thick boards that made up the ceiling. *"I tried to do the dream thing but it did not work. Is there a way that people usually figure out what their new advancements let them do?"*

Herald stepped over to the stack of barrels that divided the room, climbing up and turning around so that she sat looking down on me, her head nearly touching the ceiling. *"Instinct, mostly. We get visions or strong impressions when we choose, and then we can usually let instinct guide us. Thought it might take some triggering event. Mak knew immediately that she could heal, but it took until she was in the dark before she found that she could give herself and others darksight. I knew immediately when I woke up that I could change my sight and shift into the shadows, and that I could move them and make them darker . . . though, knowing you helped with figuring out the second part. I still had to figure out myself how to push magic into the shadows or the lightstone.*

"You told me once that you have an actual voice telling you your options. The, uh . . . Well, you. Your dragon side. Is that still true?"

"Not with my last two minors. I got some very strong impressions about what my options would do, but no voice. But then I got my major right after the second one, and the voices were back. I . . . am not sure what to make of it."

Herald looked up in surprise. *"Voices? More than one?"*

"Yeah. Have I not . . . ? I have been hearing the other voice, the human, I think, ever since I woke up in that prison. It has been acting as my conscience, sometimes, keeping me from going too far. Have I not told you about this?"

"No!" Herald said indignantly. *"I cannot believe that you would keep something like that from me! I thought you were two minds sharing a body! What does that mean about you if you hear both sides of yourself talking at once?"*

Yeah. That was something that had been worrying me, too. But it felt like way too heavy a subject to discuss just then, and we had things to do. *"We can talk about whatever is going on in my head once the Night Blossom is dealt with, yeah? I was not done. Before, I had the dragon guiding me, helping me figure out how to do things with my magic. She could be snarky about it, but she was generally helpful. Now it is all emotions with her. She has not said anything for days, since I received my second major."*

Herald didn't look at all happy about me refusing to talk about the voices in my head, and that was fair. She was worried about me, and I loved her for it. But when I made it clear that I didn't want to talk about it she only sighed and nodded, relaxing a little. *"All right. Some other time. What did she say about your new major, then? How did she describe it?"*

"Ah . . . I don't remember her exact words, but it was something like fear is our tool, the shadows are ours, no matter where they are, and our enemies cannot hide, even in their dreams."

Herald rested her chin on her hands where she sat, looking at me thoughtfully. *"Well . . . you could already make people afraid. So it seems to me that something should have changed with that. You know that you can . . . I do not even know what to call it. Dreamwalk? See the dreams of others, interact with them somehow? But you have not figured out how yet?"*

"Right."

"So you need to do that, preferably tonight. The part about the shadows, though. Being yours, wherever they are. That definitely sounds like a change. You have only been able to affect shadows that you are in, right? Like me?"

"Right again."

"So, have you tried to command a shadow far away from you?"

I thought about it and stared at her in utter disbelief. Some old human impulse made me want to bury my face in my hands out of sheer embarrassment, and only the length of my neck stopped me from doing just that. *"Damn it, Herald! How could I not think of that?"*

"It has only been a few days, big sister." Her voice was kind and soothing, but I was having none of it.

"It is right there in the description! 'No matter where they are!' It is so obvious, now that you have pointed it out! I cannot believe—"

"Draka!" Herald's tone was sharp, but not unkind. *"If talking about what is going on with your head can wait, then so can self-recrimination, hmm?"*

I snorted. *"I suppose."*

We spent the next hour confirming that, yes, I could indeed affect shadows that I was not directly touching. Starting slowly, I focused on the shadow of one of the pillars closest to me, and just like I would with my own shadow or one that I was touching, I commanded it to deepen. It took a bit more effort than usual, but dark tendrils limned in gold quested out from me, pushed through the light separating me from the shadow, and burrowed into it. It responded, growing darker and deeper. At my will it shifted to the left, then to the right, then grew wider, pushing out the light and plunging that part of the cellar into complete darkness.

"*Interesting,*" Herald said. "*When I look normally all I see is the shadow chang-ing, but with my shadowsight I can see the tendrils connecting it to you.*" She stopped and thought for a while. "*Can you control the shadows that it touches?*"

I tried, bending the shadow of the pillar into that of a shelf, and yeah! I could now control that shadow as well, separate from that of the pillar. It took consider-ably more effort, though, far more than controlling the pillar from a distance. As I was messing around with that I discovered two things. The first was that if I moved the shadow of the pillar so it was no longer touching that of the shelf, then I lost control of the latter. If I drew back my tendrils, of course, I lost control of both, each shadow snapping back to its natural state. But when I was testing the limits of that, I made my second discovery.

I was trying to find if concentrating extra hard on the second shadow might let me keep a tendril in place from the first. I put nearly all of my focus into keep-ing the shadow of the shelf extra deep. Nothing fancy. I focused so hard on that, poured so much of my magical energy into it, that it came as a sharp shock when the first shadow lost contact. I instantly lost the ability to sense and control the second shadow—but it remained as it was. I felt suddenly exhausted, but I heard a sharp intake of breath from Herald, and knew that I wasn't just imagining it.

The need I'd been feeling became stronger. It wasn't bad, but definitely noticeable.

Herald walked over with long, purposeful strides, looking closer. "*The shadow. It did not change back!*" She hurried over to one of the lanterns placed on the floor and brought it over to the shelf.

The shadow moved and grew more shallow, but that was all. It didn't vanish. It *resisted* the light, drinking it in and leaving the items on the shelves in an unnat-ural darkness no matter how close Herald brough the lantern. "*Draka,*" she said, a note of awe in her voice. "*This is—Did you* enchant *the shadow?*"

"*Touch it.*" I had a sudden urge to see what would happen if Herald tried to manipulate the shadow that I had set in place. "*Try to move it, deepen it, anything.*"

Herald reached out with her hand, physically touching the shadow, and when she commanded, it responded, but sluggishly. "*Oh, this is hard! So much harder than anything else I have tried. Like it is fighting me!*"

She laughed and moved the shadow a little to the left, then right, and when she let go it snapped right back to the same place and the same depth that I had left it.

A simple test showed that I could remove the effect. And we discovered just as easily that I didn't need to go through an intermediate shadow to do it. It took a little trial and error to figure out just what I had done, but once I had that down it was simply a matter of commanding the shadow to do what I wanted, focusing on keeping it there, and then withdrawing. It was exhausting, and the unnamed need I felt increased slightly each time, but the shadow would remain fixed just as I had left it. I was about to end the effect again when there was a knock on the upstairs door, making us both jump.

"Missus Herald?" a boyish voice called. "I'm sorry, Missus Herald, only the kitchen is out of cloves!"

"*Oh, dammit!*" Herald hissed, looking around. "*I have no idea . . . Hide for a moment, will you? I will have to let him come down.*" As I shifted she turned to the stairs and called up. "Come on down, Rel!"

The door opened and a stampede rolled down the steps. I hadn't known it was possible to make so much noise walking on stairs, but the teenage boy, whom I recognized as Relki—one of the two street kids I'd terrorized—coming down managed it.

"Sorry, Missus Herald, won't be a minute," the kid said, picking up a lantern and going for some of the back shelves. I drifted out of his way as he looked around. "Sorry, coulda sworn . . . fuckin' . . ."

I looked on in confusion and saw Herald do the same. Then realization dawned on both of us as he kept looking, his obvious embarrassment growing as his eyes just slid past the shelf with my frozen shadow on it.

After a moment's amusement Herald went over and rummaged through the shelf, and that seemed to break the spell. When she bent to check one of the lower shelves I wished I had eyes to roll in shadow form, as I caught the kid staring at her for a few seconds before he nervously stepped up next to her, reaching in to grab a lidded clay jar. "Sorry, Missus Herald," he squeaked, his voice breaking as he blushed.

"Do not worry." Herald backed up and gave him a smile. "I have only been here a few days longer than you, and I cannot find everything down here, either."

"Yeah, but . . ." he looked at the shelf, then shook his head. "Right, Missus Herald. Thanks. Sorry."

He fled up the stairs, as noisily as he had come, and I couldn't help but laugh once I'd shifted back. "*So you all decided to start a collection of your own?*"

"*A collection . . .? Oh, Relki and Sana! Yes, well . . . some of the staff were unhappy with the new ownership and left. And we thought the kids could do better with a roof over their heads and some food in their bellies. So. But this!*" She went back to the shelf. "*You saw the same thing I did, did you not? How he just could not seem to see the shelf?*"

I grinned. "*I have a lovely new toy to play with.*"

We did some more experimenting, finding that as long as Herald saw me set a shadow she had no trouble finding whatever it was I'd been trying to hide, but if she looked away when I did it she had much the same experience as Relki. Unless she used her shadowsight, in which case whatever it was stood out.

There was a tiny bit of drama when I decided to mess with Herald, stretching and kind of bending her shadow, then setting it in place when she was still lost in fascination with what I'd done to the shelves. When she walked into the light of the lanterns and realized what I'd done, she yelped!

"*Draka! Not funny! Please, this is . . . I hate it! It is like the whole world is wrong. Draka, please!*"

It took a minute of me laughing and her pleading before I undid my work, with a dear and holy promise on our friendship that I would never do it again. It did, however, show that the effect remained when the object casting the shadow moved, adapting to the lights around it. In Herald's case, it was as though she herself had been stretched and bent, with the shadows cast by the multiple light sources reflecting that.

It was an amazing thing to be able to do, and I laughed with undiluted delight as I reversed what I'd done to Herald. "*Thank you, little sister. If not for you, I might not have discovered this for months, if at all.*"

"*Thank me by keeping your promise and never doing that to me again.*" She laughed with relief as her shadow snapped back, and then she immediately started shaping and moving it. "*It was a horrible feeling, when my own shadow resisted me. Like a limb going numb. Perhaps we should be satisfied there?*"

"*Yeah. I am exhausted. Setting shadows like that really takes it out of me. A break, and then we continue later?*"

Herald looked at me, then turned her face away, embarrassed. "*What?*" I asked.

"*I have promised some friends to meet them this afternoon. At the Guild.*"

At those few words jealousy raged through me, quick and hot, like fire on the wind. With it came the urge to find these others, and to show them beyond a shadow of a doubt that Herald was *mine*. But she would never forgive that. No, better to just grab her, to fly her to my nest and leave her with my hoard, where she belonged. She'd understand. It was better that way. She'd be safe there, and no one could—

No!

The single word snapped me out, like I'd been dunked in a pool of freezing water. One word that carried all the context and guilt and shame that I needed to fully realize where my mind had been going. A place that would at best have been nearly impossible to come back from, no matter how much my little sister loved me.

Herald must have seen something in that split second, because she continued, almost without pausing, "*. . . but I can send someone to tell them that I cannot make it! Really, I—*"

"Nah, you go." I turned away from her, trying without success to sound relaxed. The warring jealousy and guilt were so strong that I couldn't even look at her, and the need nagged at me. "I should check on Jekrie and Tinir and the rest of them. Maybe have a look farther north and see if those trolls they talked about are coming south. But you'll be safe, right?"

She looked at me with concern, but nodded. "I will be at the Adventurers' Guild. Safest place for me in the city. And Tam will be with me. And I thought I might take Kira . . . ?"

"Good idea. It'll probably be good for her. See if you can get her a license to use magic in the city, too. Just don't let anyone know too much about her. Make something up, I don't know."

"I will."

"Could you . . . ?" I gestured at the cellar doors with my head. "I may as well head out."

"Draka? Are you sure? Are you all right?"

"I'm fine," I *almost* snapped at her, then sighed. "I had some bad thoughts that I need to deal with. And I've had this feeling that I need something ever since my advancement. I need to figure that out, and I really *do* need to see if I can find whatever drove Jekrie and his people south. Go. Have fun with your friends! Just . . . stay safe."

She looked like she wanted to argue, but like so often she decided to let me have my way. She opened the doors, looking outside to make sure that the yard was clear. "You be safe, too. And that need you mentioned? We will talk about that when you are back. Fly high!"

"I will," I promised. Then I shifted, wrapped myself in shadow, and left as fast as I could.

What the *fuck* was wrong with me?

I got into the drains, then left the city through the sewers. Shifted, I made my way two miles or so up the coast before I took to the air, so that it wouldn't be obvious where I'd come from if anyone saw me. Then I just kept going. I climbed, but I didn't turn inland. I just kept following the coast north, with no goal in mind.

I'd been getting more and more possessive, and I didn't like it. That was the long and the short of it. Whenever the prospect of being separated from Herald came up my fear and jealousy reared their ugly heads, and I needed to be talked down or shamed into relenting. And it had been getting worse in the days since I received my new major. The need drew me north, but even then I had a constant urge to just turn back around and follow my sense of where Herald was. Grab her and stick her somewhere safe. The strongroom, maybe. I could have Mak and Ardek and Barro look after her, and Kira on hand in case anything happened and . . . God damnit, my thoughts were going there again!

She's a person, not a thing, I reminded myself. *I'm not some storybook dragon stealing away princesses. It's not Instinct taking over. I'm worried about my friend. That's all.*

I reassured myself with the fact that I'd let her leave my hoard twice now. I'd let her leave me in the forest to make her way into the city with Kira, and I'd left her so that she could go spend time with her *other* friends. I could handle the separation. I just didn't like that I kept feeling this possessiveness.

I kept going north for an hour, then two, going farther north than I ever had, even on my expedition with the others. With *my family.* As high up as I was, almost kissing the lowest clouds, the few ships that I saw were only little specks on the water. Even sailors avoided the north, I'd been told, afraid of coming close to the un-reclaimed and reputedly cursed ruins of the capital city of the Old Mallineans. Anyone I saw up here would be someone who'd crossed the Sareyan Sea and ended up slightly off course, and now they'd be trying to make their way south as quickly as they could, sails full or oars creaking.

I wasn't sure if the ruins being "cursed" meant anything beyond just having a bunch of monsters around them, but I had seen myself that there were plenty of monsters in the north, and as I understood it, they would only get more common the farther I went.

And now those monsters were coming south in greater numbers. Rallon had made it sound like a general problem, driving people from their homes and forcing them to flee south, just like Jekrie and his people. And it didn't exactly seem like Karakan had the resources to deal with them, if they were relying on mercenaries to patrol their roads. I had no idea how many people there may be coming south, but I wouldn't be surprised if there would be more bandit problems in the future. Desperate people do desperate things.

And God, I almost hoped for it. It would feel good to get my claws in someone or something that deserved it! I'd been forced to flee from the archer, and I was still pissed about it. When I'd helped the Barleans I'd held myself back from getting violent, so that the damned judge or lady justice or whatever they'd called her wouldn't get pissy if she heard about a dragon stalking the alleys.

When I slaughtered the Night Blossom's pirates, though, oh, how glorious that had been! I'd been able to truly cut loose and let myself be a dragon. It had been so simple. Bad people trying to hurt good people that I liked. Not a peep from my conscience. Just claws and teeth and venom, screams and hot, sweet blood in my mouth and—

And I needed badly to find some kind of outlet for my draconic side that didn't involve slaughtering people every few days. I needed to hunt, and fight, and kill something terrible.

Maybe that was the need gnawing at me? A need to just be a dragon? Perhaps just letting loose for a while would fix me? It was worth a shot. And whether it worked or not, I knew that I'd enjoy it. But first, I needed something to let loose on. I needed gremlins. Valkin. Trolls.

I needed monsters.

CHAPTER TWELVE

Heart of Darkness

High above the coast of north-eastern Mallin I turned toward the mountains. I ignored the need that pulled me north, and the jealousy drawing me back south. I beat my wings, angled myself down, and just let my speed build until I was screaming through the air, then worked hard to maintain the highest speed I could. I crossed the forest in record time—twenty minutes, twenty-five at the most. By the time I reached the high hills I was practically kissing the trees, and only then did I steer south in a long, wide curve; at the speed I was going, even my strength didn't hold my wings stable enough for a tight turn, my joints creaking and my muscles trembling when I tried it.

When I was going the right way, on the right side of the forest, I tried to let go. I took all my worries about what was right, and what was smart, and long-term consequences, and I tried to stuff them down into a corner of my mind. I tried to just let Instinct take over, to think like a dragon, to act like a dragon, hoping it would relieve the pressure that had been building up these last few days and prevent me from exploding and doing something awful when it mattered. I tried to find an outlet. Luckily, I knew where to start.

My new people had been driven from their homes by monsters. That was, of course, very convenient for me, but it also demanded a response. It didn't matter that the offense had been committed before my new humans belonged to me; the guilty party, trolls in this case, must suffer the consequences nonetheless. Both because they might wander south, into my territory, and to show my people what I was willing to do for them.

I was being responsible, really.

I knew myself well enough to understand that I might not be able to kill a troupe of trolls on my own, but it would be good to know where they were. Taking a look wouldn't hurt. I could have taken Jekrie or some other human and had them show me where Piter's Clearing and Sweet Creek were, but humans were so slow and fragile. If I could not find the ruined settlements, I might have to fly one of them up to show me, but for now I would rather not be held back.

I amused myself on the way by swooping after birds. I knew from before that most animals were just regular, non-advanced examples of their species, even here in the north, but the monstrous versions were far more common. The thing with birds, though, was that I was bad at identifying them. Back home I was all right; cockatoos, lorikeets, magpies—swoopy bastards that they were—and bin chickens, I could recognize on any given day. Here, though? If I saw a bird, chances were good that I had no idea what kind it was. On top of that, many bird species were small enough that I had a hard time deciding if I was looking at a monstrous example of one species, or just a regular specimen of a larger one. Except for something like an eagle, of course, but they steered clear of me, as they should.

Not that it mattered either way. Dragons did not prey on birds. I knew that now. Hunting birds was simply too much effort for too little food. Most birds that I could catch were too agile, and those that weren't were too fast. Of course, once I started, pride demanded that I keep going until I succeeded. I had to try over and over and over again before I managed to grab some kind of long, skinny waterfowl out of the air. It was deceptively fatty and delicious and it satisfied my pride, but that didn't justify spending nearly an hour doing aerial maneuvers when I could have taken a deer or a goat in half the time.

My little hunt had taken me to the vicinity of the bandit camp I had helped destroy several months ago, and while that brought with it a surge of pleasant memories of enemies slaughtered and plunder taken, it also told me that I had gone too far to the south. Jekrie had estimated that they'd traveled forty to forty-five miles from their homes to reach my mountain, and by my estimations that meant I'd need to backtrack a dozen miles or more.

That was easily done, of course. I had a fair sense of distance, and soon I decreased my speed and began searching the ground for streams. I had little to go on besides the names of the settlements and an approximate distance from my mountain, but it was only reasonable to assume that they would be in clearings near water.

I followed the first stream I found east into the forest. It soon joined a wider and faster one, which picked up more water as it went. When I'd followed it halfway to the coast it was a proper little river, but I was also much too far east. It was getting dark by then, but that didn't bother me. I turned around and followed it back upstream, flying long zig-zags across the area. I saw plenty of likely breaks in the trees that caught my interest, but one by one they turned out to be bogs, fens, natural clearings, or old, old ruins that nature had not entirely reclaimed yet. I was becoming increasingly annoyed with my lack of progress when finally, after more than an hour of searching, I found the remains of Sweet Creek.

The settlement lay on the bend of a gentle creek, and it had been torn apart. Houses lay collapsed, walls torn out or broken in, and stains and the smell of old blood combined to tell me well enough what I already knew. Not everyone had escaped Sweet Creek alive.

The only living beings remaining were animals. There was a complete lack of human remains, but otherwise no sign that the trolls had returned since the place had been destroyed. I returned to the air, searching slowly and carefully. I knew that Piter's Clearing was close, so I stuck to an area a few miles around Sweet Creek, and it paid off.

Piter's Clearing lay on a different, faster tributary to the river that I'd followed east. It was a larger settlement than Sweet Creek, but it had fared no better. The only building still somewhat whole was what I assumed to be a communal barn, a large structure on the edge of the settlement. And there, as I stalked through the ruins of the village, I found the trolls.

There were six of them, and they had turned the barn into a charnel house. The gnawed bones of humans and animals alike were strewn across the floor and lay in piles, and among those piles the trolls slept, safe in the knowledge that nothing on this island was stupid enough to attack them. For once that included me. I watched them dispassionately. I looked at what they had done, and I refused to let my human side drive me to violence. It was funny, in a way. For once it was Conscience that screamed and raged and spat bloody oaths of vengeance and death in the name of the victims that we would never know, that should be nothing to us; and it was Instinct that held us back. *"Why should we risk pain and death for these unknown humans?"* she said, and since she chose to speak, I listened. *"They are long gone. We know where the trolls are, and we have minions who know well how to kill the creatures. So long as they are content to remain here and deplete the local wildlife, there is no rush."*

Coward! Conscience spat as I forced myself to leave the trolls behind. I walked out of the village and followed the water downstream, gritting my teeth. She was being ridiculous, of course. I was being smart. Patient. We would be back, soon, to destroy the creatures. And walking away had not been easy. I had wanted to leap in and do as much damage as possible to the closest of the bastards, then run off into the night as they woke in the confusion. But I remembered Tiny. I remembered how quickly a troll could go from sleeping to beating the ever-living hell out of me. And now there were six of them.

If I had not been trying so damned hard to be a dragon, we would have been weeping bitter tears of impotent rage. But I was, and I was not going to risk our life over some unfortunate souls who I had never met. I certainly wouldn't feel any guilt about postponing their inevitable vengeance.

But I remembered Tiny. Tiny had beat the hell out of me.

Tiny had lost.

Tiny had been smaller than average. But I had been smaller then, too.

And I wanted so very, very much to destroy something.

Sunrise found me, like so many sunrises, in a tree. Again, I had failed to dream-walk, but I didn't let it bother me. I had other concerns. I was well rested and a little hungry; the need was stronger than ever, and I was filled with anticipation.

I watched the trolls leave the barn. Much like Tiny's troupe, this one consisted of one huge male and several females. And they behaved the same as well, their morning ritual of wrestling, smacking each other around, and roaring in each other's faces being comfortingly familiar to me.

When they each went off in a different direction I chose to follow the smallest one. Not only because I wanted to kill one of them with as little damage to myself as possible, but because she was going in the opposite direction from the male, heading north.

Her behavior quickly struck me as odd. It was the way she moved. As I followed her in the treetops I didn't see any of the hunting behavior that I'd observed in Tiny. There was none of the sniffing or stalking. Instead, this troll moved with purpose and direction, along a crude path of trampled undergrowth, broken branches and torn out bushes. She wasn't looking for something to eat, I decided. She was going somewhere.

I hadn't seen that kind of purpose in a troll before, and I was understandably curious. Where was she going, along an already broken track? And why was she so eager? As she got farther she picked up speed, and soon I couldn't stay close enough to see her in the well-lit forest, forcing me to shift back and follow her at a distance by long, flying leaps.

I decided to call her Speedy.

I felt the answer before I saw it, though I had no idea what it was. The draw I'd felt, the need, the urge to go north, became a kind of pressure. Not against my skin or muscles but, for lack of a better explanation, against my soul. Not uncomfortable, just . . . there. As we followed the pressure it was soon accompanied by a sense of location, not much different from the gentle pings I still felt from the south and southeast where my hoard and Herald and Mak were. Finally the sense became strong enough that, rather than following Speedy, I let my curiosity and hunger get the better of me and flew ahead on my own.

It was only a short hop of less than a minute. There was nothing special about the location. The trees surrounding the small glade were perhaps a little denser, the forest floor a little darker. The undergrowth might once have been a little thicker, but it had been torn and trampled. The only thing that made the place truly special, the source of the pressure and the sense of location, and the troll's goal, was what I found there.

Suspended in the air, about a foot off the ground and wreathed in swirling shadow, was a Nest Heart.

I had only ever seen one, months before, but it was unmistakable. Sitting out in the open the way it was, in the middle of the day, I could see that the area around it was much darker than it should be. The light around it seemed to fall into it, gently distorting as it got closer to the swirling mass of shadow before vanishing as though the Nest Heart drank it in.

When I switched to shadowsight it shone. It was a swirling lens of pure light, fixed on a beam of gold that passed through it from the earth into the sky. It was, beyond any doubt, one of the most beautiful things I had ever seen, and I *needed* it.

When Speedy arrived she did so at a run, crashing into the glade and skidding to a halt before the Nest Heart, giving off a sense of having made it just in time. Once there she began to circle it, giving off soft crooning sounds as she reached out with a gentleness that should be impossible for such large, shovel-like hands. She traced her fingers through the wisps of shadow, and in my shadowsight the Nest Heart responded.

I didn't see any magic coming from her, but as she crooned and caressed the Nest Heart, the golden beam that pierced slowly pulsed, brighter with each cycle, and it responded by swirling just a little faster with each pulse. I couldn't say how long it went on. I sat hidden in my tree watching, frozen by fascination as the Nest Heart grew brighter and brighter and swirled faster and faster, until it was so bright that it should have been blinding; it whirled so fast that it and everything for several feet around it was a blur and then, without warning, the world went white. I blinked away my shadowsight, and even with my excellent night vision the area around the Nest Heart was as dark as the deepest depths of my mountain.

When the darkness cleared there were two trolls in the glade.

The Nest Heart still hung in the air, the shadows spinning around it lazily, but it looked diminished. Thinner, almost, as though there was less of it. And beside it, groaning on the ground, lay a troll. A male. It was only a little larger than Speedy, though nowhere near as large as the two I'd seen before, but it was, for anatomical reasons, unmistakably male.

My curiosity had cost me my chance to kill Speedy. I was sure of that. I was not going to attack two trolls at once, even if one of them was groggy on the ground. I valued my own skin too much for something like that. But the Nest Heart called to me, so I sat patiently in my tree as Speedy shuffled over to the male, grunting and crooning softly as she pushed at his shoulder. After a short while, the male finally turned his face to look at her, growling in annoyance.

Speedy popped him. One long arm rose, and the shovel hand came down, palm flat on his face. His hands went up to cover himself and he growled angrily, so she popped him again, and that, it seemed, was that. He gave a petulant groan that I could only interpret as, "Okay, okay!" and then, with Speedy's help, he got unsteadily to his feet.

Speedy looked around, seeming unsure of herself. She looked back the way she'd come and huffed disdainfully, then sniffed the air as the male took some stumbling steps, tearing at the bushes and branches around the edge of the clearing.

With a grunt Speedy seemed to make up her mind. She took the male by the arm and pulled him toward the northeast, away from the other trolls, away from the Nest Heart, and away from me.

I watched them go, wondering what exactly I'd just seen. A new troll being, what? Born? Created from nothing, or brought here from somewhere else? Was this how all trolls came into the world? Did it matter? Where before there had been six trolls there were now seven, but two of those had taken off, away from the others. Was I seeing the birth of a new troupe?

I knew two things. First, I needed to ask the others, my *family*—I grinned at the thought—about this. Second, I was finally free to indulge my curiosity, and satisfy my need.

It was time to take a closer look at the Nest Heart.

I'd been curious about the things when I first saw one in the gremlin nest, back when I'd first met my family. That curiosity had only grown when I realized how much my own tendrils of shadow, limned with the golden glow of magic, resembled what I'd seen. I'd been somewhat disappointed when I hadn't found a Nest Heart in either the valkin-held tunnels or near the trolls we'd killed; I'd wanted to see one again. Now I had one right in front of me, and it was gorgeous.

It was a little less than it had been, sure. Thinner, less substantial. Lesser even than how I remembered the gremlin's Nest Heart. Bringing a whole troll into the world must have taken a lot out of it. But it was here, and it was mine, and it awakened a whole new kind of desire in me. I descended the tree, and the closer I got to the Nest Heart, the stronger the urge became to *eat* it.

I couldn't describe it any other way. I wanted to take this beautiful thing and consume it, to strip it layer by layer and draw it into me, make it part of me, like the nest-killing crystal had done.

The pressure that had led me here had never gone away, though it had reduced in strength when the Nest Heart was depleted. Like the heat of a flame it increased exponentially as I got close, and I got the impression that it *wanted* me to consume it. It wanted to be in me, to become a part of me, and all I had to do was . . .

I reached out with one trembling finger, touched the swirling wisps of shadow, and let them flow into me. It was as easy as breathing in. Layer by layer the Nest Heart spun, unwinding itself, flowing in through my palm, down my arm, and into my chest. I felt it settle around my heart, wrapping it in a warmth that began as quite pleasant. It was almost comforting, and the act of drawing the stuff into myself was pleasurable on a level only matched by burying my face in my hoard. But as I drew in more and more, the heat grew more intense, quickly turning into an uncomfortable tingle and then into a painful, burning heat. But I didn't stop. I refused. Instinct didn't speak, but I felt her eagerness and excitement. The desire to devour the Nest Heart entirely, the pleasure of taking it into myself, was so great that I forced myself to clench my jaw and endure the fire that seared me from the inside, body and soul. The Nest Heart grew thinner and thinner, less and less substantial, and in my shadowsight the pillar of light that pinned it to the earth became as thin as a needle. The pain grew to the point where I almost lost my resolve, almost began to fear that the heat inside me would turn me to ash, or burn out my soul, or something equally terrible.

Without fanfare, the needle of light vanished. The last wisp of shadow streamed into my hand and settled around my heart, and for one blessed moment the pain became so intense that I couldn't feel it anymore.

Then the miniature sun around my heart exploded outward, filling every part of me, and I passed out.

CHAPTER THIRTEEN

Satisfaction

When I awoke, the need was gone.

I couldn't have spent more than a minute or two on the forest floor. When I came back to and forced myself to my feet the sun and the shadows were just where I'd last seen them, though the glade was brighter now that the Nest Heart was gone. There was a strange silence about the place, and it took some time to figure out what it was. No birds. All the birds had taken off.

When I moved, my body felt different. Not bad, and not by much. It wasn't larger or anything like that, as far as I could tell; if anything, it felt too small, like I didn't fit in my skin anymore. Yet I felt light on my feet, alert and full of energy in a way that I usually only experienced after a long nap on my hoard. And when I looked around, it wasn't just that the glade was brighter because the Nest Heart was gone; everything outside was brighter as well, the colors more vivid. Not by a huge amount, but it was enough to be noticeable, and I looked around in wonder.

Slowly the birds returned, their songs clearer and more distinct than I'd ever heard them. It all felt incredibly tranquil, and I felt at peace in a way that I hadn't in many weeks. My bloodlust was gone. My fears and worries about losing Herald or anyone else seemed completely ridiculous. No one could *take* them from me, because they weren't mine to lose. They were my friends, even my family now, but they didn't belong to me. How could I ever have thought that?

It lasted for a few minutes. A few wonderful minutes of peace and beauty that slowly faded away. The intensity bled out of the world, and the sense of peace was replaced with my normal sense of the present. But I didn't regret their passing. The anger, the desire to destroy, that didn't return. Nor did the need. It felt sated, somehow. And while I got used to the feeling of not quite fitting in my skin, I still felt like I was more than I had been.

It couldn't compare to the peace that I'd felt, but I had a sense of nearly complete contentment as I took to the sky and headed south.

I decided to check on my people. Not because they needed a reminder of who they belonged to, or because I feared for their safety, but because I genuinely wanted to see how they were doing. It had been two weeks now since I took them in, and I hadn't really talked to any of them. The exception was when I left a few days ago, and that had been mostly them declaring their loyalty to me. I wanted a conversation, and I was feeling magnanimous.

I did what I always did, coming in low and landing a thousand feet or so north of the gate, so that I could approach stealthily on foot. My caution was unwarranted, though. I watched the nascent hamlet from the trees, and everything seemed calm and peaceful. Skins dried on racks, meat smoked over a fire in the old fireplace. Some people sat in a circle by the single, proper building they'd finished, a log longhouse. I was impressed that they'd built something like that, out here, in only two weeks, but they had Advancements and a couple of generations' know-how to draw on. They were talking, sewing, and weaving baskets, while others did . . . something, preparing a fair-sized plot of land for a garden where they'd cleared some land. And they were smiling. Not too far off I could hear children laughing among the trees.

Satisfied that there were no outsiders around causing trouble or who might freak out, I simply strolled into the camp.

The people preparing soil for planting were the first to see me, and a murmur went through the half-dozen men and women as they stopped what they were doing and stood, lowering their heads respectfully. Jekrie was with them, so I gave them a "How ya going?" and asked him to follow. The rest stood and stared at me, but that was no surprise. They'd just have to get used to it.

To give them all some exposure to my terrifying self, I went and laid down near the big, smokey fire where they were preserving meat. The little crafting group froze as I came near, Jekrie stood silent, and it became clear that if I didn't speak, no one would.

I waved at the closest log bench. "Go on, sit!"

Jekrie practically fell onto the bench in his rush to obey me. I sighed. This might get annoying.

"Relax. I'm here to look in on how you're all doing, nothing else. And it looks like things are going well! Didn't see that gardening patch last time."

"Yes, Great Lady! We're settling in well, thank you, Great Lady! The hunting is good and the forage is plentiful, and no monsters spotted as of yet. We had some visitors two days back, but they gave us no trouble and moved on in the morning."

"All right, good. Good." I nodded toward the garden. "What are you growing?"

"Some hardy roots and greens, Great Lady, that might have time to grow in before second harvest ends."

"Yeah? No herbs or anything?"

He hesitated. "This is all we have seeds for, Great Lady."

"Ah, right. Makes sense. You had to leave in a rush."

"Yes, Great Lady."

"All right . . . say you could go back to Piter's Clearing. Do you think there are seeds and such there that you can use?"

I was delighted to see a careful hope fill his eyes. "If the trolls ain't eaten them, Great Lady. And there is much we might be able to salvage, if only—"

"Would you move back there, if you could?"

Jekrie raised his hands in a fervent denial. "No, Great Lady! Never! We're yours so long as you'll have us, and anyway the north is too dangerous for us now, few as we are!"

"If I may, Great Lady . . ."

A voice came from the crafting circle, and I looked over as Tinir got to her feet. She walked over to me, hand clasped and head bowed.

"We're in no place to ask for anything. I know this. But, Great Lady, do you mean to clear the trolls from our home?" She quickly corrected herself. "Our old homes, I mean."

"I was thinking about it. I don't like having them so close. And they hurt *my* people. I can't just let that go unpunished."

Tinir wrung her hands. "Of course, Great Lady. We would . . . It would be a great kindness, if you made it so that we could recover what we can."

"I'll take that into consideration." I hadn't decided how to go about getting rid of the trolls. My options at the moment were to try and pick them off, one by one, or to just ask my humans to help out. All I could offer was my gratitude and anything they could harvest from the trolls, but I was sure that they'd agree if asked. "Did you want anything else?"

Tinir was still fidgeting after my answer, and at my question she looked at me with eyes full of worry. "Great Lady, I . . . I know that we swore ourselves to you, and I regret naught, but the children . . ."

I wasn't sure where she was going, so I held her gaze until she finished her thought, her voice coming out in a tremor.

"Do you claim them?"

I stared at her in silence. I could only hope that I looked contemplative, because I was completely dumbfounded. The thought hadn't even occurred to me.

"You're not slaves," I said, slow and clear so that there was no room for misunderstanding. "This is not some inheritable sin or condition. I hope your children will want to serve me, but . . . Tinir, is it so terrible to belong to me?"

Jekrie looked at his wife. There was a silent plea in his eyes, and regret in hers as she looked back at him. Then she turned back to me and straightened her back. "I'll not break my oath, but we've always been free. Losing that is . . . bitter."

That, I could understand. Their forebears had fled north to avoid taxation, after all. Freedom and independence must be deeply ingrained in them.

The whole village was listening to me anxiously at that point, and some things clearly needed repeating.

"I will demand very little of you," I promised. "Nothing unreasonable, and nothing for selfish reasons. I demand no tribute that is not affordable and freely given. The only thing I demand of you, absolutely and without compromise, is secrecy. Other than that, you're free."

"And the children?"

"As long as they swear to keep my secrets, they can leave, if they want. If not . . ."

I left the rest unsaid. I didn't want to make any threats I couldn't go through with, but she quieted, her eyes flicking around me. Mercies' sake, did she think I'd hurt kids? I was pretty sure even Instinct wouldn't do that. It stung. She didn't actually know me, but still.

"In exchange I'll do what I can to give you and yours a safe and happy life. Which is why I'm here, now. I've already heard that you lack seeds. Is there anything else you need urgently?"

One of the other women spoke up. "If it please, Great Lady, we lost many tools. We have some, but work is slow and hard from their lack, and some things we cannot do at all."

"And Jemi's anvil," a man agreed, then hurriedly added, "Great Lady! If we had that . . . Well, Jemi is gone. But my boy Foren here was his apprentice, of sorts."

A broad shouldered teenage boy ducked his head at me.

"And we have few bows, and are running out of arrows," Jekrie added.

"So what I'm hearing is that the sooner you can salvage your old home, the better. That makes things simple, if not easy. If there's nothing else you need, then, I'll go."

The mood had relaxed a little, but ever since I walked into the village I had noticed people looking . . . not at, but around me strangely. They kept doing so as I got up, and when I looked at the ground beside me, following Tinir's eyes, I saw why.

My shadow was dancing.

It was near noon. The fire beside me was nowhere near high enough to rival the sun, and my shadow should have been firmly planted beneath me. Instead, it was a living thing, still attached but moving independent of me. Its neck stretched out toward one person or another, and its tail lashed in irritation as someone shuffled away from it. And I had no idea what was going on.

I couldn't show my ignorance in front of my people, though. So I focused, and I brought the unruly thing under control. It obeyed, of course, but I got the impression that it did so reluctantly, flowing back under me only because it was me demanding it. Then it sat there, still and shapeless. If a shadow could sulk, that's what it was doing.

I considered setting it in place, and it relented, returning to its normal shape and following my movements naturally. But I got the impression that it rolled its eyes at me.

I'd stood there for a few seconds figuring everything out when I remembered the humans. They were all staring at me. Not sure what to do, I just said the first thing that popped into my head. "Don't worry about her! She just gets a little excited sometimes."

As confused as any of them, I left as fast as I could.

I had enough presence of mind to not take the most direct route back to the city. That would have taken me past where the archer had shot at me, and there was no way to know whether they would still be there or not. By flying south along the mountains and then taking a sharp turn toward the coast, I hopefully eliminated any chance of running into the same person. The forest was huge, and it had been plain dumb luck that put them in that tree as I was flying by. At least, that was what I hoped. And while twelve hours earlier I might have considered trying to bait them out so I could fertilize the forest floor with their remains, now I was feeling far more pragmatic. If I passed close enough for them to take a shot at me, they would see me far sooner than I saw them. And last time I'd only seen them thanks to Herald's warning. If there was a next time, I might not be so lucky, and the next shot might get me in the wing, the gut, the chest, the neck . . . Hell, even if it didn't get me somewhere lethal, the poison might take me down before I could get to Mak or Kira. No, it was much better to minimize the risk and hope that we could find them in the city.

I still wanted to find them. There was still the risk that they had seen Herald on my back and might recognize her, and I hadn't gone soft, all of a sudden. If I could get a believable promise out of them not to take it further, and an apology, then I might leave it at that. If not . . .

They'd shot an arrow at me. They'd poisoned me. The fact that I was considering mercy at all was a good sign, in my mind.

I made my way into the city the usual way. Shifting and moving while shifted was nearly effortless, and I sped along the narrow tunnels almost gleefully, easily making it into the storm drains without taking a single pause. My excitement was tempered a little when I realized that my sisters, though together, were nowhere near the inn. Without them there, no one would know to let me in.

All right. Fine. I'd just go to them.

I followed my sense of where they were until I was within a few hundred feet of them, and unlikely to get any closer. A few minutes searching brought me to a drain in the shadow of some tall building, only a hundred or so feet away. The drain was narrow, but as full of . . . something as I was after consuming the Nest Heart it wasn't too big of a challenge to stretch and thin myself to the point where I could fit through.

My first thought when I popped out was that I might have made a mistake. I was in a large public space. I only knew that because of the sound of hundreds of voices, a constant susurrus in the blackness before me. I had exited in the shadow of some large, official-looking building, and I could only think of one place that I might be—the Forum, probably the busiest part of the city besides the north and south docks. My sense of where my sisters were pointed into the blackness, but I had a pretty good idea where they were.

I considered going back down, but that felt like an old, overly cautious way of thinking. To anyone looking, I was just a patch of deeper shadow. What did I have to worry about? As long as I didn't get too tired to stay shifted, no one would be any the wiser. And, perhaps I wouldn't even need to worry about that?

I scanned the building I'd come up beside. It had columns, decorations, windows, even a balcony or two. In short, it had all kinds of things sticking out of or recessed into the walls, which made it perfect for anyone with the will and reach to try to climb it.

Getting to the roof didn't even take me a minute.

I did what I always did on roofs. I found a nice, shadowy spot. Then I shifted back, settled in, and just watched.

I'd been right, of course. I was indeed on the Forum, and below me hundreds of people milled about, coming or going or standing around in groups. Some of the groups were just circles of people talking to each other, while others were clearly one or two people soapboxing to whatever small crowd gathered before them. And I'd been right about where my sisters were. Now that I could see normally, my sense of them pointed me clearly to the Palace, the center of government for the city.

It was a relaxing way to spend the hour or so that it took before I felt my sisters moving. From the sheer number of people, it felt like half the city must have passed through the Forum. The soapboxers came and went, and some people seemed to be there only for them, joining new crowds as they formed. Small groups of armed people, who were clearly adventurers, would sometimes pass through, go into one of the three large official buildings, or use the place to meet up. And once a tight knot of uniformed guards cleared a wide path through the throng, a single well-dressed man approached my building at a relaxed pace among them. Some important official, I assumed, probably one of the councilors.

I felt them moving, and soon a stream of people left the Palace. The session must have been over. When my sisters came out, dressed in their finest clothes, I expected them to come to me. I was a little miffed when they didn't! What could be so important that they didn't come and say hi? They knew where I was. As distant as they were I could see them both looking my way every so often, even as they kept moving at a steady pace through the crowd. This was easier for Herald, of course, as she was a head taller than most, while Mak and I only had line of sight when the crowd happened to thin out. Despite that, it was most often Mak that I saw with her face turned my way, while Herald kept her face pointed straight ahead, as though she was fixed on something.

It occurred to me that they might be following someone.

I had no idea who that might be. I had a guess and a hope that it might be the Night Blossom or someone belonging to her, but I had no way of picking them out in the crowd. It made no difference. As Herald and Mak showed no sign of slowing and coming to me, I'd just follow them instead.

CHAPTER FOURTEEN

Before You Go

The afternoon sun was still high and bright enough that the moment I shifted my world was reduced to a patch of shadow around me. I quickly sent out a streamer connecting my little island to the shady side of the building where I'd come up, then flowed over the edge. To anyone watching as I poured down the wall and settled on the pavement below, it might have looked like some large bird had lazily passed in front of the sun.

As I flitted along the streets, keeping to the shadowy side, I felt an almost perverse anticipation. I *wanted* someone to spot me, to cry out in fear or confusion. But no one did. Either the combination of my magic and my instinct for staying hidden were just that good, or anyone who saw a patch of shadow moving in a way that it shouldn't simply kept their mouth shut. Which made sense, I supposed. I'd been told more than once that my shadow magic was something strange and unknown. Anyone who thought they saw the shadows moving might question their sight or their sanity.

Ah, well. A hue and cry would have been a problem. My sisters were trying to follow someone, and I assumed that they didn't want to be spotted if they could avoid it. The pair of them stood out as it was, so anything that drew attention to anywhere near them would likely ruin their chances.

Still, it made me bolder in my movements, and I soon caught up to Mak and Herald. The way they kept to the shady side of the street let me mostly keep them in sight, and as I got close Herald drifted toward me. She focused, gathering magic in her heart, and nothing happened. Then she frowned, her brow knotted, and an impressive mass of shadow tendrils flowed from her to deepen the darkness around us. She looked around quickly, flashed a smile in my direction, and then burst into a bright glow as she also shifted.

"*We spotted someone in the open session,*" she whispered without preamble. "*It may be the Night Blossom. We are not sure.*" Then she got a funny look in her eye and reached out and carefully touched me, or whatever the stuff was that I was currently made of.

For once, it didn't feel terrible. She didn't pass through me, either. She just . . . touched me.

"*You look good, big sister. More like yourself than you normally do while shifted.*"

I kind of wiggled at her in appreciation. Whatever had happened to me recently, I still couldn't speak. She gave me another fond rub on what felt like my neck.

"*I need to shift back, but it is good to have you here. Mak said that she has felt all kinds of things from you, and it had her worried. She was very relieved when we felt you returning to the city.*"

With that she looked around, picked her moment, and shifted back, joining Mak closer to the middle of the street. Staying close to them I heard her voice, speaking in a reassuring murmur.

"She looks fine. Healthier. It is hard to explain. But there is nothing to worry about."

"Oh, good." Mak breathed out a sigh, then flashed a relieved smile in my general direction.

Along streets and up stairs, through small parks and across little plazas, we followed the perhaps-Night Blossom into the upper city. Not Cloud Street, where I'd been before, but some other, smaller street. The houses here were still significantly fancier than most in the city, from my limited perspective, but less lavish than where we'd been held months ago.

"*They just went into a house on the northern side of the street,*" Herald whispered then, "*across the street from here,*" as we presumably passed the house in question. Since it was brightly lit I saw nothing, but I noted the small private sculpture fronting the house on the southern side, which I could see. We never slowed down, continuing and then turning to connect with some other street, which took us back down the hill, from where we continued straight to the inn.

Mak grinned where she sat on a barrel in the cellar, her legs dangling.

"Three days of standing around, feeling my mind rot. Four hours today of listening to incessant bickering about cloth tariffs and forestry taxes. I was going to give it the week out and then give up. But finally we may have gotten something out of it! Can't do anything hasty, since I'm not entirely sure that it's the right woman, but at least we can take a closer look."

I snorted in agreement and grinned, feeling a vicious hope take root. "We should have Barro see if he can find out who owns the house, and if he can find anything about them. Then, we can pay them a midnight visit."

"I cannot believe that you put up with *that* for *three damn days*, Mak." Herald yawned and stretched where she sat on the stairs. "I was ready to give up after that first hour! Arguing about bits on the dragon! I cannot imagine a bigger waste of time!"

I snorted at "bits on the dragon," which got me a satisfied smile from Herald, and a good natured eye roll from Mak. Getting serious, I asked, "If it's so boring, why are there so many people at these sessions?"

"It's a chance to get your voice heard. That's why it takes so long. Anyone from a family in the property rolls, *like us*"—Mak grinned at Herald, who did a happily little shuffle where she sat—"can go to the open sessions to raise concerns and make suggestions. If there's any merit, the council will discuss them. Which is why two points of discussion can take *four fucking hours*!"

"By how packed it was, I would say that every cloth trader in the city was there today," Herald grumbled, though she was still smiling. "Including our woman of interest, who suggested that Marbek may be willing to lower their tariffs on dura-wood if we lower ours on the import of fine wool. Or something like that. Mak?"

"Yeah, you've got it. I'd guess her House trades in one of the two."

"Which means that they must have ships, or at least contacts with someone who does. And warehouses, and perhaps shops. Anything we can do with that?"

"Legally? No. If we just want to hurt them and don't mind taking some risks, sure. But let's make sure we have the right people before we torch their livelihoods, yeah?"

"I suppose." Herald turned to me. "So, Draka! Where did you go? What did you do? You were glowing before you left, but now . . . you're so bright! Something must have happened!"

"Nah, yeah! Herald, you remember how when I left I mentioned a need for something that's been nagging me the last few days? Well . . ."

We filled Mak in on what we'd found out, how I could set shadows in place to conceal things. Mak was used to impossible things by then and took us at our word. Instead of protesting, I could see her mind immediately go to work on ways we could use my new ability.

With that out of the way, I told them about how I'd been feeling more possessive and jealous lately, skipping the details, and about how the need had been calling me north. They both nodded along. Herald had been with me when I had my crisis the previous day, and Mak had felt my emotions swinging wildly, to the point where she'd been worried for both me and Herald. Mak clearly wasn't happy about me stalking the troll the way I had, but she didn't say anything. When I got to the part about the Nest Heart, though, they both exploded with excitement. They glossed over the part about my shadow moving on its own as expected Draka weirdness—it had been calm and still since I returned, anyway—but destroying Nest Hearts? That was apparently amazing.

"You *ate* it? You can *eat* Nest Hearts? And it made you *stronger* somehow? Could you always do this?" Herald's face was a mix of amazement and incredulity, while Mak kept asking, "Like a Nest killer? Just like that? Just like a nest killer?"

"Yes, yes, no idea, yes, and yes!" I said, satisfied that I'd kept track of the rapid-fire questions. "Slurped it right up, just like a nest killer. And when I woke up the need was gone, or at least satisfied, and everything I've done with my magic has been just a little easier since then. I haven't tried linking or setting shadows yet. I wanted to wait until I was back with you. But I imagine that'll be easier, too."

"Well?" Mak said, watching me expectantly.

I glanced at Herald, who looked back and hissed, "Don't you dare!" I ended up demonstrating on a regular old boring barrel, but Mak was suitably impressed anyway. And it was easier, like I'd suspected. Smoother in a way, with less resistance.

Then I told them about going to visit Jekrie and the others, and how they were very excited about the idea of someone clearing out the trolls.

"I'm sure they could get everything they need from Pine Hill and the other villages in the area, but they don't really have anything to trade, and they seem a little leery about it in general. So I was hoping we could have a repeat of our adventure. Just . . . probably no big treasure this time."

Mak chewed on her lip. "If we're prepared for trolls, and take the right reagents and containers to harvest their blood, we could make some good money. Herald and me, we both have some new tricks that I at least would love to try out, and if we ask, I'm sure that Tam and Val would be up for it. What do you say, Herald?"

"When are we going?" Herald jumped up with an excited grin, which turned slightly guilty when she turned to Mak. "I, ah . . . I may have bought some new arrows that I want to try out."

"New arrows? Oh, no, how much did you—?" Mak sighed. "Go on. Bring them here."

It took Herald a minute or two to run upstairs and return with a sheaf of six arrows. The things were long and thick, with wide heads and long, brown and white striped fletchings.

Mak held one, drawing her finger along the shaft, and gave Herald a knowing look. "What enchantment, and how much?"

"Razor-sharp broadheads, and entirely unbreakable."

"How much?"

"A dragon each?"

Mak's relief was palpable. "Okay. That's not so bad. Could be worse. Could have been so much worse. I know it's your money, but . . . Yeah. I'm assuming you had Tam with you, to find a deal like that?"

"Yep!" Herald beamed. "Turned out that the seller was an old friend of his and Val's who just returned from Tavvanar. They *just* missed each other there, too! He came here when they left! Anyway, he wanted a dragon and five eagles each at first, but when Tam showed up and the guy realized that I was his sister he went down to a dragon!"

"Yeah, okay." Mak gave Herald a wry smile. "You realize that each of those arrows could have fed all three of us for a year, when you were a kid?"

"I . . . well . . ." Herald blushed. "I just always wanted something enchanted."

As Mak gently scolded Herald while admitting that, as splurges went, this wasn't so bad—at least it was something useful that was unlikely to lose much value—and Herald promised up and down that if she loosed one of her new arrows, she wouldn't return home without it, I just watched. My heart was full to bursting. They both just seemed so . . . normal. Sure, they were talking about spending gold coins on magic arrows to kill trolls and other monsters, but that *was* normal here. Expensive, but normal.

The important thing was that they were both happy and relaxed. Neither of them had struck me as terribly worried, anxious, or fearful for weeks now. I knew that they both still had trouble sleeping, but they were healing. If this lead worked out, or if we got something useful out of Tark when we grabbed him, we should be able to deal with the damned Night Blossom and finally put that awful chapter behind us. We'd have to deal with the consequences of what had happened, of course, but I liked to think that we, and our relationships, were all stronger for it.

When we got back to the topic of the trolls, Mak brought up one pretty big concern.

"The most pressing problem, except for the trolls themselves, is time." She had a contemplative look on her face as she spoke. "You told us it was about forty, forty-five miles north of the cave. Assuming that we can follow the forest road for most of the distance, we're looking at sixty miles or so of marching. We'll need to count two days each way, and add one to be safe. Then, if everything goes well, we'll still need to count three or four days to deal with the trolls. So we're looking at eight or nine days away from the city, right after we've acquired a big, hit-us-here-to-hurt-us piece of property. Garal and Lalia and the Terriallons have been going above and beyond what we could possibly ask of them, and Rallon is sure to want his cousins back on duty soon." She bit her thumb and came to a conclusion. "If we're going, we'll need guards, so it'll be in a few days at the soonest. We'll need to talk to Tam and Val about this."

Tam and Val were out, since Tam had decided to take his role as part-proprietor seriously and was trying to track down a supplier for a certain wine he liked. "What was the point of owning a tavern," he'd said, "if you can't serve whatever you want?" While we waited for them to return, Mak took Herald with her upstairs to do something business related. Mak insisted that Herald should learn to help run the place. Herald was not at all excited about the idea, but she had a hard time resisting her older sister when she was being reasonable.

I spent most of the time until Tam and Val returned catching up, first with Kira, and then with Ardek. Once he was awake, that is; he'd turned into quite the night owl. "I never used to like the dark too much," he told me. "But ever since you, uh, recruited me, it's not so scary anymore, you know?"

It was well into the evening when Mak came down to let me know that Tam and Val were back. They turned up in a fine mood, having found a lead on a supplier for that wine Tam was after. It soured somewhat when I told them about the

Nest Heart. After that, they were more than up for hunting some more trolls, if not for the potential money, then out of a sense of civic duty.

"When I heard that those refugees had been run out of their homes by trolls," Tam said, "that was worrying, yeah? A troupe of trolls wandering that far south doesn't happen normally. But a troll Nest Heart no more than twenty leagues north of the city? I know that we can't prove it—and no blame on you, Draka. Bless you for dealing with it—but we should report that to the Guild. That's a serious danger. Even if the one you found is gone, where there's one, there may well be more. Sorrows be kind! Nest Hearts, that close to the city . . ."

They had some ideas for how we could handle security while we were away, though it might take a day or two to arrange. That wasn't a problem, though. Tam wanted to meet with his prospective supplier, and the family would need to arrange supplies, as well as whatever it was that they needed to harvest the trolls. All of that would take time, and just as Mak had predicted it would be a few days before they'd be able to go anywhere.

That was fine with me. I hadn't had a good torpor for . . . gods, I didn't even know how long.

When we were all done Tam offered to be the one to let me out. That was unusual, but I was looking forward to a nice, much too large meal and didn't think much of it. Then he stopped in front of the doors as the others hurriedly left, turning around with an anxious look in his eyes. "Before you go, can we talk?"

"Nah, yeah, sure," I said, feeling a little wary. I wasn't in any hurry, but the whole situation felt off.

"Good. Thank you." He rubbed his neck awkwardly. "Right. Draka, we're family now, yeah?"

"Yeah?"

"And if you can't trust your family, if you can't let them know what's going on, who can you trust? Right?"

I had known plenty of people in my life who'd disagree vehemently with that, but arguing the point didn't seem like it would get us anywhere. "Right."

"Right. So, I agree completely with the decision to invite you to our family. I want you to know that. Mak suggested it, but it was a unanimous decision, with no argument. You've done so much for us, and asked for so little in return. And I truly believe that you'd sacrifice anything . . . well, almost anything, to protect us. I don't think it's even *possible* for you to give up anything from your hoard, from what Herald's told me."

I shuddered. I tried to imagine giving away some of my treasure, but just thinking about it put ice in my spine, while my stomach turned somersaults. "Probably not," I agreed. "But I'll risk my hide for any of you, if I have to."

"Right. But trust, yeah? We have to trust each other, let each other know what's going on. And our sisters have been acting odd since me and Val came back. I know they've been through something horrible, but it's not just that. The way they defer to you . . . Let's be honest here, the way Mak *obeys* you—that's not normal.

Herald, maybe, but not Mak. So I've been talking to them, but they won't tell me what's going on. Say they *can't* tell me. You see how that worries me?"

I could see that, yeah. To an outside observer, especially one who loved them and who hadn't seen the whole process, the change in the sisters' behavior must be striking. Mak's especially, and they hadn't even seen Mak at her lowest.

I didn't want to lie to Tam. I also didn't want to tell him that, "Hey, I broke your sister's will and now she's my unquestioning minion, literally unable to refuse to do what I tell her to, or think ill of me." There were things I thought he could handle without doing irreparable damage to our relationship, and those were not among them. So, since we were talking about trust, I decided to be selective with the truth.

"Tam," I said, settling on the floor, "how much *have* they told you about what happened to us while you were away?"

"Not much more than what Mak told us that first night. This Night Blossom's people grabbed Mak off the street, then Herald when she went looking. They've spared us the details. I'd rather not—" His voice quavered, and he stopped to gather himself before he continued. "Then they captured you, but you got loose. You got Mak out of whatever prison they had you both in, then you both saved Herald together, and you made it to the Wolves. They've told us more about what happened afterward, and Garal and the others have filled us in a little, but . . ." He raised his hands helplessly.

"All right. There are some things that aren't mine to tell. Things that happened to Mak and Herald that I'll leave to them to tell you when they're ready. But me and Mak, I can tell you most of that.

"What you need to know, the reason Mak follows me the way she does, is that they broke her. They used Herald to do it. Don't think about it too much. It was bad. I know what happened, and you're better off ignorant. But you need to know that they broke her, to the point where she helped them capture me. And after I broke us out, she was so ashamed and remorseful that she swore to do anything to earn my forgiveness and my trust. And then, well, you know about her advancement. She's bound to me. My strength is hers, and her loyalty is mine."

As I spoke his face had slowly hardened. Worry and fear turning to anger, first against the Night Blossom, but then, at the end, toward me. I could see that he was about to speak, to vent that anger, and I continued before he had a chance to say anything unfortunate.

"Listen, Tam. Mak and me, we understand each other. She chose this. I won't pretend that I've completely forgiven her, or that I never treated her poorly. There was a short period, a few days, where my anger made me cruel to her, and she bore it because of her guilt. But I promise you, that's over. I trust her, and I love her. When she invited me into this family . . . I don't think I can explain to you how grateful I was. She doesn't want me to be her master, or her friend, but her *sister*. So I will fight for her, like I will for any of you. I will not let anyone take any of you from me, and I will stop anyone who tries."

"Like you stopped the pirates?" Tam asked, the storm on his face passing.

"Exactly like the pirates. Does that make you feel better?"

He looked at me silently for a long time before he answered. "What you've told me about Mak, it's hard to swallow. It's not like I've seen you mistreat her or anyone else I care about, but the idea of Mak bending to anyone's will is just . . . I'm going to need to talk to her, I think, and see if I can get her side of it. But, yeah. I might not like what you have told me, but knowing makes me feel better. Not good, but better."

He opened the doors for me. I could have done it myself, of course, so it felt kind of symbolic. "Go, with my blessing!" or something like that.

"Talk to her," I said. Then I walked out into the yard and disappeared around the corner, leaving him with his worries.

CHAPTER FIFTEEN

Dreamwalker

I set out that night planning to be away for a few days, and I'd told the others as much. I'd made a point of telling Kira and Ardek, too. I wanted them to feel included. Ardek didn't care much about me coming and going without a word, since he was "enjoying all this sneak-around-corners and investigation dreck," as he put it. Kira, though, seemed genuinely pleased that I'd thought of her and assured me that she would be just fine at the inn. She'd been getting to know the staff, apparently, though they could barely speak five words to each other. She really could get along with anyone, and with not a single advancement to back her up, either.

She'd found a way to contribute, too. Mak had set her up with a magic license, claiming her as a refugee from Tekeretek and a guest of House Drakonum, which was mostly true. Now, with Tam, Mak, and Herald's help, she was healing people in the inn a few times per day. The patients paid whatever they could afford—with an occasional nudge from Mak—and Kira seemed happy with that. Of course, offering cheap healing brought with it the risk of a line out the door, and she could only heal so much before exhaustion set in. It was a balancing act between letting her feel that she was doing what she could, and not inviting trouble from people who were angry that she couldn't help them until she'd had some good rest. The others were gatekeeping access to her pretty hard, as I understood it, and asking her patients not to spread the word. I figured it was only a matter of time before we started seeing that line, but I wasn't going to complain or get in her way until there was an actual problem. She'd been setting aside a third of her earnings as my cut, too. I wasn't sure if that was her own idea, or if one of the others had suggested it. Either way she didn't seem to mind, and I was very, very pleased.

Before my talk with Tam, I'd almost changed my mind about going more than once. Mak and Herald had to insist and reassure me that they'd all be fine. That I always had a place there, and that I was always welcome and wanted, but that I didn't have to be nearby all the time. When I kept dithering, Mak dropped some reality on me. If something happened, unless I was *right there*, I was unlikely to make a difference. They needed to move around the city during the day. Was I going to stalk them in the shadows all the time? I'd been about to say that I could easily do just that, but thankfully I stopped myself. Thinking it was creepy enough.

Once I was in the air it got easier. There was something about being at that inn that made me want to stay. Perhaps it was the sense of familiarity of just being inside a building, ancient as it was compared to everything I remembered from Earth. Perhaps it was just that I could smell my people there. Whatever it was, high up in the cool night sky I could tell myself that they would all be fine, and that I'd be back in a few days, so I steered north.

Rather than going straight back to my mountain and hunting in my own territory that surrounded it, I decided to go farther afield. I had my village to consider now, after all. While there weren't many mouths to feed, every animal that I killed and ate was one less for them, making each of their hunts just a little harder. Their situation was precarious as it was, and while I wasn't going to step in and do everything for them unless they were truly desperate, like with their tools and seeds, there was no reason I shouldn't try to avoid making things worse.

I took a young buck a few miles from the coast. I eviscerated it and ate the best bits on the spot, carrying the rest with me back to the cave. I didn't bother with a fire. I'd eaten enough cooked food lately that I was sick of it. It was nice, for sure, especially when I was with the family, eating the same things as them. Being a big social ritual and all that, it was a nice thing to be a part of. But even if my mind felt mostly human, I was still half dragon, and sometimes I just needed to *rip* and *tear* and *devour* my meat raw, hot, and bloody, and that was what I did. I sat under the stars on the ledge outside my cave, with the forest stretching out before me and my shadow dancing around me, and I laid into that deer until all that remained were cracked and bloody bones. I shifted myself clean afterward; I loved being able to do that. Then I dragged myself down into the cave and curled up on my hoard. I snuggled into my bed of coins, running my fingers over and through them, listening to them clink and jingle as I breathed deeply of the wonderful scents of silver and gold. Gods above, this was what it meant to be a dragon!

I let myself drift off and was dead to the world.

Jekrie was dreaming. His dreams were more settled than the last time I saw him like this, but still filled with worries about monsters, armed strangers, and a cold, hungry winter. That annoyed me more than it should have. I had *just* told him that I was going to do something to help them, and here he was, worrying!

I needed to send a message, or reassure him, or something. My words to him last time had affected him deeply, and when I spoke to Barro he'd gotten my message to come see me at Her Grace's Favor. Talking clearly worked. It just didn't feel like enough, and I wondered if I could do more.

I stilled my mind, and let Instinct guide me. It was such a wonderful thing to be able to do. I remembered being fully human and sometimes having a horrible stream of noise in my brain, one topic after another, and no way to make it stop other than making myself so exhausted I fell asleep. That or drinking far too much. Being able to just not have to listen to that was a blessing.

I looked at Jekrie's dream, and it offended me. And why should I tolerate that? Without my useless doubts telling me that what I was doing was impossible, and with just the slightest effort, I inserted myself into the dream, the confusion settling down around me.

I towered above Jekrie. This was no longer his dream. With two swipes of my mighty claws I reduced the enemies he feared to steaming meat, and with a flex of my will I made the fields grow green with crops.

"Jekrie," I purred, and he prostrated himself before me on the bloody earth, my shadow stalking around him. "Wasn't I with you just yesterday? Has anything threatened you since then, for you to be so afraid?"

"No, Great Lady!" He spoke into the soil, but I heard him perfectly.

"Didn't I tell you that I would clear the ruins of your old homes? Won't that let you take what you need to prepare for winter?"

"With luck it will, Great Lady."

"And if not, don't you trust that I will provide for you some other way? Do you think that I'd abandon my people to freeze and starve?"

"No, of course not, Great Lady!"

I huffed at him. His tone didn't match his words. He clearly still doubted, and I was annoyed. But I'd forgive him. We hadn't known each other for long, after all. I'd just have to show him.

"In a few days we will deal with the trolls, and you'll see that you have been right to join me," I told him. "After that, if anything threatens you, let me know. If you lack anything that you can't live without, let me know. I've promised to protect you, and I will. Now, is there anything you need to tell me?"

"No, Great Lady. Nothing important."

"Anything unimportant?"

He hesitated. "The children, Great Lady. They miss Kira."

I laughed. "I need her to stay in the city, for now. But I'll tell her. I think she liked them."

Without waiting for a reply, I kind of . . . stepped back. I was outside Jekrie's dream again looking in, and whatever stability I'd brought into it dissolved back into the confusion of a normal dream. But I saw with satisfaction that it was a much calmer and less anxious confusion. Not *calm*, but calmer.

But I didn't move on automatically, so now what? Last time I'd just kind of floated, with no direction. Now I seemed to be stuck here with Jekrie, with no idea of how to move on or even end this lucid dream I was in.

Herald had been very disappointed in me for not even making an effort to figure out my limits. I wasn't going to repeat that mistake. And I was rapidly becoming bored, so I decided to work on that.

I thought about Herald. That on its own wasn't enough, but a little push was all it took, and I was looking at her and some man I didn't recognize in a soldier's uniform. Kissing, and thankfully nothing more.

I turned and ignored the dream with equal parts jealousy and embarrassment. I was *not* going to be telling her about this. Frantically I tried Mak instead, but nothing happened, no matter how I tried. Maybe she was still awake? It didn't matter. I needed to move on before something mortifying happened. My thoughts went to Kira, and I threw myself at the image of her, willing myself—

Kira walked in a field of bone and ashes, looking lost. She didn't cry, or scream, or make any sound at all. She just looked empty, her face blank, like she'd given up.

In a fit of indignation I broke through. I descended on her, picking her up before she could protest or even react, and took her away. Not to anywhere in particular, just away from this awful purgatory she'd made for herself.

"Draka, what is this?" Her voice came strong and clear, the wind doing nothing to dampen it.

"I'll not have one of mine give up. I don't know if that's what this is, but I won't have it. Things will get better for you. I'll make them better."

"How?"

"Friends and purpose, I guess. We'll start with the first, and then we'll figure out the other. Ah, there!"

The inn sat in a green, peaceful field in the middle of nowhere. Which made perfect sense in a dream, of course. It's location didn't matter. It was full of warmth and life, and it was a familiar place, which was what I wanted for Kira. I set her down outside. No one inside the open door remarked on the fact that there was a dragon outside.

"Go on. Inside with you. Have a drink. Laugh. Flirt with someone. I'm sure you'll all understand each other just fine. It's your dream. And when you wake up, make sure to keep working on your Karakani."

She looked inside with trepidation. "As you wish."

I turned to leave, then remembered something. "Jekrie says that the kids miss you."

"Oh!" Her worry melted into a smile. "That's sweet of him."

I stayed and made sure that she went inside. I had no way of knowing if her dream would continue where I'd left her once I was gone, but if nothing else, it would be interesting to see what she'd have to say. I hadn't actually asked Jekrie or Barro about their experiences. Would they remember anything, or would they only be left with impressions, perhaps subconscious directions pushing them to do what I wanted? I'd have to speak with them.

Herald would be terribly disappointed with me if I didn't.

In the name of science I tried just drifting. Without any particular person in mind, I tried to let go of Kira, to see what would happen. Even if I just woke up, that would still be useful to know. The field and the inn slowly faded.

The whole dreamscape lurched. I was looking down on a street, infinitely long, stretching to the horizon in either direction and with indistinct buildings on either side. A man was running, alone, but his legs were moving slowly and with great strain, solid shadow-like globs of tar making his feet stick to the cobbles. Like when I'd dreamt of Ramban, his face was indistinct, but no matter how his features shifted, there was wild-eyed panic, and he tried to stay in whatever little specks of light he could find, cast by street lights and the occasional window. One of the thugs who'd attacked the Barleans, perhaps? But again, just like with Ramban, the whole dream felt slick. I might be able to hold onto it with some effort, but it didn't feel worth it. Relki and then Sana flickered past, the two kids my family had taken in, and even Simdal, whom I hadn't thought about since we let him go, but they were all too slippery to grasp.

I decided to make one final effort and try Barro, but when I did I just, for lack of a better word, stuttered. I didn't have the gas. I let go entirely and tried again, in case that made a difference, but nothing happened. Instead, I felt myself losing my grip on my own dream. I didn't feel tired; I was already asleep. But my control slowly slipped, until the dream turned from lucid to normal, and then to nothing.

I couldn't tell how long I spent in my cave digesting my meal. When I wasn't lucid it was hard to tell dreams from reality with that much meat in my belly, but I kept going from sleep to brief wakefulness and back. When I woke properly the need was back. At the same time, I was the most well rested I'd been for weeks. My body felt strong and healthy, and my mind clear. Taking advantage of that clarity, I didn't rise right away. Instead I stayed on my hoard, thinking about what had happened.

I had gone dreamwalking again, stepping into people's dreams. I'd been trying to do it, and I'd had some measure of control. I really did need to know why it worked this time, though, so I decided to see if I could figure anything out.

It could have been a complete coincidence that it happened, and I couldn't discount the possibility. But assuming that it wasn't, three things were different from the other times I'd slept since the first time it happened. The first was probably not a factor. I'd eaten a ton of meat before I slept, but there was just no way to connect that to the first time. The second difference was that I'd slept on my hoard, which I'd also done the first time. That did already have an effect on me, allowing me to heal and recover faster, so maybe it did more. The third, which seemed most likely, was that I'd eaten that Nest Heart. It had filled me with *something*. That something was gone now, and I felt that hunger that I could finally put a name to. I wanted another one. It wasn't overpowering, but I felt like something was missing. And after the first time I dreamwalked I woke up with the same need. Perhaps these dreams used some kind of resource or energy, and the first time I dreamwalked I'd spent whatever I had. Then, and now, I needed to replace it.

That felt right, but not with the certainty that I sometimes felt other things. I'd just have to wait until I found another Nest Heart and see what happened.

I got off my hoard and returned to the entrance. I emerged to a dark, dreary afternoon, with heavy rain cutting visibility to a mile or less. Absolutely miserable, in other words, but I was far too proud and lively to let it stop me. I'd just have to suck it up and endure. I'd had a plan of going to find another Nest Heart, but while I didn't know how long I'd been in torpor, I knew that it must have been two or three days, and making sure that everyone was all right had to take priority.

First, after having a big drink at the stream and then taking care of necessities, I checked on the village. They were right there, after all. Another log house was finished. Getting a whole house built in a few days was amazing to me, even if it looked simple and possibly temporary, but I didn't know anything about construction, here or anywhere else. Maybe that was completely normal. Either way, no one was outside, to my complete lack of surprise, and I decided to leave them be. Talking to Jekrie wasn't important enough to drag them outside, or go in and drip water onto their hopefully dry floors.

Instead, I got back up and made my way to the city. I didn't bother with the sewers or the tunnels, which were beyond a doubt flooded by now. Rather, I relied on the rain to cover me as I flew to the abandoned garden, where I shifted and then made my way to the inn. Being shifted in the rain was an unpleasant experience. Whatever I'd taken from the Nest Heart was gone, and I no longer had that effortless lightness it had given me. Besides, the drops fell through me, and every single one just felt *wrong*, like a pin being pushed softly through my soul. Not painful, but deeply unsettling. Luckily, I could feel that both of my sisters were at the inn, and it didn't take long before Mak opened the cellar door for me.

One advantage of moving in the rain while shifted, unpleasantness aside, was that I didn't drip on the floor.

"We were starting to wonder," Mak said as she closed the door behind me. When she turned around she looked a little harried, but she gave me a knowing smile. "Three days is a long time for you to be away from Herald."

"Don't pretend that you wouldn't sleep for three days straight if you could," I countered, heading for the strongroom. "Sit with me for a while?"

"Sure. Herald's busy with Reben. He's teaching her to handle accounts."

"He's turning her into an accountant? The horror!"

Mak grinned as she fished out the keys and unlocked the heavy door. "I doubt that. She hates it. But she also went out alone yesterday, and this is her punishment."

Inside I plopped down on my little nest of cloth and stuffing and Mak, for the first time that I could remember, sat down with me, leaning against my side.

"Mercies, but you're warm!" she said, snuggling in closer. "I can see why Herald likes this so much."

"That's me, yeah. Just a big heated cushion for chilly girls. Here." I wrapped my wing over her so only her head was visible. "How's that?"

"Should have tried this months ago, that's how it is."

"What's gotten into you, anyway? You're not usually this bold with me. I'm not complaining, mind, just surprised!"

"We're family now, aren't we?" She looked at me impishly from the cocoon I'd made for her. "Honestly, though, Herald keeps pushing me to be more familiar with you. She's pushing all of us. Thinks it's good for you. And you felt like you wouldn't mind."

I snorted. "That girl knows me too well. I do like it. I remember being human, you know? It hasn't been that long. And I miss the contact, just sharing closeness and body heat with someone I like."

Mak looked at me hopefully, quirking an eyebrow.

"Yeah, that includes you. You've been off my shitlist for a while now. Don't you know that?"

She sighed, closing her eyes and leaning her head on my shoulder, looking peaceful and content. "Feeling it and hearing you say it aren't the same."

I was glad that she didn't ask if I'd forgiven her. I wasn't sure, myself. I definitely cared for her deeply. Hell, I might even love her. But I still bore the scars of the rage and the hate that I had felt for her in the days after her betrayal. Perhaps it would be as simple as saying those three, simple words, but I wasn't ready, and she didn't push.

She'd told me not so long ago that she wasn't sure that she deserved to call herself my friend. I couldn't imagine her working up the nerve to ask me to forgive her.

"So, what's been going on while I was away?" I asked, wanting to take my mind off it. "How are you doing? Did you talk to Tam?"

"After your talk the other night? Yeah, and Val. Thank you for telling him the things I couldn't. It'll take them some time to understand, and I don't know if we can ever tell them the full truth, which I hate, but I think they'll accept the situation soon enough."

"Great. Other than that?"

"Running the inn, mostly. Had to fire one of the girls for stealing this morning, and turn her over to the guard, which felt terrible. We caught her in the act, and she didn't even seem ashamed of it, so the decision was easy, just . . . Yeah. Other than that . . . keeping up with regulars, meeting suppliers, renewing agreements. Tam made a good deal with that wine merchant. Business is stabilizing. It's down a little, but not too bad. On track to be nicely profitable for the month, and Kira's helping with that—it looks like she'll be contributing a few silvers every week. And the rooms we can't fill are coming to use, anyway. Tam and Val couldn't kick Ardek out of theirs and into an empty one fast enough once the place became ours."

"I guess you stuck him in one of the cheap rooms?"

"Draka, please. Do you think so little of me? I stuck him in a regular room. The cheapest and the most expensive rooms are always rented out. It's the regular ones that we always have two or three empty. Anyway, the kids seem to be settling—"

"Relki and Sana, right?"

"Right. They're doing all kinds of things right now, though mostly cleaning and running errands. We'll figure out what they're good at as we go, besides keeping their eyes open and picking pockets. And Kira, besides making us money, seems to be doing well. She's learning new words every day, and getting along with the staff.

"But, most important, Barro found some things about the woman we followed. Looks promising. The house is owned by a merchant family, but a minor one. House Tespril. And that House, he says, has more money than their business can easily explain."

"Like maybe they're doing some heinous, illegal shit, or own a bunch of stuff through intermediaries?"

"Something like that, yeah."

"Think we should pay that woman a visit?"

Mak grimaced. "If you can avoid implicating us . . ."

"I know, I know," I said soothingly. "I'll go on my own, yeah? And then I'll bring her somewhere nice and secluded, where no one can hear us, and I'll wait for you and Herald."

"All right. Thank you." Mak relaxed against me, then tensed and looked up at me urgently. "But only if it's the right woman! Please be absolutely sure before you do anything!"

"I will, I will! Have a little confidence, will you?"

"I do, just . . . every time the Night Blossom comes up I feel this wave of excitement and anger from you. Don't be hasty. Please?"

I sighed. "Yeah, fair. I promise."

"Thank you. Now, if this lead on the Night Blossom turns out to be nothing, we could leave to deal with the trolls tomorrow. Though we should wait until the rain lets up. Val's talked to some adventurer friends of his who'd be happy to watch the place for us in exchange for free room and board for a couple of weeks, and Reben knows some people he's worked with before who don't charge too much. Kira offered to contribute with free healing for whoever we hire on, as well, so they'll watch her when she's working. Between that and the supplies, the cost should still be low enough that we can turn a nice profit on five trolls. I know that isn't the point, but . . . well, an eagle's an eagle, right?"

"Right." She was entirely correct, and I approved. "Any trouble?"

"We've had some people hanging around, possibly watching the place. Hard to say. Don't want to throw them out as long as they're paying, either. Nobody's tried anything, thank the Mercies. Some of the staff have been getting curious about what's going on when we shut ourselves up in the cellar. Otherwise . . . no trouble."

"And you?"

Mak's eyebrows rose. "Hmm?"

"How are you doing? You've talked a lot about everything that's going on, and nothing about yourself."

"Me? I've been keeping busy taking care of things, don't worry. I'm not slacking off. I've been trying to manage the others, like you said, and—"

"I know. And it sounds like you're doing a great job. But I'm not asking *what* you're doing, I'm asking *how*. You look tired. Are you all right?"

"Am I . . ." Mak blinked. "I'm . . . okay? I'm worried, I suppose. About what the Night Blossom might do. I don't like that she hasn't tried anything."

"Yeah, me neither. She's being too careful. Anything else?"

"I'm . . . yeah. I'm tired." She laid back against me again.

"Not sleeping enough?"

"Not enough, and not well, no. Midnight to sunrise, maybe. A short nap here and there. Too much to do. And there's still the nightmares."

"I think the inn can manage without you for a while, if you want to stay here."

She lay silent against me for a few seconds. "I'd like that."

She closed her eyes. I pulled my wing closer around her, and after less than a minute her breathing became slow and even.

CHAPTER SIXTEEN

Leverage

Twenty minutes after Mak went to sleep, warm and safe under my wing, Herald found us. She kept looking at her sister with a loving smile on her face as we talked softly about what she'd been up to, and I told her about how the need had come back after my lucid dreams. I carefully did *not* mention how I'd seen her dreaming about swapping spit with a man who I assumed was Maglan.

Our talk got slightly heated, turning to hissed whispers when I told her that I intended to go investigate the house that night. She didn't object to me going. On the contrary, she was excited about it; what she got upset about was me going on my own, specifically without her. She wanted to come. But I'd promised Mak, and Herald finally gave in and promised not to try to go after me.

"It's pissing down outside anyway," she grumbled, making a last ditch effort to pretend that she hadn't wanted to go anyway as she went off to have a sook.

Mak never stirred from her sleep until it was time for me to leave. It was near midnight when I went back out into the pouring rain. Instead of making my way back to the abandoned garden, I stuck to the streets. I didn't even bother trying to be stealthy. Anyone with the shit luck to be out was rushing so quickly from cover to cover that even if they could have seen me and my shadows flitting around, they weren't paying any attention.

Finding my way was something of a challenge, and I had to backtrack a few times before I was sure that I was on the right track, heading up the hill to the high city. But the houses steadily got more expensive looking, the surroundings more familiar, and before too long I recognized the house with the sculpture garden that was right across from the house our target had gone into.

The house I was looking at was large for the area. It had two stories and was wide, with a sizable private garden surrounding it. A fountain overflowed in the rain, the water in its center pouring from a wide bowl held high by a naked woman carved from some stone or other.

How did that even work? The hill I was on rose above the landscape on all sides. You had to go for miles and miles before you hit the same elevation, and there weren't any aqueducts. How the hell did they have a working fountain? For that matter, how did the sewers work up here? I assumed they did, or the houses probably wouldn't be so fancy. Who'd choose not to have plumbing?

The clouds had been growing brighter—well, darker, in the real world—as the day passed. My world was plunged into absolute darkness for a split second before thunder rolled across the city. If I'd had a mouth, I would have grinned.

Above the closed gate two covered lanterns hissed and spat in the rain, casting a weak light over the only entrance to the property. A guard sat huddled on the covered porch, dry but clearly bored and unhappy. He saw nothing as I drifted over the wall into the garden and began slowly circling the house. I wasn't too hopeful about open windows, and my pessimism turned out to be right. There were plenty of windows, and even a balcony, but everything was shuttered tight.

That wouldn't stop me, though. I settled in, watching the doorman; there'd be a change or something sooner or later. With no idea how long I'd have to wait I chose a nice, shadowy place where I could see him, and shifted back.

I regretted my choice instantly. Being outside in heavy rain was truly miserable. It had felt strange as the drops passed through me, but once I was solid again I had to deal with being wet and cold, which was infinitely worse.

The doorman stirred, looking around the garden from where he sat, then settled back, apparently satisfied. After close to an hour of wretched cold and water getting under my scales the door opened, and another man leaned against the frame. He held out a mug to the doorman, who took it gratefully as the two chatted in low voices.

I shifted. The only light came from the gate and a weak glow leaking out the door, each dancing and flickering. If either of the men saw me, neither one showed it. I surged past the newcomer's feet, doing my best not to touch him and failing.

He shuddered. "Damned nasty night, ain't it? Like it's got teeth," he commented to his friend, who mumbled agreement into his mug.

Just inside the door was an oil . . . lamp? A wide tray with some kind of wick in the middle that gave off a weak light. It didn't even slow me as I continued into the building. Though it was large, it didn't come close to resembling the house where we were imprisoned. There was no open central hall here, no pool in the floor. Instead, I left the small vestibule for something more like a large sitting room, with low tables, pillows, and divans tastefully arranged around the floor, mosaics between the doors along the walls, and a wide staircase at the back, which split and curved to the sides. One of the doors stood open, soft voices and light spilling out, but that didn't interest me. The house was settled for the night. If the woman was here, I was sure that she'd be in some study or bedroom, and those, I was sure, would be upstairs.

As I studied the room I heard the front door close behind me, and I surged to the side, settling in a corner while the original doorman walked past me toward the open door in the hall, carrying both mugs. Once he'd passed, I climbed the stairs to the upper floor.

Up there was a wide hallway, running most of the length of the house. Most of the doors were closed, though one was simply an empty archway leading to something like a combined sitting room and study, with a wide desk backed by shelves of scrolls, and a low table surrounded by pillows. Another led to a bathroom.

I stopped at the door at the end of the hall. I assumed that this was where the mistress of the house would sleep. With no real mass I couldn't open any of the doors. I'd just have to be careful.

I shifted back. The fine wooden floor settled but didn't creak under my weight. My nose was tickled by the faint scent of jasmine.

The wood protested as my claws dug in. I could feel Instinct fighting me, trying to take over as thoughts of caution and mercy fled before the memory of *that woman*. It was all I could do not to tear the door open, consequences be damned, and my shadow flickered and waved, though weaker than it had before I last dreamwalked.

My hand trembled with suppressed rage as I slowly lifted the latch on the door. Conscience fought to help me hang onto some semblance of humanity. *It might be a coincidence*, she told me. *Jasmine is a popular scent. We've smelled it in other places. She might just look similar and wear the same perfume.*

I couldn't turn the bedroom into an abattoir. I'd promised. I wondered what Mak was feeling from me in that moment, if she was still awake. She must have been sick with worry that I was about to do something incredibly irresponsible.

The door swung open smoothly. The scent didn't get any stronger, but I could hear soft breathing coming from a large bed against the wall to my left, drawing my eyes to a shape among the sheets, the swell of a hip telling me what I already knew. The woman was curled up on her side facing away from me, but I remembered her silky black hair. Straight hair was such a rarity here, it might as well have been a neon sign.

I shifted. I was so close. I wasn't going to risk ruining everything by stepping on the wrong floorboard and alerting her. There was a large, shuttered window on the wall, and I opened it, the weak light of the gate spilling in and barely illuminating the room. I was not going to kill her. I was not going to display her eviscerated corpse on the Forum. Not yet. I was going to grab her and leave, and let my sisters do whatever they felt they had to do.

My prey groaned as the sound of the rain got louder, then rolled over and pulled a pillow over her head. I didn't bother shifting. I stalked over to the bed.

I looked down at the defenseless woman before me. The scent of jasmine was still faint, dominated by something else. Orange blossoms. Some kind of soap, perhaps? A scented bath before bed? It didn't matter.

I let my shadows flow out and envelop her, and I *squeezed*, pouring all my hate and rage and pain and fear into it. She froze, her breathing locked up. When she gave off a low, moaning wail, the sadistic satisfaction that filled me was everything I'd imagined it might be.

I reached into the shadow, around her head, and my hand closed over her mouth, claws just barely retracted as I turned her to face me.

She jerked, jolting awake. I dropped my shadow so that she could see her end. Wide, terrified eyes stared at me, and my rage mixed with confusion.

"You're not *her*!" I growled in absolute outrage. I lifted her by the face, and the sheets slid off her as she scrambled to follow, to sit and take the weight off her neck. Her hands closed feebly around my wrist. It reminded me of that day in the cell with Mak. I didn't like it.

I switched to a grip on her throat so I could see her face properly, choking off a scream in the process as I turned her left and right. The nose, the lips, the jaw and chin, the cheekbones. Everything was almost right. But the hair was too short, and the eyes were wrong. The Night Blossom had brown eyes, like most people in Karakan, while this woman's eyes were green, like Garal's. And she was too young. Lalia's age, maybe. But I'd bet anything that she was family.

I pulled her face close to mine, easily grabbing both of her hands in my free one when she tried to push me away. I wouldn't have bothered, but once the shock wore off she had a surprising amount of fight in her.

"Where's the Night Blossom?" I said, my voice trembling with frustrated anger.

Oh, I was on the right track. There was recognition there, a fearful widening of her eyes at the moniker. That was a relief. But of course, I was doing the same thing as I had with Mak. She couldn't speak with my hand on her throat.

"If you try to run, or scream, I will take you with me." I held her so that she could see the open window. "You probably won't enjoy flying naked through the rain, but that's not my problem. And then we'll continue this somewhere else, with me in a much worse mood. And no one will ever know what happened to you. Do you understand?"

She just stared at me, so I gave her another dose of shadow, then asked again. She tried to nod, and I dropped her.

"Now. Where is the Night Blossom? Don't pretend you don't know who I'm talking about. She's been here, hasn't she? I can smell her."

She rubbed her bruised neck. "No," she managed in a stammering croak. She stared at me with such terrified defiance that I felt a glimmer of respect for her. The woman had some real fight in her. Simdal and Jekrie had folded after half of what I'd given her.

"No?" I advanced on her, and she scuttled back desperately as I stepped onto the bed after her.

"No!" she squeaked. When she reached the edge of the bed she scrambled off and kept backing up until I had her cornered.

"What is she to you, that you'd throw your life away for her?" I was genuinely curious, though I had a guess.

She squeezed her mouth shut. She was breathing quickly. Her eyes flitted around the room in desperation, but she didn't scream. She was clearly taking my threat seriously. But when she looked at me it was still with that mix of terror and defiance.

My shadows smashed into her, making her gasp and her knees buckle from the intensity. "Who? Is? She?" I asked, again putting my face right in front of hers as she sat with her knees drawn up between us.

"My sister! Zabra's my sister! She's all I have!"

It came out in a pitiful squeak, and when she realized what she'd said, she clamped her hands over her mouth like a child.

That was what I'd thought. That, or her mother, but there wasn't enough of an age difference. And the knowledge of how much I could hurt the Night Blossom by doing something terrible to this woman was almost enough to push me over the edge.

No. Not "the Night Blossom." Zabra. I had a name for her now.

"Tespril Zabra," I said slowly, tasting it, and she stared at me with guilt and horror. "Tell me where to find her."

She shook her head, and I almost snapped. I almost slaughtered this woman where she cowered in the corner, to vent my frustration and to leave a message. But Conscience, that persistent little voice of restraint and mercy, held me back. Instead of doing something terrible, I pulled her hands from her mouth and asked, "What is your name?"

"What?" She stared at me as I waited. "My name? My . . . Kesra. It's Kesra."

"And how much do you know about your dear sister, Kesra? Do you have any idea what she might have done to bring me here?"

"No!" she squeaked. I let my shadows swirl up around her. "I don't!" she insisted, frantically trying to press herself further into the corner. "I only deal with trade, I swear! She doesn't tell me about the rest!"

"But you know about it."

"Gambling, drink, whores? I know it happens! I know that we own some places, but I don't know anything about it!"

"What about slaving? Kidnapping?" I grabbed her throat almost gently with my claws, letting them barely prick her skin. "Torture?"

She'd held out admirably. I had to admit that. She'd been terrified, but she hadn't screamed or cried or begged. Not until then.

"Please," she whispered. Tears spilled down her cheeks. "Please don't."

"Please don't, what?"

"Torture. Please just kill me if—If she's done something so—Please don't!"

"Just tell me where I can find her, and you'll never see me again," I promised.

She squeezed her eyes shut, sniffled, and managed a single sobbed "No."

And despite my anger and frustration, Conscience just wouldn't let me hurt her.

I jerked my talons away, and Kesra gasped as they scratched her, five thin lines appearing on the smooth skin of her neck. She took a shuddering breath, relaxing just a fraction as she realized that she was still alive, then opened her eyes and looked at me, fear and uncertainty warring with hope.

"Your sister tortured my friends," I told her coldly, and her face began trembling with renewed tears. "She made deals with monsters to sell free Karakani citizens into slavery, and when my friends interfered, she had them taken off the street and tortured. So tell her this. Tell her that I'm going to find her, and when I do, everyone around her will die. And if she hurts anyone close to me, if she even tries, I will find *you*, Tespril Kesra. Whatever hole she sticks you in, wherever she tries to hide you, I will find you, and I will take my anger out on you. Whatever happens to my friends, far worse will happen to you. Will you tell her that?"

"I don't believe you," she breathed. She sounded far less certain than she probably meant to.

"I don't care what you believe," I growled into her face. "Will you tell her, or do I need to carve it into you? My writing's messy. The claws, you see. They're no good for curved lines."

I left Kesra crying silently in the corner of her bedroom. She was probably being truthful about not knowing anything, but she was also protecting her sister. Admirable, but if you put yourself between two monsters and refuse to move, you can fucking well deal with the consequences.

She did promise to pass along my message.

I had no idea if I could find her if the Night Blossom—Zabra—hid her somewhere. Perhaps I should have just killed her. It was frustrating that I hadn't allowed myself to do so, but Conscience was probably right to hold me back. Zabra had an idea what I was capable of. I'd escaped her chains and her cell. I'd killed fifteen or more of her people. If she'd been hesitant to act against my friends and family before, this should make her think extremely carefully about escalating.

On the other hand, feeling her kin's blood spurt across my face would have been so very, very satisfying.

When I returned to the inn both of my sisters were waiting. Mak must have warned Herald about my mood; they were both cautious as they let me into the cellar.

"How did it go?" Herald asked, standing far enough away as not to crowd me but not so far that it would signal fear.

"It wasn't her," I growled, letting my frustration show plainly. "But it was her sister."

"Is she . . . ?"

"She's alive. Mostly unharmed. I asked her to pass on a message."

"Why didn't you take her?" Mak wasn't criticizing, just asking.

"I didn't want to provoke the Night Blossom. I doubt she'd come herself, but she might have thrown everything she has at us. Or not. Who knows if a woman like that cares about her own sister." It wasn't a lie, exactly. I *didn't* want Zabra to do something that might threaten my family or the inn. But the main reason that I hadn't taken Kesra with me was . . . I wasn't sure myself. Pity, perhaps?

"At least it wasn't a waste of time," Mak said soothingly. "We know which House the Night Blossom belongs to. We know that she has a sister."

"And we have a name," I added. "Zabra. Tespril Zabra. Her sister is Kesra."

I told them the message I'd left for Zabra. We all agreed that it could have been better, but they insisted that I'd done well enough under the circumstances. And then, together, they slowly and carefully soothed my anger, coaxing me with gentle touches and talk about happier things.

We fell asleep together in the strongroom, with my sisters cuddled together against my side and me hoping that I hadn't made a royal mess of things.

CHAPTER SEVENTEEN

Damn Bloody Trolls

We gave it two days before we left to deal with the trolls. I spent most of that time watching Kesra's home, only returning to the inn to check in with people and to rest. In those two days I never saw Kesra or the Night Blossom come or go, though I did see Kesra on her balcony and in her garden once or twice, so I knew that she was there. She always had at least one guard with her and jumped at shadows, though she didn't let that stop her from going outside. I kind of admired that. It was too bad that she had the sister she did.

When I was at the inn I stayed in the cellar, sleeping or practicing my reading while doing my best to ignore the need. Reading materials came in both books and scrolls, with books being, by far, more expensive, and you could easily tell how much more care was put into them. Scrolls rarely had illustrations, and the ones I'd seen were sloppy things, nothing like the careful, full-color art in my bestiary. No, scrolls were clearly churned out as quickly as they could, intended for consumption. Almost everything that might be called pure entertainment was on scrolls. Herald had a sizable collection of those, which she left with me in the strongroom when she went out. She had Tam with her for safety, but I got the distinct impression that the scrolls were partially there to distract me from her excursions.

I didn't let it bother me. I knew that she wouldn't hide anything too important, and it amused me to no end that, in her haste, she'd forgotten to sort out her collection of "romance" scrolls before bringing the lot to me.

I tried to dreamwalk, but nothing. People came and went as they wished, and I managed to speak with pretty much everyone—my new family, the Wolves, Ardek and Kira, even Barro made an appearance late the second night, and I took the opportunity to thank and praise him for the good work he'd been doing. He seemed to enjoy that, though he also admitted that Mak had been paying him "well enough," with no sum mentioned. I didn't ask. I'd rather not know.

The rain let up the evening after I'd visited Kesra, and then we gave it another day to get our guards ready. The family agreed we had no control over whether the Night Blossom would try anything, but we couldn't let that control our lives. We'd take what precautions we could, and then trust the Mercies and sisterly love that nothing would happen. Ardek was tasked to keep an eye on the house without being obvious. I still expected the Night Blossom to move her sister somewhere, and I'd like to know where, but it wasn't like Ardek's minions were the height of professionalism.

On the morning of the third day we set out, me shifting and taking the sewers out of the city and the family walking with Stalwart the mule and their packs. Stalwart was mostly loaded down with big clay jugs, carried in net slings and full of some reagent, in which we'd collect the trolls' blood. Each was the size of a small keg, but with the size of the average troll and with five trolls that needed killing, that looked about right. Anything smaller would have been silly, and we had eight of the things. With the relative rarity of trolls' blood, Mak told me, they'd negotiated a price of fifty eagles per filled jar, and since they'd only needed to pay a deposit on the jars and the reagent, they'd grabbed extra just in case.

We met at the edge of the forest, and then we were truly on our way. Everyone was wearing noticeably heavier clothing than the last time we'd gone north, and when I thought about it, that had been true of nearly everyone I'd seen for a while now. It had just been so gradual that I hadn't thought about it, and while I'd seen the leaves slowly change I hadn't noticed the drop in temperature. It really drove home that we were heading into autumn now, with what they called first harvest giving way to second planting.

Traffic on the forest road was unusually heavy, and even though I stayed in the trees, I frequently had to go deeper or even shift as we met groups of travelers coming from the opposite direction. Two of the groups we met were clearly refugees, ragged people in low spirits traveling with all their possessions. We didn't know where they were going, and we didn't stop them to ask.

Even two nights and one day after the rains had finally stopped, the road was a churned, muddy mess. I pitied the humans in their sandals; walking on all fours in the forest I rarely sank down anywhere, while my siblings were constantly cursing and struggling against the sucking mud. By the time we made it to the exit for the lake and the campground, the decision to stop for the day was unanimous.

It felt oddly nostalgic being back there, but also painful. I went down to the tree. This was where I'd first met Garal. This was where Herald had come to meet me when she felt abandoned by her family. And this was where Mak had betrayed me.

Herald joined me by the tree, and we talked a little about those early days, only months and yet a lifetime ago. When I mentioned the days that she'd spent waiting for me, she looked suddenly embarrassed.

"There is something I should confess," she finally said after some prodding. "Do you remember back in the beginning? When you lost your horn?"

"Yeah. Not something I'm likely to forget."

"I came out in the morning, after Mak had healed you. And when you scratched your head a chunk sort of . . . came off."

"Something that'll haunt my dreams until the end of my days, yeah."

"And it startled you so much that you threw it at me, and I caught it."

"And . . . ?"

"I sort of . . . kept it?"

"Herald, I love you. That's disgusting. Why?"

"I thought I might not see you again! I guess I wanted something to remember you by, and then we became friends and it sort of became important to me, because I could not see you so often but I always had it to remind me of you, and—"

"All right! All right. Stop. Herald. That's weird, and it's gross, but oddly flattering, I guess. I get where you're coming from, yeah? Just . . . Please, tell me you don't still have it."

"So, the thing about that . . ."

"Herald, no," I pleaded.

"Well, the reason I thought of it now was that when I was here, waiting, I had it with me. And then again when we went north, like we are now. And when I was packing for this trip—"

"Oh, Herald," I shook my head theatrically.

"Well, I could not find it. I have not even looked at it for so long that I do not know where I put it. I have not even thought about it, since I get to be with you so much now. But, yeah. I supposed I wanted to confess that I . . . kept a piece of you. And I may have lost it. Or misplaced it."

"You're forgiven?" I wasn't entirely sure how I felt about the whole thing. It was a worryingly stalkerish thing to do, and it made me wonder how early I'd been in her head, but it wasn't like it changed anything. She was still my little dragon. I had to make one thing clear, though. "Just, please, if you find it, burn it. Please! I don't want to see it."

"Yeah," she said awkwardly. "I promise."

Mak never went near the tree. As we were leaving, I saw her look toward the path where she had lured me into the ambush. There was such regret in her eyes that I nearly told her that she was forgiven right then and there. I wished that I could; I wanted so badly to forgive her. But the words would have been empty. I didn't feel it. I still experienced that surge of anger whenever I thought about what she'd done, and until I dealt with that, I couldn't honestly tell her what she wanted to hear.

I had no idea how to get myself to that point. I suspected that it wasn't in my nature to forgive. My human side had been fairly unforgiving to start with, and the dragon . . .

Mak looked at me and gave me a weak smile. She was getting too damned good at reading me.

The second day was sunny, and the mud finally dried to the point where it only slowed everybody down a little. At Lalia's request, we took a detour to Pine

Hill, only a few miles north of the lake, to check in on her family. To everyone's relief nothing truly monstrous had been spotted in the area. They'd seen a few more advanced animals than usual, but no trolls or goblins or the like.

I made sure to ask Herald to bring Lahnie outside while "the grownups" talked. For once Herald had no problem being treated as the junior member of the group, and Lahnie was beyond happy when she saw me. We both marveled at how big the other had gotten. I had Herald lift her onto my back and walked around as she chattered excitedly about things Lalia had told her, and how her granddad had shown her how to carve a fox from wood, and how silly Soldier, her dog, had been. I barely got a word in, and I loved every moment.

It took the rest of the day to make it to the river. I recognized the sturdy stone bridge from when I'd been looking for Piter's Clearing. From there, we'd be following the river west through uncleared forest, with our destination about fifteen miles upstream.

The need still called me north. I told the others about it, and they all agreed that if I wanted to go, I should, but it wasn't so strong that I couldn't resist it. It was never a compulsion, just an itch, and I stayed with them.

It took until noon the next day to reach Piter's Clearing. About five miles in, the first signs of trolls appeared, which had everyone putting on their armor. Tam and Val were both still in the same old stuff I'd always seen them in, but Mak had gotten a suit of black leather scale to match Herald's. Despite the situation, I couldn't help but grin at my two little dragons. They both looked absolutely lethal.

On the way we hit a wide swamp, which turned out to run along much of the river. I hadn't noticed it when I passed, since I'd been flying at the time, and unlike the other treeless wetlands I'd seen, I hadn't known what to look for. It took hours of wet feet and uncountable mosquito bites before we found ourselves on the other side. It wasn't like anyone blamed me for not warning them, but I couldn't help but feel a little bit embarrassed about the whole thing. At least I could always go up and check how much farther we had to go, which kept spirits pretty high despite the rough going.

I left the group at the edge of the swamp to go check on the ruined village, though far enough away that the mozzies weren't so bad. There was still plenty of daylight. In our limited experience the trolls only returned to their lair once the light began to wane, and we had no reason to think that this troupe would be any different. The trolls were all out, of course. That meant that there were at least five of them roaming the area, which was all I'd wanted to confirm.

I returned to the family and reported what I'd seen, and then we set off. We needed to choose a place to camp, far enough away that the trolls were unlikely to disturb us but close enough that we wouldn't have to trek for hours to hunt them. We'd settled on Sweet Creek. It was about three miles from Piter's Clearing, across a quick stream that had to be forded and had already been torn to pieces by the trolls. With any luck, all these factors would combine to make the trolls unlikely to bother us. Besides that, I'd seen one building in Sweet Creek with most of its four walls and a roof, making it a far better place to store our supplies than hanging them from a tree or something while we were away.

The group was pretty somber as we made our way through Piter's Clearing, keeping close to the river so they wouldn't have to look too closely. The grass was getting long around the ruined buildings, and the scattered debris left no doubt that something disastrous had happened there. At least the long, heavy rains had taken care of the blood.

We followed a path from the village to the ford. There was no bridge, and no sign that one had ever existed, but two thick ropes hung over the rushing waters. The water was normally shallow enough to cross, but with how swift and deep the stream was after the rains, the family was happy to have the ropes, as well as a member of the party who could fly across with their gear. Poor Stalwart had to brave the waters the hard way, and he did so only under loud, braying protest and with lots of coaxing. In the end, though, everyone and everything got across.

We made it only three hundred feet from the stream before we came across our first troll. So much for the water keeping them away.

As soon as we got away from the water we heard crunching, snapping, and rustling sounds that made us cautious, but Herald was the one to spot it and stop us. A small clearing was almost entirely overgrown by some kind of bramble bearing small, red berries, and the troll was tearing entire branches out of the ground and crunching them down, thorns and all. From the churned soil we could tell that it had made its way through quite a lot of the stuff. It was honestly kind of impressive, but also cemented trolls in my mind as nature's garbage disposals.

There was no discussion about *if* we were going for it, only a quick brainstorm about *how* we'd approach it. Our plan of attack was simple—Mak and I would circle around to the left. When we were in position, Herald would start loosing arrows, with Tam and Val between her and the troll. The moment the troll moved, either to attack or retreat, Mak and I would hit it from the side, tie it up, and let Tam come in to do the real damage with his magically charged sword strikes.

When we were getting into position, Mak moved like a wraith through the undergrowth. With her agility, smaller body and lower weight, and my stealth helping her, I was pretty sure she was less visible and making less noise than I was. I was jealous and extremely pleased all at once.

When we were in position and ready to strike, Mak raised her spear in the air to signal the others.

It took only a second for the first of Herald's enchanted arrows to find its mark, sinking deep into the troll's back. It jerked and stumbled, seemingly in confusion rather than pain for the first few seconds. When a second arrow took it near the spine, the troll gave off a wailing roar, rounding to see two humans ready to meet it and a third with an arrow already nocked, bow taut as she aimed.

The third arrow took the troll high in the throat as it charged. It never reached Tam and Val, though. The moment the troll moved, Mak and I exploded out of the bushes, Mak digging in her feet and driving her spear into the troll's hip as I leapt onto its torso, bringing it crashing down ten feet from them. The troll landed on Herald's food-for-a-year arrow which, instead of breaking, continued right through the thing's neck under its weight. The damn thing almost got me in the process!

That wasn't enough to kill it, but the troll was dazed and injured enough that finishing it off was pretty much a formality, with Herald quickly grabbing one of the large jugs and Tam waiting to take its head off until the jug was ready.

Collecting the blood was just as messy as I'd imagined. Trying to maneuver the carcass so that more of the stuff hit the target than not was nearly impossible, but we still managed to get one jug full and another halfway. Val, who was the only one who'd done this before, was delighted with the result as he cleaned the jugs and sealed the full one with wax. At this he said, "A troll must normally be worn down, as we all know, and killing them without cutting the head off is risky and difficult. To get more than a jug from a single troll is better than I'd expected!"

All in all, everyone was very happy with how our first fight of the expedition turned out. None of us got hurt, Herald's arrows performed just as she'd hoped, Mak got to show off her new strength, and we had gallons of troll blood. Nobody even had to get their clothes too messy, since I was the one holding the jars. I could just dunk myself in the stream, and then quickly shift when the men weren't looking.

We got out of there as soon as we were ready, just in case the noise had attracted another troll. No one wanted a repeat of the Big Boy incident.

As I led the way to what remained of Sweet Creek, I thought about the fact that I was still keeping secrets from Tam and Val. I'd told Herald and Mak that I'd tell them, but I just never felt comfortable with it. It bothered me, but just like with forgiving Mak, something was holding me back from trusting them completely, and I wasn't sure what or why. The first thing that popped into my mind, the first possible reason, was fairly obvious once it occurred to me. It came back to Mak. Mak had known as much about me as Tam or Val did now, and that might be the only reason that I was still alive, and they were free.

But while that felt like a perfectly valid reason, it didn't feel right. I tried to think of any kind of trait or behavior in either man that might make me distrust them, but I couldn't think of anything. From what I could tell both of them respected and liked me, and they had made no secret of their gratitude for my part in making them rich and freeing our sisters. Besides that, I trusted Herald and Mak to let me know if the men voiced any concerns, to protect everyone involved.

So, there was nothing about Tam or Val themselves that stopped me from letting them know. The reason had to lie with me. I thought about who I'd revealed my powers to, and who I hadn't. Those who were still alive, that was. My best theory, after some pondering, was that it came down to control.

I had only shown my powers to one person because I wanted to. Herald. I knew in my bones that she would never do anything to hurt me. If I asked her to do something, she'd do it, unless it hurt those she loved. Probably. I hadn't had a reason to test that. So, though my feelings on it were as mixed as ever, I had more than a little control over Herald. About as much as she had over me.

No, that wasn't true. If she asked me to kill someone, I would ask if she was sure, and then I'd do it no matter who it was.

Everyone else who knew about my powers did so because I hadn't felt that I had an option. Mak had been there when I had to shift to get free, and I hadn't bothered to try to hide what I was doing because I hadn't been sure if I was going to let her live or not. I'd told her about my past later on, but only once I felt like I controlled her completely. With Ardek it had been the same as with Mak. When I shifted in front of Kira I'd been too distraught to think, and I'd kept her firmly under my thumb since. Rib and Pot might have been avoidable. I could have dropped them off somewhere safe and gone down through the tunnels myself. But again, I hadn't been thinking clearly; my only objective had been to keep everyone safe. Rib and Pot had sworn a pretty serious oath before I showed them, true, but I knew that I wouldn't have done it if I didn't feel like I had to. I liked them. I really did. And I liked Garal and Tam and Val. But that wasn't enough.

My conclusion was that I needed to have near absolute control of the person, or a lack of control of the situation. Otherwise, I would never choose to reveal my secrets, and that was that.

When we reached Sweet Creek the mood again turned somber. The creek bubbled peacefully down a gentle slope. Birds sang and bugs buzzed. It was peaceful. With the sun and the breeze, it should have been nice. The hamlet was much as I'd last found it. In the eight days since I'd been here, the grass had grown a little taller and the wind and rain had caused a little more damage. A fox fled as we entered the center of the small community. Homes gaped empty, entire walls staved in, and birds perched on collapsed roofs. It was difficult to walk into a place where you knew that much of the community had died. The way they'd gone was just plain awful to think about, and as though to remind us, clean-picked bones lay where they'd been discarded, shining brightly in the sunlight.

We stood before the mostly intact house that had been someone's home. Mak swallowed thickly, and in a voice that was almost a whisper, as though she was afraid to disturb the silence in this dead place, she said, "Right. Let's get ready to kill these bastards."

CHAPTER EIGHTEEN

Retribution

The remaining daylight was spent doing two things. First, we set up camp, with Mak and Val rigging up a simple sliding door for the hole in the wall of the house we'd be using. That should keep anything out that wasn't a troll or some other absolute monster, and nothing short of a stone wall would stop one of those.

When that was done, and without discussing it beforehand, they began collecting bones. It started with Tam picking up a cracked femur. He looked sadly at the others, and without saying a word he put it down near the smashed well, then looked around and brought another. Then Herald joined him. Mak and Val were still busy rigging up the door, but they joined in when they were finished.

Once they got started, I just stayed out of their way, feeling awkward about not helping sooner. A shovel came out, and they all took turns digging a sad little mass grave for the pieces, holding a joint prayer to the Traveler, the Mercies, and the Sorrows once it was filled in. I hadn't even considered doing something like that. The bones themselves hadn't bothered me, so while the others were busy setting up camp, I'd nominated myself for troll patrol, and that was where I stayed until they returned to the house.

As the sun touched the mountains I returned briefly to Piter's Clearing and verified that there were now four trolls. I stuck around for a while and no extras showed up, so I was satisfied that Speedy and her boyfriend, or possibly son—it was a weird and disturbing situation—were truly gone.

We rose and set out from Sweet Creek well before sunrise. Hunting the last troupe of trolls had taught us well, and we were stronger now than we had been. We still planned to do this carefully. It took a little over half an hour to reach Piter's Clearing now that the humans were moving without their full packs. We could have done it faster, but the biggest limit was how fast we could keep Stalwart moving, and he was not a fan of running.

Outside of Piter's Clearing we hunkered down. We didn't have to wait long. Just like before, as the sun rose, so did the trolls. The four of them, appearing entirely unconcerned about their missing member, had their morning brawl and set out in different directions. We picked our quarry, waited, and followed.

We had decided to knock off the largest threat first. We were fresh, and Big Boy surprising us last time had an effect on all of us. It was best, we'd decided, to get rid of the male first. That way, any surprise would be less threatening. An unexpected troll was still a hell of a problem, but the females were at least a foot shorter and two hundred pounds lighter. If we could choose our problems, we'd choose the lesser ones.

What followed was three days of grim satisfaction. Tam and Val fought as well as ever, and with Mak's mix bag of new strengths, Herald's unmatched stealth and improved gear, and my increased size, we took the troupe apart. One by one, slowly and patiently, we hunted them down, harvesting their blood as best we could and avenging the two destroyed outlaw communities in the process. I ate well those days, only taking the best parts, though only Herald could stand to watch me. Even Mak got queasy once I tucked in. It was their loss. Troll was good eating!

We killed both of the last two trolls on the third day. With four dead, we simply ambushed the final one as she returned at sunset. Herald put all six of her enchanted arrows in the creature, the broadheads tearing her up inside and slowing her to the point where we could easily get her on the ground, and I gave her a face full of venom. Then we just stood back and waited. Once she was dead, we hoisted her into a tree and bled her like a pig, getting two full jars out of one troll and making seven and a half in total.

My family was clearly satisfied with the results. They were happy with the fact that we'd gotten rid of a threat so close to the more settled parts of the forest, and that we'd avenged the dead of Piter's Clearing and Sweet Creek. And, of course, that we'd gotten so much trolls' blood to sell. But it was clear that the fate of the villages, something that could potentially happen to any village in the north, weighed on them. We'd all seen the scattered bones, the inside of the barn.

Our trip back was easier than the one there. The roads were much better, and we made it from Sweet Creek to the lake in one day. There I left them. I returned to my refugees to let them know that the trolls were gone and so I could check on my hoard. I spent the following four days escorting eight of them north to salvage what they could. Just because we hadn't seen Speedy and her boyfriend didn't mean the area was safe.

There were a lot of tears and haunted faces. Of course there were. And they didn't even give themselves time for proper funerals. I would have stayed with them, but they all agreed that this was not their home anymore, and they worried about the few people left behind at the mountain with the children.

They gathered what remains they found at Piter's Landing in the barn, cleared it out of anything useful or valuable, filled it with scraps of wood, grass, and other fuel, and burned it to the ground. That would have to do.

Once they were done gathering what they could, and I'd seen them past the tributaries of the river and on their way home, I turned back and headed north once again. The need was always there, calling me north, and now I was here, and I had time to do something about it.

From the air I tried to actually listen to the need. I'd been trying to do that for days now, ever since we came north. I wanted to make sure that there were no other nests nearby, but I'd usually been busy with something else. Now I could focus.

The need was drawing me somewhere. Last time, when I'd followed Speedy, it had changed from a general draw toward the north into a pressure with a general direction to it as I got within some unknown distance from the Nest Heart, and then into a specific sense of location when I got close enough. Now I cruised, keeping my speed just fast enough to stay aloft with minimal effort, and I tried to feel that pressure.

I didn't. But after a long while of focusing on nothing else, other than making sure I didn't accidentally crash into a tree or something, I noticed that what I felt wasn't one single draw. It was a multitude of little threads—hundreds, perhaps thousands—all pulling me in their own direction, and it all averaged due north. North, where all the monsters and all the Nest Hearts were.

Well, then. I landed in a massively tall tree, three hundred feet at least, a real queen of the forest that towered even above the already giant specimens that grew around it. There I settled in and tried to isolate those threads, to find one that pulled harder than the others. The more settled I got, the more I focused, the better I was able to distinguish between them. The directions I felt were not exact. Not all of them were north, either. I felt some weak pulls to the west, to the mountains, and even a few to the south.

That was concerning. I'd have to see if I needed to do anything about that. But it was a problem for a later day, because after sitting in that tree for hours I'd finally picked a thread to follow.

I turned toward it and opened my eyes. I was facing east-northeast, the sea glittering in the failing light. I leapt from the tall tree and followed the thread, focusing on it and nothing else, adjusting my heading whenever it felt like my hold on the thread was slipping.

I was flying north-northeast by the time I felt the pressure. Only this time I was flying, going far faster than I had been when I was following Speedy, and the feeling changed from pull to pressure to location in no more than two minutes.

Once I knew where to look it was obvious. There was no glade this time, but even in the long shadows of the mountains I could see the deep, swirling darkness among the trees. I went straight for it. The closer I got, the more excited I became. The thought of drinking in the substance of the Nest Heart, of finally sating that need, scratching that itch after two weeks of doing my best to ignore it, was overwhelming.

The leaf work of the canopy was open enough to see the darkness through, but the branches were too dense to pass comfortably. I didn't let that stop me. Like I'd done when I first brought Kira to Karakan, I shifted in the air, catching the high branches of one of the taller trees and making my way down below to where I could see the ground.

There was a village there. A village of goblins. It was a very crude little village, of lean-tos and hide tents, but it was a village, far too large to be called a mere camp. The inhabitants were sitting or lying around, eating, talking, and laughing. Settling in for the evening, basically.

I felt a little bad for a second. The goblins I'd met when I'd been with Herald had been reasonable, and these ones didn't seem like the horrid little monsters of Earth's stories, either. But I also remembered what Jekrie had said about goblins that made no bargains, taking all that they could. Also, they had the Nest Heart, and I wanted it. I wanted it so bad that I could taste it.

I shifted and dropped.

There was a camp-wide twitch, there was silence, and then there was pandemonium. Most of them fled screaming into the forest. Some stood rooted to the ground, staring in wonder or in terror. A few picked up weapons that they pointed at me doubtfully, but a growl and a hiss made them think better of it, and they backed off.

"Can any of you speak Trade?" I asked them. That was what Nalleeka, the leader of the goblins I'd met, had called Karakani. "Answer me!" I demanded when none of them spoke, but there was no sign of understanding or recognition on any of their faces. Nalleeka had learned the language from somewhere. Clearly, none of these goblins had, and as wondrous as my very first advancement was, it only enabled me to speak all *human* languages. What the goblins spoke might as well have been Martian to me.

Since none of them had the courage to approach me, I walked up to the Nest Heart. That got some nervous chattering from the remaining goblins. It was near the center of the camp, by a large central firepit, and it swirled and twisted just as beautifully as the last one had. I didn't hesitate. I couldn't hold back. I reached out, put my hand inside it, and drew it in.

The goblins' voices grew steadily more unhappy as they realized what I was doing. As I stripped layer after layer of shadowy streamers off the Nest Heart, some of them even mustered the courage to approach me, screaming angrily, but none dared to get close enough that either of us could hurt the other. Unless I spat venom at them, of course, but as long as they didn't try to stop me I saw no reason to. And it was hard to pay attention to them, anyway, with a little sun forming around my heart, burning my soul so good. One did get a little too close for comfort, but in my mercy I only wrapped it up in its own shadow, which was enough for it to run screeching off into the trees.

The beam of light fixing the Nest Heart to the earth winked out. The final shreds of darkness vanished into me, and I felt it all collapse into a little ball around my heart.

Oh, right. In my excitement, I'd forgotten the last part.

The ball exploded.

When I awoke, the need was gone.

So were all the goblins. As I came back to my senses I could hear them screeching in the distance, and I thought I smelled some hiding nearby. That might just have been the camp, though. I'd been so eager that I'd been unforgivably careless, but I'd been lucky. I was pretty sure that I had only been out for a minute at most, but that would have been more than long enough for some goblin warrior to drive a spear through my eye, if they had the minerals to get that close.

I would not make the same mistake again. I needed to be protected when this happened, or I needed to resist whatever knocked me out, to be strong enough to stay awake. And to learn that, I would need practice.

"Or we can make sure to exterminate whatever we take the Nest Heart from," Instinct whispered, as my shadow danced, wild and free. If there were no threats around, a little nap wouldn't matter.

I stood up, and Mercies, I felt good. The feeling of fullness, of strength and vigor, of being *more*, was back, as was that fleeting sense that the world was unfathomably beautiful. I took one look around the camp. The explosion didn't seem to have done anything except scare everyone off, and I was thankful for that. It would have been terribly sad to ruin the place.

I shifted, climbed to the top of a tree, and made my way into the air.

The need was gone, but when I focused I could still feel the threads that would lead me to other Nest Hearts. They felt fainter. Perhaps they were just harder to focus on, now that I was satisfied. But they were there, and I was glad for it. Happily, none of them seemed to overlap with my hoard, the closest being in the mountains many miles to the north of my nest. I'd have to keep checking, though. If a nest popped up anywhere close to my mountain, I wanted to know about it as early as possible, before there was a risk of some little gremlin bastard getting its grubby mitts on my treasure.

I headed for Karakan, taking the long way around so that I could check on the salvage team. I found them easily enough, camped in a gully but easily visible from the air with the fire they had going. After making sure that they were safe, I continued southeast to the city, and when I got there I didn't bother with the sewers, going straight to the garden and from there on to the inn.

It was Mak who came to let me in. Of course it was. I could feel her rushing down to the cellar, and she practically threw the door open.

"Thanks," I said. "Trouble sleeping again?"

"Forget about sleep! Thank the Mercies you're here!" she said, relief dripping off her. She stepped out of the way to let me in. "I was working my way up to going back out to find you!"

"What happened?"

She let me in, then quickly closed and barred the door before speaking. "Sempralia wants to meet you, is what happened! And Ardek stumbled in here two nights ago, beaten half to death with a message from the Night Blossom, *and before you do anything*—" she rushed to say as outrage flared in me, "I don't think she ordered it!"

"Explain," I commanded. I was shaking. My shadow was going wild, straining to go back out, and I was holding back from ordering Mak to open the door so that I could go and do something terrible. They had hurt one of mine. My servant. Someone had to pay for that, and I had told Kesra what would happen. I needed to make good on my threat, or I'd look weak. They'd think that they could do whatever they wanted, and the next time they might go after the actual family.

Oh, I wanted so very badly to send a message. And if I ordered Mak to open that door for me, she would. No matter what she herself wanted or thought best, she'd do what I told her to. I'd been careful the last few weeks not to tell her to do anything that she wouldn't want to anyway, to frame things as requests rather than commands, but in that moment . . . no. I'd asked her to tell me when I was being crazy and to help me if I was giving Instinct too much control at the wrong time. I especially needed to trust her and the others when it came to judging people's actions. If I didn't listen to her now, what was the point?

"It doesn't make sense," she hurried on. "The message is almost conciliatory. Posturing bullshit, yeah, but if you read between the lines, I think you've scared her, so why would she try to provoke you? No. It doesn't make sense. Unless the bitch is unstable, which we can't assume that she isn't."

I forced my anger down, then moved, deliberately putting some distance between myself and the door and sitting down by the stairs. "If you don't think the Night Blossom ordered it, then who?"

"One of her minions. Maybe . . ." she swallowed. "Maybe that little shit Tarkarran? Maybe someone else who was supposed to bring us the message and recognized Ardek? The fact that they left him alive at all . . . They must be furious that he's still alive, and working with us. If they wanted to provoke you, it would make more sense to just kill him and dump him here with a letter."

"What about his minions? Those friends of his that he recruited? Was anyone else hurt?"

"All fine, as far as I know. They weren't even around. Some guys he didn't recognize cornered him, kicked the shit out of him, and told him to bring us a message."

I laid down, hearing my claws scrape against the stone floor as I flexed them, slowly bleeding my anger out where it couldn't cause permanent consequences. "And he's all right now, yeah?"

"Don't worry, sister." Mak's voice was soothing as she sat down next to me. "Kira and me, we healed him right up. He's fine."

"Want to tell me the message? Or would you rather have him do it?"

"Well . . . he's the one who suffered for it. Might as well let him tell you."

"All right. And Sempralia? That's the lady justice you met, yeah?"

Mak heaved a long sigh. "Yeah. That's her. Simple enough. We got a letter, with a seal and everything, while we were all out killing trolls. I could read it to you."

"Just summarize it."

"Right. Apparently, the lady justice has decided that she wants to meet you. That's it. No reason given, no hint of what she might want to talk about. She wants to meet you. Wants us to suggest a time and place. And, while you certainly *can* refuse . . ."

"You'd rather I didn't?"

"I *beg* you to do as she asks. I still don't know if she's any kind of ally, or just someone who's treated us fairly, but I am desperate not to make an enemy of her. We just got somewhere! We're a family, a House, we've got this inn, which could secure our futures for generations! If we anger, or even just annoy a councilor . . ."

She went on for a while, speaking as she let me into the strongroom. I'd decided almost immediately to do it. Like Mak said, it would be crazy to upset one of the most powerful people in the city, and there was no reason I could see to refuse, as long as I could choose a place where there was no risk of an ambush or a surprise attack. But I let Mak finish. From the way she went on she had obviously been thinking about this, preparing her pitch. And there was something about how earnest and anxious she was that was, quite frankly, adorable.

"Please, Draka?" she finished. "Would you do this for us? Just meet with her?"

I couldn't tell from her expression how well I'd kept my emotions in check, but I made a show of considering her arguments. Perhaps it was patronizing, in a way, but I wanted her to feel that I was listening to her. And, honestly, she'd made some good arguments. We had done, and would continue to do, some things that were very much illegal, and having a councilor with a grudge against us, especially one who was a notorious stickler for the law, was a guaranteed way to have those illegal acts exposed sooner or later. And that was besides the many small ways Sempralia could make my family's lives difficult, no matter how carefully they followed the law. On the other hand, if someone like the lady justice had a good impression of us, of me, that could be a real blessing. Hell, I might even be able to gain legal recognition!

Or perhaps not. Hundreds of years of prejudice probably wouldn't be that easy to overcome. But that was no reason not to try, and a girl could dream.

"I'll talk to her," I said finally, to Mak's undisguised relief. "Can you pick a place and a time? You know what I need."

She thought for a split second, then nodded. "I can do that. I'll send a reply to the lady justice in the morning and let you know when everything's decided, yeah?"

"I knew I could rely on you. Now, that message from the dead woman. I don't know what she could possibly have to say that would interest me, unless she's offering to turn herself over to us, but I'd like to hear it. Is Ardek around?"

"He might be asleep, but I think so. Should I get him for you?"

"Please. And Mak?"

"Yes?"

"Get some sleep, would you? I know it's hard, but you're still obviously not sleeping enough. Hell, you're welcome to come down here and stay with me if it helps. I don't mind it. It's nice, and I need you in good shape, yeah?"

She looked at me in surprise then turned to leave, but I saw her smile as she did. On the other side of the door she stopped and turned around. "I might take you up on that." Then she was gone.

CHAPTER NINETEEN

Ambush

I didn't have to wait long in the strongroom, but I wouldn't have minded. I could have spent all night there and been perfectly happy. There was a bunch of new money in the magically sealed, red lacquered box, and it smelled absolutely divine. Some of it was already set aside for me in a small leather pouch. Mak and the others must have gone to the Alchemists' Guild when they got back, and they'd been paid a tidy sum for the trolls' blood we'd harvested. Fifty eagles per full jar, if I remembered correctly, which should make somewhere around three hundred and seventy-five eagles in total for the seven and a half jars, depending on how full each had been. I wasn't sure what the expedition had cost in preparations and security for the inn, but less costs . . . I opened the small leather pouch and poured its contents into my palm. In the warm glow of the lightstone, one gold dragon and twenty-two silver eagles gleamed at me, filling my vision.

I put them back in the pouch, then ran my hand through the coins in the box, which were mostly silver. The way they clinked and tinkled was as hypnotic as ever. I could have amused myself like that for ages if I had nothing else to do.

One thing struck me as odd, though. While I had the same strong urge as always to bring my share to my hoard immediately, I couldn't say the same for the rest. The desire to take the whole treasure with me was there, certainly, but it was manageable. Clearly, even Instinct understood that my servants, my friends, my *family* needed money.

A thought flashed through my mind. Perhaps a memory: "What's mine is mine, and what's theirs is ours." And they could be trusted with it. I knew that, without doubt. It just felt right, and it made leaving all that silver in their hands acceptable no matter how easy it would have been to take it.

Alas, I could not play with coins all night. When Mak brought Ardek to me he was yawning and bleary-eyed, though he made an admirable effort to straighten himself, despite how tired he obviously was. "Sorry, boss," he told me, flushing with embarrassment after yawning right in my face, "only, I've been doing some pretty long nights. I always thought the higher-ups had it easy, but keeping an eye on Tark and that house you say belongs to the Night Blossom's sister, and trying to keep track of the kids, it's a lot of work!"

"I'm sure it is," I said. "Are you all right? Mak told me what happened."

"Yeah, boss, thanks for asking. Makanna and Kira fixed me right up. Set my jaw and unbroke my wrist and everything." He grinned, and glanced at Mak. "Can barely believe it, honestly, having two pretty healers taking care of me like that. Made me feel like a rich man!"

Mak just rolled her eyes.

"So, what's the message?" I asked. "And are you sure it's from the Night Blossom?"

That poured some cold water on his mood. "I'm sure, yeah. I didn't recognize them, but when they were done kicking me around, the leader called me a traitor and told me to 'tell my new boss this . . .'" He cleared his throat and closed his eyes. "'The Night Blossom says that if any of you lot go near her people again, she will fucking grind you into the gutter. Don't start shit, and she'll forget about you little fucks and your little inn or whatever, and you can all go on with your little lives.' Then he kicked me in the jaw and they left. Only, I don't think the Night Blossom would have said it like that, 'cause when I heard her talk she was pretty well spoken."

"I do believe you're right," I told him generously. I was pretty sure that almost anyone would have been more eloquent than that. "Was that the whole message?"

"That was it, yeah."

"All right. Thank you, Ardek." I considered him for a moment. He looked tired, yeah, but for all that he'd just been beaten within an inch of his life, there was an excited energy about him, like he was expecting something. "What do you think we should do about this? What should our response be?" I asked.

He grinned wolfishly. "Can't let that stand, can you? I mean, me getting beaten up, fair enough. Can't say I didn't hate it, but that was just a warning. But the message, that's a challenge. Wasn't an offer or anything; it was a demand. Disrespectful, too, to have a subordinate tell me so I passed it along. If she didn't mean nothing by it, she should have sent you a letter or something. A messenger maybe. But this way, she's saying she's got all the power. So yeah, nah, you've got to respond to this."

I looked at Mak. She didn't look happy about it, but she nodded, saying, "It might escalate things, but if we do nothing, the Night Blossom and her people will think that they can hurt us with impunity. That we're too afraid to respond."

"That's what I thought," I agreed. The anger was boiling again, at the insult of hurting Ardek, and the disrespect in the message. But it wasn't just the instinctive rage of the dragon. It was a controlled anger that belonged to all of me. "She thinks she can hurt us and we'll let it go. That after all she's done, we'll be happy to accept a truce. We're going to show her just how wrong she is."

"What are we going to do?"

"What are we going to do? She hurt one of mine. We're going to kill one of hers. That's what we're going to do. I told Kesra that anything her sister did to one of mine, I'd do worse to her. But I think she's the wrong target."

"Who, then?"

"Mak, I promised you revenge, and you've been very patient. It's about time that I deliver."

Ardek and Barro had done a good job, tracking down Tark and establishing the way he usually moved around the city. There were variations, of course, but they were regular variations of a solid pattern. He had a home where he usually slept, a few high-end establishments and a bath he liked to visit, and the estate outside the city where most of his House lived. Exactly when and how he talked to the Night Blossom was something we hadn't figured out yet, but my bet was on him meeting her in one of the taverns.

For the next few days we had eyes on him constantly. A big part of that was me. He often moved during the night while sleeping the days away which, of course, suited me just fine. Shifting, I followed him in the shadows, learning his movements, seeing for myself the places he went and choosing the right moment to strike. Herald helped during the nights, although staying shifted for too long still took it out of her, so she couldn't stay as close as I could. Still, it was good practice for her, both with her shadow magic and the basic skills of surveillance and sneaking. In the daytime, we had Ardek's minions watching wherever Herald or I had left Tark, and for four days we never lost track of him.

On the fifth night, after hours of planning and preparation, we struck. If we'd just wanted to take him, we could have done it earlier. But I didn't want to take him in front of witnesses. I didn't want anyone running to the Night Blossom or the guard or anyone else, screaming about how one of the city's upper crust had been taken by a dragon or, even worse, by a group of Tekereteki. I wanted him to disappear, to vanish suddenly one night as he went about his business. I wanted the Night Blossom to wonder, to suspect, but not know what had happened to him, until the time was right.

I wanted her to be afraid. And if that led to her doing something rash, or even stupid, so be it.

Tark always had guards or companions with him, and we would have to deal with them no matter when or how we grabbed him. What made things awkward was that he almost always moved in public. Every other day, however, and Ardek's minions had confirmed this, he liked to visit a certain brothel in the southern part of the city. To get there he crossed one of the two bridges that spanned the wide river and cut through the city. He'd go down a major street, turn onto a smaller one, and then he always took a shortcut through a certain narrow alley rather than go all the way around a block of apartments. The guy was careful, but that block was ridiculous, so I couldn't blame him. Unfortunately for him, that alley was the perfect place for an ambush—dark, rarely trafficked, and easy to close off.

We had the when and the where. All that remained was the how.

The Wolves, of course, couldn't risk being involved. I couldn't blame them. In this case, they wouldn't even be able to argue that they were defending their friends; this was abduction and premeditated murder, pure and simple, and the less any of them knew, the better.

Ardek wasn't a fighter. His role was to keep his minions in line and minimize the risk of any nasty surprises. Barro could fight, which Val could vouch for, but he wasn't close enough for me to involve him. And Kira, as I'd promised her, wouldn't even hear about what we were doing unless something went horribly wrong. All she knew was that we were up to *something*.

My family, the precious four who'd be with me, were nervous. Of course they were. Tam had killed one of the pirates because he'd had to, but he was no more comfortable with it than Mak had been. Herald and Mak would be facing the man who'd tortured them for days, and who'd been the catalyst for so many changes. And Val had to watch three people he cared for more than his own life go up against trained killers. While they would all be wearing their armor, hidden under heavy cloaks, there was a real risk of severe or even lethal injury. If they hadn't been nervous, for each other if not each for themselves, they'd've been insane.

But none of them complained. Not once did anyone express any doubt about what we were doing. This was about revenge, honor, justice, and hopefully even healing. It was necessary.

"Are you sure that you can do this?" I'd asked Mak privately as we made our plans. "You froze last time."

"I know. I'd never seen Simdal before that night. I'd heard that he was an awful man, but him, and his guards . . . I just couldn't make myself hate them like that, to injure or even kill them when they'd done nothing to me. This bastard, though . . ." She swallowed, her breathing growing quick and shallow. It was hard for her to even talk about him. "Tark," she spat, once she got herself under control. "After what he did to Herald. What he did to me . . . Anyone standing between him and me has made their choice. If I have to kill them, so be it."

We put her at the entrance to the alley, to close it off once Tark and his guards entered. Her job was to make sure that no one escaped back the way they came. At the other end would be Tam and Val, blocking Tark's path, trapping him.

As for Herald, we practiced her part over and over, improving her control and stamina as much as we could in preparation. She would be hiding in the shadows in the alley itself. We'd placed a barrel about halfway, and I had hidden it in permanent shadow, which should hopefully make the barrel itself less noticeable and give Herald a place to shift. When our target arrived a shadow would stretch out. Two quick stabs with a short, wide blade, and she'd escape as I fell from the sky. Hopefully she wouldn't need to stand and fight at all, but once she'd launched her surprise attack she'd retreat back to Mak, in case things went to shit and someone tried to escape that way.

And me, I'd be taking Tark. I'd fought him before and won, and I had no doubt that I could do so again. I was bigger this time, a little more experienced. I knew myself and what I could do better. Maybe I'd have to break him a little, maybe not. I'd need to disarm him at least. Once he was dealt with, I'd fly him out, hopefully alive. While I'd settle for dead if he put up too much of a fight, we had questions to ask him. More importantly, I'd promised Herald that she could finish him off. I knew that she'd understand if it didn't turn out that way, but that was no excuse not to keep my promise if I could.

When we took Simdal we had brought him to the inn. That had been an unnecessary risk, in hindsight, so this time we were prepared. Instead of bringing Tark somewhere that someone might hear him, a place he might recognize or where he might be found, or somewhere we'd have to clean up when we were done with him, I was taking him into the drains.

I intended to bring him in via the outflow by the docks. It had the benefits of being easy enough to get to unseen in the middle of the night, and if anyone should hear him yelling, they wouldn't be able to easily locate the sound or be able to do anything about it. Being able to fly, I could get to it easily compared to my family, who'd have to row out to the opening.

For that reason I'd shown the family to the Barlean woman Tellee's house on the west side of the city. The window was closed tight but could still be opened, if you only knew to try. Solely using it as an entrance to the tunnels felt a little off, especially when the woman clearly had some emotional ties to the place. We had talked about buying the place from her, but her ship was long gone. Maybe next time, if I ever saw her again. There was also the huge Karakani man, Tor-something, who we might be able to use to get in touch with her, but the urge to make things right were nowhere close to strong enough to want to explain why we wanted the house, and why we thought that he could arrange it.

Legality and morals aside, I'd taken them through the house and down into the drains. Herald had been less than amused with how much she had to stoop down there, but she'd managed. Mak could just barely walk upright, which was fairly amusing to everyone else. We hadn't had much time, so I didn't show them around, but thanks to the regularity of the tunnels, and the fact that Mak and Herald could feel my location like I could theirs, it was easy for them to find their way to the sea cave where I was taking Tark.

On the day we grabbed the bastard, I posted up on a roof across from the tavern he usually visited after leaving his home in the city. I saw him come, I waited, and I followed him to the next place, and the next, and the next, as the sun dipped behind the mountains.

As he and his three guards left the baths and began their walk south, I took off into the night sky and went ahead to tell the others to get ready.

By the time the four of them arrived at the alley, everyone was in position. Mak was hidden on the side they would be entering from, practically invisible in the shadows and ready to close off that end. Herald was hidden behind the barrel we'd prepared, ready to become literally invisible once our targets approached. And Tam and Val awaited my signal at the far end.

The plan met reality at that point, and it did not survive impact.

CHAPTER TWENTY

A Foot of Steel

The alley where we trapped Tark was about ninety feet long. By the time his party had made it twenty feet in, about halfway to Herald and her barrel, the lead guard stopped, holding up a hand. He looked around, seemed to listen, or to almost feel the air. Then he turned to herd the others back out, hissing, "Ambush!"

I had started shifting back the moment they turned. I hadn't made or executed a lot of plans, but I could recognize when one turned to shit, and I refused to let them get away. I was on a roof above Herald near the middle of the alley and was almost ready to leap into the air when Mak stepped out in front of the four men, her sword held almost casually at her side.

If the four had rushed at her in that moment, I don't know how she could have survived. She was saved by the pipsqueak's arrogance.

"Tarkarran," Mak said as I took off, her voice trembling noticeably. With fear or anger, I had no idea.

"*Miss* Makanna," Tark sneered in his high tenor, holding up a hand to stop his guards as he drew his sword with the other.

That was as far as they got before I landed, instinct putting me between *my* valuable servant—*my* sister—and the man who had harmed her and who threatened to take her from me. Perhaps it would have been better to pounce on the whole group, but I couldn't take the risk. I'd once been willing to use Mak, to throw her away if the payoff was worth it. Now I could not risk losing her.

Of course, introducing a dragon to the situation did not make things calmer, or less violent.

Mak's expression when I landed in front of her, what I saw before I whirled around, was a mix of relief and reverence. The four men behind me had leapt back, wide-eyed, and as I faced Tark for the first time since we freed the slaves he bought from the valkin, he growled, "The dragon! Kill it!"

Well, he tried to growl. It didn't really work with his voice, but it was still a sound that would have sent chills down the spine of any human. There was a malice bordering on madness in it that was reflected in his eyes, a promise of violence and suffering to anyone unfortunate enough to end up in his power, which Herald and Mak knew so well. But I was only barely human at that moment, hanging on by a thread and a hope as I faced the man who had tortured my friends. I wanted so very much to just rip him apart, but I had promised, so I would try and hold back.

That was assuming I had the choice. The moment he finished speaking he was coming at me. He hadn't lost a shred of the speed I'd seen the first time I faced him, and he either didn't feel fear, or he recognized that he didn't stand a chance at a distance. He closed with me in the blink of an eye, scoring more glancing cuts than I'd care to admit as I dodged, slapped, and snapped at him. His cronies were no slouches, either, coming at me and Mak with swords and desperate courage.

I sprayed my venom wide at them, but they were prepared. When I let loose they all closed their eyes and held their breath, falling back and covering their faces. I only got one of them who was too slow, and who started groaning and coughing as he tried to blink away whatever got in his eyes. Mak went for him, but the guy next to him jumped in to fend her off, and they ended up locked in a furious exchange. Tark's man had the advantage when it came to skill, but they were matched for speed, and Mak was, quite frankly, cheating. When the guy had to parry, it became clear that she was strong as hell, her attacks driving him back despite his skill. When she defended, she moved with a dancer's grace, but despite her agile dodges, a thrust slipped through, aimed at her neck.

Time seemed to slow to a crawl as the blade slid along her skin, blood welling as it went. But that was it—a shallow graze, a thin line of bright red on brown where her neck should have been cut open.

That was the turning point. When Mak realized that her borrowed draconic fortitude really meant something in a fight, she went on the offensive. She attacked furiously, dodging most of what the guy could throw at her, accepting shallow cuts on her arms and legs when it made sense, and only parrying the most clearly lethal stabs.

As Mak went on the offensive, so did I. Tark and the third guy, the one who wasn't partially disabled, had recovered. I saw Tam and Val enter the alley from the far end, but it would take them seconds to reach us, and I needed the initiative. I let myself go wild, forcing them back into the alley, not expecting to do any damage but keeping them busy until we could overwhelm them. A quick glance at Mak showed that she was winning her duel, but that might change in a second. It was still one-on-one, but the last guard, still coughing and blinking furiously, had recovered enough to join the fight and was moving to flank Mak. If Mak went down—

A shadow reached out and wrapped itself up along the man's body and around his head. He cried out in surprise and wiped ineffectually at his face, never seeing the length of steel that appeared from nowhere. It cut halfway through his neck, lodging in his spine.

Herald's sword jerked loose from the dying man, seemingly of its own accord, and followed that up with a slice to the back of the knees of the man Mak was fighting, who stumbled and fell as his legs stopped carrying him. Mak only hesitated for a heartbeat before closing in. He cut at her, but she caught the wrist of his sword arm in her free hand and drove her sword clean through his throat, kicking him off her blade in one smooth motion.

That left two, still focused on me as I pushed them back. Things were going well. They were both quick and had reach on me with their swords, and I wasn't getting at them, but that was fine. It was five on two now, or would be in about two seconds when Tam and Val joined the fight. But no matter how skewed the balance was, we were still facing two desperate men with fighting advancements, and I didn't want any last second reversals to lead to one of my humans getting hurt. When the rhythm of our exchange would have had me attack, I fell back, instead sending shadows to envelope my two opponents, to terrify and blind them.

Tark quickly showed me that I had underestimated him.

His remaining companion froze. Tark himself was made of sterner stuff. Perhaps he was truly fearless. Perhaps his fight, flight, or freeze was permanently locked to fight. Whatever the cause, he launched himself out of the shadows, a cornered animal throwing everything into a last ditch effort to, if not survive, then at least cause as much damage as possible. Roaring with surprise and outrage I reared up and away from him, swiping at him with both hands and dodging back and to the side. He accepted a glancing blow from one set of claws and dodged under the other. As he did so he followed me unerringly, put his free hand on the pommel of his short sword, and thrust.

The thrust was perfect. The aim was off. He missed my heart by inches. It was still the most horrible experience of my life.

The sword took me straight on, low on the right side of my chest, through the flight muscle. Scales slid and cracked, and the pain and the horrid, cold sensation of steel sliding into me, cutting through flesh and organs, was like nothing I'd ever imagined. At first I wasn't sure what had happened. Tark himself seemed stunned, shocked beyond comprehension, that his attack had worked. It slowed him enough that he didn't have time to pull away when my head snapped down, almost reflexively, and my jaws sheared through his wrist, bone and all. I barely heard his shrill, horrified scream as he fell away from me, clutching at the stump, or how the others cut down his last guard and subdued him. I just stared stupidly at the hilt of the sword hovering in front of my chest, connected to a gash in my scales by about five inches of steel. I tried to take a breath to speak, but that made everything shift around the thing—the sword—stuck through my lung, and I hated that, so I forced myself to hold my breath.

I ended up lying on my side, not sure how it had happened. There was a lot of blood on the ground, but I was pretty sure that very little of it was mine. The sword that had been driven almost all the way through my chest was still in there, after all. If you got stabbed you were supposed to leave the blade in so it could block a lot of the bleeding. They'd included that in my first aid training back on Earth for some reason, and I remembered wondering why.

I had a detached sort of realization that I was in shock. Dragons could go into shock. Or could they? I felt very human in that moment, small and vulnerable and scared, and somewhat betrayed by the fact that Instinct, with all her rage and arrogance that could have made the fear go away, was nowhere to be found. But then my family was all around me. That made things a little better.

Someone was holding my head.

"Herald," I gasped with some of my last, hoarded air. The word came out wet, and I tasted blood.

"Hush, big sister," she said. She sounded terrified, like she was barely keeping it together. I hated that. Then her grip on my head tightened, keeping it from moving while her hands clamped my jaws shut. I wasn't sure what was going on, but I didn't like it at all. "Don't worry," she said. "We're going to fix you up, all right? But I need you to lie very still, and keep your claws in. Can you do that, Draka? Keep your claws in. That's it. That's good. Just like that."

Her speech wasn't the careful style she usually used, but the rush that came out when she was very emotional. I didn't like that. I wanted to comfort her. But she'd asked me to lie still and be quiet. And to keep my claws in, for some reason. And she was Herald. If I couldn't trust her, if I couldn't do as she asked, then who?

I distantly heard Val ask, "Ready?"

"Ready," Mak and Tam both answered.

"It's going to hurt a little bit, okay?" Herald said, in a quavering tone I *really* didn't like. "Only a little. Just be still."

Then she clamped down on me as hard as she could. Out of the corner of my eye I saw Val grip the hilt of the sword that was sticking out of me. There was some pressure as he braced one foot on my chest, and then he pulled the sword out in one smooth motion.

The world was pain. I would have howled if I'd had any air. As it was, I just contracted my chest as hard as I could, which was lucky, because if I'd tried to take a breath I would have filled my chest up with air through the two-inch gash that went right through my lung.

I tried to lie still. I really did. I still couldn't stop myself from scrabbling at the ground and trying to cover up my wound. Luckily, Mak only caught a glancing blow when she dove in past Val, and she recovered quickly and shoved her palms onto either side of the gash. "Heal!" she pleaded, and I felt a warmth, followed by a beautiful numbness that spread through my chest. At the same time someone was pouring something on the wound. "Heal, you gods-damned lizard, heal!" she said as she continued pumping magic into me, a steady stream of light from her heart to mine.

As I got my limbs back under control Herald released her grip on my head, and I gasped with relief. Then I started hacking and coughing, globs of blood coming up with every wracking spasm, spattering onto the ground and Herald's lap. She stroked my jaw as I gasped weakly, recovering from my coughing fit. "You need to drink this, all right?" she said, her voice a little steadier. I felt a bottle against the side of my mouth. It was weird. I hadn't drunk from a bottle for . . . half a year, maybe? "Just open your mouth, and swallow," she said, tilting my head back and pouring a slow trickle of burning liquid onto my tongue. Alcohol! The healing potions were mostly alcohol; I remembered that. I hadn't had a drop of alcohol since I came to Mallin, but last time I drank I'd been chugging pink Moscato straight from the bottle. Classy as hell. Nowhere near as strong as this stuff, but it was still funny how that worked out.

I carefully swallowed the trickle, and it burned all the way down. I really hoped that healing potions weren't toxic to dragons. That would be embarrassing. Surviving a sword through the lung and then dying from potion poisoning.

"Getting her out of here will be difficult," Val said. "I can't imagine her flying in this state."

"Yeah, how do we carry her?" That was Tam. "Especially if we don't want her to be seen?"

I agreed. Moving me anywhere would be tricky. I was large, and probably somewhere between three or four hundred pounds. I'd just have to move on my own.

"Tark?" I said weakly, remembering what we were doing here. I was supposed to fly him out.

"Alive, but out," Mak said wearily. She was sitting back against the alley wall, breathing heavily.

"Oh. Good."

"I'm sorry, Draka," Tam said. "I don't think we can keep you hidden."

"All right. It's all right. Needed a kick in the bum anyway. You wouldn't betray my secrets, right, Tam?"

"No, of course not! You know I wouldn't."

"And you, too, Val. You wouldn't tell anyone if I showed you something crazy, yeah?"

"I swear that I would not."

"All right. Good. Thank you. Mak? Do you think that I'm all right to move?"

I shared a look with her. She knew what I was planning. I could see it in her eyes. Finally she gave me a sharp nod.

I shifted. It was hard. Harder than normal. Harder to focus. It felt like there was a lot of resistance, and I wasn't sure that I could have done it without the fullness of the Nest Heart I'd eaten. But it was still far easier than it had been those first few times, and the way Tam and Val jumped back was amusing.

"I'll go with her. Leave the bodies, and figure out what to do about Tark," Herald said, almost commanded, then went from a mid-gray in my vision to shining bright as she followed me into the shadows. She didn't wait for them to argue or acknowledge. She just shifted and went with me.

"I guess you knew about this?" I heard Tam ask Mak as I made my way north.

Perhaps I should have stayed with them, but I was in no shape to fight. I was woozy, and getting hungry, and desperately tired. There was no way that the sounds of fighting wouldn't attract someone, and the sooner I left the scene, the sooner the others could do the same. Besides, I was not planning on being out in the street when something like four shots of pure grain alcohol kicked in. I didn't know if dragons could get drunk. I didn't want to know what might happen if one did, but I was about to find out.

Our walk back toward the inn was halting and occasionally uncertain. Once I was stopped by something as simple as one of the weak street lights, when I forgot to use the shadows to make a passage through the light. After that Herald kept an eye on me, making sure to guide me around the light with careful nudges. She also blocked my way once or twice to keep me from passing unnecessarily close to some late-night pedestrian. Not that they'd be likely to see us, or believe their eyes if they did, but Herald took keeping me hidden pretty seriously.

I ran out of steam about halfway there and had to stop behind a wall and shift back. I just lay there, panting through my exhaustion, Herald watching over me until I could shift again and make it another few thousand feet, then another few hundred. The last time I had to stop we were almost in sight of the inn. We didn't bother with the yard and the cellar door. Herald just went in the front, and I followed.

One of Barro's friends was keeping an eye on the place while we were all out. He hadn't asked for much, either, just a free night's stay with meals, so he didn't deserve the way Herald just shooed him out of the way, storming through and doing her best to play a pissed-off princess to keep his attention on her as I slipped past into the kitchen. Once she'd opened the door to the cellar, though, and I had slipped down the stairs, I heard her sigh theatrically and begin to apologize as she closed the door.

I had no idea what she was going to tell him. She was a bad liar and couldn't act for love nor money. But I was too wrung out to worry about that. In the dark of the cellar I shifted back and collapsed. The world spun. I felt like I could barely breathe, and I was getting frighteningly hungry. I'd been healed, by magic and by alchemy, but I still felt like I was horribly injured. The memory of steel sliding into my chest was still fresh, and it was difficult to accept that I wasn't pumping blood onto the floor.

Now that the pain was gone I could feel Instinct creeping back in, the coward. I wanted to hide, to crawl into a crack somewhere no one could find me, or where they could at least only come at me from one direction.

I desperately wanted my hoard.

I settled for the best I had available. The strongroom was locked, but I still dragged myself into the short corridor, settling down the best I could with my back to the massive door. My face felt numb, and I was so tired, but something told me not to sleep. I was hurt, and I hadn't killed the one that hurt me. They were still out there. The archer. No, that wasn't right. It hadn't been an arrow this time, but a sword. And my humans had the little bastard, didn't they? So I knew that I was safe, but I wasn't with my hoard. I couldn't sleep yet. I needed to get to my hoard. I'd be safe there, safe to sleep and heal. Not here. My humans were out; they weren't here to guard me. I mustn't sleep. I mustn't—

CHAPTER TWENTY-ONE

Calm

I woke with three bodies breathing softly around me. The surface I lay on was comfortable, and there was the smell of silver in the air.

It came to me slowly that I was in the strongroom, laying on the nest of pillows and blankets that my family had made for me. They must have brought me in there, somehow, sometime. They'd added mattresses, more pillows, and more blankets, and now Herald, Mak, and to my surprise, Kira lay around me in a protective half-circle, between me and the barred door. Herald and Mak both had their swords and daggers in easy reach, and while Kira was unarmed she still lay there, looking determined to at least make herself a speed bump if necessary.

I was hungry, but I wasn't as hungry as I should have been. I didn't know how long I'd slept, but I had healed a terrible injury, and experience told me that I should have been properly ravenous. There was an empty box in one corner, though, smelling vaguely of fish. I couldn't remember much of anything since we'd left the alley, but my best guess was that they must have gotten a bunch of fish in me when they moved me into the strongroom.

I looked around me again, and I was at once both satisfied and touched by how loyally my humans were guarding me. Even here, behind a heavy, locked door in their own home, my sisters, my little dragons, were prepared to fight. They were wearing their armor, their weapons ready nearby, and there was no way that anyone could get in here and get to me without going through them first. The thing was, I could understand them doing it. But Kira had put herself in the same position. She had slowly become more accepting of her position here and the power I had over her, but I would never have expected her to put herself at risk for me. The fact that she did so with only her body to put in the way of any attacker was flattering, to say the least.

Mak was the first to wake. I couldn't say if that was because she was more alert than the others, because she slept poorly, or because she felt me waking up through our bond, but soon after I awoke, her eyes blinked open, and she looked at me blearily before giving me a tired smile and reaching out to touch where my wound had been and sending a pulse of golden light into me. "Good," she whispered, running her finger over the irregular line of broken scales that now covered it. "Very good. It's healing nicely."

"How long?" I said softly, trying not to wake the other two.

"A full day. I'm not sure what the time is, but with how rested I am I'd guess late afternoon, or early evening. You're healing quickly."

"Any response from the Night Blossom?"

"Not yet, though she may not have heard yet. We'll have to wait and see."

"Yeah, all right." I paused for a bit. "Thank you. For the healing and all."

"No need. I did what I had to. And, I mean, not because of your power over me, but because I wanted to. You're family, yeah? And you were hurt. How could I not?"

"Still. Thank you, Mak." I gestured around the room with my head. "How did this happen? I don't remember coming in here."

"We found you asleep outside the door. I think you must have been confused, because you got scary when we woke you, rambling and growling and hissing and all . . . yeah, pretty scary."

"I didn't hurt anyone, did I?" I asked anxiously, but she waved it off.

"No, everyone's all right. I could feel you, you know? You didn't want to fight. Not us. So we backed off and slept on the floor in front of you, and in the morning we sent Ardek down to the fishing docks, and he got a big box of fish for you—that box, there—and, ah . . . we kind of used it to lure you in here."

"'Lure' me?"

"Sorry, but, yeah. Talking to you didn't work. I'm not sure that you understood us at all. I think you were delirious, talking to us in some language we couldn't recognize. That 'English' of yours, maybe. But Herald got you away from the door by giving you a couple of the fish, and then we brought the rest of them in here and got you in that way. Not very dignified, I know. Sorry. But we just had to get you in here."

"Why? Thank you, but why?"

"I . . . I'm not sure. It didn't feel safe, I guess? We all agreed that we needed to get you in here, so you could rest safely. Herald wanted to try to get you back to the mountain, to your hoard, but how could we get you up there? So this was the next best thing. Ardek's outside, too. He insisted someone needed to stay outside, to warn us if . . ." She looked away, slightly chagrined. "You know, it seems ridiculous, now. Warn us of what? Protect you from who? You're in the safest place in the city. But you were hurt, and we felt that we had to watch over you."

"Dragon magic? Messing with your head?"

"Probably."

"I didn't mean for that to happen," I said, suddenly embarrassed. "You know that, right? You know I don't like to make you do things."

"I know. But I don't mind. It was nice, in a way. There was no uncertainty, just 'Protect Draka, and damn everything else.' Very direct. Uncomplicated."

We both knew that she *couldn't* mind, as long as it benefitted me, and she was at peace with that. It still felt weird, but it wasn't like I could do anything about it. I had that effect on some people. It had something to do with strong emotions, like love or terror, but I wasn't completely clear on how it worked. I didn't know why Barro had become so loyal to me and not the scholars, Ramban or Tavia, who'd been with him. I'd terrified the crap out of Jekrie, and he practically worshiped me, but Simdal couldn't get far enough away from me. But, no matter how it worked or why it happened, I had a responsibility to those I'd mind-whammied, at least those who were essentially good, well-meaning people. *My* people.

"Well," I told Mak, "I'm happy to hear that. And again, thank you. For your efforts and for your kindness. I really do feel like I can rest safe with you here."

"That's all I wanted," she said, giving me a wide, proud smile.

Soon, Herald and Kira both awoke and, just like Mak, the first thing each of them did was check my wound. *"Another scar,"* Herald commented, running her thumb over the irregularly placed scales.

"Another mistake," I snorted. *"Perhaps I will learn from this one?"*

"What did you learn from the previous ones?" Kira asked curiously. I'm sure she didn't mean to sound sarcastic, but I sure heard it that way.

"Pay attention to the strongest opponent," I said, pointing to the nub where my left horn was slowly growing back. *"Do not rush into combat with multiple, prepared opponents."* I lifted my wing to show the scar there, where I'd been stabbed while cleaning house in the Night Blossom's prison. *"I am still working on that. And this new one . . . never underestimate a cornered enemy, perhaps? I really did not think that little shit had it in him. Speaking of Tark, what happened to him?"*

"I stopped the bleeding from his arm," Mak said. *"Nasty amputation, by the way. Well done. Then we bound and gagged him and stuck him in that barrel. We have kept him there since, under guard in the other room, where we talked to Simdal."*

"In the barrel?"

"We did not see any reason to get him out, since . . . Oh, hells. Sorry, Kira."

Our short exchange about Tark had Kira looking fairly miserable, and Mak had picked up on it much more quickly than I had. *"Draka,"* Mak said, *"If it is okay with you . . . Kira, perhaps you could go upstairs and send down whichever of Tam and Val is not on guard? We will need to talk about some things that you would be happier not hearing."*

"Please," Kira said, giving me a desperate look. *"I understand that you need to do this, but—"*

"Go ahead, Kira," I said. *"And thank you for watching over me as I slept. I appreciate it. Mak, would you open the door for her?"*

Mak tried to do as I'd asked, but when she pushed on the door there was a light *thump* and a startled cry from Ardek, who had apparently been sleeping with his back against the door. Once he got out of the way Mak let Kira out, who left with a relieved smile my way.

"Poor Kira," Herald said, looking out the door after her as she left. "She cannot stomach even talk of violence. Her time with the Silver Spurs must have been hell." Then she turned back to me and Mak with a predatory smile. "Now, what do we do about the monster in the barrel? I have some ideas, but I suppose we should try to get some information out of him first."

The little room where Val was guarding a barrel became terribly crowded once Herald, Mak, Ardek, and I had crowded in there; and when Tam arrived he had to stand in the doorway by virtue of being last on the scene.

I opened our meeting without preamble, tapping the barrel with a claw. "Suggestions?"

"Throw some rocks in there and sink the bastard in the river," Tam suggested.

"Interrogation is usually the first step with prisoners," Val said. "But I don't think that this is an ideal place for it."

"I agree with Val on both points," Herald said. "And, sorry to say, brother, but simply drowning him does not sound nearly satisfying enough. So, if not here, then we go back to the original plan, yes?"

"I think so," I agreed. "The important question is: Herald. Mak. Do you feel up to talking to him? Or would you prefer that we do it?"

"I need to be there," Mak said softly. She was staring at the barrel like Tark might break out and start abusing her at any moment. "I need to."

"Me, too," Herald agreed. "Seeing you take his hand off helped, but I need to see this monster made human."

"That's agreed, then. I'm taking him, and you all know where I'm going and how to get there." I knocked on the barrel. "You hear that, you little shit? We're going flying, you and me!"

There were some angry, muffled groans from inside that delighted the darkest parts of my heart to no end.

Since it was still evening, it was a few hours before Val carried the barrel down to the abandoned garden. I followed him in the shadows, then grabbed the barrel and flew with it to where the drains emptied into the harbor. Carrying it was surprisingly easy; the barrel plus the man inside didn't weigh all that much more than Herald, and since I could dig my claws in, I had a nice, strong grip on it. Landing, though, was hard. Still feeling uncomfortable after my earlier experiences, I didn't want to end up in the water, and the drain opening was too small for me to fly inside. I considered approaching at speed, folding my wings as I approached, and then shifting as soon as I was inside, but that might kill Tark. He was a tough little monster, but I'd need to be going twenty miles per hour at the very least. In his state, the impact might just be too much. If the barrel landed just right and rolled he might be sick but otherwise all right, but I didn't want to take the risk.

Not that him dying was a problem in itself, but we wanted to at least try interrogating him. Besides, I'd promised his life to Herald, and I intended to deliver.

I'd been worried about how to get him to the cave. Flying with the barrel had been all right, but I wasn't sure exactly how to move it through the drains. Carrying it wouldn't work, since I needed all four limbs for walking, and dragging it seemed like a hassle. I'd been on the verge of just opening the barrel and making him walk when something occurred to me—getting him there was only difficult *if I cared about him.*

Once I realized that, it was easy. The whole long way from the harbor to the cave, I simply rolled the barrel in front of me, hearing the occasional thud or muffled groan from inside. I hummed happily all the way.

In the cave, I stood the barrel up on the little jetty that extended into the water. The boat was where it had been the last time I saw it, still in the dark, placid water. My sense of Herald and Mak told me that they were somewhere in the direction of Tellee's house, and it would be a while before they made it to me.

"Listen, Tark," I said, speaking into the side of the barrel. "Can you hear me?"

There was no reply, so I shook the barrel a little until I heard a groan, then put my head against it. "I said, Tarkarran, can you hear me?"

Another groan, somehow managing to sound indignant this time.

"Great. I want you to know what's going on. You're underground right now, in a place where no one will find you. No one will even know to look for you here. Not that it matters, since you won't be here for long. What does matter is that no one can hear us down here. And that's going to be very important in just a little while, because Herald and Mak are on their way here. You remember them, right? Tekereteki, one of them tall, the other one short with really pretty long hair? You spent a couple of days with them, about two months ago? They killed two of your guys last night? Anyway, they're very excited about seeing you. They've got all kinds of ideas about what to do with you, and I'm pretty sure that you gave them most of those. But it doesn't have to go like that, yeah? It can be quick. Clean. As much as I hate you—and I really do hate you—and I want the girls to get to take their frustrations out on you, the one I want is the Night Blossom. You know her, right? Your, what? Boss? Mistress?"

The next groan sounded very rude.

"Or maybe you don't call her that. Zabra, then? Tespril Zabra?"

With a little bit of imagination I could almost think that I heard a sharp intake of breath.

"You know, finding out who she actually is took some work, but less than I'd expected. Do you know if she got my message? I had such a good talk with Kesra, and I thought that we understood each other. I said that anything you scum did to any of my people, I would do worse to her. To Kesra, I mean. And then some of your morons went and beat up one of my boys. I can only imagine that you never got my message, because now I have to pay Kesra another visit, don't I?"

That got a reaction out of him, and what a wonderful reaction it was! He must have been screaming, but the guy was gagged in there so it all came out as muffled nonsense. At the same time he was moving around so much that the barrel was shaking.

I picked the barrel up and shook it, then put it back down. That settled him. Then I kept pulling on the little thread I'd found.

"I don't know why you're so upset. I was very clear. All you had to do was leave my people alone. Now, I don't know if Kesra never passed the message on, or if Zabra just doesn't care about her sister, but it doesn't matter. I have been insulted, and there need to be consequences."

The angry groaning started up again, if a little weaker this time.

"But, Tark, I'll give you a choice. You can think about it until the girls get here. I'm afraid your time is likely to run out fairly quickly at that point, though not nearly as quickly as you may wish once they get warmed up. So, here it is: Zabra, or Kesra. Give me the one, or I'll take the other. And don't think that all those guards at her house can stop me. I walked out of your little prison, and I walked right into her bedroom as she slept. I can do it again, and no one will ever know. So. Think about it."

Then I left him there to stew. It would be at least half an hour before the others showed up, so I leapt up to the alcove in the cave wall that I'd scoped out for sleeping and settled down, with one eye on the barrel in case Tark tried anything.

It was nowhere near as comfortable as either of my nests, but you can't have everything.

CHAPTER TWENTY-TWO

Tarkarran

I spent almost an hour listening to the water drip from the ceiling, which condensed on the cold stone and slowly gathered on the stalactites that hung there before plunging back into the pool, where it had originally evaporated from. *Drip, drip, drip* it went as the girls made their way through the drains, slowly getting closer.

The barrel rocked a few times, but it didn't do Tark any good. The boys must have trussed him up good when they shoved him in there.

When Herald and Mak arrived I was surprised to see only the two of them. The first was in a foul mood, while the second was grinning smugly. "Could you not have picked an easier place to get to?" Herald complained in my general direction as she stood up straight, then bent backward, popping her hips out with a groan. "I do not think that my back has ever been this damn sore!"

"Divine justice for every time you've joked about me being short," Mak told her cheerfully. "And are you really going to whine like this in front of Draka? Toughen up and take it!"

"You being short enough to walk upright in these worm holes is not something to be smug about!"

They both sobered up, the reality of the situation catching up with them, when they saw the barrel. It was still sitting on the jetty where I'd left it. I winged over, silently joining them as they walked down the wooden stairs. They circled the thing, Mak looking almost sick. Herald gave it a kick every so often.

"*This is it,*" Herald said, switching to Tekereteki. "*It is not the Night Blossom. It is not the woman who gave the orders. But this is the bastard who held the knife.*"

Mak stopped, her hands clenching and unclenching, and a shudder went through her. "*And the hammer, and the pliers . . .*" she whispered. "*And other things.*"

Herald knelt by her sister, putting her arms around her. "*You do not have to do this,*" she said. "*You do not have to be here. Not if it will cause you more pain.*"

"*I do. We should ask him questions first. Perhaps you can do it, Draka, but I think I have a better chance of getting something out of him.*"

She looked so scared and vulnerable that it was painful to witness. She'd looked nervous in the alley, but she'd done well. Now we had the guy tied up in a barrel, and she looked like she'd rather be anywhere else. Still, she was right. Not only did she have my charisma, and possibly command, backing her—however those worked. She was just more social than I had ever been, more used to talking to people, and she knew the culture and society of Karakan far better than I could have possibly picked up in my time here.

I felt more worried about Herald losing it than anything else. Otherwise, I was as calm as could be expected, considering what we were about to do, and I tried to project that onto Mak. What I felt didn't replace her own emotions but influenced her to some degree, and I figured that, whether trying to affect her actively worked or not, I could always try.

"*I will leave it up to you,*" I said. "*I know that it is hard for you, but I agree. I think if I try, I may just kill him the first time he resists or says something unpleasant. Better if I stay back. You should know, though, that he seems to respond to threats against the Night Blossom's sister, Kesra.*"

She gave me a sharp nod. "*All right. I will remember that. Shall we open this thing, then?*"

"*Do we want any light?*" Herald asked, producing a lightstone from the simple bag she had slung over her shoulder.

"*I think so, yes,*" Mak said. "*Better that he sees our faces.*"

Herald nodded, then channeled her magic into the stone, which ignited with a cold, blue light.

When they closed the barrel, Tam and Val hadn't sealed it shut properly. Tark might have been able to open it from the inside, if he wasn't constantly being watched and also tied up, knocked around, missing a hand, and most likely suffering from some serious blood loss. It was convenient for Mak, though, as she didn't need to worry about the bands that would normally have kept the head of the barrel in place. Instead she simply hammered on the edge of the head with her fist until it turned, the opposite edge popping up and allowing her to wrench the whole thing out.

The stench that hit us as the air inside escaped was foul enough to make the two women back up, their faces twisting with disgust, and even I pulled my head back before unceremoniously shoving the barrel over, then lifting it by the bottom end and dumping Tark onto the rough wood of the jetty. He lay there, gasping and groaning, with his legs tied together, the knees firmly folded and his arms tied behind him above and below the elbows—they couldn't be tied at the wrists, since his right arm ended in a blood-soaked, bandaged stump. *Oh, yeah,* I thought to myself with some satisfaction. *I did that.*

You sure did, Conscience whispered. I ignored her.

He barely got a moment to orient himself, looking up at us with murder in his eyes, before I grabbed him and dunked him as deep as I could in the water, holding him by the ankle. I brought him back up, let him snort and sputter and catch his breath, then repeated the process a few times until I'd gotten most of the filth off and dumped him back on the jetty.

Herald squatted next to him, grabbed him by the hair, and lifted his head toward her. "Hello, Tarkarran," she said, trying and failing to keep the anger out of her voice.

Where Mak smelled of fear every time we spoke of the man, and especially now that he was in front of her, all I felt from Herald was a deep, churning rage, her control tight but already slipping. I knew that the fear was still there. I'd soothed her back to sleep enough times when she woke in the middle of the night weeping, begging some unseen tormentor to stop. But with Tark helpless in front of her, there was only a struggle—one that I recognized all too well—to not lose control and kill him before we even got a word out of him.

For a moment I thought that she'd lost that struggle, as she brought up her dagger. I expected her to slit his throat, but she only slid it in under the gag, removing the cloth with one sharp, jerking cut. With a retching cough Tark spat out another wad of cloth that had been stuffed in his mouth.

I don't know what I expected, but the first words out of his mouth were "'Teki whores . . ." and that set the tone for our conversation.

Herald hissed indignantly and knocked him in the teeth with the pommel of her dagger. "I want to hurt you," she said, teeth clenched, her voice trembling as he grinned at her.

"How lovely." His voice was lower than normal, hoarse and rough, and he spat some blood. "We have something in common. I never thought you two would miss my attention so much that—"

His snark vanished into a high-pitched groan as Herald split his lip, her own lips peeling back. "Shut up, filth!" she snarled, then smashed him in the nose for good measure.

"*Back off,*" Mak snapped, putting her arm between the prisoner and her sister. "*The idea is to get him to talk!*"

Herald, it turned out, was not interrogator material.

I was mostly there for moral support, so I sat back and let them handle it. While Mak dragged Herald back a foot or so and gave her a stern look, though, I took the opportunity to wrap Tark up in shadows and give him a good squeeze. To my extreme annoyance the little bastard just shrugged it off, somehow getting to his knees and spitting more blood toward my sisters.

That only further infuriated Herald. "You disgusting—!" she screamed and threw herself toward him, but Mak wrapped her arms around her sister's waist, set her heels, and stopped Herald dead.

"*Stop it, Herald!*" Mak said. "*You are smarter than this! He is trying to provoke you, and succeeding!*"

Herald stopped straining, then settled back on her haunches. "*Fine,*" she snapped, scowling past Mak at Tark. "*You do it!*"

"*Thank you*," Mak said, giving her shoulders a quick squeeze before turning back around. When she saw Tark on his knees her lips curled, and with a sandal to the chest she pushed him back over.

"Like my sister said, she wants to hurt you. I don't blame her. I want to hurt you, too. I want to hurt you in every way that you hurt me, and every way that you hurt her. But we have questions for you."

"You don't have it in you," he sneered. "The righteous and honorable Tekereteki adventurer. You don't have what it takes to break someone. And I do not break as easily as you do."

"I never said that I did. But Herald does, as much as it pains me to say it. So I'm going to ask for one thing. Just one thing. The Night Blossom. Tespril Zabra. Tell us how to get her, and if I believe you, I'll cut your throat. Quick and clean."

"Fuck you, whore. Tell her to do her worst!"

I saw Mak jerk back just a little at the insult, and I wanted to tear the bastard's throat out for it. "Fine," she said. "Herald—"

Tark just continued. "That wasn't the first time we met, down in the cells. Did you know that? Did you even know that you were working for the Night Blossom, in the end? Hells, Hardal even recognized you. How many guests did you offer 'private performances' to before you disappeared on us? You were popular, I know that. Why—"

"Shut! Up!" Herald roared, and lunged for him, leading with her dagger. There were tears of anger in her eyes, and I have no doubt that she would have simply killed the bastard if Mak hadn't gotten between them and wrestled the dagger from her as Tark shrieked with laughter.

"Enough!" I commanded, as Herald went to her knees, crying with rage as Mak tried to calm her. "We all know how to make him talk. We know what the worst torture he can imagine is. Why else would he have used it on you two?"

All three heads turned to look at me.

"Wait here," I said. "And don't fucking kill him, yeah? I'll be an hour, maybe two. I don't know if Kesra sleeps in her bed anymore, so I might have to look for her. You brought a healing potion or three, didn't you?"

"Yeah, we did," Herald said, her fury briefly replaced with a dawning shock at what I was suggesting.

"Great. Bye, Tark!"

"Wait!" he shouted as I leapt onto the ledge where the short tunnel opened into the drains. "Wait!" he screamed, louder and shriller, as I ducked in. "I'll give you Zabra!"

I stopped, backed out, and looked at him. "And why would you do that? Why would a loyal little weasel like you give up his boss?"

"That's no concern of yours, lizard!" he spat. "Leave Kesra in peace and I'll tell you where you can find Zabra."

I made a show of considering it, hemming and hawing before saying, "All right. But understand this: If you lie, I'm taking Kesra. If you clam up,

I'm taking Kesra. If I think that you're stalling or if you bore me, I'm taking Kesra. And if that doesn't make you talk, I'm questioning her when we're done with you."

"She can't tell you anything," he sneered. "She doesn't know where the money comes from, or where Zabra goes when she's not at home. You'd be wasting your time."

I descended the stairs to where he lay and put my face right in his. The light-stone was the only source of light, and a weak one at that. To Tark, unless he had some advancement that let him see in the dark, it must have looked like two golden eyes and a hundred teeth just appeared out of the shadows, and for all his fearlessness he pulled his head back at that.

"I wouldn't be wasting my time," I growled. "Her blood would be the next best thing to her sister's, wouldn't it?"

I was bluffing so hard that I had imaginary cold sweats. Even Instinct wasn't interested in killing some girl just because of who her sister was. I would take her, and I would question her. I might traumatize her in ways that would never heal. I might use her to draw Zabra out. But I wouldn't torture her, and I wouldn't kill her. Not to make him or her talk. But Tark couldn't know that. He was quick and strong, and I suspected that his complete lack of fear was an advancement of some kind, but he couldn't tell if I was lying. And once he'd agreed to answer our questions, Mak took over. She was cold. Distant. She spoke like she was some-where else, speaking to someone else, but she was effective. Every time she thought he was trying to deceive her she repeated her questions, then again later. The third time he gave a different answer to the same question she stood up and turned to me. "This is pointless. Get Kesra, and let's start over."

Something about how emotionless she was in that moment convinced him, and he became much more cooperative after that.

As morning approached we had a pretty comprehensive list of the places Zabra might be found, as well as when she would usually be in each place. Herald, who'd been taking notes, asked, *"Are we done here? Do we need him anymore?"*

"We could use him if it turns out that he lied after all," Mak said, still distant. *"Otherwise, no."*

With that Herald walked over, grabbed him by the scruff of his tunic, and hauled him up to a sitting position. He stared at her, silently but with utter hatred, as she smiled and patted his cheek.

"Thank you, Tarkarran," she said. "We'll be sure to tell Zabra how helpful you've been. And if anything is wrong, if one word is off, we will ask Kesra to correct it for us."

"You lying cunts," he growled. "Just wait! Once our roles are back as they should be, when I have *you* locked to my table again, I'm going to make you hurt in ways you can't imagine. Your sister was fun, but she broke too fast. You? I won-der if you'll beg like—"

His words cut off suddenly, his eyes bugging as Herald silently drew and slammed her dagger into the side of his neck, hard enough to pierce all the way through and knock him on his side.

"SHUT. UP!" she roared, tearing the blade out, then slamming it back in at a different angle as blood pumped and poured from severed veins and arteries. Tark tried to speak. He looked genuinely surprised, as though he'd truly expected to leave that cave alive. But all that came out of his mouth was a gout of blood, joining what was already leaking between the wooden slats of the jetty to splash into the water below.

As I stood in stunned silence and Mak looked on dispassionately, Herald leaned in, heedless of the blood still spurting weakly from his torn throat onto her face. She grabbed a fistful of hair and growled into his ear. "Listen to me, you worthless filth. You hurt us. You broke us. Hells, I don't know if the night-mares will ever go away. But you did a piss-poor job of it. You half-assed it. You didn't destroy us. And we have healed, and gotten stronger, and we are whole again. We are richer and doing better than ever. And you, you little shit, are bleeding out in a cave, in the dark. And soon your precious Zabra will join you. So fuck. You."

With a final snarl she tore her dagger free, reversed the grip, and slammed it through his temple.

Tark jerked once. He shook for a few seconds, the blood at his throat bub-bling, and then he was still. The only sound coming from him was the blood still dripping into the water.

Herald was not done. She sat back on her heels, panting until a sob tore from her and she started punching the corpse, screaming and calling him names I hadn't thought she knew. Only when she again wrenched the dagger loose, having to brace with her foot to get it out of the bone and nearly stumbling back into the water, did Mak and I rush in to stop her, Mak disarming her and wrestling her, crying, to her knees.

"I hate him!" Herald choked out as she wrapped her arms around her sister, pulling her down and holding her like she was the one protecting Mak rather than the one in need of comfort. "I hate him! I hate him so much! What he did to you . . . what he said . . . I don't care what you did or didn't do. I love you, Mak. I love you so much!"

"Hush, sweet sister," Mak mumbled from somewhere inside Herald's arms. "I know. I know. I love you, too."

Parvion Tarkarran ended his days far out at sea, dropped from a great height. The next night I delivered a letter, sealed inside a leather tube so that I could carry it inside my mouth while shifted, into Tespril Kesra's bedroom. She wasn't sleeping there, but the message was hopefully clear enough.

I had considered dive bombing Tark through the balcony door, but the thought of Kesra, who was probably innocent in all of this, being woken by a corpse crashing into the room made me feel bad, so the hand-delivered letter would have to do.

The letter was short and to the point, written painstakingly, and after several tries, in my own hand:

To Tespril Zabra,

I look forward to our next meeting.

Draka

Sunset

Zabra's reply came swiftly. It was one of two letters we received the next day. In the morning, a letter arrived from the lady justice Sempralia's office, confirming the suggested time and place for our meeting. In a week I would be meeting with one of the rulers of the city, and I was all at once proud, nervous, and excited. The fact that I was important enough to rank a meeting where she essentially came to me tickled my pride in all kinds of ways. At the same time, it was a meeting with someone who had the power to make my family's lives far more difficult than they already were. I wanted her to think favorably of me, but what if she made a bunch of demands I couldn't accept? I would need to tread a careful line between being on my best behavior and appearing cooperative on the one hand, and not making unreasonable concessions on the other.

There was also a non-zero risk that this was a setup for an ambush. If Sempralia or someone else that she had confided in decided that I had done some kind of unacceptable damage, or that I was an unacceptable risk or complication in the political landscape, a prearranged meeting would be an excellent time to try and knock me off. I had no doubt that the council had access to people who could hurt me if necessary. Hell, for all I knew that archer who'd been after me was on their payroll. For this reason, all the places Mak had proposed had me arriving from and spending the entire meeting with my back to the sea. Sure, there had been solemn assurances from both sides that the meeting would be entirely peaceful, but Instinct didn't trust anyone we didn't control, and Conscience would see us dead before she trusted a politician.

This would be the most politically powerful person I'd ever met in either of my lives. That reminded me that I hadn't met with Rallon for months, which was no way to maintain a working relationship. He surely knew where I could be found, and I met his officers and cousins regularly, so there wasn't any risk of us falling out of touch. But I still felt that I really should have a word with him soon. I was just so busy! Refugees and revenge had been taking up all my time lately, and I still wanted to see what Ramban might know about my mountain's past, and perhaps that of my draconic father. And there was still that damn archer. They may be hunting me, or I may just have been unlucky, but either way, we had seen neither hide nor hair of them since I took an arrow to the leg. I wanted to know who the hell I was dealing with, and if it was someone I needed to keep worrying about. And I wanted to hurt them a reasonable amount. Not kill them, necessarily. I just wanted to make my displeasure unmistakable. But if I could be sure that they weren't likely to be a threat in the future, that would do.

So, busy, busy. And this was what Herald and I had been talking about, late in the afternoon, when Kira came down, knocking on the door and anxiously telling us that Mak had called an emergency meeting.

When we got into the cellar all the others were already there—Mak, Tam and Val, and Ardek. With the addition of Herald, Kira, and me, the whole core gang was there.

A peace had settled over Mak since the previous night. While I got rid of Tark, the girls had returned to the inn. There they got cleaned up and were fussed over by Tam and Val, who'd stayed at the inn with Ardek in case there were any reprisals for our abduction of Tark. When I returned, the whole family had joined me in the strongroom. There hadn't been any discussion. We hadn't reflected on what we'd done or what had happened. There had been a lot of tears and comforting words as some deep-seated, months-old tension was finally released. Then, in the early morning hours, Tam and Val had left, and us girls had gone to sleep.

Their sleep wasn't dreamless or entirely free of nightmares, but both of the sisters got a full, uninterrupted eight or nine hours, and Mak had awoken with a smile. She had seemed lighter since then. Unburdened and unflappable. We weren't done, though. There was still Zabra, the damned Night Blossom, to deal with. But while she'd been the one to give the orders, Tark had been the one who'd hurt them, and he was the one who haunted their dreams. That was over now.

When we entered the main room of the cellar Mak was holding a scroll in a relaxed grip. "*Thank you, Kira,*" she said, nodding to us all. "*We will probably be speaking in Karakani, for the men's sake, but you are welcome to stay if you want.*"

Kira looked around the room, then nodded and settled down next to Ardek on one of the two sturdy benches, which currently sat along one wall. With how and how often the room was used, Tam had recently decided to add some seating. I'd had no idea that he was so handy, but he'd put them together by himself in a few hours.

"This," Mak said, holding out the scroll, "is a letter from the Night Blossom."

I let my surprise show, settling in to give Mak my full attention. I hadn't expected a response so quickly, and from the reactions of the others it was clear that I wasn't the last to find out. Val simply scowled, while Tam curiously asked, "Well, what does she want?" Ardek looked at the rolled up letter as though it were a snake that might decide to go for him at any moment. Kira looked anxious, probably more at the mood in the room than anything else, and Herald crossed the few steps to her sister and took the letter from her hand, unrolling it and reading out loud.

To the incomparable Draka,

Forgive my brevity. I only just received your message, and have much to do.

I can only imagine that my previous message was ill received, either in its contents or its delivery. To avoid further escalation and unpleasantness, I suggest a meeting on neutral ground, at a time convenient to you. My messenger will return tomorrow, at the same time. Please reply with a time and place. I am confident that I can rearrange my schedule to accommodate you, within reason.

Needless to say, if you choose not to reply, or indicate that you do not wish to meet, I will be forced to take other measures.

Zabra

"She wants to negotiate." Herald's voice was somewhere between incredulity and anger. "We have shown that we can hurt her, and now she wants to *negotiate*!"

"That is generally the time to do it," said Val. It was a reasonable observation, but not one that Herald wanted to hear.

"*Fuck* her and her negotiations! She can hand herself over to us, or to the lady justice if she prefers being thrown from the rock to having her throat slit, but—!"

"We will meet her," Mak said, quietly yet somehow cutting through Herald's building rant. "We will see what she has to say and what she has to offer, and then we will decide how to move forward."

Herald stared at Mak like she'd just announced that she was marrying Ardek. "You cannot be serious!"

"I can, and I am. And Draka agrees with me."

And, well, I did. I didn't intend to make peace, or even a truce, but I wanted to face Zabra. I wanted to know how much she was sweating. I didn't know if Mak had the same reason, but she could read me easily.

Herald wasn't about to give up. "What is even the point? There is only one acceptable outcome of this conflict, and that is us spitting on her corpse. We know where to find her, and we know how to hurt her. Why waste our time?"

"We know little of our enemy," Val said. "Mak has met her once, while drunk. Draka also once, while enraged. Neither, I would think, had an opportunity to take her measure. I agree with your sisters. We should meet with her."

"What we do know," Mak added, "is that she's made a name for herself and survived as a criminal. We killed Tarkarran, who seemed entirely fearless and convinced of his own invincibility up until the end. Even then, Draka got hurt terribly. Two inches to the left, Herald, and no magic in the world would have saved her. If she had someone like that working for her, do you not think that she has worse available? We will talk to her. We will see if we can learn more about her. And when we are confident and prepared, we will strike. Not before."

Herald snorted. "Tam?"

Her brother shrugged apologetically. "Mak makes some good points."

In a move of utter desperation she finally turned to Ardek, who just held up his hands. "I'm just a minion," he said without a shred of embarrassment. "Pretty sure I don't get a vote."

"Fine. We will *wait*, and *talk*," she spat, and stormed off. Not upstairs, though, but to the strongroom. Kira looked around the room, hesitated, then followed her.

"I'll talk to her," I told the room. "I'll try to cheer her up, and leave it to you all to decide on a time and place. Just give me at least three days. There's something I want to do first."

Mak looked at the door Herald had left through, then sighed and nodded to me. "As you say."

Ardek spoke up as I left. "I've got some ideas, actually . . ."

When I reached the strongroom, barely a minute behind Kira, a conversation had already begun. Or, rather, Kira had tried to start one, and Herald wanted nothing to do with it.

"*Oh, good! Draka! Please send your pet away,*" she said petulantly. "*She is trying to convince me that I should be ashamed of killing bastards who deserve it.*"

"*I said no such thing,*" Kira said calmly, not rising to the petty insult. "*I only asked why you are so eager to take a life when there may be an alternative.*"

"*Did you understand the conversation?*" I asked. I didn't think she knew more than a few dozen words at most of Karakani.

"*No, not at all. But Herald kindly filled me in. I believe she said, 'We have a chance to kill that disreputable woman, and they just want to talk.'*"

"*That is not what I called her,*" Herald muttered. "*But sure.*"

"*And I understand your anger. I have heard what she and her people did to you all. You have every right to be angry, to hate her even, and to want to hurt her back. But can you not be satisfied? The man who held the knife is dead at your hands. Draka was almost killed in the process. Now you may, perhaps, have a chance to end this without risking anyone else. What if she is more difficult to fight than you expected? What if your information is wrong? What if someone you love dies in the attempt? What if you die, leaving the others to grieve?*" Kira sighed. "*I just do not understand.*"

Herald had listened in silence, looking more and more embarrassed as Kira talked. "*I just want it to be over. I want her to be gone. How can we be sure that she does not come after us again, or keep hurting other people, unless we end her?*"

"*Perhaps you cannot. You will not know until you have studied her.*"

"*Thank you, Kira,*" I said, and she took it as a dismissal. On the way out she held her hand to my almost completely healed wound, looked to me for permission, and then put a strong pulse of healing into it before leaving.

I sidled up to Herald, who was sitting on the table, running her finger along the carvings on the red lacquered box. "I've got an idea that might cheer you up."

"Yeah?"

"Yeah. Did you ever get those warm clothes I told you about? The hat and gloves?"

Herald looked up, and her face slowly broke into a wide smile. "Yeah!"

"Get them and anything else you'll need, and tell the others that I'm stealing you for a day or two."

It couldn't have taken her ten minutes to get her stuff together. Heavy clothing and some necessities in a light pack. No armor, but she took her sword, her bow, and her arrows, both fancy and regular, with her. And my share of the trolls' blood money, of course. That was way overdue to join the hoard.

Simply flying out with her on my back was an extremely tempting and monumentally dumb idea, so instead we made a game of shifting and racing down the back streets. Since it was still daylight I had a serious advantage. I was pretty sure that I was simply stronger, but I also had a lot more practice using my magic in daylight; and on top of that, I still had a Nest Heart pumping through my magical veins. It felt like it had weakened since I ate it but still made my control of the shadows near effortless, even when fighting the sunlight. Herald didn't give up easily, though, and cleverly chose to tail me, staying close on my heels and using the same shadows I was pushing to conserve her own energy. It wasn't enough for her to get ahead, but it got her much farther than she would have managed on her own.

She, of course, had the advantage of being able to shift back and rest without causing a scene. A tall girl taking a breather in the shade didn't raise any eyebrows, beyond the looks my tall, dark, and pretty friend usually drew. Me, I had to find some place to hide every time. I preferred tall roofs. It wasn't like I was invisible—anyone with a high vantage point and sharp eyes would be able to see me—but I wasn't causing a panic around my little sister, which was the important thing.

We went a few rounds like that, making it most of the way to the gate before Herald simply couldn't shift anymore. Then we separated, and like usual, she walked out the Forest Gate, while I made my way through the drains and the sewers to the coast. From there I made my way north until I was far enough from the city to shift back and fly the rest of the way.

Thankfully, it was my regular pectoral and not my flight muscle that I'd been stabbed through, because even that still twinged a bit as I took to the air. I couldn't imagine that I'd have been able to fly for another day or three if I'd taken that sword lower.

We met up near the edge of the forest. "*I saw you, you know,*" was the first thing out of her mouth. "*I waited out among the fields, and I saw you fly in.*"

"*With your eyes, I can believe it,*" I told her. The forest sloped gently from north to south, and I had come in close to its edge, with little to hide me. I was being responsible and avoided being seen flying over the city, but here, miles away? I was taking basic precautions, and that was it. I wasn't going to let one pesky archer drive me back into hiding.

I brought her a few hundred feet into the trees, where there was a glade we both knew. "*You brought everything, right? The hat and the gloves, as well?*"

"*Yes! But it took quite some time to buy everything.*" Her eyes shimmered with excitement as she unpacked her warm clothing. Well, as warm as you could buy in this place, where I'd been told that the water never froze and only the mountains ever saw snow. What she had was a fur-lined jacket and trousers to wear over her regular clothes, as well as woolen gloves and a hat, and proper boots to take the place of her sandals. I honestly wasn't sure if it would be enough, not having much experience with proper cold even before I came to Mallin, but we'd know soon enough.

I did know that she looked pretty funny wearing her winter clothes in the warm autumn afternoon, but this was supposed to be something fun and exciting for her, so I did my best not to laugh. We needed to get going. I could tell that she was already starting to sweat, and while I didn't know too much about dealing with freezing temperatures, I was pretty sure that getting sweaty could be deadly if it was cold enough.

With Herald's equipment properly secured and her holding on tight on my back, I threw myself into the air, heading north for a few miles before I started climbing, and climbing, and climbing. I made a long, lazy turn west toward the mountains and kept going. My heart fluttered at Herald's laughter as we hit the lowest wisps of cloud, and when we broke through the thick layer I grinned at her awed gasp when she gazed out upon the white hills and valleys that spread out beneath us, with the highest peaks of Mallin's mountains ahead.

"*This is amazing!*" Herald shouted over the wind. "*Where are we going?*"

"*Somewhere I have wanted to go for a while. I just never took the time!*"

With that I turned north a little. Soon we were over the mountains, and I could feel Herald leaning to the side to better see the high grassy valleys, the low forested ones, and the scattered mountain lakes that we passed over. And there, straight ahead, was our destination. The snow-capped peak rose so sharply that it was practically vertical in places. I'd spotted it during my flight home after skimming the eastern edge of the mountains, and while I wasn't completely sure, it might be the highest peak on the island. At the very least, it was the only one I'd seen bearing snow so far.

"*It is white!*" Herald exclaimed once I convinced her to look ahead.

"*It is covered in snow,*" I shouted back.

"*I know that! But it is barely second planting! How can it have snow? Do mountains not only get snow in winter?*"

"*Not if they are tall enough! Some mountains have snow year round. And there are lands where I come from where even the ground is covered in snow parts of the year, and where the lakes and rivers freeze over in winter!*"

"*That sounds horrible!*"

"*Oh, yeah, sure! That is why we are going back to my mountain once we're done here!*"

I landed as close to the absolute peak of the mountain as I could, my feet sinking into the powdery snow. I'd seen and touched the stuff before, when my parents took us all out to the mountains during a rare weekend when the forecast called for snow.

Herald, as it turned out, had not. It didn't snow in Karakan, not in her lifetime, and why would anyone go up into the mountains unless they had a job
that called for it? Either my lair or the silver mine was the highest she had ever
gone, but that was still miles below the snow line. Now, here she was with me,
twenty thousand feet or more above the sea. When she slid off my back, her feet
sank and she promptly lost her balance and slowly fell over sideways with a small
puff of white.

"*Oh, Mercies!*" she laughed, getting onto her back. "*It is so soft! And cold!*"

I took that opportunity to shovel two full hands onto her, making her shriek
and flail around as some of it got in her face and more got in through the neck of
her jacket.

"*Why?*" she wailed as she struggled to get up, the loose snow sliding and breaking under her. "*Oh, gods! It is melting!*"

I just laughed until she, still on her back, started furiously flinging snow back
at me with both hands. And she was strong. And accurate. I kept laughing, but
finally had to throw a wing up to cover my face after getting one too many
mouthfuls.

"*All right, all right! I give up, yeah? Here.*" I carefully stepped over next to her
and flattened myself on the snow, so that she could use the base of my wing to
pull herself back to her feet. She did, then made her displeasure clear with one
final handful planted directly onto my head. "*Blah! I deserved that. Come, let us
get to the highest point.*"

Right by us was a small rock formation, large enough to climb onto fairly easily, but too narrow at the top for me to want to try to land there.

"*Why?*" Herald asked, breaking my heart with a single word as I realized that
there was not a shred of a climber's soul in her.

"*Because that is what you do with high places,*" I explained. "*You find a way to
the top.*"

She shrugged and followed me up. It wasn't so much a climb as a clamber,
but soon enough we were both seated at the very top of Mallin, looking out
across the clouds and the mountains, and the distant farmland and the sea in
the cloudless southeast.

"*I think I understand a little better like this,*" she conceded after a minute of
silence. "*But can you not see this whenever you want, when you fly?*"

"*Not like this. Flying is amazing, but when I am flying, there is always the sound
of my wings, and I am constantly moving. Like this . . .*"

I let the serene stillness finish my sentence for me.

She nodded thoughtfully, and we spent another few minutes just looking out
in every direction. She huddled up to me against the cold until I covered her with
my wing, my shadow all on its own curling up protectively around her, and she
gave a contented little sigh.

The clouds covered most of the north of the island, moving southwest and
stretched out toward the west. "*Look,*" I told her, and she twisted to look in the

direction I'd indicated. She gasped, covering her mouth with her hand as she turned around properly to take in the view.

"*Oh!*" was all Herald managed.

The sun was setting, painting the tops of the clouds in pinks and purples and oranges as the sky turned an ever deeper blue above the fire at the horizon. "*Yeah,*" I agreed. This was something I'd seen a few times before, but always on the wing, and I'd been eager to share it with Herald. Sitting like this, miles away from all our problems, her huddled up against me and just watching the sun paint the clouds as it dipped below the western horizon, was better than I could have imagined.

"*I have never seen a sunset that was not behind the mountains before,*" Herald whispered as the sun finally vanished, leaving only the pinks and oranges of twilight between the clouds and the night sky. She huddled up even closer, putting her arms around my neck and leaning her cheek against my shoulder. "*Thank you.*"

"*Thank you for sharing this with me,*" I replied, bringing my head down to press my cheek against hers. "*Do you know what is in the west? I can feel a lot of Nest Hearts there.*"

"*A few small villages, far to the south, I think. And then nothing. Forest, ruins, and monsters, like in the north. The mountains cannot be crossed, and Happar has not wanted to fund any real colonization effort, as far as I know.*"

"*We should go there someday, yeah?*"

"*Yeah.*"

We sat looking across the dark clouds for a minute longer before I broke the spell. "*It is time to go, I think. It should get bitterly cold up here now that the sun is gone. Did you pack any food?*"

"*Ah . . . not as such,*" she admitted.

"*No worries. We will figure something out.*"

CHAPTER TWENTY-FOUR

Promises

The mountain may or may not have already had a name. Herald didn't know of one, so to us it was Sunset Peak. We left a small cairn of stones that Herald had collected to mark our visit. As we left, we descended far faster than we had climbed. Herald was shivering lightly on my back, and I wanted to get her back into the warmer air below. On the way back we stopped at a clear stream to drink and for Herald to fill her waterskins, and then it was straight back to the mountain.

I left Herald by the entrance. There was still a pile of firewood there, and I left her to start a fire and warm up as I went off to hunt. It took me only half an hour, flight time included, before I was back with a small boar, gutted and bled, but it was still late into the night before Herald declared the meat she'd sliced off to be cooked well enough to eat. Not that the time mattered. Neither of us had had much of a sleep schedule for the last several months.

"All right, time to spill," I told her after she'd glutted herself on wild pig. "You've been sneaking out. Why?"

I couldn't see her blush in the low light of the fire, but I knew her well enough to know what it meant when her face went rigid and she looked away the way she did. "I have no idea what you mean," she lied terribly.

"I can literally feel what direction you're in at all times. I know you keep going to the same place. And it's not like no one's ratted you out. They just won't tell me what you're up to, but I'm pretty sure that Mak knows. And you know she'd tell me if I asked, I just haven't. So . . . ?"

"Dammit," she muttered, looking away. "You'll be mad."

"Yeah, nah, I promise I won't. But I am dying to know. I'm worried about something happening to you, escort or no, and you know I can't just let that go. So do you want to tell me, or do I need to figure it out on my own?"

"Urgh!" Herald groaned and put her face in her hands. "I do not know why I thought . . . Okay. Fine. So, I do not know if you have noticed that there are more soldiers around than normal?"

"More than I'd expected, yeah."

"The border is apparently a little more stable, and the new regiments have been deployed, so they are rotating the regiments. Letting the soldiers come home for a few weeks."

"Right."

"And Maglan—"

"Oh. Oh! And you're embarrassed about it, so . . ."

"Yes?" I could almost feel the heat coming off her. "We missed each other!"

"Nah, yeah, I get that! But sneaking out for . . . damnit, *booty call* doesn't translate . . . Sneaking out for late-night trysts with your beau? And your brother's escorting you? He's okay with this?"

She smiled helplessly. "I do not know what to tell you. He is a romantic, and he never teases me about . . . what Mag and I might be doing. Also, 'trysts'? 'Beau'?"

"I've been reading your romance stories. Anyway, why not just invite Maglan to the inn?"

"Do you remember when we talked about him? Down by the gate, only a short time after . . . you know? And I was worried about keeping you secret from him?"

"Yeah." She'd been afraid of what I might do if I couldn't trust him. "But the secret's pretty much out now."

"And you have some issues with jealousy."

"Yeah," I admitted.

"So . . . I did not want to risk introducing you two. I wasn't sure how to handle it yet, and even if the secret slipping is not a big risk anymore, I did not want to make it difficult for you."

"Yeah, I get it," I said, looking away. This was the one thing she didn't seem to trust me on, and as fair as it was, it still stung.

"Oh, no, Draka!" she said gently. "I trust you! I do not think that you would harm him, but I also know you. You will do what you must. You would break him, if you had to, and I do not want that. I do not know if this is something that will last, but I do love him, in one way or another."

"I said I get it!" I pouted, getting up. "I just don't like it. And if you're running around the city at night, at least do it shifted. I know Tam would fight like a demon to protect you, but on the streets at night you'd be safer alone, in the shadows."

She looked like she was about to object, but stopped herself. "You are probably right," she admitted. "This power is so new to me, I often do not consider it."

"Yeah, well, sometimes it feels like it's all I think about," I huffed. "I want to meet him before he goes back to the border. Now come on. Let's go sleep."

It wasn't like I could stay mad at her. Once we got to the nest, and Herald had aired out the pillows and the blankets and poured my troll money on the mat of coins, we snuggled up as cozily as ever. She was right to worry, I thought as we settled in. I was jealous and possessive. I hated the idea that this guy I'd never even met was taking even a crumb of her affection away from me, as though her love was a finite resource. And if I felt like I couldn't trust Maglan, I *would* break him. I didn't care about his silence, but if I thought that he was hurting Herald . . .

Don't tempt yourself, said Conscience, at the back of my mind. *What's to say that your jealousy won't find you a reason not to trust him?* And she was right. It was better for Herald to keep us apart. And it would be best if I could leave it at that, but that wasn't happening.

Then she rubbed my neck affectionately, and all my jealous worries melted away.

"Hey, Draka?"

"Yeah?"

"I will bring him to the inn, once everything is settled, all right?"

"All right."

"Good night," she said, snuggling up under my wing. "Sleep well."

"You, too, little sister," I murmured, and soon I drifted off to dream.

I drifted in a lightless void. Instead of falling into someone's dream, I was in a still and comfortable emptiness, but just as aware as I had been the previous times I walked among people's dreams. And this third time pretty much confirmed what I had suspected. I'd found what I needed. I was sleeping on my hoard and had a Nest Heart burning inside me. The right place, and the right fuel. Now to do something productive with it.

Spending some time out with Herald, taking her to see the sunset, those were things I had wanted to do. And the hoard always called to me, so checking up on it, making sure that it was safe and whole, that had been a weight off my shoulders. But this, diving into the dream world, had been my real purpose in leaving the city.

I had one specific person in mind. I didn't know if it would work, but I thought it might. All the pieces seemed to be there. She knew me, and I'd certainly put the fear in her. I'd done much less to the thug whose dream I'd accidentally fallen into, so I figured it was worth a shot.

I focused. Her face, her voice, even her smell were as clear in my memory as they had been the night I'd visited her. I focused, and I pushed, and when I found the barest hint of a connection I grabbed on with all of my will, and dragged myself along, and then—

Kesra looked just as I'd seen her that night in her bedroom, but she was smaller. Child sized. She sat on the floor between a wooden wall and a dressing screen, wearing only a worn, oversized tunic. Her eyes were screwed shut and she held her hands over her ears, pressing hard, trying to block out the grunts, the sounds of flesh on flesh and of a young woman pretending to enjoy herself that came from the other side of the screen.

She looked like she was trying not to cry.

"Oh, hell no!" I growled. I'd wanted to leave a message for Zabra. I had not expected to get kicked right in the heartstrings by dropping in on Kesra's childhood trauma.

I did the first thing that came to mind. I picked up the tiny woman in front of me. "Think of a safe place," I commanded her, and then I left. I just took a step at a right angle to reality, taking her with me and letting her guide me to a better place.

We emerged into a field full of ripe yellow grain. I could just see Karakan's walls in the distant north, and a villa with some accessory buildings to the south. Wherever this was, it sure as hell beat the place I'd found her.

Kesra herself had grown to her full size as soon as I dropped her, and she was staring at me in absolute horror. Her mouth was opened like she was trying to scream, but couldn't find her voice. At the same time she was trying to crabwalk backward, but not going anywhere. She may have picked the destination, but this was my dream now, and she was going to listen to me. I willed charisma to help me choose my words and be convincing. I still didn't know if it worked like that, but it couldn't hurt.

"Kesra," I said, leaning in close. "I came here with a message for your sister. But what I just saw, honestly . . . If that was how your childhood was, you have my pity."

I scowled mentally. That wasn't the right way to start. That wasn't the tone I needed to set. I tried my hardest to bring out Instinct, to channel that smug, ruthless superiority. To quash the little voice of Conscience telling me that Kesra was probably mostly innocent, and that there was no way I could go through with the threats I intended to make. There was no room for guilt or doubt. I needed her to take me deathly seriously.

Her mouth worked soundlessly, then she managed, "How? How are you here?"

"Does that matter? You're dreaming, and here I am. What you need to understand from this is that you can't hide from me. Ever. Wherever she takes you, I can find you. I want you to tell her that, and be sure that she understands, because I don't think that she understood the last message I left with you. Do you remember what I said?"

"Yes," she whispered. "Anything she did to you, you would do worse to me."

"Right. Now, she fucked that up, but I chose to show a little mercy. When she had one of my people beaten, I took Tarkarran instead of you. Wasn't that nice of me? Next time I won't be so kind."

"You . . . took Tarkarran? What did you do to him?"

"I killed him, of course," I hissed. "Don't pretend like he didn't deserve it! Now, here's my message. Listen carefully, because if she 'misunderstands' this one, I'll come visit you, flesh and blood, and it'll be a much nastier conversation than these last two, yeah? Tell Zabra that if she wants to live, to continue to spoil you and enjoy her current lifestyle, she needs to think long and hard about what she can offer me that'll make up for what she's done to me and mine. She wants to talk. Fine. I'm willing. But the only thing my friends want from her is her still beating heart in their hands, and I like to spoil my friends. Tell her that."

As I spoke Kesra had been growing smaller and smaller, until she was back to the size of a child. Now she sat hugging her knees to her chest, weeping as she asked me, "Why are you doing this?"

I snorted, pushing away the guilt nagging at me. I didn't owe her anything, and she'd already dismissed my reasons, but I decided to indulge her. "I already told you. You chose not to believe me, but the truth is the truth. Your sister, whatever she means to you, is a monster. I don't know everything she's done, but I've seen kidnapping, slaving, and torture for myself, and two women who are important to me are among her victims. Vengeance and retribution. That's why."

I looked around. We were clearly outside of some wealthy farm south of the city, unless the location in Kesra's mind was wildly off from reality. "This looks like a much nicer place than where I found you," I told her. "I think I'll leave you here. Sweet dreams."

"Wait!" she shouted after me, but I had already begun to step out. By the time she finished that one word, I was already gone.

I woke with a start. Herald grunted unhappily where she lay half flopped on top of me. The need was back. I was surprised, and a little annoyed, that I hadn't been able to try to go to anyone else's dreams after Kesra, but the energy of the last Nest Heart I ate had been growing weaker the last few days. Perhaps it had gone into my healing somehow? I had healed rapidly, thanks to Mak and Kira, but I hadn't needed to eat as much as I would have expected after the kind of wound I'd received. And now, even the slight remaining twinge in my chest was gone, so that was nice.

I looked down at Herald, who'd relaxed back into me almost instantly. There was no reason to wake her. We weren't in such a hurry that a few more hours of sleep would make any difference. I readjusted my wing over her, laid my head on the mat of silver coins that made up most of my bedding, and went back to sleep.

The next time I woke, Herald was gone. I forced down the familiar panic that something was missing. A quick check with my dedicated find-Herald sense showed her up by the cave entrance, so I got up and headed that way.

I smelled smoke before I got there, and when I arrived I found Herald sitting by a cheery little fire, warming up leftover boar from the previous night. "Good morning, great sleepy one," she said, grinning. The sun was falling straight into the cave, the angle wrong for it to hit the back wall. "I hope you do not mind me leaving you alone. Nature called, and it was either the ledge or deeper into the cave."

"Mmm. How'd you sleep?"

"Wonderful. No nightmares! And you?"

"I don't dream much anymore. But I did dreamwalk!"

"Oh?"

"Yeah. I'm pretty sure I need to have a Nest Heart in me, and to be sleeping on my hoard. That's how it was the last two times."

"Sounds plausible," Herald said, turning one of the large skewers of meat a little. "You know, I have been eating more and more meat lately. Greens and bread and such just do not taste as good."

"Good on ya," I said, encouraging her. "You have the money now, and you're a great huntress. Barbecue for every meal, I say."

"So, do you want to tell me about your dreamwalking?"

"Hmm? Oh, yeah. I scared the piss out of Kesra. The Night Blossom's sister."

Herald blinked at me in silence for a while, the pause becoming slightly uncomfortable before she asked, "Why? And how? I thought you could only do that with Kira and Jekrie and me and . . . you know. Those of us who are loyal to you."

"I don't think that's it. I've found Ramban, the scholar, before. And remember how I told you about those Barleans, Tellee and her nephew? The one whose house you used to get into the drains? I found one of the thugs from that night, by accident. So I think it might have something to do with how big of an impact I've had on someone. Something like that. Not sure. Anyway, I found Kesra, and I left a message for Zabra with her."

Herald considered my words, handing me a skewer of meat, then picking up one of her own and chewing a piece of pork thoughtfully. "They are still all people you have touched with your magic, correct?"

"Yeah."

She nodded. "Perhaps you are right. What was the message?"

"Eh . . . that she can't hide Kesra from me—almost a total bluff there—and she'd better think of something more valuable to us than their lives if she wants our meeting to go anywhere. Something like that."

"Mmm . . . not awful, I suppose. Shows that you are confident and that you feel you are negotiating from a place of strength. Though I may not be the best person to give an opinion on this. Most of my experience comes from stories. You should perhaps have run it by Mak first, but what is done is done."

"I figure that either it scares her and she brings that energy to the meeting, or it makes her do something stupid. Worst case she ignores it, and I have to do something to Kesra. Which, honestly, I'm not sure how to handle that. I'll have to grab her and stick her somewhere, I guess. Maybe leave her with Jekrie. Probably couldn't bring myself to actually hurt her."

"And that is why you are my favorite dragon."

"Wow. Beating out all that competition? I'm flattered."

"Still, you need to do something about this habit you have of kidnapping young women. Try kidnapping an old man to break the pattern, perhaps."

I experimentally worked my hand into the correct shape to flip her off, but the gesture didn't translate. We finished most of the rest of the cooked boar in silence, with Herald wrapping the best of the leftovers up in waxed cloth.

"I need a Nest Heart before we meet with the Night Blossom," I told her when we were done, "and I need to practice finding them. Want to come?"

"Do you think I would ever forgive you if you went without me?" she countered. "Let me check my gear."

CHAPTER TWENTY-FIVE

Sharing

I cannot help but notice that we are not in the northern forest," Herald said drily after I'd landed outside a crack in the rock many miles north of my mountain. "Is that not where the Nest Hearts are?"

"The two I've eaten were, yeah. And there's more of them there, and they get denser the farther north you go. But do you remember when you camped out at the lake, waiting for me? And I told you how I'd gotten lost in the tunnels?" I waved to the crack in the wall. "That's where I came out. There's gremlins in there, and a Nest Heart. I can feel it."

"Ah! Could they not get to your hoard, then? Theoretically?"

"Yeah. I've been meaning to do something about them for ages, and now I have the perfect reason to take the time. Want to help me make sure that they never make it to our part of the mountains?"

She gave me a vicious grin and started walking. "What are you waiting for? Come along, then!"

After passing through the long, narrow crack, the passage slowly widened enough for us to walk side by side. "If you would have told me when we left the Favor, I would have taken my armor," Herald chided lightly.

"I don't see you needing it, but you're right," I admitted. "If some of 'em sneak up on you, let me know and shift. But with any luck they'll never know you're there. We'll find their nest, I'll cut loose, and you can take shots at anything that tries to get at me while I eat the heart."

"What about . . ." She reached out and scratched around the bump where my left horn was growing back. She couldn't hide the worry in her tone. "Gremlins have hurt you before."

"That was ages ago. I'm bigger now, with an advancement that lets me shrug off swords and arrows—" I faltered at the look she gave me. "Fine. *Most* swords and arrows. I don't see the gremlins bringing anything to the table that can threaten me."

"Do you think that we will find any treasure?"

"Hopefully? I was not in the best state of mind the last time I came through here, so I don't remember smelling anything. But they do seem to love shiny stuff, so with any luck they'll have collected something over however long they've been here."

Soon we entered the larger cavern I'd found on my way out. It was nothing so grand as the one we'd found by the mines, but patches of glow slime shining on the walls and lighting up a few shallow pools of water gave the place an other-worldly appearance.

We stopped there. This was also where I'd found the gremlins, though they had wisely kept their distance. And as we looked and listened, there was the dripping of water but also, in the background, a distinct scrabbling on the stone and hushed chattering from deeper into the cave. The same direction as the pull of the Nest Heart.

"Eyes open and head on a swivel," I told Herald. "Perhaps you should even shift. Can you shoot your bow when you're shifted?"

"Sure. Though the arrow becomes visible the moment I loose."

"That's still awesome," I muttered. "Real life stealth archer, invisible in the shadows . . ."

Herald preened theatrically. "I am rather amazing, yes."

We both shifted. Her for safety, just in case, and me so I could see where she was. The uneven cave floor made the going slow. Herald had no special advantages when it came to mobility and had to go around and sometimes over obstacles that I could practically ignore. The sounds of movement and hushed conversation in the gremlins' chattering language became stronger, until we were suddenly next to a couple of the creatures who were straining to see back the way we'd come, completely unaware of our presence. Herald's shifting did strange things to any sounds she made, which might have thrown them to our benefit.

Herald carefully loosened her sword in its scabbard, then turned to me. I couldn't see any details of her face, since her entire form was radiant when I saw her like this, but the question was obvious. I nodded with great exaggeration and turned to the gremlin closest to me.

We'd discussed fighting like this in passing while planning our ambush of Tark, and she'd done well, even if our plan hadn't worked out as we'd hoped. Since we couldn't speak while we were both shifted, the idea was to position ourselves so we could see each other. Then, since Herald could strike while shifted and I couldn't, I would attack first.

We each circled around our targets. Herald raised her sword like an executioner, and nodded my way.

I shifted back. The moment I was solid I grabbed my gremlin and twisted its head halfway around with a pop and crackle of tearing cartilage. At the same time a shadow moved, and the other gremlin's head jerked off its shoulders.

There was a dull thud as the head hit the stone and rolled, and the sound of liquid spattering. Then there was only the water dripping from the stalactites, as

Herald silently shifted back to being visible and sat down on a mostly flat stone, away from the blood spray.

"That was"—she spoke quietly, pausing for a few quick breaths—"surprisingly strenuous. No extra resistance when the blade struck, but it drained me quickly."

"All right. Let's take a second for you to catch your breath, then we'll continue."

"Yeah. Thanks."

As Herald rested for a few heartbeats, I noted that both gremlins had belts. A quick inspection didn't reveal anything fancier than a few bits of rusty iron and what might have been native copper, but I stayed optimistic. These were the poor sods who'd gotten stuck with the worst job, so they couldn't be expected to have anything nice. Then, when Herald indicated that she was ready, we both shifted and continued into the depths of the caverns.

We were death on black wings as we moved. We encountered another three groups of gremlins in twos and threes and dealt with them just as silently as the first two. We found an easy way for Herald to save energy. While she *could* strike from the shadows, it was far more efficient for her to simply position herself so she wouldn't be seen, then shift with her sword ready and strike. It was, unfortunately, also the messier option, though she didn't seem too torn up about it. When one of the gremlins sprayed her pretty bad after she cut its throat, she just grimaced and wiped her face the best she could on the short sleeves of her tunic.

"Starting to wonder if it would be worth losing your gear to get clean when you shift?" I asked, and she rolled her eyes at me.

"A tunic like this is cheap. And I'd never be able to show my face again in the city if I shifted in the wrong place, so, no. I am quite happy as it is." She followed that by scowling unhappily as she wiped at her eyes with the back of her hand. "I just never expected such a small creature to bleed so much, or with such pressure."

As I looked at her, it struck me how completely unconcerned she was about killing these creatures, compared to how annoyed she was about the mess they'd made when they died. Back when we first met she had killed a bandit on the road, and at least one more when she led the Wolves to attack the bandit camp, and it had haunted her for weeks. Recently, though . . . I didn't see what happened after I grabbed Simdal off the street, but according to Ardek she had killed his guards without hesitation or remorse. It had been the same with our ambush of Tarkarran. She had discussed killing one of his guards from the shadows almost casually, as though she were talking about going to the market or something. When that failed due to one of those guards smelling danger, she had killed one man and crippled another, and I'd never heard a word of regret from her. She'd been an emotional mess for a while after killing Tarkarran himself, but as far as I could tell it was not killing him that was the issue. If anything she'd seemed upset that she couldn't kill him *more*.

I was so proud of her. *You shouldn't be*, Conscience insisted. *This change in her, it isn't healthy. It's not good for her. You should be worried, not proud.* But she didn't sound convinced. Who could say that this wasn't who Herald was always meant to be? She was my little dragon; strong, confident, and free of doubt. I had seen a glimmer of that even at the bandit camp. The wild joy in her eyes had been unmistakable. Wasn't that better than being wracked with guilt over every life she took? Would she be able to hide away and be left in peace if she didn't want to fight? I doubted it.

She couldn't have ignored what was being done to those poor people we'd rescued from the valkin any more than I could, and all of our current problems stemmed from that. She hadn't chosen violence; she and the others had simply refused to back down when violence came to them. If some of the Night Blossom's people died, that was on her, and if Herald could play her part without guilt or unnecessary pain, I would smile and praise her for it.

"You have been staring for a while," Herald said quietly, breaking me out of my thoughts. She wiped at her face again. "Did I miss anything?"

She'd missed plenty. The situation with her face was not something that wiping would fix. But I didn't tell her that. There was no point, and she looked appropriately fearsome with blood smeared across her face. "I was just thinking how impressed I am," I said instead.

"Impressed? With what?"

"With what a warrior you've become."

She looked away with a smile, clearly pleased. "Where did this come from, all of a sudden?"

"It's not sudden. I just don't say it enough. Now come on. We've got a nest to kill, on the other side of that wall and down a bit."

"Yeah. I think I can feel it. Mak always described it like standing near a fire, feeling the heat of it on your skin as you move around it, but I think it is more like . . . pressure, I would say. Or as though there is a gentle wind coming from it, through stone and all." She pointed, and I snaked my head around to sight along her arm. She was pointing almost exactly in the direction that I knew the Nest Heart to be. "There, right?"

"Right! Can all magic users feel Nest Hearts?"

"Not all. Mak can, but Tam cannot, for whatever reason. Perhaps it is because his magic only affects himself. I never bothered to find out more about it, but it is a well-known phenomenon, so information should not be too hard to come by. I could ask at the Guild, maybe?"

"Please. It would be interesting to know, if nothing else."

The Nest Heart was close enough at that point that I could feel its exact location, no more than three hundred feet away. It ended up being more like twice that, since the caverns twisted and split, but soon we were looking at the nest. Due to how the caverns had turned, we ended up looking up at it, with crude dwellings lining a wide incline, a hundred and fifty feet long, bathed in the faint light of the glow slime and with the Nest Heart swirling and flickering at the top.

We sat still and silent and observed for a while. There were about two dozen gremlins that I could see. The ceiling was too low to fly effectively, so I'd just have to slog through, dealing with anything that was crazy enough to come at me. There was no way of telling how enthusiastic they'd be, considering how much bigger I was than the first time I fought gremlins, but the one that I'd have to fight for sure was the brute leading them. Standing almost five feet tall and thickly muscled, it was much like the one that had taken my horn, though this one was female. It lounged near the Nest Heart, open and visible, while tearing meat from the bone of some unidentifiable creature. Goat, perhaps. Or gremlin, for all I knew.

"Want to do the honors?" I asked Herald, who had already strung her bow and taken out one of her one-month's-profits-for-a-successful-inn arrows.

"Whenever you are ready," she answered, her eyes shining as she drew back and sighted along the arrow.

"I'm good to go. Let's see how many shots you can get off before they realize what's happening!"

Herald grinned and loosed. Some gremlins turned their heads at the snap of her bowstring, but the brute wasn't one of them, and she ignored them. She immediately nocked a second arrow, drew, and loosed that one, as well, before the first struck home, taking the gremlin brute high in the chest. A moment later the second arrow followed, which hit close enough to the first that I couldn't distinguish them from the distance we were at.

The brute stared stupidly at the two shafts sticking out above her breast. She pawed at them, stood unsteadily, stumbled, then fell over, all in complete silence. She rolled and slid twenty or thirty feet, then lay still.

While that happened Herald had put five arrows in the air, hitting three gremlins. I was just watching, silently impressed and wondering if I would have anything to do, when eight of the bastards screeched and charged down the incline toward us.

Two fell to Herald's arrows as they came. That barely slowed them down, but the fact that they'd only seen Herald and not me became abundantly clear when they immediately screamed and tried to reverse course as I leapt out. They scattered, so I ran down the ones I could, confident that Herald could deal with the rest if they tried again. Then things got hazy.

I had a tendency to simply cut loose and let Instinct take over when a fight felt entirely one sided, and that was what I did now. It was barely even a fight; it was a mop-up. I was a dragon, with strength and fortitude, faced with gremlins who were armed with, at best, stone hammers, small picks, and crude knives. I let Instinct take the wheel, and when conscious thought faded, back in the cavern was full of the smell of blood and the screeches and whines of the dying, the voices growing fewer as Herald moved among the scattered bodies and silenced them.

Looking down the slope, I saw fresh blood spattering my friend, and several small bodies lying where she had stood at the bottom. They'd tried another attack, after all. Or perhaps they had just been trying to get out. Either way, they had met Herald, and it hadn't gone well for them. As she moved between the bodies, using her dagger to make short work of any that were still breathing, it again struck me how casual she was about it.

"Are you all right?" I asked.

"Hmm?" She looked up from cutting a throat, then looked down at herself. "Oh, yes. They came at me practically in a line. No trouble at all."

"You're looking pretty relaxed with all of this."

She smiled. "Should I not be? They are gremlins. Or, well, they were. And I am with you, so it is not like there is any danger. If anything, this all reminds me of how we met. Fighting gremlins under a mountain, you keeping me safe . . . Not sure if the payout here will be as good as back then, but we spent most of that on freeing Tam, anyway."

She stood, wiping her dagger on a rag. "Now, I have been dying of curiosity. Will you eat that Nest Heart?"

"I guess." I looked around. There weren't enough bodies. Something like a third or a quarter of the gremlins were either hiding or fled, but I didn't see them trying anything after this massacre.

"Have you heard of anyone else absorbing a Nest Heart?" I asked Herald as we approached the swirling mass of shadow, brilliantly bright in my shadowsight. "Did Mak ever try, for example?"

"I have not," she said thoughtfully. "And I do not think that she ever tried. But it seems to me that it should be known if it were something some people could do."

"Well, you're different, right? Your magic is like mine. Do you wanna try?"

"Me?"

"Yeah, why not?"

"But you need it, do you not?"

"Nah, yeah. But I can find another one. Shouldn't take too long. Go on, give it a shot!"

"But . . . what do I do?"

"I just put my hand in it and focus on pulling it in. Like the opposite of pushing magic into a lightstone."

"Oh, like when you make them dark?"

I looked at her, embarrassment slowly creeping in. "You can make them dark?"

There was a silence. "Yes, Draka," she said finally. She was grinning, very carefully not laughing but not hiding her amusement nearly well enough. "You can make them dark."

"Right. Yeah. Good to know. You may feel some heat, from inside you, as you take it in. If it works, that is. Just try it, all right?"

"All right."

She approached the Nest Heart with her left hand out, moving tentatively. She looked at me and I nodded in encouragement. She steeled herself, then plunged her hand into the outer layer of the Nest Heart.

She didn't gasp. It was more controlled than that, a long, sharp but even inhalation. "I can feel it. It is streaming over my hand, hot and cold at once, and it is . . . like it wants to stick to my skin, almost."

"Try to draw it in," I said. There was a short pause as she focused, and a thin stream peeled off the Nest Heart, a trickle of magic that flowed into Herald, to her heart and from there out into the rest of her body.

"It resists me," she said with some strain. "It does not want to come. Was it like that for you?"

"No. For me it just flowed in."

"Not for me. But the fact that I can do this at all is amazing. We have to have the others try this!"

Her face twisted with concentration, and the streamer grew a little thicker, but not by much. Suddenly Herald stopped, withdrawing her hand. The Nest Heart wasn't much smaller at all. "I cannot take any more. I have nowhere to put it!"

"How do you mean?" I hadn't felt anything like that. I wanted more and more, no matter how intense it got.

"Just what I said. I feel full to bursting. Painfully so. I cannot take any more because there is nowhere for it to go." She took a deep breath and swung her arms. "I do feel marvelous, though!"

"We'll have to see what it does for you. Now step back, and I'll finish it off."

I stuck my hand in the slightly diminished, swirling mass and drew on it as Herald took a few steps back, watching with interest. It was pretty much the same as the previous times, if perhaps a little quicker. I lost myself in that feeling of fulfilling a need, in the growing heat, and in the hypnotic swirling of the Nest Heart as it shed layer after layer, which flowed into me. The heat reached the same intense peak, the same explosion—

CHAPTER TWENTY-SIX

Hunted

Herald gently shook me awake. "Intense experience?" she asked, with only mild concern in her eyes. "You have been out for about a minute."

"Intense, yeah," I replied as I got to my feet, luxuriating in the feeling of fullness, of oneness with the world that came with the absorption of the Nest Heart. "But it feels so good afterward. So, how did that look to you?"

"Strange! There was the same wave of silence as when you destroy a Nest Heart with a nest killer. The interesting thing, of course, was you."

I preened happily. "Of course."

"You shine when I look at you with the shadowsight, but I could see the magic clearly. It gathered in you normally, around your heart, like when you use it to move shadows, or when Mak or Kira heals someone. Nothing strange so far. Then it got more and more intense as you absorbed the Nest Heart. Brighter. Bigger, too. And then," she said with great excitement, "after the Nest Heart vanished, the ball of magic around your heart collapsed on itself!"

"That's kind of how it feels, too," I commented.

"Yeah? So it collapsed. Then, when the wave of silence came, the magic burst outward into your whole body, filling your whole body with golden light. Not like how it always looks, but like the whole thing was liquid gold, just concentrated magic! Then it vanished, all at once, and you passed out."

"Huh. It kind of feels like I explode when it happens, so that makes sense, I guess. What does it mean, though?"

"Does it have to mean anything? You feel full, do you not? It looked like it filled you."

"I mean, yeah. But it's magic. When magic makes me feel like I'm blowing up, I kind of expect it to do something."

"Filling you with a sense of well-being, allowing you to watch and invade the dreams of others, and allowing you to permanently change the way items block light, while also hiding them from sight even when they should be clearly visible. That is nothing to you?"

"Well, when you put it like that . . ."

We took some time to gather whatever loot we could, Herald collecting belts and me sniffing around in the crude dwellings. There wasn't much to find. We found a handful of badly tarnished eagles and some green peacocks, so it wasn't nothing, but otherwise it was all corroded metal or shiny rocks. I almost started to feel a little bad about wiping the gremlins out, but finding some old, weathered, yet clearly human bones put an end to that. My guess would be that whoever those people were, and however they got up here, they were the source of the coins and other pieces of worked metal. I hoped that they'd died in some kind of accident, but I doubted it. Damn gremlins.

We emerged from the cave with plenty of daylight left. I took Herald down to one of the forest streams, where it was a little warmer, so she could wash up. Then, once she was as clean as she was likely to get, we went to check up on the villagers.

Progress was as impressive as ever. There was a new cabin, with another well under way. Little green shoots dotted the rows of the garden, which had been given a simple fence, and skins and meat hung to dry by the central fire.

Jekrie told me that they hadn't had any trouble, as such. Several people had come by since the last time I visited, but two had stood out. Both groups had seemed satisfied with their tale of having been driven south by monsters, but they had also asked if anyone had seen a large, winged lizard in the area.

"Lying did not seem the right course," Jekrie said, "with none of us skilled at such things, or with advancements for it. It would look suspicious to be caught in a lie, I thought. So I told them all that aye, we had seen such a creature, and it had flown south, and that was all I could tell them."

I asked them to describe the visitors, and none of them matched the magic archer, which was my greatest concern. "I don't think you could have done better," I told them. "Hunters and adventurers have looked for me here before, so I doubt they learned anything new. But I guess I'll need to remember to be careful flying in and out of here. I'd rather not have to kill anyone if it can be avoided, you know?"

"We know your mercy well, Great Lady."

One great thing about Jekrie was that he could say something like that and sound completely honest, with not a bit of simpering or insincere flattery. It was nice.

We hung around the village for the rest of the afternoon, until the sun reached the mountaintops. I mostly just lounged around in the sun, staying out of sight from the forest in case someone came by. Herald, meanwhile, had taken it upon herself to try and teach three interested villagers how to read, Tinir among them. I watched with amusement at how she scratched letters in the dirt, telling them the sounds of each and then stringing them together into words. She'd done the same with me only months ago, and she'd done a pretty good job of it. My writing left something to be desired, but she could hardly be blamed for that—I lacked a knuckle on each finger, and I was still relearning how to hold a pen or brush. My letter to the Night Blossom had taken me ages, and several tries. But I *could* read and write again, and it was all thanks to Herald.

Idly, I used a claw to scratch my name into the dirt. My old name, my human side's name, in the Latin alphabet. I didn't feel anything when I saw it. I didn't identify with it; it was just a word to me. I wiped it out, and instead wrote out my new name, my real name, in the Sareyan alphabet. *Dah-ruh-ah-kah-ah*, properly connected and with the correct little accent marks on the *ah*s. Then I added *Drakonum* before it, like they did here, family name first, and I grinned to myself. Draka of House Drakonum. That felt better. It felt right.

As I admired my work I noticed a little head watching me from around the corner of the longhouse. I watched the boy out of the corner of my eye, before slowly turning my head to look at him. At first he barely reacted. Then my shadow reached for him. His eyes went wide, and he vanished behind the house.

"Should we be going?" Herald asked, coming over. Her little group had broken up, and she had her gear next to her, ready to go.

"I guess," I said, looking up at the setting sun. "Did you see a kid run away around the longhouse?"

"Oh, Trem? Yeah. Was he giving you trouble?"

I looked at her incredulously. "What kind of trouble can a little kid give me, exactly? No, I think he was just curious. Any chance you could find him?"

"Should be easy," she said, but her tone was doubtful. "I do not know what his mother will think about it, though."

"Just tell them that if he's curious, if he's got any questions or anything, he's welcome."

"Yeah, all right. Wait here."

It took five minutes before Herald returned. "Next time, perhaps?" she suggested sheepishly.

"Let me guess. Kid's terrified?"

"Yeah. And it took me a couple of minutes to convince Madalla, his mother, that it was an invitation and completely voluntary, not a command."

"All right. Maybe next time."

I was a little disappointed. I liked kids, and I didn't exactly get many chances to interact with them. It had been nearly three weeks since I last saw Lahnie. Maybe I should swing by Pine Hill? But no, it was getting dark, and I couldn't very well drop in there with Herald out of nowhere. They knew Herald, but her randomly dropping by, alone, and asking Lahnie to come outside for a while would look sketchy as all hell.

Someday soon I'd go visit, though. Maybe after the meetings with Zabra and Sempralia.

As we said some quick goodbyes, I saw the kid, Trem, watching me again. This time he stood in the doorway of the longhouse. I raised a hand, claws in, and waved. His eyes went huge and he vanished inside.

Ah, well. I tried.

For the return trip to the city we decided to try something new. One of my concerns had been someone seeing me taking off from or returning to the city with Herald on my back. So why, Herald wondered, couldn't she just shift when we got close, and remain unseen that way?

Some testing was in order, and we moved back up into a grassy valley in the mountains above the village. Neither of us wanted to be five hundred feet up when we found out that shifting made it so Herald couldn't hold on to me, so we started on ground level. That worked with absolutely no fuss or drama at all, and then it was just a matter of working our way up from there. I ran around with her shifted on my back, which worked just fine. I took a low, flying leap, and she didn't report any trouble. Then I shifted with her still on me, and she, predictably, fell right through me with a distant yelp of surprise, while I felt like . . . well, like someone had fallen right through me. Not a pleasant sensation.

That led to Herald wondering what happened when I shifted in the air, and her special brand of gentle, encouraging disappointment when I confessed that I didn't know. I'd only tested it when I was coming in to land. With her cheering me on, we did some experiments and found that while I could shift just fine, I couldn't fly while shifted, instead just falling as though I'd folded my wings. Which was fine as long as I shifted back in time to recover, but a low-altitude test with hitting the ground was unpleasant enough that I didn't want to try the real deal. Still, it was good info.

Then we moved on to flying with her shifted on my back, and it seemed to Herald that only speed might cause problems. Holding on was no harder than normal, but the faster we went, the more draining it was for her to remain shifted. Everything we'd learned put together made it simple enough. We'd go straight to the city. I'd slow down as we came in above it, and she'd shift, and then we'd land in the abandoned garden or somewhere equally out of the way. Then I'd shift on the ground, and we'd make our way back to the inn together.

What we actually did was fly around like fools for hours, testing how fast I could go before she could barely remain shifted, or even hold on. It was exhilarating, my own simple pleasure and Herald's unfailing joy at flying combining to make me never want the night to end.

Our peace shattered suddenly and quite rudely, when magic flared like a beacon in the treetops below. "Dodge!" Herald screamed, seeing the same thing as I, and I took a sharp high-speed turn as a shard of light streaked up at us.

From the corner of my eye I saw Herald lose her grip with her legs. For an eternity she slid sideways, sending her flailing off my back and only hanging on by her arms around my neck, then falling to dangle beneath me as the turn ended. While moving at highway speeds, five hundred feet off the ground.

Mercies be blessed, the next shot missed, no thanks to me. I didn't dare do any fancy flying while trying to wrap all four limbs around her. I just descended while putting distance between us and the archer. We landed and stayed on the ground for a few minutes after that, with me letting go of Herald and her holding on to me for dear life while alternately laughing or crying hysterically.

"We should—We should probably be more careful," she hiccupped once she'd calmed down a little.

"Yeah," I growled. My blood was boiling. "Or find that fucking archer."

"How about we go home? We can look for them tomorrow?"

I pulled back and got a good look at her. She was seriously rattled, her face still wet with fresh tears despite her brave smile. "Sure. No need to rush. Tomorrow. Yeah."

After that we made our way back to the inn. Carefully.

It was midnight when we got back to the inn, and late morning when we woke up. Mak had been sleeping at a reasonable hour for once, and while my panic hadn't woken her, she apparently had a part of her brain dedicated to keeping track of where I was. Despite Herald's best efforts not to bother our sister, Mak came down to the cellar as Herald was letting me in. After sleepily opening up the strongroom for me, she went back to bed, and Herald went with her. She was apologetic about it, but I shooed her on. I could understand wanting to sleep in a bed. And after being shot at and nearly falling to her death, I could definitely understand her wanting to be near Mak, who was, in practice, as much of a mother to her as a sister. I knew that she loved me, but our friendship couldn't replace seventeen years of care and affection.

I mean, I would have liked some company. I'd been shot at, too. But I was a big girl. I could handle it.

Once I awoke it didn't take long for Mak to join me. I'd barely unrolled one of the "romance" stories when there was a knock on the door, and when I unbarred and opened it there was Mak, looking anxious.

"Morning, Mak," I said, backing up to let her in.

"Good morning, Draka. Would you care to explain why my sister insisted on sleeping with me in my bed last night? She was too embarrassed to tell me."

"Gods above, let a girl wake up before you ask something like that!" I settled back down on my comfy little nest of pillows and blankets. "Did she tell you anything at all about what we were doing?"

"She told me that you cleared out some gremlins, and that you ate another one of the Nest Hearts. Though she was cagey about it."

"Well, ask her some more about that, for one thing. But the reason she might have needed some comfort is probably that we got shot at again."

Mak's eyes grew large at that. "Neither of you got hurt, did you?"

"No, we're fine. I'd bet it was the same guy, though. And thank the Mercies we can see magic, because that was the only warning we had. Might have got hit, otherwise."

"That bastard! And we're no closer to finding out who it might be. No one seems to know about anyone matching the description."

"They may just be hanging around the forest," I suggested. "I don't see how they could have just happened to be in the right place to take a shot at me twice if they spend any time in the city."

"Maybe you're right, but it's been a month since the first time! If they spend all day in the forest, watching the sky, that's one hells of a dedicated hunter. I'd be bored out of my mind!"

"Twice could be a coincidence, I guess. Just doesn't seem bloody likely. Even if there's more than one of them, and at least two who can imbue their arrows with magic."

"They'd have a better chance if they have some way of knowing when you'll be out of the city."

I looked at Mak with distaste. "Please don't say that. I can only think of a few ways for that to happen, and I don't like any of them."

"Betrayal, spies, or some kind of strong advancements," Mak said, nodding unhappily. "Yeah. Unpleasant, but I don't think we can afford to discount any possibilities."

I sighed. I didn't want to do this, but it was necessary. "All right, let's think about it. Betrayal. There are only a few people who know that I exist. Not all of them know that I'm ever here. I'd say the list is limited to you, Herald, Tam and Val, the cousins, Garal and Lalia, Ardek, Kira, and Barro. Did I miss any?"

"The kids may suspect it," Mak said, "but they've never seen you here as far as I know."

"All right. Now, out of those, I trust the four of you in the family implicitly. I'm pretty sure that Ardek can't try to harm me any more than you could, and I don't think that Kira wants to, though she might be hiding a grudge, I guess. I have no reason not to trust the Wolves, and they're rarely here when I leave, but it could be possible that one of them is telling someone when they know that I'm gone. Same goes for Barro. Do any of them ask about me when I'm gone?"

"Barro mostly talks to Ardek, so you'd have to ask him, but the Wolves ask for you sometimes, yeah. But they'd have to be hiding their intentions from me somehow, and I know all of them. As far as I can tell, any time they ask for you it's because they want to check in on you, that's all."

"And if I can't trust them, I should have bigger problems than some archer taking shots at me in the forest," I mused.

"And that. But either way, unless this archer is just waiting in the forest all the time, looking at the sky, they must have some other way of knowing when you'll be out there. And another thing, they need to not only know to look for you, but they need to be in the right area. The two times you were attacked weren't in exactly the same place, were they?"

"Nah, I came in from different directions. The actual spots must have been dozens of miles apart."

"So that means they must have ridiculous speed, luck, or some way of predicting where you'll fly over. I don't see them spotting you, then running several miles to be in position before you pass over. But luck, or prediction . . ."

"Really?" I said incredulously. "That's some ridiculous luck. That, or fortune telling. You think an advancement could do that?"

"I can heal people from lethal injuries. Herald can turn invisible. Tam has luck that borders on the unbelievable, and that's a *minor* advancement. Is it so hard to imagine that a major could let them regularly chance upon or predict where their prey will be?"

"Magic is bullshit, sometimes," I muttered, and Mak laughed at me.

I couldn't even bring myself to scowl at her. I knew that I was being unfair and petulant. My own majors let me turn into a literal cloud of shadow and invade people's dreams. But the difference was that this time, I didn't benefit. And that, Instinct insisted, was utter bullshit.

CHAPTER TWENTY-SEVEN

Nowhere to Hide

It was two nights until our meeting with the Night Blossom. Most of the day after I returned with Herald was spent going over what Tarkarran had told us. It painted a picture of a cautious woman who rarely slept in the same bed two nights in a row and always had guards with her. The fighter with the scarred lips, a man named Hardal that we had taken captive and who had later escaped the Wolves, was usually one of those guards. We had all seen what he was capable of, holding his own against multiple opponents at once. Tarkarran had freely admitted that the man was damned good, and that he would not want to try to face him in anything resembling a fair fight.

Well, his words had been more like, "Killing is all that street rat is good for. Hells, *I* wouldn't fight him unless he was asleep and unarmed. You two? He's gonna cut you up beautifully before he cuts you down."

Same difference.

One thing we got out of him was the reason for his visits to the particular brothel he'd been headed to when we took him. It wasn't that he had a girl there he was sweet on; that brothel was where he usually met with the Night Blossom. Which would have been very useful information, except that, with how careful he made Zabra sound, it seemed unlikely that we'd find her there in the future. Still, she hadn't hidden Kesra away until we took Tark, so maybe he'd exaggerated. If things went poorly at the meeting, we'd have to check that brothel out regardless, together with half a dozen other places he'd said she might be found.

The day passed. We talked. I read and I rested. I wouldn't sleep that night; I had a solo mission planned.

When night fell, Herald saw me off with an insistent, "Be careful! Watch the ground for flashes of magic!"

"I will," I promised, and then I shifted and set off for the garden. I still avoided flying out from the inn, just in case.

I headed south, flying high and scanning the ground. I knew where I was going. At least I knew where I wanted to go. I just didn't quite know where that was, so I was trying to find it. My destination, if it existed, was Kesra's villa in the country.

I might be wasting a night. The place might not even exist, or if it did, it might just be a place that Kesra had visited once. But no one had seen her since I delivered my letter into her bedroom, and when I wanted to hide people, I took them out of the city. Why couldn't Zabra do the same? If that villa in Kesra's dream truly was the safest place she knew, weren't the odds good that she was there now? I thought so, and my sisters agreed that it was worth investigating, so I wanted to find it. I wanted credible leverage.

In the dream the villa had been in sight of the city's walls, but that may or may not be true. There was no way of knowing how many liberties Kesra's dream image of the place took with reality. In the end, what I was looking for was an estate, a central villa surrounded by accessory buildings. It should be somewhat out of the way, and not too far from the city. And while that didn't narrow it down much, there weren't too many estates that fit the description. Besides, I knew Kesra's scent, and I had all night to search.

So, search I did. It reminded me a little of when I'd been looking for the raiders who turned out to be the Silver Spurs mercenaries. I flew from estate to estate, watching, listening, sniffing at doors and windows, and generally invading people's privacy. I checked both large estates and smaller ones, in case Kesra's memories made the place grander than the real thing. I caught the scents of jasmine or orange blossoms more than once, and I spent a long time investigating those places before I was satisfied.

Sometime in the small hours, only a few miles from the coast and with the city just barely in sight, I was sniffing around a likely looking place. It had twice as many guards patrolling as was reasonable, and at an open window I caught a strong scent of orange blossom, together with a weaker one of jasmine.

It took me an hour to get inside and find Kesra, and another to get out. Not because there were any problems, but because I took my time, memorizing everything that I could of the place, inside and out. The long pergola covered in grapevines, the fruit of which must have been harvested already. The dry, crumbling well at one end of the courtyard that was slowly being filled with household refuse. I spent extra time on the murals and mosaics on the walls and in the central pool of the villa, trying to pay attention to little details, like how many dogs there were, and what kind of fruit a man was feeding to the woman next to him. I made absolutely sure that I'd be able to describe Kesra's bedroom in detail. Which way the windows faced, what furniture she had, and how the rugs were placed. Things like that. I wanted to be able to describe the place so meticulously that there could be no doubt I'd been there.

On a nightstand by the bed where Kesra slept fitfully I saw a necklace that I'd seen her wear before. It was a simple thing, a leather thong with a small ceramic pendant of a bird in flight. I silently shifted, taking it and putting it in my mouth before turning back into shadow. I felt like a creep—which, fair enough; I was being one—but I wanted to be utterly convincing if I had to. And then, satisfied that I'd done as well as I was likely to, I was on my way back to the city, with no one the wiser.

"I only want Mak with me at the actual meeting."

The muted sound of a lone, mournful string instrument bled from the common room above, lending some unexpected gravitas to my words. I'd questioned my family's choice of musician at first, but the woman was some adventurer they knew who wanted to practice playing in front of an audience, and people who came in to drink in the afternoon appreciated something downbeat, apparently. It was their world. If they said that the music was appropriate, who was I to argue?

The family, along with Ardek, the cousins Terriallon, and even Barro, were gathered in the cellar. It was well into the afternoon. At midnight I was meeting with Zabra, the Night Blossom, at a derelict brickyard in the slummy southwestern part of the city, and we had little idea of what to expect, besides treachery. "Sorry, Herald," I continued, "but Mak, you're better in a negotiation. And if we need to bail, I need someone I can just grab by the collar and fly, without worrying if I'm hurting you."

Mak understood me perfectly and just nodded. Herald looked unhappy and gave me a curt "Fine." The others did not quite understand me, and there was an uncomfortable silence.

"Ah, bad phrasing. I mean that I'm confident she's tough enough that I won't hurt her if I just grab her by the collar and fly off."

"Oh, right, that's what I thought," Tam said unconvincingly. "Good."

"Herald, I want you hidden somewhere you can see what's going on. Rib and Pot—and, again, thanks for doing this—I want you to make sure that no one sneaks up on us from behind. And Tam, Val, and Barro standing by somewhere close. If the shit hits the fan . . . uh, I mean, if things turn ugly, I need Herald to go alert you that you should get back to the Favor as quickly as possible, or come help if I can't get us out. Use your discretion. If there's a dozen of them suddenly and there's nothing you can do, don't risk yourselves. Ardek, you're not fighting. I want you and your minions scouting the area, letting us know if they've got anyone set up ahead of time. Everyone all right with that?"

"Quick question," Pot said before anyone else could speak up. "Do you want us slitting throats or just running people off? Because we're fine with the first, but it'll be a lot harder to explain if we're caught."

"Cousin Mordo will not be best pleased if we're locked up with good cause," Rib agreed. "We can afford the fines. But we're still Wolves, and it's his ass unless he punishes us convincingly. Which might mean us getting on a boat back to Tavvanar."

"And that would be damned annoying," Pot finished.

"I mean . . . if you *can* run them off without things getting bloody, do it," I said. "I'd prefer if you don't get in any unnecessary shit because of me. But if they're expecting a fight . . ."

Rib nodded. "Likely to cause trouble, and not likely to back off. Right. We'll get messy if we have to."

"Right. Anyone else?"

"Retreat, abandoning Mak and yourself, are unpalatable," Val said, a slight scowl backing his words. "As you say, we will use our discretion. Will you agree not to argue with our decision, if worse comes to worst?"

Instinct was not happy that he'd argue the point to start with, but Val was the most experienced combatant in the group. "Yeah," I agreed reluctantly. "It's your call. Whatever you decide needs to be done, I'll accept it. But, hey!" I grinned. "Maybe it'll be fine and Zabra *won't* try anything stupid!"

The only one who didn't scoff or roll their eyes was Ardek. "What're you thinking?" I asked him.

"Just, you know, don't take her lightly? She's got this far, yeah? She didn't do that by being stupid. She knows you got out of a locked cell. She knows what you did on your way out, and what you did to a whole boat full of fighters. She won't be meeting you without protection, but I don't think you can assume that she wants this to get violent. I've never heard of her fighting anyone who wasn't much weaker than her."

"You think she really just wants to talk?"

He shrugged. "I don't think you should be so sure she doesn't. She underestimated you pretty bad, yeah? And she's been hurt for it. She might just want to cut her losses." He looked at the others in the room, settling on Herald and Mak. "If you'll let her or not, that's not up to her. But she may want to try. I'm thinking, be prepared for her to come in good faith, just as you are for her to try something."

"All right. The point of even going to this meeting is to get a read on her. If she wants to keep things peaceful, fine." I looked around the group. "But a straight up truce is still out, right?"

Herald, of all people, looked thoughtful. She'd been so sanguine up until then that it took me by complete surprise when she said, "That depends on what she is willing to give up, does it not?"

Mak looked at her incredulously. "Her life would be a good start!"

"I do not think we will get her to agree to that. But if she is willing to consider reparations . . ."

Mak turned to face Herald fully. "You're not seriously considering this, are you? Even if she's willing to negotiate something closer to a surrender than a truce, you know where that money comes from."

"Silver is silver. I do not think that she is likely to give us anything, but with a good enough offer . . . we should keep our minds open."

I loved Herald. I really did. She was my dearest friend, my closest confidante. We understood each other in a way that no one else could compare to. So why, oh why, did she have to go and make things difficult?

"She will never agree to paying tribute in exchange for peace," I said, but I could feel my conviction wavering. I wanted Zabra dead. I did. I wanted vengeance for what she'd done to my sisters, to myself, and to the unknown number of people who'd been enslaved and otherwise harmed on her orders. But silver was silver, and gold was gold.

A crime lord paying me tribute, growing my hoard . . . I was sorely tempted.

"We'll see what she has to say," I decided. "*If* she tries to buy us off, her offer will tell us how desperate she is. But we won't agree to anything. And I still think it's more likely that she'll try to use the opportunity to kill me, anyway."

"And if she does, I will try to take *her* out, along with as many of her people as I can," Herald stated. "I will not use the expensive arrows, though," she added thoughtfully. "I have full confidence that you can get yourself and Mak out safely, Draka, but I doubt that I will be getting back any arrows I loose."

Again, she was so *casual* about it, and I couldn't make my mind up if I should be delighted or concerned.

The day passed quickly after that, and I was excited. I wanted to face this woman. She'd been a ball and chain on my life, a constant threat hovering in the background, and I wanted it to be over. I wanted the threat to my humans, to my family, gone, by any means necessary. Even if that meant letting her buy us off. Maybe. Silver was silver, but blood was blood, and I had wanted hers for months.

We rested, we ate, and we talked, and the evening passed. Then it was time. Mak opted to forego her armor, taking only her sword. Her argument was that against the kind of people the Night Blossom was likely to have with her, armor wouldn't help much. The others, though, wore theirs, covering it with cloaks. We made our way down to the garden, my preferred place for take-offs and landings, and after a quick check to make sure that it was clear, I had Mak get on my back.

She was nervous about the whole idea of riding me, of course. I was pretty sure that she had a fear of heights, flying, or both, but she pulled on her big-girl britches and did it anyway.

Her arms tightened around my neck like she was trying to choke me out. "Think of it this way," I cajoled her, gently pulling on her arms to try and get her to loosen her grip. "You might be the fifth person in decades, maybe centuries or even longer, to ride a dragon!"

"The *fifth*?" Mak asked, her voice unsteady. "I thought Herald was the only one! Who else?"

"Well, Lahnie. First time was way back when—Have I told you about how I saved her from a monster boar?"

"This is familiar, to me at least," Val said, and the others nodded.

"She was too scared to climb down from the tree she was in. So I went up there and had her cling to my back."

"She was so eager when we met her in Pine Hill," Herald laughed. "Sat on your back quite naturally, too!"

"Yeah," I said fondly. Lahnie was a sweet kid. Of course, I hadn't actually *flown* with her, but Mak didn't need to know that. "And then there were Rib and Pot back during that whole monster bear debacle. Had to get them out of there somehow. They turned it into a whole spectacle; you should ask them about it sometime. *Anyway.* Are you settled in there, Mak? I promise I'll go slow and easy."

Mak had her face pressed into the back of my neck, and I just assumed that she had her eyes screwed shut. "Just get it over with, please."

"All right. You know I'm going to need to circle a bit, to let the others get into position?" I gave the others a look, and they understood perfectly, hurrying off to do just that.

"Don't remind me. Just—Let's just go."

I obliged, leaping into the air and climbing steadily. Mak stiffened, her grip tightening, but I was not the least bit concerned. Being generally smaller than Herald, Mak actually fit better on my back, and with her heels locked under my hips, I was pretty sure that she was more secure than her sister ever was. If only she could learn to enjoy flying. Letting someone ride me wasn't nearly as much fun when the person on my back was terrified.

Once I'd reached my preferred cruising altitude, where I could see practically the whole city beneath me, I tried to take it as gently as possible. "You should try to open your eyes!" I shouted back at Mak. "It's absolutely beautiful at night!"

There was a short pause, and then Mak's strength-enhanced grip became, somehow, even tighter. "Mercies, Draka! How high are we?"

"Not sure!" I choked out. "Three thousand feet, maybe? High! But don't think about that! It doesn't matter. Above a hundred feet you're done for anyway!"

"Why would you tell me that?!"

"Think of it like this! This high up I have plenty of time to catch you if you fall! But you won't!"

"No! No, Draka, it's time! It's time! Take us down!"

The wind swallowed my muttered "Where did you get bossy from, all of a sudden?" But she was right. It was time.

I turned and descended slowly, heading south, then corkscrewed down until we were only a few hundred feet up. Then I searched the cityscape for our destination, and swept in.

The brickyard was a large, roughly square space bracketed by buildings. Broken down wagons and other litter were piled by the walls. Someone had taken the time to line the place with torches on poles driven into the ground, with more of them making a square in the center of the yard. And at one side of that square, looking up at our approach, were about a dozen humans. Most of them stood with long spears at their sides. One, dressed in fine silks, sat with perfect posture on a tent chair, looking like a queen on her throne.

The Night Blossom was there, and she'd been waiting.

CHAPTER TWENTY-EIGHT

The Night Blossom

The fine layer of dust that covered the disused brickyard billowed under the force of my wings as I came in to land. I'd put some thought into my entrance, and I was rewarded for my efforts. Some of the heavies who'd accompanied the Night Blossom put their hands up to shield their eyes. Some of them stepped back. Only one didn't react. Hardal, the plain-faced man with the scarred lips. He looked bored with the whole situation, but his eyes were sharp.

The Night Blossom, to my annoyance, was holding a fan, which she used to keep the dust at bay. The corners of her lips even pulled back in a small, infuriating smile.

The moment I settled on the ground Mak leapt off my back. She didn't slide or climb, she vaulted, pushing off against the base of my wing with one strong leg and putting every bit of her grace to good use as she landed lightly beside me, all nearly five feet of her straightening to face our opposites.

As the dust settled, the Night Blossom stood. She snapped her fan shut, tucking it in the sash of her silk wrap, then faced us with her hands down, palms out as though to welcome us into her home.

"Draka! Lady Drakonum!" Her voice carried easily across the fifty feet separating us, and I hated how warm and inviting it was. She took a few steps forward, looking completely at ease, her guards staying where they were. "We've already met, of course, but we haven't been properly introduced. I am Tespril Zabra. Thank you for joining me here tonight."

"Did you get my message?" I asked, ignoring her pleasantries. "Are you going to make it worth our time to hear you out?"

"I got your message, yes, though I'm curious why you'd leave it with my sister instead of sending it to me directly. Was it intended as some kind of threat?"

Is she messing with me, I wondered. Was she pretending like the fact that I waltzed into her little sister's dreams just to leave a message didn't worry her? Or did she not know? But she was moving smoothly on.

"Whatever your reasons, I'm sure that once we're done here, you'll agree that a peaceful coexistence is in everyone's best interest." She turned her back to us, returned to her chair, and took a seat. "Now, let's make sure that we all agree on the foundation of this . . . relationship that we have. You bear me a grudge. I get that. It's pointless, but understandable in your position. We didn't exactly get off to a friendly start, did we? And while I might childishly point out that *you started it*, I understand that you may not see it that way."

Even with Instinct screaming at me that we had our enemy right in front of us, that we should kill her *now*, that there was no point in waiting, I was still hanging on her every word. Something about her made me want to listen, to hear her out. But it was only strong enough to nudge me, and not so strong that I didn't realize what was happening. I loved magic and all the messes it made, but sometimes it was a real pain.

Mak, though, seemed entirely unaffected. And when I didn't speak up, she did.

"I've been told that you're not stupid. And it must be true, on some level, since you've gotten to the position you have. But what makes you think that we'd let this go? What could possibly explain or justify your crimes against us and so many others? You had your goons shackle me to a table, then had my sister tortured in front of me! What do you think could possibly be worth more to me than your head?"

Zabra snapped her fan open with a dismissive gesture and resumed fanning herself. "I'm not here to explain myself, and I'm not going to justify anything. I've done what I had to, to keep myself and my sister safe. If you took the time to speak to Tark, then you know where I came from. You've had a taste of that life yourself. You know what it's like. You did what you could to keep your sister out of it, and I did the same. Let's leave it at that."

I finally managed to speak. "You said that you had some reason we shouldn't just kill you. Spit it out."

"You're even more magnificent than the first time I saw you, you know?" she said, with undisguised admiration. Despite myself I preened at her praise. "The first reason is simple, something that I hope everyone will understand—lives, dear dragon. I've lost quite a few, and I don't want to lose anymore. But I also haven't been trying to kill anyone close to you. Since the mess in the harbor I've been restraining myself, hoping that we could work this all out. If we can't come to an agreement here, tonight, I'm sure that you'll try to kill me. You'll fail. Draka, I know what you are, and when I say that scarier people than you have tried, I mean it. So you'll try, and you'll fail, and then I'll have to retaliate. I'll start *really* hurting the people you surround yourself with, and the people important to them. Now, you may think that you can keep them safe. Perhaps you can, for a while, but for how long? How long until Lady Drakonum's sister goes to visit that soldier of hers? Perhaps she finds him dead. Perhaps she meets an arrow somewhere on the way, far from help. Even if you all stay in that lovely inn of yours, how long before one of you steps in front of a window at the wrong time? And that's not even getting into poisoned goods, legal mischief, or a dozen other ways I have ready to hurt you."

I started growling, an unconscious warning from deep in my chest that rolled out across the brickyard.

"Oh, don't be like that," Zabra said. "I know what you're thinking. You're big and strong, and your scales are ridiculously hard to pierce, I'm sure. And you have that suffocating venom that you can spray. I know. But even trying would cost you more than you could possibly gain. Do you think I would come here without safeguards, without already having given orders? If I don't return and cancel those orders, little Miss Herald's soldier will be dead before sunrise. So will Mister Tamor's singer friends and those old acquaintances from your former life, Lady Drakonum, some of whom still work for me, that you try so hard to keep hidden. And those are only the easy targets, you see? You have friends, acquaintances, employees, and suppliers, and loyal guests. In the following days, who knows what might happen? And even if you did manage to kill me, my people are very loyal. They'd want to avenge me, and the people you care for would die anyway. So, you see, it's much better that you don't try. There's no point in posturing or making threats. If anything, you should be aware of how lucky you are that I'm not interested in taking this any further."

"Well," Mak said, "that's pretty clear, isn't it? You've done your research, and there's nothing we can do to threaten you. We have no leverage, and we should be glad to have this opportunity to make peace. Is that about right?"

"That's about it, yeah," Zabra said, her face settling into a satisfied smile.

"Draka," Mak said, looking up at me. "How long would it take you to reach Kesra? Right now?"

"About fifteen minutes."

Zabra's smile froze on her face.

"If you wanted to bring her back here, how long would that take?"

"Half an hour there and back. Then it would take me a minute to get her out if I went through the front door and past the mural with all the dogs. Or I could go through the eastern window with the white roses. Then it would only take thirty heartbeats, but getting Kesra out that way would be much less pleasant for her." I looked at Zabra. "You know how thickly the rose bushes cover that window. Like a damn blackberry bramble. The shutters don't even open all the way anymore."

"You're bluffing." Zabra's face was confident, but her voice wasn't. The fact that she said anything at all in response told me that I'd gotten to her.

"Am I?" I wondered if I should ask Mak to take out the necklace I'd stolen from Kesra. She was currently wearing it around her neck. "Has your sister not been passing on my messages properly? I told you both that I could find her anywhere. Did you think that taking her to some villa a few miles south of the city would be enough to hide her from me?"

Zabra's face twitched. It was just a heartbeat of uncertainty, but Mak seized on it immediately. "You see? We do have something to threaten you with. And Draka can cover those few miles much faster than any rider you might send out. So, do you want to have a serious talk, or shall we see who is better at making good on their threats?"

Zabra scowled, just a little, and before I caught myself, I thought that it was a terribly sad thing to see on such a face. "Very well. Tell me what you want, and I'll explain why it's impossible. I suppose you'll want to start with my head and work your way down from there?"

"No," Mak said. "What *I* want is to be alone with you in a room for a few days, with some shackles, a knife, and a shelf full of healing potions. *That's* the starting point."

"Well, that's a little ambitious, don't you think? How about I offer you an apology and a promise not to destroy everything you love so long as you all behave, and we leave it at that?"

Zabra's smile was gone, but she still radiated confidence, and I didn't like it. She couldn't possibly think that her men could keep me from her if I decided I'd heard enough, so what was her game? She couldn't still think that we were bluffing, could she? Did she think that we'd back down? If she did, she was about to be sorely disappointed.

I was about to speak, but Mak beat me to it. "Tarkarran talked, you know," she mused, changing the subject. "He talked a lot. Didn't care much about protecting you, but once we threatened to bring in Kesra, we could barely shut him up. About you, about your businesses, your . . . I hesitate to call them friends, but acquaintances."

Zabra scoffed. "That's no surprise. As besotted as he was with me a few years ago, the man had preferences that became clear once Kesra got a little older. And I've made sure that he never touched her. I can only assume that he still kept his hope burning. What's your point?"

"My point, you insufferable bitch, is, why not? We know where your money comes from. We know who your most valuable people are. Why not just start destroying each other, and see who suffers more? You may not think much of us, but I *hate* you. Draka *hates* you. You may think that you have the upper hand, but Draka, in case you forget, despite her presence, is a *dragon*. Are you sure that you know how much we're willing to sacrifice for the sake of vengeance? To know that you'll never hurt anyone else? To tear down everything you've built? How well do you really know us?"

I could see Zabra's mouth move, just a little, like she was about to speak. But she hesitated. She studied Mak for a few seconds then looked at me, then back at Mak, and when she spoke her tone was surprised, intrigued, almost respectful. "You truly want that! You want a *war*! You want everything to burn, to see how much you can hurt me before you have nothing left!" She laughed. She actually *laughed*, the same musical sound that I'd heard in that prison of hers.

"Mercies be kind to us all. Tark fucked you right up, didn't he? But, no, Lady Drakonum. We will not be doing that. Not unless you truly force my hand. And I can't help but notice that the dragon in question doesn't seem nearly so excited about the idea."

She looked at me instead. "So, tell me, my dear Draka. What will it take—"

I only had a moment's warning. A glimmer in the corner of my eye. A light in the second-story window of a building to the south overlooking the brickyard. A glimmer of gold.

I grabbed Mak and threw her in the direction of the south wall, getting out of the path of the arrow in the same movement. My roar of "Archer!" was nearly drowned out by the outraged yells of Zabra's guards, who all lowered their spears toward me the moment I moved. The arrow *thuk'ed* into the ground just past where I'd been, but the window shone gold. The next one was almost on its way.

There was a whisper in the air above us, and the golden light in the window shuddered and flickered. A streak of gold flew wide, nowhere close to us, and the light in the window disappeared.

Zabra was yelling furiously as her guards tried to bundle her away, demanding that everyone just "Stop! Stand down, you shits! That's not one of ours! Draka, that's *not* one of ours!" I barely heard her over the sound of blood in my ears, red rage creeping into my vision. I leapt the short distance to Mak, preparing to get out, fighting to control myself as Instinct clawed at my mind and tried to take full control and spit and rip and tear until there was nothing but blood and steaming meat left of the treacherous bitch and her men. I was facing a wall of spears, but Instinct didn't care. Let them try to stand before me!

Mak was getting to her feet, staying crouched and moving toward the wall, but I swept her up in one arm. "Zabra," I hissed, turning to look the Night Blossom in the eyes. For the first time, a moment I knew that I would treasure, I saw actual fear there. Hot fury and cold malice fought for control inside me. "I told you what would happen." I grabbed Kesra's necklace, which dangled from Mak's neck. With a sharp jerk I snapped the old leather cord, and I threw it to Zabra. She caught it and looked at it mutely.

"Here," I said. "Something for you to remember your sister by."

I had barely leaped into the air when I heard a desperate wail of "Wait!" from her. I risked pausing in my ascent for a second, looking down, and I saw that she had pushed past her guards, moving toward me with her arms out, open and unprotected. The necklace dangled from her hand. "Fine! Here I am! Come back!"

I glanced toward the window where the archer had been. Still nothing.

Deep inside I was relieved. Zabra had been right. I didn't want a war. If I'd gone after Kesra, a war was exactly what I would have started, and there would have been blood shed on both sides. Zabra had said that she had people ready to go tonight, to kill people I didn't know, but who were important to the members of my family, and I believed her.

Now I had a way out. I didn't have to start something that wouldn't stop until one side was wiped out, and I didn't have to hurt an innocent woman. And despite that, despite my relief, I was still tempted to start a war right then and there. To finally get what I'd wanted for months, to drop down and tear into Zabra where she stood, and accept whatever it cost to raze everything she'd built to the ground.

It was her desperation that held me back. The way she offered herself up to me to protect her sister, and the way she held her guards back, vehemently denying that the archer was doing her bidding. But even if this had been in no way her fault, the balance of power in this conversation had changed. She had shown weakness, and I was going to exploit it mercilessly.

Rib and Pot, Tam and Val, and Barro all arrived nearly simultaneously from different directions, weapons ready. They were just in time to see me land heavily in the dust, only feet from Zabra. I set Mak down, murmuring "*Get on my back*" to her in Tekereteki. It was hard to speak. I was shaking with pent up fury and the desire to destroy, no matter the cost to those around me. "Cancel your orders," I hissed at Zabra, putting my face inches from hers. I could taste my own venom, and while she stood tall and proud, she was still forced to blink furiously as some spittle got in one of her eyes. "Then go to Her Grace's Favor. Alone. If you're not there in half an hour, you will never see your sister in one piece again."

She nodded once, her sneers and superior smiles replaced with a look of resignation.

I turned to my humans. "We're done here. Get back to the inn." Then, switching to Tekereteki, I called out, "*Little dragon, if you are out there, feel free to follow this one and make sure she does what she was told.*"

Keeping my eyes on Zabra and her men, I couldn't see Mak's expression on my back. But her voice was ice and venom when she said, "I look forward to your company, Lady Tespril." Then she leaned forward and clamped down around my neck, ready to go.

Before we left, my shadow surged forward, moving the wrong way in the torchlight. It carried with it all my boiling anger. I couldn't have held it back even if I wanted to. I let it envelop the woman before me, taking a dark delight in the way her eyes went wide before the darkness swallowed her, and only then did I take off.

It was at least twenty minutes by foot from the brickyard to the inn. Making sure that everyone got away unmolested, then flying by a roundabout path to the garden and making our way to the inn took the same amount of time. Mak and I arrived at the inn only minutes before the others.

The last few minutes until the half-hour deadline I'd given Zabra were spent in tense silence. I wondered how many plots, schemes, and contingency plans she'd manage to set in motion in that half hour, and if I'd have to force myself to make good on my threat. I'd made a real mess for myself, because this was one threat that I couldn't back down from. I *had* to act on it, and I really, really didn't want to.

For all that Instinct raged, I couldn't bring myself to believe that Kesra was anything but a victim of circumstance. I desperately hoped that Zabra would show up, but at the same time it seemed she'd given in too easily, and I was suspicious. If I were her, I'd send my fastest rider to get Kesra out of that villa. It'd be futile; even a fast horse would take too long to get there. Even with a half hour head start they couldn't beat me, but that was what I would do in her position. Then I'd gather everyone I could to mount an attack on the inn, forcing the dragon to stay and defend everyone she held dear.

But Zabra didn't do that. I couldn't tell how close she cut it. Time-keeping wasn't an exact thing, at least not without the right enchanted tools, which we lacked. Perhaps my reluctance to take one more step toward becoming a monster bought her an extra minute or two. She came alone. When Mak led her into the cellar, Zabra was dusty and out of breath, her face streaked with sweat. She stopped on the last step of the stairs, and looked around the room.

Her composure was gone, replaced with a mask of impotent anger as she looked at me. Her voice quavered as she spoke. "Do what you will. But touch my sister, and all you love will burn. No matter what happens to me, I've made sure of that. Are we clear?"

"Yeah, we're clear."

"Good. Well, here I am. Alone. Let's get this over with."

CHAPTER TWENTY-NINE

Lady Tespril

Zabra stood on the last step of the stairs, straight-backed and defiant. The effect was spoiled a little for me by the fear she hid so well but which still wafted off her, and for the others when Herald materialized out of the shadows behind her and kicked her in the back, spilling her onto the stone floor.

The tension snapped. Zabra didn't even have time to get to her hands and knees. Her earlier threat of her men retaliating meant nothing; Mak and Herald kicked the *shit* out of her, to the point where I wondered if they intended to just kill her there and then.

After two minutes there was only me left watching them, and I didn't trust myself to join in. Ardek and Pot had been dragged away when they tried to intervene, the others going with them. They couldn't stomach it anymore.

When my sisters were done, when they'd left the author of their suffering within an inch of her life, they poured a healing potion between her split lips. They bound and gagged her, and left her on the floor of the same unused room where we'd kept Simdal, and later Tark in his barrel.

"Five days." Mak broke the silence as the three of us sat in the cellar. Blood spattered the floor. Her voice was thick, the words choked. She was staring at her hands still smeared with red. They were trembling. "We shouldn't kill her. I want to. I want to, *so much*. I want to keep beating her until she's *meat*. But we *shouldn't*. I believe her when she says that her people will want to avenge her, and as much as I sometimes feel like just letting everything *burn* . . . But we can keep her for five days. Five days of hell, one for every day that she held us."

"And then?" Herald asked. Once the rage had left her she'd become emotionally flat. Empty. She sat looking at her hands as she slowly clenched and unclenched them. She'd split two of her knuckles and had refused to let Mak heal them, pulling back when she'd tried.

"Then we let her go. With . . . I don't know. Whatever threats seem reasonable. Enforceable. Maybe Draka can break her? I'm honestly too focused on keeping myself from going back in there to think of anything."

"Really?"

"I never thought I could exhaust myself beating someone and regret that I can't continue, but . . . yeah."

"And if we cannot control her?"

"Then . . ." Mak rubbed her face and sighed. "Then we'll have to find a way to strike first, before word gets out that she's dead. And we pray to the Mercies that we don't lose too much."

"Oh." Herald kept looking at her hands, and whispered, "I don't think I can do this."

Mak and I both looked at her with concern. When Herald broke out the contractions, we listened.

"Not like this," she continued. "I thought—I imagined that hurting her the way I was hurt would be . . . cathartic, I suppose. That it would make me feel better. But I just feel dirty. Hollow. Give me a dagger and I'll drive it into her heart for what she's done, but this?" She waved helplessly toward the door to the corridor, where we'd left Zabra on the cold stone floor. "I can't."

We both closed in on her, Mak wrapping her arms around her sister and me covering them both with my wings.

"You don't have to," I said into the little cocoon I'd made. "You don't have to touch her, or even see her again, if you don't want to. But Mak needs this. Right, Mak?"

"Yeah."

"Is that all right, Herald?"

She closed her eyes and gave a small, sharp nod, then abruptly shifted, fading into the darkness. When she answered, her voice was distant and hollow. "Do whatever you need to. She deserves so much worse. I just can't be there."

"That's okay, sweet sister," Mak murmured, her arms wrapped around nothing. "You don't have to do anything."

After a while Herald faded back in. "That is really hard to keep up with someone holding me," she said, with a little sniffle of laughter. "And I am being so dramatic. Sorry. Maybe I should have just shot her when I had the chance."

"Why didn't you?" I asked.

"It didn't feel right. The bitch and her guards were all as shocked as you were. And they did not attack you after, so I wanted to keep an arrow ready and an eye on that window, in case the archer popped back up."

"I think you got the bastard, though."

"Yeah!" she agreed with a feral grin. "I did. But you never know how quickly someone can recover. I could not risk it."

"Can I fix these now?" Mak asked gently, pulling back and taking Herald's hands in her own.

"Leave them."

"Are you sure?"

"Yeah."

"Okay. But you have to promise me to keep them clean. If I see them getting swollen or anything, I'll deal with it, whether you want me to or not."

"I will."

Herald was still being dramatic, but I understood where she was coming from. Killing someone and hurting them for its own sake are very different things. She clearly felt guilty about it, and not letting Mak heal her hands was some kind of self-flagellation. But like Mak, I wasn't going to interfere as long as it was only painful. She was a big girl. If this was how she wanted to deal with her feelings, fine. I still gave her fifty-fifty odds of going to Mak or Kira for help within a day or two, once she'd processed the night's events.

Ardek came down soon thereafter and told us what I'd already suspected. There were people, a lot more people, and rougher looking than normal skulking outside the inn. He'd pulled his younger minions back inside, just in case. Two guests had come and gone unmolested, but none of our people were going farther than a few steps out the door. We were, effectively, under siege.

We hadn't been actively trying to hide anything from Kira, but I'd asked everyone who'd seen Zabra come in not to mention her to anyone else. Kira still figured out pretty quickly that something was going on. She came to me in my little nest in the strongroom the next morning.

"*Who are you keeping locked up in the other room?*" she asked me bluntly as she stood in the doorway.

"*What makes you think there's anyone there?*"

"*The meeting last night. Someone banging on the door in the small hours. Herald's hands. Mak bringing some drink down here.*" She rolled her eyes. "*Blood on the floor. A door that's always open is locked. I'm not a fool, Draka.*"

"*No, you're not,*" I sighed. "*It's Zabra.*"

"*Who?*"

"*The Night Blossom.*"

"*Oh.*" She blanched. "*Her? What are you . . . ?*"

"*She tortured my sisters, and now we have her. Mak has some very justified anger to take out on the woman. I'm going to let her.*"

"*Oh.*" She looked away from me. I told myself that she wasn't judging us, that she was just being her soft, kind self. But I wasn't confident. Conscience told me that perhaps she *should* be judging us, and I wasn't sure that I disagreed. Perhaps we should just slit Zabra's throat and deal with the fallout. Perhaps that was the smart move. I didn't think that she'd hated us before last night. Now, or in a few days . . . who could know?

"Is that why there's half a dozen dirty children hanging around the back of the common room?" Kira asked, facing me again.

"Yeah. Some of Zabra's people are out there. Ardek didn't want to take any chances."

"Can I see her?"

"Why?"

"Do you intend to let her die?"

"No."

"Then I would like to see her. Please."

I looked into her earnest eyes, and saw only worry there.

"Fine. Mak is in the . . . feels like the kitchen. Get the key from her."

Kira left. A little later I felt Mak moving to some other part of the building. I wasn't sure what was there. An office perhaps, since Mak and occasionally Herald spent a lot of time there.

When Kira came back with the key and a lantern, I was waiting outside the door to the improvised cell. We'd decided that no one should be allowed in the room with Zabra alone. We weren't sure how it worked, but she definitely had something about her that made people want to agree with and help her. Ardek and Pot were banned from interacting with her entirely after how they'd acted while Herald and Mak were beating her, trying to step in and stop the sisters. And while Herald and Mak seemed immune, I knew for a fact that I was not, though I hadn't had any trouble resisting whatever it was.

Kira looked to me for permission and I nodded. The lock opened with a rasping *tchunk*. Inside, Zabra was slumped in a back corner, looking like she'd just woken up. Magical healing took a lot out of you, after all. She blinked in the light, but gave us a defiant look that I didn't like at all. I quickly wrapped her up in shadow and considered just setting them there, keeping her in the dark until it was time to let her go, but that might make the others lose track of her for all I knew. I hadn't really experimented with setting shadows on people since I'd first messed with Herald.

"This is Kira," I told her, hearing her whine as I squeezed the shadows a little to make sure that I had her full attention. "She's a kind soul who wants to take a look at you, to make sure that you're not dying on us. You will cooperate with her, and not try anything stupid, or I'll do something terrible to you. Understand?"

I released the shadows, and Zabra slumped forward from where she'd been sitting rigid against the stone wall. She looked up at me, the defiance replaced by just a little bit of undisguised fear, and nodded.

"Good."

"Was that necessary?" Kira asked in her provincial Tekereteki, almost reproachfully. *"Look at her!"*

I did. What I could see was a mess of bruises. Blood from where split skin had barely healed crusted her face and stained her torn clothes. She looked tired. Not broken; there was still strength in her. But she was clearly in pain, the potion being either too slow-acting or not enough to heal her fully in the hours since it'd been given to her.

Was it really necessary to add magical fear on top of that?

"*Yes,*" I decided. "*With her it's necessary. I don't know what tricks she has, but she makes people loyal to her. I don't want her trying anything.*"

"*I want to untie her and remove her gag while I treat her. Can I do that?*"

I considered it. With me there it was unlikely that Zabra could hurt my little healer, especially in the state she was in. "*Go ahead,*" I told Kira, and settled back.

Kira put the lantern down close to me, and approached. "Name Bekiratag," she said to Zabra in her beginner's Karakani, putting a hand on her own chest. "Healer. Help pain, injuries. Yes?"

Zabra looked at her, then nodded.

"Turn," Kira said, making a circling gesture. "I take out . . . in mouth."

Zabra complied. Kira carefully untied the ribbon keeping the gag in, then had the other woman turn back around. She put a gentle finger on each lip near where they'd split, pushing healing, painkilling magic into them before reaching in and removing the sodden wad of cloth blocking Zabra's mouth and keeping her jaw open.

"Ah!" Zabra croaked, slowly working her jaw up and down. "Thank you."

Kira spent some time going over the bruises around Zabra's eyes and on her cheeks and neck. Then she put both hands on either side of her nose, whispered "Sorry," and with a surprisingly savage jerk straightened what the potion had begun to heal crooked. Zabra yelped and tried to pull away, but Kira simply followed her back to the wall, pushing healing in all the time. "Sorry," she repeated, though her tone was business-like. "Needed. Sorry."

"Mercies, girl," Zabra hissed, though I was sure the pain must already be gone. "Thank you, but some warning would be nice."

Kira didn't show if she'd understood or not. "Need that off," she said, gesturing to Zabra's ruined silk body wrap.

Zabra looked at me. "Your choice," I told her. "I'd probably let her heal me, in your position. Might be your last chance to be free of pain."

Whatever she saw in my eyes, she turned back to Kira. "Help, please?"

Kira untied her arms, then helped her with the wrap. The skin around her undergarments was a mess of purples, greens, and yellows, bruises of various sizes and stages of healing. The area around her lower ribcage was almost black in places, and I wondered how many of her ribs had been broken. Maybe that was why she was still such a mess; maybe the potions prioritized the worst injuries. Mak was small, but with my strength backing her, she kicked like a mule and punched like a prize fighter. I'd be surprised if they hadn't left Zabra with all kinds of internal bleeding.

Kira gave me a . . . not a dirty look, but a decidedly unhappy one, and got to work. "*Can you translate for me?*" she asked me after a while.

"Sure." I was curious what she might have to say.

"Are you the Night Blossom?" she asked Zabra, and I translated.

"That's what they call me, yeah. The Night Blossom."

"Why were you selling slaves to the Silver Spurs? Or to Tekeretek?"

"I won't admit to having anything to do with that," she scoffed, then cringed slightly under my unimpressed gaze. "That was all Tarkarran's business. The whole damn operation. I could have stopped him, I suppose, but he insisted, and he had too much leverage."

"You expect me to believe that?" I snorted, but Kira looked at me.

"Translate, please," she said.

I did, with a tone appropriate to just what I thought of Zabra's claim of relative innocence.

"If it wasn't your business," Kira asked while working on her ribs, *"why did you do what you did to Draka, to Makanna, and Herald?"*

"I was angry. Fucking furious, really. Perhaps I overreacted. They'd killed some of my best men. Some of those guys had been with me for years. And, yes, losing a whole shipment was a lot of money I'll never see." She looked at me. "And then, there was you. I didn't believe Tark at first. I thought he'd finally lost it. But then Hardal came back, and he told me the same thing as Tark. A dragon. Small, but an actual, live dragon on Mallin, one that spoke and worked together with people." She looked at me desperately. "I swear that I never intended to harm you. I let greed and childish fantasies run away with me, but I truly wanted to learn about you. Get to know you, even."

"Congratulations," I told her drily. "You have a perfect opportunity to get to know me right now. Let me tell you about myself. I love silver and gold and other pretty things, and my friends. And I destroy anything that threatens the things I love."

"Draka," Kira reminded me, and I translated what Zabra had said. *"Did you sell the slaves to the Silver Spurs or to someone else in Tekeretek?"* Kira asked once I was done.

"I don't know who those are," Zabra said, and I told her the Tekereteki name. "Oh. Yeah. Tark mentioned them. Someone called Lakatekete, or something like that."

"One of the commanders of the Spurs," Kira commented in an aside to me.

"Not the one you were with?"

"No, that's Sarahem. Lakatekete commands the ships." She turned back to Zabra. *"Did they want anyone in particular?"*

"Tark mentioned that they'd pay extra for anyone with magic advancements, but otherwise he took care of everything."

I was actually starting to feel a little bad for Zabra. Just a little. Part of me was wondering if she'd just been unfortunate, saddled with some bastard she couldn't get rid of who got her into all this. If this was all just a terrible series of unavoidable events that escalated to this point, with me and her and Kira in a small stone room. Perhaps, after Kira finished healing her up, I should talk to Mak.

Just as I finished translating, the door swung open. I'd felt Mak come down shortly after Kira. She'd been waiting outside the room, listening. She chose that moment to step into the room, as though she'd heard me thinking of her. "*You are both aware that she has been lying through her teeth, are you not?*" she asked. "*Every sentence she speaks, she has been trying to hide something.*"

I blinked. Kira sighed and nodded. "*I thought so,*" she said, "*but I hoped not.*"

Zabra scowled up at Mak. "Anything you wish to share with the room?"

"Not at all." She waved a large stoppered bottle. "I thought you might need something more to drink before tonight. And since Kira has apparently been kind enough to remove the gag, you might not spill half of it this time."

"That was hard to avoid, with you pouring it through the damn thing," Zabra replied bitterly.

"Be glad you get anything. I've heard that a person can live for three days with no water. We could try it and see, if you prefer." Mak then turned to me. "*Draka, do you feel affected by her at all?*"

"Yeah," I admitted.

"*I thought so. You felt . . . confused. Even sympathetic, perhaps, before I came in. Should I take over?*"

"*You probably should.*" I looked at Zabra, and said in Karakani, "Try not to undo all of our healer's hard work."

"*That's up to Zabra,*" Mak said. "*And how much she wants to lie to us.*"

Zabra gave me a brittle look as I went to leave. "Sure that you can't stay?" she asked, her eyes flitting between myself and Mak. I didn't answer. And I wasn't the one she should want to stick around, anyway. As long as Mak didn't send *Kira* away, Zabra was relatively safe. Mak didn't want to upset Kira any more than I did. Probably less. But Zabra didn't need to know that.

"*Now,*" Mak said as I closed the door behind me, "*let's figure out how much you* actually *knew about 'Tark's' slaving.*"

CHAPTER THIRTY

Kesra

S he told you part of the truth, as far as I can tell," Mak told me an hour later. "She knew pretty much everything that was going on, but it really was Tarkarran's operation, from beginning to end. She supplied the resources, but he ran it. And I don't think she *knew* that the Spurs were Tekereteki, but she probably suspected it. Of course, I have no idea just how good of a liar she is. If she can defeat my own ability to read intentions . . ." she shrugged. "I can't detect lies directly. I can only tell if someone is trying to deceive me."

"Did you learn anything else?"

"She was surprisingly willing to talk about her advancements, in general terms. I might have been able to get some details out of her if I'd been willing to start breaking things, but doing that in front of Kira . . ." She scowled. "Anyway, nothing surprising. She's a bit like Ardek, but much stronger. Makes people like her and want her to like them. I can only assume that's why her people are so loyal. Some minor fighting and health related advancements, too, but that's her major.

"Besides that, she's very protective of her sister, but we already knew that. It's the only reason she's here, right? At one point I offered to hand her over to the justices if she'd confess to her crimes, and she outright told me that she won't do anything that might lead to Kesra ending up destitute."

"That makes sense. However awful a person she is, those two love each other. Kesra was ready to die before she gave me anything that might hurt her sister, and Zabra's the same. If Zabra had a massive fine against her, I have no doubt Kesra would rather pay it than let her be indentured."

Mak frowned. "I think everything Zabra's become began with protecting her sister. I hate having anything in common with the woman, but I can understand that, at least."

"How's Kira doing?"

"Upset, of course. She's thankful that I never actually touched the woman in front of her, but I can't hold back much longer and she knows it." She looked away, her mouth quirking up as she said, "Kira may have gotten me to promise to bring her down once I'm done. You know how she is. It's hard to deny her anything when she's clearly hurting."

"It's the way she looks at you, right? Like she blames herself."

"Right! I used to second-guess myself about her. Wondering if maybe she lied about her advancements. But she's just so . . . docile, most of the time. If she had the advancements to deceive me, I'd expect her to have tried something by now. I honestly think that she's just a good person, and she so rarely asks for anything that when she does it's impossible to deny her."

"Yeah, I know what you mean." I stayed silent for a while, then switched to Tekereteki and asked, *"Are you sure about letting her go?"*

"If possible, as much as I hate the idea. If we could make sure that none of her people would suddenly stab Herald in the market . . . but, no. And there are her people outside. No telling what they will do if she does not come out. We need to try to extract something binding from her, though. If we cannot be sure that she will leave us alone and stay on the right side of the law once we release her . . . Do you think that you can do to her what you did to Jekrie?"

"Let us see, shall we?"

Zabra's cell was dark. Kira must have taken the lantern with her. Zabra was back in the corner, dressed and bound and gagged again, and she looked up, trying to look at us in the infinitesimal light that came in through the open door before Mak closed it behind us, plunging the room into absolute darkness.

"Haga?" she mumbled through the ball of cloth filling her mouth. I took the few steps needed to bring my face close to hers, letting her feel my presence before I spoke.

"This will not be a conversation. I don't intend to ask you any questions, so you don't need to be able to speak. What I need from you is to think. To understand what I am, and what I can do, and what that means for you. Who you've made an enemy of."

The smell of fear grew stronger, even before I wrapped her in shadows. I left her like that as I continued. "We still haven't decided what to do with you. Slit your throat, drop you five thousand feet into the sea, release you once we feel that the score is even . . . I don't know. Perhaps we'll simply decide not to heal you one day, and let your busted insides do the rest. There's a lot of factors, you know? But if we do decide that you're not worth killing, understand this: There is nowhere I can't go. No lock or guard that can keep me out. And there is no way to hide from me, not for long. Ask your sister, if you see her again. So if we do decide to let you live, you will be doing so on sufferance, until and unless you become a problem again."

I released my shadows, and Zabra slumped forward, her face contorted with fear and anger as she gasped for breath.

"Think about that," I told her, and left. Mak looked as though she considered staying, but followed me.

The next morning I went to talk to Zabra again, to try to instill in her just how careful she should be not to provoke me if we should happen to let her live.

Mak must have returned, because Zabra had fresh bruises, half healed, and I could smell blood that had spattered the walls and floor. I wrapped her in shadow and monologued at her, though this time I found myself almost using her for therapy. I told her just how much it had hurt that they had used Herald to turn Mak against me, and how angry I was about the damage that had done to Mak's and my relationship. I told her how I wished that everything could just go back to the way it had been before, when things had been simple. But that was impossible now, and it was all her fault.

"At some point," I told her after I'd released her from my shadows, "I think I'm going to take off that gag, and I'm going to let you make your case as to why we should let you live. And I want you to think very carefully about what to say, because I promise that I'll listen."

I wasn't going to tell her that we were most likely going to release her anyway. I wanted her to think. I didn't want her zoning out and just letting time pass. The way I saw it, the more she was aware of her situation, the more she thought about what had brought her there, the better. I didn't know if we could reform her or anything, but I wanted her scared enough to either give us an excuse to end her, or for her to never dare touch us again.

Or break her. She was tough. Most people would have broken several times over already. But we had time, and if I could break her, that would be fine, too.

I spent much of that day talking to the others about how to handle the meeting with the lady justice Sempralia the next day. The damn archer was probably still out there. Herald wasn't arrogant enough to assume that her one shot had killed the bastard, not in a world with magical healing and potions. The meeting place was by the coast south of the city, with the closest tree being hundreds of feet away, but it paid to keep them in mind.

Mostly our conclusions came down to the fact that we didn't know what she wanted. I would be polite, promise not to damage the city and its law-abiding citizens, and be open to any offers. And I was not to lie. They were very clear about that. Better to say that I didn't want to answer than to lie or be evasive. And I should probably not admit that we were keeping the lady Tespril Zabra in our cellar, no matter how guilty we knew, and Sempralia might suspect, she was.

I expected the day to slowly wind down after that. I was having a rather nice conversation with Kira about her life before she gained her healing when Ardek came down, his whole face alight with excitement, like he was expecting a grand show.

"The sister!" he exclaimed. "The Night Blossom's sister is here, and she is in a *state*! Makanna and Herald are bringing her down!"

I saw Kira take a second or two to translate what Ardek had said, and her eyes widened as she whispered, "Oh, no!" She turned to me, speaking quickly. "Please, Draka! Let me see Zabra before her sister does! I did what I could last night, but—"

I interrupted her. "No. I'm not letting you in there alone, and there's no one I trust to accompany you who won't be busy. She gets in people's heads too easily. You can look over Zabra once we're all in there, if it comes to that."

I got up and herded them into the main cellar. In the warm glow of two light-stones I found that Herald and Mak were there already, sitting on the bench, one on each side of Kesra. And Kesra was, as Ardek had put it, in a *state*. She had on a simple cinched tunic, riding boots, and a hooded riding cape, and was spattered with mud up to the knees. *It must have rained*, I thought idly as she raised her face from her hands and looked at me with fear and anger.

"You!" she choked out, her voice trembling so hard that she stuttered. "Where—Where is she? Where's my sister?"

"Ardek," I said, ignoring her. "Go upstairs and make sure that we won't be disturbed." He acknowledged me with a nod and disappeared up the stairs as I approached Kesra. I didn't answer her until I was only a few feet away. "Hello, Kesra. What makes you so sure that Zabra is here?"

"Har—Hardal told me! They tried to keep it from me, but he finally told me she came here! I want to see her!"

I wondered why he would have sent his employer's only living relative, as far as I knew, into the arms of her enemies, but that was a question for a different day. "*If* she came here," I said, getting closer, "what makes you think that we've kept her around?"

Horror slowly spread across her face as my implication registered. "No," she whispered. "First Tark, and now . . . Please, no!"

A little bit of shame wormed its way into me at her stricken expression. I was considering what to say when Herald took Kesra's jaw in one hand and turned her head to face her. "Tark? Are you torn up about *Parvion Tarkarran*? What could there possibly be about that animal to grieve?"

Whatever Kesra was feeling in that moment, Herald's snarl had her trying to get off the bench and away, but Mak's hand on her shoulder kept her down.

"Go on," I said, and Kesra's eyes turned to me. "Explain why we should feel any sympathy for your loss."

Fear and shock compelled her to answer. "He—He saved us. He got us out of the . . ."

"The brothel?" Mak completed for her.

"That, yes. He got us out, helped Zabra buy her first business, backed us for years. He's been so selfless, so—"

Mak cut her off with a barking laugh. "Selfless? You think—?" I expected her to go on and explain just what kind of picture Zabra had painted of the man, but then Herald cut *her* off.

"*Kind*?" Herald's hiss cut through the room. Mak went silent, and I saw Kesra's breath catch as Herald rose to stand in front of her, teeth bared and jerkily undoing the sash cinching her tunic. "I'll show you how *kind* your *savior* was to me!"

Even magical healing was not perfect. Whether healed naturally, through magic like Mak's and Kira's or through potions, wounds still left scars. I'd seen that firsthand with Garal on one of my first days on Mallin, and many times since with my friends. The scars faded with time, of course, but when Herald angrily tore her tunic over her head and threw it to the floor, hers still stood out starkly. Dozens of dark lines marred her brown skin. Long and short, alone or in clusters, they showed every cut and stab that had been inflicted on her at Tark's hands to force Mak's cooperation. I'd seen them before, many times, but it didn't matter. Even his death did nothing to soothe the rage I felt at the man every single time I saw them.

Grabbing a lightstone from where it sat on the floor, Herald changed it to a bright, nearly natural light, then went back to where Kesra sat stunned on the bench.

"Here." Before Kesra had a chance to flinch, Herald had a fist bunched in her hair. Kesra yelped in protest, her hands going to Herald's wrist, but she didn't stand a chance. "Take a good look. When I met your precious Tark, this was all smooth skin. It took him four days to give me these, or so they tell me. It took so many health potions to keep me alive that I don't remember much, besides the pain and the fear. So *excuse me*"—she released Kesra's hair with a jerk into the shelves behind her—"if I don't feel bad for your *loss*!"

That was enough for me. "Herald!" I said sharply, putting an arm around her waist and gently pulling her back, just in case she wasn't quite finished. "She is either willfully blind or horribly naive, but I don't think she's involved in . . . anything, really. Gods know you deserve to be angry, but she's not the right target."

"No, she is not, is she?" Herald fumed, not resisting me. "How about we take her to the one who is?" She shared a look with Mak that I couldn't decipher, and Mak nodded.

"Are you two keeping secrets from me?" I asked in Tekereteki.

"Not really," Mak answered. *"It was a spur of the moment idea. And it is nothing you will not approve of. Think of it as a surprise."*

Kesra rubbed her head, looking between us as we spoke in a language she couldn't understand, then replied to the part she could. "So you do have her? You'll take me to her?"

"I suppose so," I said. "In a moment. Mak, take Kira, and let her have a look at our guest. Let me know when you're done."

Kesra spent the ten-minute wait anxiously pleading with Herald and me to take her to her sister *now*, to tell her what was going on and why we were holding her, or to just let her go. She offered us money, favors, and to take her sister's place. I barely answered. Herald was completely silent. She had thrown her tunic back on and curled up against me, and I was focused on soothing the anger that Kesra's ignorance had awoken in her.

I hadn't used to think of Herald as an angry or naturally violent person, but that had been changing during the past month or so. She'd always found it easy to get excited in combat, but lately it had seemed like fighting and killing was becoming her preferred solution to a lot of problems, whether she acted on it or not. I'd been calling her my little dragon as an endearment, but she was starting to really live up to the epithet.

I wondered, again, how much, if any, of that was my doing.

Finally Kesra resorted to threats. Or perhaps a warning. "Hardal is out there, with a lot of Zabra's men," she said. "He said that if I don't come out soon and tell him that Zabra is alive, they're burning this place down with everyone in it."

That made me take notice. It wouldn't be easy, if Mak was right about the warding enchantments on the place, but I'd rather not see it tested. If they were determined enough . . .

I told Kesra to be patient.

A minute later Kira came back. *"She is . . . presentable. I've healed most of what Makanna inflicted upon her,"* she told me, her voice more judgmental than I could remember ever hearing from her.

"What did she say?" Kesra asked almost immediately. "Can I see Zabra now?"

"Yes, fine," I said, and Herald reluctantly got up as I shifted around beneath her. "This way."

I showed her into the improvised cell, and when she saw her sister kneeling on the floor, bound and gagged, her clothes a ripped and bloodstained mess, she fell to her knees and burst into tears. Zabra looked at us accusingly, but she couldn't hide the worry in her eyes.

"Zabra! Oh, Zabra, what have they done to you?" Kesra crawled forward and carefully embraced her sister, who made soothing noises through her gag. "Can I at least talk to her?" Kesra spat, turning and somehow mustering up an angry glare to fix on me.

"Take her gag out, if you want." The words were barely out of my mouth before Kesra was working on the knot behind her sister's head.

"Kes," Zabra coughed as the wad of cloth came out. "I'm sorry. I couldn't . . . What are you doing here? What possessed you—"

"What are *you* doing here?! What?" Kesra shot back angrily, switching to Barlean all of a sudden and pushing her sister back by the shoulders. For a moment I thought I saw Kesra's arm twitch and Zabra flinch back from her, with something like a flash of fear. It was there and gone again so fast that I decided I must have imagined it. "Do you know how worried I've been, do you? How scared? What could have possessed *you*—?"

"I'm sorry, I am! They were going to hurt you! I couldn't—I *couldn't* let them. I had to do something, I had to!"

"Very touching. Very," Mak said in passable Barlean while grabbing Kesra under the arms and bodily hauling her back, leaving her with Herald as she protested. She switched back to Karakani, probably for Herald's benefit. "But let's all of us have a conversation. Together."

"Why are you putting my sister through this?" Zabra asked bitterly. "It's not enough for you to . . ." She glanced at her sister and clearly changed what she'd been about to say. ". . . to keep me here?"

"Your sister came here on her own. She wanted to see you." Mak turned to Herald, giving her another of those looks I couldn't read. "Hold her there, please."

"What?" Kesra said, just as Herald wrapped her arms around the much shorter woman. I wondered just what was going on. Then it became clear, and I wasn't sure if I should be impressed or horrified.

"I want your full attention, Zabra," Mak said. She took a small pouch from beside the door where she'd left it when we came in, squatting in front of the prisoner. From the pouch she carefully took out a potion bottle, which she placed on the floor between them. Zabra's eyes went wide as Mak continued, "I'm going to make you an offer. Your cooperation—"

"No. Please!" Zabra whispered.

"—in exchange for that potion."

"What is this?" Kesra asked, looking from Zabra to me, then trying to look up at Herald, who had her eyes firmly fixed on Zabra.

"Please." For the first time I saw tears in Zabra's eyes. "Ask me for anything. Anything at all. Just don't do this."

"Anything?" Mak asked, a dangerous edge to her voice as she produced a long, thin dagger from her belt.

"Anything!"

"Then tell your sister why you're so fucking terrified of a simple healing potion!"

"I . . ."

Mak turned to look at Kesra, then stood, testing the point of the dagger. Kesra's eyes went wide and she squirmed in Herald's grip. "No! Please! I don't know why you're doing this, but I haven't—Hardal will—!"

"*Draka*," Mak said in Tekereteki as Kesra begged, and Zabra sat mute with wild-eyed indecision. "*We are not going to hurt the girl. But if her sister does not break in the next few seconds, could you blind her with your shadows?*"

"*Yeah, sure.*" I hadn't wanted to intervene, but using Kesra like Herald had been used? That was too much. Too far. I couldn't let my sisters do that to her, or to themselves. I'd fought too hard to not let myself become a monster to let them slip down that path instead. Mak's words, letting me know that it was all theater, was an enormous relief.

It was damned effective, though.

CHAPTER THIRTY-ONE

Zabra

'm sorry!" The words tore out of Zabra's throat with panic and desperation. "Please! Yes, it was me, okay? I told Tarkarran to make you talk! I told him to use your sister when you wouldn't cooperate! I didn't know exactly what he'd do, but I had a good idea. The man was ruthless. A monster. That's why I picked him! Please! Just—You wanted me to tell Kes about the bottle?"

She was getting truly desperate when Mak didn't put the dagger away, speaking quickly as her eyes flicked from Mak to me to Herald and back around, finally landing on her sister. "Kes, listen, baby, the bottle? It's an old trick used for interrogation, okay? You offer someone a healing potion in exchange for doing what you want, telling you what you want to know, whatever, right? And then you hurt them until they take the deal. Then you do it again the next day, and the next. And we had both of these women—You know Tark's house on Cloud Street? The one that we haven't been to in a while? We had them locked up there, both of them, and Makanna only gave us horse shit, so . . ."

"Go on," Mak said calmly, not taking her eyes from Kesra as she placed the point of her dagger just above the younger sister's belly button.

Kesra stood absolutely still, her eyes locked on Mak's.

"So Tark killed her sister in front of her. Not really, but . . . gut wounds. Painful, can take hours to kill if you do it right. And it worked. After two days we only had to show her a bottle and she'd do anything we wanted, not that it stopped Tark. Makanna, please. Lady Drakonum. Is that enough? Is that what you wanted to hear?"

I should have left before Mak and Herald started their little charade. I shouldn't have been in the room to begin with. As it was, my heart was breaking for the two Tesprils. Only the insistent voice of Instinct reminding me of just what Zabra was confessing kept me from removing her bindings and releasing her right then and there.

"*Please*! I've told Hardal not to do anything if I don't walk out of here! You want me dead? Fine. I'll drive that dagger into my own heart if that's what it takes!"

"Zabra, no!" Kesra snapped, but her sister ignored her, her voice breaking as she babbled in her desperation.

"You want favors? Political power? I have some sway over a few people on the council. You want a seat on the council yourself? I might be able to arrange it if you give me a few weeks. You want money? You can have it! Just leave Kesra enough to live on! Ruin me, put me on the street, kill me, anything, just don't hurt Kes!"

"*Can we stop this?*" Herald asked, stone-faced, in Tekereteki. "*I feel sick.*"

"*Yeah,*" Mak agreed, putting away the dagger. "*This was a much better idea in my head.*"

Herald released Kesra, and Mak got out of the way as Herald gave her a little push in Zabra's direction. Kesra stumbled forward, then threw herself forward and wrapped her arms around her sister. "Why, Zabra? You idiot! Why would you—?"

Zabra managed a sobbed "Thank you!" to us before she buried her face in Kesra's neck. "I'm sorry, Kes. I'm sorry. I can't let them hurt you, no matter—I never meant for you to get involved in anything. But I fucked up. I'm sorry! I fucked up!"

"We'll fix this. Don't worry. We'll fix this," Kesra whispered back. Their words were quick and desperate, like they didn't know how much longer they might have together, like every second was precious and they had to make it count.

"*Mercies, forgive us.*" Mak's tone was still low and menacing, completely out of tune with her words. I could see on her face how hard she was fighting not to give her feelings away. "*When I was beating her, she always had this defiance about her, taunting me, challenging me to do my worst. It made it hard to stop, even after she went limp. Now I understand you, Herald. This . . . This just made me feel dirty. I think I need to go to the temple and pray.*"

Herald looked down at the sisters with a forced neutral expression. "*So what do we do now?*"

"*We make sure that this sticks,*" I said gravely. "*And then, when we are sure, we let them go.*"

I grabbed the lightstone and sucked the magic out of it, plunging the room into darkness. "Wait!" Zabra cried, then went silent as I wrapped them both in shadow.

"Remember this," I told them. "Remember that unlike *some*, we show mercy if you cooperate. Now, Kesra, you're going to go out there, and you're going to tell this guy Hardal and the others that your sister is alive and well, yeah? And that she will remain that way as long as they sit back and do nothing. And you'd better convince them, because if they do anything stupid, Zabra dies first. Then you're going to come back in, and we're going to let you have some time together to think and to talk. I want you, Zabra, to tell your sister every horrible thing that you *know* that you should be ashamed of, so she can help you become a decent human being. And then, we are going to talk about reparations."

I released Kesra. Mak dragged her away from her sister and escorted her upstairs, and there were a few tense minutes as we waited for them to return.

I wondered idly if I could stop someone's heart if I squeezed my shadows enough—if I could give them a heart attack or a stroke through sheer terror. I'd find out soon enough, if Zabra's men decided to be heroes.

To my relief and disappointment, Mak returned with Kesra inside of five minutes. "He wants to see me twice a day," Kesra said. "Midday and sunset. Miss it by a minute and they're coming in."

We put Kesra in the cell with her sister and locked the door behind us.

"Kira?" I said with surprise as we stepped into the main cellar. She sat up on the bench where she'd been lying.

"Do they need me?" she asked anxiously.

"No. They're not hurt. Go upstairs and get food and drink for two, would you? Something simple that can be eaten with just your hands. And a bucket, I suppose. Zabra's been in there for a while."

Kira brightened. "Yes! Immediately!"

As she disappeared up the stairs, I turned back to my sisters. "I'll trust your judgment about releasing Zabra, Mak, and I think we should do it as soon as we feel like we have a leash on her, but do either of you feel like you don't want to kill her because it would hurt Kesra?"

They both shook their heads.

"I hesitate to kill her because of the large number of thugs surrounding us," Mak said. "We'll need a plan to strike first if we decide to do away with her. But for Kesra's sake? No."

"Just me, then. And neither of you feel affected by Zabra, either, right?"

"A little bit of pity, perhaps?" Herald suggested. "Not something I expected to feel for that woman, but it is there."

"I still want her heart on a plate," Mak said. "Although, now that you mention it, I suppose that I would feel a little bad about how that would affect her sister. Not enough to spare Zabra, if that was the only reason, but it sure seems like they've been shielding Kesra from things. She obviously loves her sister very much. I can relate, I suppose."

Herald swept her into a side hug and pecked her on the top of the head. "Same to you, little big sister."

I couldn't let the feeling that something was off go, though. I thought about my interactions with Kesra, how my anger had always turned to pity. That might be Conscience's influence. It would probably be a good thing if it was. Then there was the way Zabra had caved so thoroughly and unexpectedly, both just now and in delivering herself into our hands in the first place, when there was a credible, immediate threat to Kesra's life. That might just be sisterly love, but somehow I didn't think so.

"I think," I said, "that Kesra's got some kind of advancement that messes with our heads. Like how Ardek makes people like him, and Zabra makes people loyal to her, I think Kesra makes people want to protect her. I don't know. Maybe I'm overthinking things, but we should question her about it."

Herald looked thoughtful. "It would not be the strangest advancement ever. And with her background . . . I will admit, *actually* hurting her never came to mind when Mak and I planned this. But I doubt that it affects anything, practically, for us right now."

Mak nodded. "Yeah. The important thing now is, do we think that there's any chance of Zabra reforming, or is she too far gone? Too deeply involved to let live?"

"Do we even know the extent of her—let us not say illegal activities," Herald said. "I honestly do not care much if what she does is illegal or not, as long as it is not utterly immoral. How much do we know?"

Mak thought for a moment. "From what Tark told us, and what Ardek and Barro knew and have found out, Zabra has a lot of blood on her hands, but almost all of it is between her and other criminals. Most of her businesses are legal. There are no laws against properly run gambling houses or brothels." She sighed. "Besides, between Tam and myself I can't honestly complain about either. Their overseas trade sounds completely above board except for a few illegal things they've been smuggling. It's infuriating, really. Zabra could have been almost entirely law-abiding and still been wealthy. She might have been . . . I don't know. Inoffensive."

"If not for the slaving and the murders."

"If not for the slaving and the murders," Mak agreed, as the door at the top of the stairs opened and Kira came down with Ardek in tow, carrying a bunch of simple food, two large wooden flagons of something, and a lidded bucket. We paused for a minute or two as they delivered their cargo to our guests, with Kira, of course, making sure to leave the lightstone lit before we shut the door.

"So," I said once we were alone again. "We demand that she gives up on everything we can't tolerate, and we take some serious reparations out of her. I don't know what kinds of fines she'd have to pay if we took her before the law, but I think we'd all be better off avoiding that. Then we hope and pray that a combination of fear and shame keeps her honest, because if not, I'll have to kill both of them."

"What?" Herald exclaimed, while Mak looked at me in silent surprise. "Why both? Why Kesra?"

"You've seen them together. You saw Kesra. She was willing to walk into our hands, alone, to make sure that Zabra was here and alive. What do you think she'll do if we kill her sister? On the off chance that Zabra's people don't attack us when they find out that she's dead, do you think that Kesra won't ruin herself trying to get revenge, whether we deserve it or not? No. If we can't trust Zabra, we can't let either of them live. We'd just be back to square one—to where we started, I mean—with the same problem."

Herald looked sick about it, but she eventually nodded. "All right. But you have to tell Zabra exactly what you just told us. It should help convince her."

I did, an hour or so before sunrise the next morning. It was only me and Mak there; Herald was still feeling sick about the whole situation, and I wasn't going to force her to join us. Kesra was still there, of course. We'd offered her a room, but she'd practically spat in our faces.

Someone—I strongly suspected Kira—had brought them some blankets to make them more comfortable. That was entirely counterproductive, but I didn't comment on it.

I had Mak drag Kesra out into the main cellar so I could talk to Zabra alone. I drowned her in darkness, and then I laid out our position. "Don't tell me that you agree," I told her before I released the suffocating shadows. "I doubt that anything you say right now has any value. I'll be back this afternoon, or perhaps this evening. I'm not sure. I'm a busy lady. But when I come back, you have one task. You need to convince Mak, Herald, and myself that you are not a danger to us, or any other innocent person. If you can do that, you and your sister will leave here alive."

I didn't tell her the obvious alternative. I just relit the lightstone and left, letting Kesra back in.

As the door closed I thought I heard Zabra crying softly and Kesra speaking to her gently, and I had a brief moment of self-loathing that I tamped down on hard.

"You were right," Mak told me, "but not exactly. Kesra's advancement isn't about protecting her, not directly. It's about wanting her to be happy. I guess when you know how much she cares for her sister, that's enough to spill over to not wanting to hurt Zabra."

"You got it out of her that easily?" Kesra had looked fine when I saw her which, under the circumstances, meant no worse than when I'd last seen her.

"Yeah," she said with a shrug. "I didn't need to make any threats or anything, though I think the charisma I'm getting from you helped. I just told her that we don't appreciate our heads being messed with, and that we wanted to know what exactly she was doing. So she talked. She knows the position they're in."

I snorted. "And knowing that leaves a bad taste in my mouth. You're sure that you're not affected at all?"

"Pretty sure. And I have an idea about that, why Herald and I aren't affected."

"Hmm? Do tell."

"It's simple—we're bound to you. And not only in the way that Ardek and Kira are, but truly bound. How could their petty advancements compete with *you*?"

She looked at me with adoration as she spoke. It warmed my heart and reignited a small spark of guilt all at once.

Be good to them, I told myself, and quashed the guilt until only the affection toward her remained. It was all I could do.

It was nice to have all that out of the way. One less thing on my mind. I had an important meeting at sunrise, and I needed to focus.

I'd wanted to skip the meeting, to stay and guard the inn, but my family had insisted I go. Snubbing Sempralia was just too dangerous. So I was going, and I was going alone. The others hadn't liked that idea, but Sempralia had recommended in no uncertain terms that they should distance themselves from me. This was one small way of paying lip service to that. There was also the issue of their safety. I had no doubt that whoever Sempralia had with her would be a damn sight scarier than Hardal and Zabra's other guards, and it wasn't like anyone could expect to remain free for long if they got into a fight with one of the rulers of the city. If this was some kind of trap, or if Sempralia didn't like what I had to say and tried to have me killed then and there, I didn't want the people I cared about to get caught up in a fight they couldn't win.

I left the inn, having promised my sisters not to do, say, or agree to anything foolish. We all knew what that promise was worth, going in blind to a meeting with one of the most powerful people on the island, but I still gave it. I went through an upstairs window; there were a couple of toughs in the yard, and we didn't want to remove the barricade we'd built in front of the cellar door.

I should have been focusing on the upcoming meeting, but my thoughts kept going back to Kesra. To what I'd resolved to do if I had to. It was that same old line, one of the two that I'd hoped I would never cross. The first was eating human flesh, and that line was scuffed as it was. I'd done a lot of biting over the last several months, and I'd swallowed more blood than I was comfortable with. Especially since the urge was so strong, every time I sank my teeth into someone, to just start tearing and swallowing. I didn't *think* that I'd crossed that line fully, but when Instinct took over completely, I couldn't always remember everything afterward.

I *hoped* that I hadn't.

The other line, the one that I had decided to cross if Zabra couldn't be trusted— no, if Zabra couldn't be controlled; she certainly couldn't be trusted—was killing for convenience. No matter how I dressed it up, if I killed Kesra, it would be to make sure that she didn't become a threat. I was sure that she would, and that it would be stupid not to, but there was nothing I could do to convince myself or Conscience that it would not be deliberate and premeditated murder of an innocent woman. It certainly didn't help that Instinct agreed and approved of taking the easy way. *She* would prefer to just kill them both and have it over with. Consequences were for other people.

I flew southwest in a long circle, looking down at the twilit fields, then circled around. I passed over the coast, out above the open sea, and tried to focus on appreciating the slight rosy tint on the northeastern horizon. It'd be fine. For all her flaws, Zabra was an intelligent woman. She'd do the smart thing, and I wouldn't have to follow through on my threats.

I really should stop making threats I didn't want to act on. It was going to come back and bite me in the tail someday, for sure. But when you're a murder-lizard the size of a small horse, making threats is just so damn *effective*.

The meeting place was easy to spot. The short promontory, only a few miles south of the city and incidentally almost directly east of the Tesprils' villa, stuck out like the proverbial sore thumb on the otherwise even stretch of coastline. I passed it at a height of a thousand feet or so, easily visible to anyone with good dark vision. It both let me see that Sempralia and her party had arrived, and gave them a chance to prepare for my arrival before I landed. Smart *and* polite, I figured. There were perhaps two dozen of them, with three standing well apart from the others, closer to the point of the promontory.

One of them shone with magic. I did *not* like that, but since no arrows came flying at me I decided to give them the benefit of the doubt.

I took one last look over my shoulder, toward the horizon, and saw that telltale blaze that heralded the imminent sunrise. I turned back out over the sea, then began my approach. If I timed it right . . .

When I reached the promontory I was gliding slow and level. As soon as my feet were above solid ground I turned my wings up, braking hard, and for one glorious moment I hung suspended in the air as dawn broke behind me. It would have been more effective if the sun rose more than a fraction of a degree, but I happily took what I could get. Entrance made, I settled to the ground, and walked the rest of the distance.

The lady justice Sempralia rose from her seat, and her trio came to meet me halfway. Someone had put out a tent chair for her, just like when I met Zabra, though in this case it was entirely justified. The woman was old, in her seventies or maybe even eighties by my guess. Despite that, anyone who thought she looked frail should get their eyes checked. She held herself and moved as steadily as a woman half her age, and as we got closer to each other, details popped out. Her silver-white hair was put up in a large, tight bun—it must have been long—and she looked at me with calculating interest, complete confidence, and not a hint of fear. Everything about her, even before she'd said a word, told me that this was a woman who was used to not only seeing her will done, but to being right, too.

I remembered what the others had told me about her. How she'd been on the council for four decades. How well respected and feared she was, depending on how much you had to hide. How she was considered a master of law and rhetoric, able to cut through the lies, omissions, and half-truths of a case to render a swift and fair judgment, and do it so convincingly that most people considered it pointless to try and appeal any decision she'd made.

She had probably accomplished more in the last year than most people did in a lifetime. And I was suddenly very aware that less than half a year ago, I was a climbing gym instructor who'd barely graduated from high school, and who considered two bottles of Moscato and a Netflix marathon to be a night well spent.

Ah, well. There was no point in worrying over that. I might not have a flashy degree, or five decades or whatever of experience arguing in courts and whatnot, but I did have one advantage that she couldn't match. I was a goddamn dragon. And a dragon did not cower in front of some jumped up lawyer. The other two were nothing to worry about, either. One was clearly a secretary or scribe of some sort, carrying a simple table and a large scroll, presumably with some pens and ink somewhere on him. The other shone with a steady magical glow. A tall, lightly armored man, he carried a sword and moved like every motion was precisely calculated to be as efficient as possible. A lawyer, a scribe, and a guy with a sharp stick. I had nothing to worry about.

Then we were close enough to speak. Sempralia stopped, and so did I. She put her hand on the center of her chest and gave me a quarter bow, and I improvised something similar by bending my elbows and dipping my head.

"Lady Draka!"

Sempralia spoke. Suddenly, I was eight years old again, listening to my teacher take attendance, and God save any girl who made a racket. Her voice made it absolutely clear that while she was speaking I would listen and patiently wait my turn. "I was so glad to hear that you'd agreed to this meeting. Let's discuss the future, shall we?"

CHAPTER THIRTY-TWO

The Lady Justice

Think before you speak. Be polite. Don't lie. Don't promise anything you can't or don't intend to deliver. Don't speak out of turn.

Pray that charisma does something for you.

Mak's advice to me for this meeting ran through my head. Then I realized that I was being rude to a very important person, and answered. "Apologies! The lady justice Sempralia, I assume? I was flattered to get your invitation. My friends have spoken well of you."

She gave me a slight, amused smile. "I'm pleased to hear that. I thought I might have left them with a less than favorable opinion of myself. And you? What do you think of me?"

"Me?"

Don't lie, Conscience reminded me. *She wants to hear the truth.*

I didn't want to offend her, but if she could smell dishonesty, loved the truth as much as my family thought she did, and if she was as tough as she looked . . .

I spoke before I could chicken out. "Your reputation is good, and I appreciate that you've treated my friends fairly and with an open mind, as far as I know. But I don't know you, and calling me a dangerous animal didn't win you any points, I can tell you that much."

"I can imagine not. Though I could excuse myself by pointing out that I was only making clear the perspective of the law."

That was a cop-out answer if I'd ever heard one. If she thought honesty was so important, I hoped to get some out of her. "And you? If the law is so clear, what do you think of me? I don't see how we can have a conversation if you don't see me as a person."

"A good point. In the interest of a friendly conversation based on mutual respect, then, let me say I don't see how I could deny the personhood of anyone capable of protesting its denial. You may not be a human or, so far as I know, a citizen of any recognized state, but you are most certainly a person. Now, to answer your question, forming my own opinion of you is one of the goals I hope to accomplish this morning. It is one thing to be told about you, by my agents and by those who know you. It is quite another to see you, almost close enough to touch, and to speak with you. I don't mind admitting that so far, I've been positively surprised!"

"Oh?"

"Yes! You are clearly far more intelligent than any dragon I've heard of, or seen described in the historical record. Your size leads me to believe that you are young, and so less likely to have had any unsurmountable negative experiences with people—forgive me, with humans. And considering that you first appeared in my awareness after publicly killing thirteen of my citizens, you are far less brutish than I feared. You've made no attempts so far to posture or threaten me. These factors all lead me to hope that you are, indeed, as rational as your . . . friends indicated. Tell me, do you see yourself being a threat to my city or its people?"

"No," I answered, quickly and honestly. "Not to anyone who does not try to harm me or mine."

"Ah, good. Your . . . friends mentioned that you are quite protective of them. Most admirable."

Something bothered me about the way she said that. "You paused there, again, when you mentioned my friends. Why?"

That earned me another amused smile. "Permit me to answer with a question. What do you know of human-dragon relations, historically?"

"Not great? Lots of murder, both ways?"

"Let us call it 'conflict.' I don't think the word *murder* applies in this context, but that is quite a succinct summary, yes. It is a relationship that has been fraught with violence in both directions. But as it applies to the humans you associate with, there is also the historical prevalence of dragon cults."

Ah, right. That.

"In every part of the known world, dragons have been known to surround themselves with loyal followers, who worship them and pay them tribute. Some of these people are motivated by fear, hoping that by submitting, they will be spared. Others are drawn by the promise of wealth and power, setting themselves up as the dragon's human representatives in whatever territory it carves out. Then there are those that desire protection, and those who simply worship the dragon as a representative of the gods, or as a god itself, like in old Tekeretek. So. What are you to the humans who follow you?"

That was one hell of a loaded question. It was one of those things that I knew perfectly in my gut, but had to think about to put into words. And what I arrived at reminded me of what Mak had told me. Don't lie. Just say that you'd rather not say.

"I don't think that I can answer that," I said. "I hope that you understand. But I can tell you that while we're important to each other, they don't worship me. And while I definitely want them all to become obscenely wealthy, I'm not planning on that happening at the expense of the city of Karakan."

"Is that so?" Sempralia's smile faded. "Well, an honest answer, at least. And not in conflict with what they told me. Very well, I will hold you to that. Know that the city of Karakan will not tolerate any attempt to set up a parallel power structure within its borders. This is not a threat, merely a statement of fact. I don't know how familiar you are with human societies and politics, but Karakan claims all inhabited land on this island to the mountains in the west, the northern forest, and to our southern border with Happar, which is another human polity. To be blunt, if you wish to set up your own territory to rule as you please, I suggest you do so outside of Karakan."

That might be too late, depending on how far north they wanted to draw the line. Though I hadn't actually challenged their authority yet . . .

"Understandable, and understood," I said, which was completely true.

"Very good. I'm glad. Now, I opened this meeting by saying that I wished to talk about the future. By that, I specifically mean that I wish to talk about how we, meaning yourself and the city of Karakan, can make each other's futures brighter and more prosperous. I hope that this is something that interests you?"

"Oh, yeah, sure! But I've gotten the impression that most people would not be very happy to know that their government was, I don't know, 'consorting' with a dragon."

"Very true. So let's not discuss this under false pretenses. In a void, I would have likely given in to those of my more short-sighted colleagues who wished to see you hunted down. This is not due to any personal animus, though your existence, and especially your presence, do cause me some concern on principle, no matter how well we have gotten along so far. But for the sake of popular peace and acclaim, you see."

"That's one hell of a way to start a negotiation," I muttered.

"Indeed. Rest assured, however, that nothing happens in a void. And I believe that your appearance here can, with correct handling, be an opportunity for both yourself and the city of Karakan. Tell me, Draka, what is it you want in life?"

That was a big question. But I knew myself well enough that the answer was easy. "Peace. Safety. Companionship. And, since I've been told that you can see right through deception, silver, gold, and anything else that glitters." I shrugged without a shred of self-consciousness. "I am a dragon, after all. But mostly peace, when I choose it. I want to be able to live my life, freely and without hiding." I couldn't stop some bitterness from creeping into my voice. "I thought I'd gotten there, five weeks ago, but your conversation with my friends put a stop to that."

The look Sempralia gave me was shrewd and calculating. "What would you be willing to do in exchange for some level of protection or recognition?"

Don't agree to anything you can't deliver, I reminded myself. "Lots of things, probably. But you wouldn't be asking that if you didn't already have something in mind. Just tell me what you want."

"Very well. If the city of Karakan were to recognize you, there would be political considerations. Do you understand what I mean by that? Yes? Good. And not only when it comes to our allies in the Sareyan League, or our trading partners. You understand that public perception must come first, do you not? It is entirely impossible for the council to give you any kind of support if there is no public support first. Despite what some people may think, rulership is an illusion, sustained entirely by the belief of those being ruled. There are many things we can do that the people would simply accept. But if we were to throw our lot in with a dragon, without the people having already accepted you, we would face a public uprising. It would be chaos. Blood in the streets."

"But . . . ?"

"*But.*" That amused little smile came back. "If you were to be seen selflessly aiding the good people of Karakan . . . If word went out about a dragon aiding our brave soldiers in the south, for example, well, that would change things."

"I know about the refugees from the north," I said, "but I thought the situation in the south was getting better."

Sempralia actually gave a bark of laughter at that. "You are far better informed than I could have imagined. I suppose all the time you spend with your friends at that inn they bought has been spent productively."

I bristled at her words, the casual way she revealed that she knew where I'd been living half the time for the last month. She must have picked up on it, because she raised her hands apologetically.

"Your friends are entirely too honest for the kinds of things they've gotten involved in, Draka. I even told them during our meeting that I had them followed. I can't imagine why they would have thought that was a one-time occurrence. Yes, I know that you have been coming and going. But you have kept an admirably low profile, and so I have no objections."

Her words were calm, and on the surface they seemed like a peace offering. She was telling me something she knew, and asking nothing back . . . yet. But if she had the inn watched, what else did she know? Did she know about Simdal or Tark? Was she waiting for the perfect moment to let slip that she knew that the Tespril sisters had both gone in, and that Zabra hadn't come out yet?

How much did she know about me? I forced myself to relax. Play it cool. Volunteer nothing.

"It's convenient," I admitted. "I like it there. I can sleep comfortably, I can see my friends easily, and there are these long, thin fish I like that you can buy by the crateload at the fishing docks. Yes, I spend a lot of time there. But I thought that I had been more careful."

"Oh, don't be cross. I would not employ the people I do if they were not extremely good at their jobs. Like Kalder and Maek, here." She nodded to the shiny man and the scribe next to her, both of whom had somehow faded from my consciousness as we spoke. "I could walk through the poorest part of the city wearing nothing but my finest jewelry, and as long as I have Kalder by my side I wouldn't have a care in the world. Except possibly catching cold, I suppose. And Maek fluently captures every word we speak, every intonation, *with* annotations and other commentary. Believe me, a lady justice's investigators are no less skilled than her guards or secretaries. Ah, but I digress. My apologies. We were speaking about how you might be seen to aid the city, were we not?"

"Yes?" She had me off balance with her comments, but that seemed to be where she'd been going. "It sounded like you were going to make me an offer."

"Quite so, and it's simple. As a show of good faith, we would like you to help us find how Happar's forces are distributed along the border. We are not asking you to put yourself in danger, merely to do some scouting for us. Nothing that you've not already done for the Grey Wolves."

Again, she just casually announced her knowledge of something that was supposed to be secret. Though, frankly, that was Rallon's problem, if it was a problem at all. For all I knew he'd been keeping the council in the loop from the beginning and had just thought it best not to tell me.

But it didn't take more than a few small logical steps to connect us, did it? My family were all friends with several of the Wolves. With Garal, Lalia, Rib, and Pot all staying at the inn off and on, and Sempralia knowing that I did so as well, I could easily imagine her having simply called Rallon to a meeting and asking him directly. And I didn't see him lying to her.

Still, it was just as likely that she didn't actually know anything, and was just fishing. And I wasn't going to confirm or volunteer anything if I could help it.

"I'm not against it," I told her. "But what would I get in return? As a gesture of good faith, that is."

"Rumors and hearsay." The amused little smile was back. "If you help us in the south, we can make sure that word of your deeds becomes public knowledge. We could not recognize you, of course, but rumors are easy enough to start. For example, word might spread that a black dragon has been known to attack Happaran raiders, but sparing and freeing their prisoners. Who could object to that? Or that the same dragon has been seen attacking and killing bandits, while leaving Karakan's loyal retained mercenaries unharmed. Such tales may sound farfetched, but they will take root here and there, I'm sure. And if our soldiers in the south are already primed with such rumors, and they should happen to see you coming and going from their camps while *not* causing them any problems, that might be helpful as well, I imagine."

"How do you even know about that?" I muttered, half to myself.

"People talk. When mercenaries talk about a large, flying lizard attacking bandits and seemingly protecting the tall, dark, young woman guiding them, that is interesting. When a group of citizens from various devastated farming communities do their patriotic duty and report what they know, and careful questioning finally draws out that they were set free from their captors by a large, flying lizard that spoke to them, that is *very* interesting. And I have very good agents bringing me information. You don't think that I am *only* interested in matters of law, do you?"

"Clearly not. So I do you this favor in the south, you stealthily work on my image, and if everyone is satisfied, we take it from there? Easy as that?"

"As easy as that."

I looked at her. I took in her scent. Citrusy perfume and age, paper and silk. There was interest and curiosity on her face, together with a lot of calculation. Though, in someone whose whole life had revolved around handling people for who knew how many decades, what her face showed might be entirely up to her. But there was no fear that I could detect with any sense. Almost everyone, Herald and recently Mak being the exceptions, feared me to some degree. Not everyone was wary around me; they may not even acknowledge that they were scared. But their bodies gave them away, and I instinctively read the little cues that told me they knew that they were, in the grand scheme of things, prey. Even Tark, for all his bravado, had smelled of fear at the end.

Sempralia didn't. Not at all.

"You're interesting," I told her. "Why were you so ready to meet me, face to face? Why do you want to work with me?"

She looked at me thoughtfully, the amusement entirely replaced by something more serious. "I see an opportunity in you. There are good reasons, historically, why I should be wary of a dragon, yes. But you defy expectations. You should be arrogant and demanding, but you are not. Your friends have made claims about you that I found hard to believe, but they made them with absolute conviction. And there is a problem facing the city which I believe that you are uniquely suited to . . . perhaps not solve, but attempt to ameliorate at the very least. Let me be blunt. I want to believe that we can work together. That you can be trusted to help us. But I cannot tell you *why* until I actually trust you."

"Huh."

It was perhaps not the most draconic, or even dignified, reaction imaginable, but it was an honest one. Sempralia quirked an eyebrow, but otherwise waited patiently as I mulled over her words. She told me something important, there. Calculated to manipulate me, perhaps, but probably true. They *needed* me. Or my cooperation would make things easier for them, at least. But she couldn't tell me why until we trusted one another, so it must be big.

Did I have some leverage?

"I'll do your scouting mission," I told her. "As a gesture of good faith, like you said. I think I've already done plenty, but I'll play along. If you just want me to fly along the border, I'll need a map. More, and I'll need details. From some . . . military person, I guess."

"Wonderful! You would of course meet with General Sarvalian at the border before undertaking anything. Shall we—?"

"But beyond that, we'll have to hammer out some terms. Official recognition, no matter what, is non-negotiable. So is protection for the inn while I'm away.

We've had some trouble lately, and I can't leave unless I know that my friends are safe. Other than that, I'd prefer if you worked it out with Mak. Lady Drakonum, I mean. I trust her to have my best interest at heart."

She didn't look at all perturbed by me cutting her off with my demands, though that could of course just have been her controlling her facial expression.

"Making something 'non-negotiable' is rarely productive, and it is rarely as non-negotiable as the one making the demand believes. But if that is what you wish, I would be delighted to speak with Lady Drakonum again."

"In that case, are we done? You know how to contact me. Send me some specifics about this mission you want me to carry out, and I'll see to it as soon as I can."

"I suppose that we are. Thank you again for meeting with me. I hope that this is the beginning of something profitable for all of us. And, one more thing before you go . . ." Sempralia said the last part with obvious hesitation, like she thought that she shouldn't but couldn't help herself. It was odd, coming from her. Mildly endearing, even, and I wondered what she might want.

"Forgive an old woman her rudeness, Lady Draka, but . . . may I touch you?"

CHAPTER THIRTY-THREE

Frustration

I couldn't help but grin as I leapt off the cliff, spreading my wings and quickly turning my dive into a glide, then climbing out across the sea before beginning my turn.

The lady justice Sempralia, one of the senior councilors of Karakan, had asked, almost timidly, if she could touch me. I'd let her. There had been a child-like glee in her eyes, a smile splitting her face as she'd carefully touched my nose, then run her hand over the scales of my neck and the leathery membranes of my wings. Her bodyguard Kalder had looked the closest to nervous I'd seen him during the whole meeting, like he might explode into violence at any moment. I'd sat very still and patient until Sempralia backed off, a little flush of what I could only imagine to be embarrassment decorating her face as she thanked me.

It was so easy to forget what I was, sometimes. Or rather, what I was to everyone else. While I always knew that I was an amazing, marvelous creature, powerful, beautiful, and deadly, to them I was truly fantastical. Most humans in history would have never seen a dragon, and many would have wondered if we ever really existed. Even if they saw one, judging by how dragons were described, I imagined that most humans would count themselves lucky if it was only at a great distance. So, to have a friendly conversation with one, to have one wait patiently as you gently, almost reverently put your fingers on it . . . I couldn't fault the lady justice for asking when she had the chance. Neither of us knew if we'd meet again. I hoped that we would, ideally in the Forum or some other similarly public place, but it wasn't for sure.

Maybe she was being a crafty old politician, trying to flatter me. Job well done, if she was. But there had been a casual honesty about her when she asked that made me sure she truly just wanted to be able to say she had touched a dragon.

I finished my turn, coming a full one hundred eighty degrees and heading back toward Sempralia's party. The lady justice, her bodyguard, and her scribe had rejoined the larger contingent of guards that she'd brought with her. I saw several of the guards pointing at me, and lady justice turned to look just as I got close enough to see some detail on her face.

She was grinning as I passed less than a hundred feet above her, and I had the sudden impulse to show off. I was going fast enough, so I whipped out one of my favorite aerobatic moves. It was one which I should really be higher up to try, just in case I messed it up, but I decided to throw caution to the wind. Twisting my wings in opposite directions I pulled myself into a series of tight rolls. Once, twice, three—

I felt a burning sensation in the membrane of my right wing, like the worst papercut imaginable, in the middle of my third roll. With a hiss I stabilized and looked at it in disbelief, seeing a ragged tear in the middle of the membrane between the second and third fingers. My membranes didn't tear! That just didn't happen, especially not in the middle!

The adrenaline that had spiked at the pain flooded my brain as I looked around, searching the ground. And there, among the ripe grain of a nearby field, I saw a shimmer of gold.

That *fucking* archer!

I turned toward them. They'd made a serious mistake, and judging by the distance, I had about five seconds to decide if they should die for it. There were no trees to hide in now. They'd gotten careless. Greedy. A field full of grain may be excellent cover from anything on the ground, but from an enemy that could fly, you may as well be on open ground. Hell, the field was probably worse, since it would slow them down.

I dodged a second arrow, then a third. As long as the archer kept using their magic, I could see clearly how the golden glow went from their body to the arrow the moment they loosed, making it almost trivial to avoid as long as I was paying attention. Ironically, they would have had a better chance of hitting me without the magic. Of course, the arrows might not do anything in that case. The best solution was to not put an arrow in a dragon at all, but it was far too late for that.

After the third arrow they realized that I was too close and moving too fast, and they turned to run.

Yeah, nah. Not happening.

My talons closed on air as they threw themselves to the ground at the last moment, but I threw my wings up, beat hard, and stopped dead in the air, flipping myself around to face them before hitting the ground.

Thirty feet away, my nemesis was getting up from the ground. He—and now that I had a second to look at him, I could see the light stubble, the boyishly youthful, rather than feminine, features—stared me in the eye. His expression was eloquent, telling me that he was fully aware of just how well and truly he had fucked himself.

There was a standoff, lasting all of a fraction of a second, in which I had time to realize just how damned *pretty* he was. He had the androgynous beauty of a runway model, and while Instinct straight up did not care what any human looked like, Conscience was intrigued, to the point where I actually started second guessing myself. Should I really hurt him? It would be a damn shame to destroy something so beautiful, after all. Sure, halo effect and pretty privilege and all that crap, but damn!

Thank the gods that Instinct was in charge right then, because the stalemate was broken as he lit up like a bonfire. He didn't even have his arrow fully nocked when my wing-assisted leap bore me into him, one foot catching him square in the chest and bringing him down hard, pinned under my full weight. Even then he drew a knife from somewhere, but I caught him by the wrist and squeezed until I felt bones break and he spent the last of his air on a wheezing scream, dropping the blade.

"Lie still!" I growled, my face two inches from his. When he squirmed and tried to grab at my leg with his uninjured right hand I took a firm grip on his vest, then with the help of my foot lifted and slammed him down. "Why? Why are you doing this? I was having a perfectly nice morning!" I slammed him again, a high-pitched wheeze exploding out of him. He stared up at me groggily, looking dazed from the impacts. "I had a nice conversation. The weather is shaping up to be great for flying—"

I heard voices and the sound of grain being trampled, and looking up, I saw some of the guards approaching. "Back off!" I warned them. "This bastard's been trying to kill me for weeks! Mine!"

"Lady Draka!" The voice was unfamiliar, but as he approached I recognized Kalder the bodyguard. "Whoever you have there, please release them to me."

"Oh, so you speak? And what are *you* going to do with him? Let him go? No law against trying to kill a dragon, is there?" I looked down at the archer, who looked mildly concussed. "No, I think I'll be keeping this guy. We have a score to settle."

"Lady Draka, he fired several arrows over the head of a councilor. We have to take him in for questioning, in case he was following us and not you." He looked back over his shoulder and nodded, then continued. "I can promise you, on behalf of the lady I serve, that he will not be released without consulting you first. Is that acceptable?"

"*Kill him!*" Instinct snarled as I looked again at the bastard beneath me. "*Tear him to shreds! Eat his heart!*"

I was oh, so tempted. The smell of his blood from where my claws had dug in filled my nose, so strong that my throat twitched in anticipation. But I held back. I really thought about it. How angry was I? How badly had he injured me? He'd poisoned me, but that had healed. My wing smarted, but I could handle that, and the cut didn't seem to cause any real problems with flying. He'd made me worry about Herald and Kira, but neither had been hurt. Same with Mak, a few nights ago.

He'd been trying to kill me. He'd failed. I wanted to hurt him. I wanted to kill him. But if Kalder's word was good, he wasn't going anywhere, and mostly, I wanted to know why he was after me, if anyone was backing him, and how the hell he kept finding me.

"Will my friends be able to question him? Can you promise me that?"

"Easily and without hesitation, yes. Anyone we know to be associated with you will have access."

I looked at Kalder. He looked at me. Mercies damn it, perhaps it was time to cultivate some goodwill.

I threw the bastard toward the guards with a snort of disgust, sending him rolling among the stalks. "I'll trust you on this, Kalder. You and your lady. Don't make me regret it."

As I was about to leave, I saw the bow lying there among the trampled grain, where he'd dropped it as I struck him. I picked it up. It looked nice. Expensive. Looking back, the knife also lay where it had fallen after I crushed his wrist. It looked completely ordinary, but I grabbed that, too. I wasn't going back empty-handed, and there was something satisfying about taking my enemy's weapons. Like a little consolation prize.

"You'll hear from us soon," I told Kalder, and took off.

My first impulse was to give the bow to Herald. I didn't know much about bows, but there was something about it, a luster that just screamed "high-quality," as well as some decorative swirly patterns. Basically, it looked nice and expensive. There were some problems with that idea, though. The first was that I'd need to carry the bow into the city. I couldn't bring it with me through the sewers, so I'd need to fly in at night and then sneak along the streets, or stash it somewhere and have someone fetch it. Which, admittedly, wasn't insurmountable, but it was a hassle. Second, I knew that Herald liked her current bow. It wasn't a masterpiece, sure, but she'd had it made to order so the length, the grip, and the draw were all just right for her. Lastly, I just kinda wanted to keep the bow for myself. The archer had been trying to kill *me. I* had taken it. It was *mine.* I could do anything I wanted with it. I wouldn't *mind* giving it to Herald. I was sure that she'd be happy and touched that I was giving her a present. I just didn't see her loving it, or even using it. It would end up as a back-up somewhere, and only used when, for whatever reason, she couldn't use her *real* bow.

At least those were the reasons I gave myself as I added the bow to my hoard, carefully unstringing it and wrapping the string around one end the way Herald had shown me. And when I did, it felt right. It belonged there, beautiful and mean-ingful and valuable all at once. I left the knife as well. It was just a tool, but it might come in handy someday.

With plenty of morning left I decided to visit my little village. It had been a couple of days since I'd seen my people, but they worked hard and fast, and I was curious what they might have accomplished. I didn't want to arrive empty-handed, though. While I was supposed to be the mighty protector and ideally the one receiving tribute in this relationship, I felt a responsibility toward these people. Besides, I was starting to feel hungry.

Hunting down a boar took me just over an hour, but it was ridiculously easy compared to my first attempts. I knew what scents to look for now, I knew my own body, and I could stay shifted for far longer than it took to sneak up on a sleeping pig, so close that I could tear its throat out before it knew what was happening.

When I arrived at the village I did so with my customary caution. I was dragging a bled and gutted boar, which wasn't ideal for stealth, but I was sneaky enough that it shouldn't be a problem. When I got close, though, something felt off. There was a pen of those super-sized turkeys that a lot of forest communities raised, and those were new, but that wasn't it. The houses were coming along nicely, though it didn't look like any new ones had been finished lately. Fair enough. They couldn't spend all their time building, after all. But . . .

I realized what the problem was. Where were they? Where were my people? There was no one sitting around talking and making crafts. There was no one working in the gardens, and no sound of trees being felled and split. The kids weren't playing and screaming. It was halfway through the morning, yet there was no one to be seen or heard at all.

Not until someone stepped out of the one finished cabin. A tall, rough-looking guy with long, wavy hair and several days' worth of stubble, he was completely unfamiliar to me. As he stretched in the late morning sun I saw an axe strapped to his belt. He was followed by a woman, another stranger, who was nearly as tall as he was. She finished buckling on her sword belt, then ran her hand up into his hair. He turned around and kissed her, then groped her, which got him a light slap, a playful grin, and a kiss back.

I started getting excited. Not because of anything they did. I wasn't a voyeur. I didn't care what they got up to. But other base instincts and desires were getting all fired up. There was a good chance that those two wouldn't live much longer, unless I got some very satisfying answers to some very important questions. Such as, who the *fuck* were they? Why were they in *my* village, and where were *my* people?

I dropped my catch and shifted, bringing the shadows of the forest with me as I stalked forward. Around the corner of the longhouse I shifted back and sniffed. I smelled smoke on the air. Standing still and listening, I heard murmuring from inside the longhouse, low voices that made no sense during the late morning. It didn't make sense that they'd be cooped up in there at all.

The two strangers were still necking—and by the look of it, considering doing a whole lot more—by the cold firepit that had become the center of the village, not paying any attention at all to the world around them. They were armed, but their weapons were at their belts, and their hands were very, very busy.

I struck.

I didn't kill them. I took them completely by surprise, but I hit them with my claws in; I wanted answers, after all. I could have used my shadows, but I didn't need them, and in case there was a perfectly innocent explanation, I didn't want to accidentally make another couple of Jekries. I didn't hurt them *too* badly, but I did slam into them at high speed, and I was getting to be a big girl after months on a solid diet of meat and hoarding precious things. Entwined as they were, they went down in a screaming heap, and I quickly tore their weapons away, then pinned first the man, who'd been slower to react, then the woman, who almost scrambled away before I wrapped a hand around her ankle and reeled her back in. They were strong—fighters, both of them, no doubt about it—but I was stronger, and they were not lifting several hundred pounds of *me* off them, not in the position I had them.

I had the man pinned pretty well with just my weight, though he was still trying to hit me. The woman was snarling and kicking as I pulled her closer. I felt the punches and the kicks, but they didn't *hurt*. As long as they were unarmed and didn't have any crazy magic, they couldn't really harm me. There was no point in maiming or killing them unless they became useless or too annoying, or found another weapon somewhere. But there was a question of pride, and of putting them in their proper place, that place being beneath me, silent and cooperative.

The man was at an awkward angle beneath me, but I had my foot on his belly and flexed my claws. I wasn't sure if I drew blood, but I could tell by how he jerked that he felt it. "Stop!" I growled, but they didn't seem to be listening, instead punching, kicking, and screaming. They both finally froze when I wrapped my hand around the woman's throat, letting my claws prick her a bit. They were both dead if I so chose, and they knew it. "Lie still and be silent, or die!"

I heard a door slam open behind me. I whipped my head around, ready to face this new threat, ready to finish off these two and turn on—

"Dar, Elem, *Mercies so help me*, if you don't quiet down—!"

Tinir stood in the door, her infant daughter in her arms. Her voice cut off as she saw me, then the two humans under me.

Tinir was not one to stand paralyzed and speechless in a crisis. After taking in the scene for all of a second, a sickly, almost desperate smile swept across her face. She either couldn't or didn't even try to stop her voice from trembling as she spoke. "Great Lady! What a—a lovely surprise! May I introduce my cousin, Darvellan, and his wife, Elem?"

CHAPTER THIRTY-FOUR

I Don't Think I Like My Selves

I looked down at the two humans under me, finding myself disappointed. "Not bandits, then?"

"No, no!" Tinir said frantically. "Adventurers, if anything. Just two friendly, harmless, *trustworthy* adventurers." Her eyes pleaded with me to believe her.

My shadow moved restlessly back and forth, as though it was pacing, and I didn't bother reining it in as I considered what my senses had told me. There hadn't been any blood or fear in the air, no sign of a struggle at all. Just smoke, from a cooking fire, perhaps vomit—which was, Mercies help me, *interesting* rather than disgusting—and the distinct smell of sex on the couple that I'd considered killing.

I still hadn't made my mind up about that, either, though I did make some small adjustments—shifting my weight to mostly take it off them, pulling my claws in, relaxing my grip on the woman, Elem's, throat. Little things like that.

"Where are the others?"

"Away, trading. Or in the longhouse sleeping off last night." She laughed nervously. "Dar and Elem had some strong drink with them, you see, and . . . well."

Trading? "You didn't mention going to trade when I was here a few days ago."

"It wasn't planned!" Her tone was frantically defensive. She was trying to talk me down. I knew that. But I didn't want to be talked down. "When Dar and Elem found us, and offered to stay and help keep the children safe, we thought it was an excellent opportunity. Please, Great Lady, can you let them go?"

"Found you, huh?" I looked down at my prisoners. "How, and why, exactly, did that happen?"

The man, Darvellan, found his voice. I imagined that Elem was still a little nervous about moving her throat too much.

His voice was deep, quick and clipped. A little breathless, probably from the pressure. "You're, ah . . . That was you, at the harbor, wasn't it?"

"I asked you a question." I flexed the claws holding his wife, drawing a choked whine from her.

"Sorry! Please! I heard about the trouble in the north, and I was worried about my family. That's all, I swear! I took the same way back north as I did south when I left, way back when, and we just found them here!"

"That's been going on for months! Why now?"

"You!" the woman, Elem, choked out, and I turned my attention to her, loosening my grip on her throat again. She had a slight accent, similar to the Terriallons, marking her as Tavvanarian.

"Explain."

"We saw you in the harbor! Scary, yeah, but we didn't think too much of it. Or so I thought. Turns out this one's been worrying about it for weeks. If there's something that nasty—shit, sorry, didn't mean anything by that. But if there was a creature like you in the city, what's going on in the forest? That kinda thing. And he finally wore me down a week ago, we settled what we needed, and headed out a few days ago."

I wasn't sure if I believed them. It seemed too convenient. But it wasn't like these were the only people ever to stumble onto the little village. Pretty much every week one or more wanderers would turn up, and either avoid the village or say hi and move on, trade, or stay the night. And if Tinir vouched for them, perhaps I should trust her. But I had to be sure.

"These two are a problem. You understand that, right, Tinir?"

"What! Why?!" she exclaimed, a look of near panic on her face as she took a step toward me. She stopped, visibly forcing herself to calm, but her voice still shook when she continued. "I mean . . . how so, Great Lady?"

"They've seen me here, talking to you. They've heard you speak to me with respect and deference. If they spread that around, if someone hears and tries to use you to get to me, you're all in danger, yeah?"

"But . . . but he's my cousin! She's his wife! They're family!"

"And if they're careless? If they get drunk, and their tongues start wagging down at the Guild, or something like that?" I looked down at the two. "Convince me. Why shouldn't I nip that problem in the bud and just get rid of them?"

Because of the line, Conscience reminded me. *The line that we don't want to cross. The one that we shouldn't cross even with Zabra and Kesra, no matter what we've decided. That line.*

But they were a potential problem. They could endanger the whole village. *I should just kill them*, I thought, and my shadow drew itself in, like it was preparing to pounce.

"Because—because—" Tinir stuttered to a halt, her eyes full of pleading, then rushed up and knelt beside me, head bowed and her baby still in her arms. Curious, frightened faces had appeared in the doorway behind her. "Please, Great Lady! Because they're family, and we have lost so many already. And Dar was always a good boy, and I've only had him back for a few days, but I'm sure that he's as good a man as he seems, and though I've only known Elem since they came she's been nothing but wonderful! I will vouch for them. I will take responsibility for them. They won't do anything to put us or yourself in danger. I swear!"

Begging. My biggest weakness. She was even holding a baby. How was I supposed to be cruelly practical in front of a woman begging with her baby in her arms? And if that wasn't bad enough, little Alda chose that moment to start crying.

I felt a flash of frustration, and suddenly things became crystal clear. I *wanted* to kill them. And not even them, specifically. I was searching for an excuse, anything good enough to convince myself just long enough to kill *someone*.

I stopped everything, holding myself completely still as I forced myself to analyze that. I didn't even breathe. This was not a revelation I could put off for later. I needed to deal with this *now*.

It wasn't Instinct. Instinct did want to kill them. Of course she did. That was the easiest solution, and long-term consequences rarely figured into what she wanted. But what I felt didn't come from her. I could always tell. Nor did it come from Conscience, who definitely and emphatically *didn't* want to kill them, because they hadn't done anything at all to deserve it. It came from *me*, the weird mish-mash brain baby that had grown out of my two halves being forced together in one head.

I'd never—since coming to Mallin—had a problem with killing, before or after the fact. I didn't know how much of that was Instinct muting my horror and guilt—probably a lot in the beginning, and less as time went on. But now I just wanted to kill someone. I didn't much care who. I didn't like that, but I couldn't think of any other way to relieve the frustration. I'd been fantasizing about killing Zabra for months, and now I'd been denied. Not that I couldn't just go and do it; no one would try to physically stop me. They might try to talk me out of it, but they wouldn't get in my way. But I had promised myself and my sisters that I would trust their judgment, and Mak had said that Zabra should live if possible. Hell, Mak wanted to kill her worse than I did, and she still insisted on sparing the woman. Then there was the archer. After three attempts on my life I'd *had* him, I'd been gearing up to vent my displeasure on him, but nooo! Sempralia was right there, and I had to be *reasonable* and *merciful* and to *think of my reputation*.

And now I'd thought, hoped, even, that I had two new bastards in front of me, deserving of my wrath. And here was Tinir, telling me that they were family. That they were good people and could be trusted. Begging me on her knees to spare them.

I should have been relieved that all was well in the village. Instead, I was just frustrated.

"I need an oath," I gritted out. I resisted the urge to use my shadows on them to really drive the point home. "I need you to swear that you will never speak to anyone about my relationship with this village, or do anything else that might put the people here at risk. If I even suspect the tiniest attempt to deceive me, if either of you so much as hesitates, I will kill you both, no matter who your family is. I've promised to do what I can to keep these people safe, and I take that promise extremely seriously. Do you understand?"

Darvellan was first to speak. I'd barely shut my mouth before he was talking. "I understand, ah, Great Lady! I swear, on my honor and on my life and on my love for Elem, that I won't put my cousin or anyone else here in danger, through word or deed!"

I couldn't tell if he was lying, of course. I wished that I could. I wished so badly that I had something similar to Mak, where I could tell what someone's intentions were. Or even what Sempralia was rumored to have, where she could just straight up tell if someone was lying. I wished that I had something like that, and that it would tell me he was lying through his teeth. But I didn't, so I just had to assume that he was scared enough, and loved his cousin enough, to mean what he said. It wasn't like I could change my mind if I acted on the alternative.

"And you, Elem?"

"Yeah, yeah, same!" As my silence and stare grew longer, she quickly added, "On my honor, and my life, and my love for Dar, I won't do or say anything to anyone that might put these people in danger. Truly. I'd never want that anyway, but I swear it to you!"

"Fine." I carefully transferred my weight fully to the limbs that weren't on them, then stepped off. My shadow withdrew, turning away from me. I got the strangest feeling that it was sulking. "You can get up. Pick up your weapons if you want. They can't hurt me anyway."

"Gods and Mercies, thank you!" Elem said, first to scramble to her feet. She gave her hand to Darvellan, who took it and let her pull him up. They stood there, leaning on each other for support, watching me warily.

"Well?" I said as the silence started bothering me. "So you're all hung over? *That's* why you worried me enough to almost kill these two? What do you even have to get drunk on, here?"

"Ah, that, Great Lady, would be my fault," Dar said, and Elem's eyes flashed with fear and concern. "I didn't want to arrive empty-handed. We could always provide for ourselves before I left, but there was never anything stronger to drink than honey-wine, so . . ."

"So you brought some of Karakan's finest, and these poor bastards never knew what hit them," I finished for him.

"Ah, yeah, Great Lady. That is about the whole of it."

"You don't think that endangered the village? What if something happened while you were all drunk?"

"With respect, Great Lady," Tinir said, "I did not drink, for the baby's sake. And these two were quite sober when they went to . . . sleep. But I admit that Madalla and Sarhos may have been overly fond of the stuff."

I looked at the two women who'd appeared in the doorway; they both looked exceedingly embarrassed.

"So it's just you five and the kids here? Everyone else is away trading? No threats, nothing bad going on, just bad timing and unexpected visitors."

"Yes, Great Lady."

I sighed. "Fine. Whatever. Get a fire going. I brought meat to feed a village, so I hope you're hungry."

I didn't bother waiting for a reply. I just walked over to my kill, taking my sweet time, and dragged it over to the fire before laying down behind the long-house. The whole way I stewed in my own thoughts. I couldn't deny what I'd just discovered about myself, and I didn't like it. But the more I thought about it, the more I became convinced that there was at least one mitigating factor. I did not, in fact, just want to kill someone. When I imagined killing someone who wasn't by any stretch of the definition an enemy, I recoiled. Even someone like Simdal, who'd been, and possibly still was, one of Zabra's creatures, didn't do it for me. I was convinced that he was permanently neutered, as far as I was concerned.

It had to be an enemy. That was the only conclusion that I could draw. I wanted someone in front of me who was unarguably a threat to myself or those I loved, and I wanted the satisfaction of destroying them.

That felt better. It was easier to accept that some non-specific murderous need. But I still didn't like it.

I stayed at the village for a few hours, and the people there left me to myself. But even if no one dared to approach me, I enjoyed listening to the few people holding down the fort go about their lives. On some level, I wanted to reassure myself that I could be around them. That I wouldn't fly into a murderous rage just because someone made a loud noise and woke me from a nap, or something equally insane and ridiculous.

At least I got to enjoy being stared at by curious children. I hoped one of the two little ones would work up the courage to approach me one of these days.

Before I left I called for Darvellan and Elem. I made it clear to them, making absolutely sure that they took me seriously, that if either of them gave me any reason at all to distrust them, I would kill them both, starting with the non-offending party. Telling them that crossing me meant that they would see the love of their life die in front of them seemed very effective. The fact that I felt like shit the whole way back to Karakan was just something I'd have to deal with.

I returned to the inn the long way, through the sewers. Herald opened an upstairs window for me, welcoming me back, telling me how worried she'd been when I didn't come back immediately after the meeting. How Mak had reported the storm of emotions that she'd felt from me. Then she ran interference for me to let me sneak into the cellar.

"Do you want to tell me what happened?" she asked.

I gave her a tired glare that I immediately regretted. "Later. Let's deal with the Tesprils first. Could you get Mak down here?"

"Yeah, sure. It is time to let Kesra out to talk to that Hardal guy, anyway."

With Herald and Mak backing me up, and Kira waiting anxiously in the main cellar—she was a clever girl; she knew what might happen—I stepped into the makeshift cell. It was dark, and it smelled pretty bad, but Kesra had refused to leave her sister.

I didn't bother with light, but they both moved in their corner, each trying to protect the other. I guessed that they'd been sleeping. There wasn't much else for them to do. Zabra was neither bound nor gagged, which I probably should have punished them for, but I didn't care. I recognized the looks on their faces, the way they felt, or smelled, or however I should describe it. Zabra was done, her resolve shattered. Kesra wasn't, but she was close, and terrified enough that she wasn't a concern.

"Mak," I said, and she knew what I wanted.

"Come on, Kesra," she said. "Time to show you off to your people."

Kesra reluctantly let go of her sister and got to her feet. She gave me a hard look, but she didn't argue. She knew what would happen if she didn't cooperate, and if Hardal made good on his promise to attack. "I'll be back," she promised her sister, who watched her leave with silent desperation.

"Do you think she means it?" I asked Zabra. "Or will she take the chance to run?"

"I hope she does." Zabra's voice was tired. "I hope she takes our money and gets as far from here as she can."

"I could still find her."

"Maybe. But I don't think you would. Not if she's no threat to you."

"I've seen how much she loves you. She'd always be a threat."

Zabra didn't respond. She just slumped back against the wall.

Kesra, of course, returned promptly. I would've been terribly surprised if she hadn't. And despite her words, the relief in Zabra's eyes when her sister came into the small room and joined her in the corner was a wonder to see.

"Now that that's taken care of, let's settle this." I said. "Zabra. I want to kill you."

They both tensed. It was the tension of two women who saw death coming and who knew that they could do nothing to stop it, but there was a subtle difference between them. Zabra looked like she just hoped that it would be over quickly. Kesra didn't look any more hopeful but shifted to put herself between us, making herself, if not a shield, then at least a speed bump.

"I want to kill you in so many ways. I want to tear your throat out with my teeth. I want to spray your face full of my venom and watch you struggle desperately for breath on the floor. I want to tear you open and spill your living guts on the Forum for the crows to peck at. But I won't do any of that. If anything, I'd give you to Mak, and it's a coin toss whether she'd beat you to death or stab you in the gut and leave you like that until blood loss or infection got you. Understand that. I want to kill you. I want you to die.

"But we're going to let you go."

Zabra let out the breath that she'd been holding with a long shudder. Kesra just stared at me, rapidly blinking away her silent tears of relief.

"You are not forgiven. There will be consequences, and there will be conditions. Mak will tell you the details."

Mak gave me a questioning look, but I had faith in her. There was no way that she hadn't been thinking about this since the moment she decided Zabra should live.

"If you don't accept Mak's conditions, or if Mak tells me that you're not being honest, or if you go back on whatever the two of you agree on at some later date, I will kill Kesra. I'll kill her in front of you, so she can see the person who threw her life away when I do it. I don't want to. She's innocent in this, but there need to be consequences, you understand? And when she is dead, when you know that the person you sacrificed your soul to protect is gone, then I'll kill you.

"Kesra, I don't expect you to do anything stupid enough to force me to kill you regardless of what your sister does. I honestly believe that you're not a bad person. You just have a sister who loves you, and who doesn't care who she hurts to protect you. But if you do, if you try to be some kind of hero, then the same applies to you. Zabra will die first. You will watch her die. Understood?"

"Yes," Kesra whispered.

"Zabra, are you ready to listen to Mak?"

Zabra pulled her sister close. "Yeah."

There had never been any doubt about her answer. I could feel it. Zabra was as broken as Mak or Ardek had ever been. I didn't know if she knew that yet, but I doubted that she could, or could even want to, do anything against me now. The words were just a formality.

I turned to my sisters and switched to Tekereteki. *"Deal with this. I beg you. I do not like to just drop this on you, but I am exhausted, and I think you can handle it better than I. I am going to the strongroom, and I do not want to see these two again for a long while unless it is because you need me to kill them. The key, please."*

Mak wordlessly removed the key to the strongroom from her keyring and handed it to me, and I left the four of them there, in the dark.

CHAPTER THIRTY-FIVE

What Makes A Monster?

When the knock came, both Mak and Herald were outside the door. I'd felt them moving around, in the cellar and above me, and it had been a while since I left them with Zabra and Kesra. I wasn't prepared for them to have everybody with them.

"May we come in?" Herald asked, and I grunted and went to lie back down.

Herald and Mak, Tam and Val, Kira and Ardek. They all crowded into the small room. It wasn't what I'd imagined for the conversation we needed to have, but neither did I want to send anyone away. It felt good to have them all there, even if it was a little awkward.

"Are they gone?" I asked once everyone had settled in. "I'm guessing you wouldn't bring everyone like this just to have them watch me kill two women."

"They're gone," Mak said, "and they took their people with them. There's been someone skulking around watching Hardal, too. They took off as well. Don't know for sure who that might be, but I have some guesses. Anyway, they're all gone now, best we can tell."

"Probably one of Sempralia's people. What happened with Zabra and Kesra?"

"They, or rather Kesra, accepted everything. Zabra didn't say much. She tried to protest, once, and Kesra gave her this *look* that shut her up. After that she just agreed when Kesra told her to. Every demand and condition. I could have gone farther but . . . Zabra's *important*." She spat the last word. "If she becomes too weak, things will become unstable. And since we're going into business with them—"

I cut her off. "We're what now?"

"Perhaps that's the wrong way to put it. Since they'll be *paying tribute* from now on, we want them in a strong, stable position."

"Right. That sounds better, yeah. What're the conditions?"

"They'll drop all the heinous shit. The legal businesses, the gambling, the taverns, the brothels—that all stays, unless you say otherwise."

"Just make sure that no one's forcing anyone to work or take predatory loans or whatever. You know what I mean."

"Yeah."

"Damages?"

"I honestly had to pull a number from thin air, so . . . I figured an inn would be a decent start. Two hundred dragons. Half of that's yours."

In spite of myself, a low, slow rumble rolled out of my chest. A hundred dragons was . . . a lot.

"Kesra insists that they're good for it, but that it'll take a little time to bring together. And they'll be paying us half of their profit in tribute, monthly. Don't know what that's going to add up to. She's going to get their books together. *And* they're going to try to find and buy back the slaves they already delivered, if possible. Not much hope of that, but they'll try."

"And you believe them?"

"They . . . Kesra wanted us to believe her, in a way that made me think that she desperately didn't want us to think that she was lying. Does that make sense? It's the best I can do. Sorry. Zabra was hard to read, but I don't think she's in charge anymore."

"It's fine. Zabra's broken. I could smell it on her. And Kesra . . . she's not stupid."

"Broken?" Val asked.

"I don't know what else to call it." I didn't care who knew anymore. I could barely remember what I'd already told Tam, and I didn't know if he'd told Val, but it would surprise me if he hadn't. "Something inside her has broken. She can't fight me anymore. She won't want to. She *can't* want to. That part of her is . . . smashed. Gone. Broken. In some messed up way she may even love me, once she's had a chance to recover from all this."

I looked at Mak, and she gave me a sad smile back.

"Hey, since everyone's here—and I want an honest answer—am I a monster?"

The room went silent.

"Is that why you've been in such a pit ever since this morning?" Mak asked.

"Yeah. All day I've been burning with this desire to kill someone. There were two adventurers at the village, and I thought they were making trouble. When Tinir convinced me not to kill them, I was so disappointed. And now . . . I've been lying here, hoping that you would come in and tell me that Zabra spat in your face, or give me some other reason to tear her apart. And it's not the first time. Killing, permanently removing a threat like that, it's so . . . satisfying. After I killed her people in the harbor I felt more alive than I could ever remember. So, am I a monster?"

There was a short silence, then a storm of denials from Herald, Mak, and Ardek. Kira joined in once Mak translated for her. And I was grateful for it, but those four literally couldn't think ill of me. So, while I didn't ignore them, exactly, I looked at Tam and Val.

"I," Val began slowly after giving the question due thought, "have seen you kill. We all have. I won't lie; it's a primal thing. Hard to look at. There is none of the hesitation in you that must be trained out of a soldier. Your whole being seems built to cause fear, from your teeth and claws to the way you meld into the dark, even without your magic. If you did not speak, if you could not reason and show emotion, I wouldn't hesitate to call you a monster. But you do, and you can, so besides your form, there is little that makes you different from many veterans. I know men who have killed more than you, and who show less concern or remorse. Some few show pride in the number of lives they've taken, which I've never seen from you in the context of killing. Are they monsters, then?

"You say that you want to kill. I think most of us have desired the Night Blossom's death, Kira perhaps being the exception. You say that you are disappointed. Frustrated. I can understand that. You have been expecting an emotional release, and been denied. You are not the master of your emotions. None of us are. We can only control what we do with them. Have you harmed anyone who didn't deserve it in some way?"

"I've been needlessly cruel to Kesra."

"That is childish, not monstrous. But Draka, you could have maimed or killed her to hurt the Night Blossom. You could have killed both of them. You could have gone outside and torn your way through their men watching the inn. You didn't. You went to be alone, until they were gone.

"I can't tell you if that is the best way to handle what you've been feeling, but it is not a bad one, I think. And while I would not claim that you are a saint, neither are you a monster. At least no more than many people I consider friends. Does that answer your question to your satisfaction?"

"Not a monster, just not a very good person?"

"Better than one might hope, under the circumstances. You at least think about killing. You don't just do it."

His words were kind, and true enough. I did think about it. Far more than I was comfortable with but, sure, maybe constantly wondering if this was an appropriate time to kill someone, actively looking for excuses, was a better thing than just doing it. But I was in a self-flagellating mood.

"The way I've treated Kesra, it's unforgivable. Her only crimes are being naive and Zabra's sister. And I know that. I knew it before I hurt her, repeatedly threatened her life, and promised to kill her only family. That's not something a halfway decent person does."

"What do you want from us?" Tam asked, a tinge of annoyance to his voice. "Do you want us to condemn you? Or to tell you that it's okay? Yeah, you probably messed Kesra up. It worked, didn't it? We've won, hopefully. You've won. Assuming that you're right about them, of course. You can stop worrying about them burning down our inn, or trying to kidnap or murder us, or anything else. They're even paying reparations. And if you're worried about this Kesra woman, are you sure that she's entirely innocent? That she knew nothing about their finances? That she had no idea where the money came from? Are you sure that she didn't simply turn a blind eye to the things her beloved sister did?"

"That—" I started to retort, but then I thought about it. Tark and Zabra both insisted that Kesra didn't know anything. But while I didn't know her, she never came across as stupid to me. From what I'd been told, she basically ran the trading side of the sisters' business. Could there be something in what Tam said? Did she simply refuse to wonder where the extra money came from?

And there was something not quite right about how Zabra had reacted whenever Kesra raised her voice, when she was angry or frustrated. There was something there, but I couldn't quite see it, and it never felt important enough to worry about in the moment.

"I don't think that you're supposed to make me feel better by making the victim look worse, but thank you," I told Tam. "That does help. And so does having all of you here. So thanks, all of you."

"Are you ready to tell us what happened during the meeting now?" Mak asked after a little while. "You felt very pleased for a short time."

"Yeah. It was good. We came to an understanding, the lady justice and me."

I filled them in, trying to remember as many details as I could of what Sempralia had said. I still wasn't feeling great about myself, so I made extra sure to tell them how she'd asked if she could touch me at the end. I was feeling very smug about that, and I wanted them all to know that even a powerful old lady like her thought I was awesome. Their smiles and laughter at that definitely helped.

The mood grew tense when I told them about how Sempralia had been having the inn watched, even though they were hardly surprised. If anything, they'd been expecting it on some level. The fact that no one had come for them over the disappearance of Tark and our other less-than-legal nighttime activities was accepted as a good sign.

Tam explained. "If the lady justice had us followed, besides watching the inn, she might know about Tark. She might even know what you all talked about when you met with the Night Blossom. But if she wanted to have us put on trial, she wouldn't be so cordial, would she? At least that doesn't seem like her, not judging by her reputation. So yeah, she might try to use it as leverage, and we may even have to bend to that, but it doesn't look to me like we're in any real trouble."

Then I got to the part with the archer. Herald was literally bouncing with excitement when I told them about catching the bastard, and they reassured me that my decision to hand him over was the right one. I finished off with my visit to the village. I'd already touched on Darvellan and Elem, so I gave the full story, how I'd found them in a worryingly quiet village and was going to kill them until Tinir intervened.

Tam was the first to speak up. "Darvellan? I know that guy! And Elem, she—Val, she's the Tavvanarian woman who was with that spear fighter before, isn't she? Soren? Sorem?"

"Sorben."

"Right! So her and Darvellan, huh? Can't have been married for long . . ."

"Yeah. They smelled . . . newlywed, if you get what I mean," I told them.

Mak rolled her eyes at that, and Herald looked confused. Tam gave a snort and short laugh before continuing. "*Anyway*, you gave them a chance to explain themselves and you *didn't* kill them, which is what matters. And I'm glad you didn't, because Darvellan's a good-natured guy. A little rough when we first met him, but if he was from some outlaw village outside the city's reach . . ."

"What do you mean 'smelled newlywed'?" Herald interrupted when Tam paused, but I skillfully dodged the question by moving on, and no one else seemed inclined to answer her.

"I'm going to need someone, and I guess that someone should be Mak, to send a letter to the lady justice. Both about talking to this damn hunter who's been trying to kill me, because I *really* need to know how he's been tracking me, and about when and where they want me helping out on the border."

"Are you sure about doing that?" Mak asked as Herald pestered Tam and Val to explain. "I know that it sounds easy, but you'd still be getting involved in the trouble that's brewing. Is that something you want?"

"Mak, this is your city, yeah? All of you."

"It is."

"Then I want it to be mine, as well. Easy as that. And I should help my city, yeah?"

"I think you should wait for the city, or at least its rulers, to do something for you before you get patriotic. But as long as you are sure."

I didn't point out that the city of Karakan had already given me so much. It had given me Herald and the others. What else could I ask for? Except a big pile of coins, of course, but the city had contributed a decent bit to my hoard, too, so even there I had good cause to be gracious. Possibly even grateful!

But saying all that would have felt overly mushy after all the whining I had already done about myself, so I didn't say any of that. "I'm sure," I said instead. "But I appreciate the thought. Will you take care of it, Mak?"

"Of course."

"And the archer? Can I trust you all to talk to him? I'd like you to take Ardek along as well."

The man in question, who'd been spacing out in the back, looked up. "Me, boss?"

"Yeah, you! You did wonders with Simdal. I'm guessing you don't have any history this time, but I want you there."

"All right, boss, if you say so." He smirked. "Got to say, being some kind of interrogator for a dragon was not where I thought my life would go!"

"Yeah, well, here we are. I'd do it myself, but I suspect getting in unseen wherever he's being held might be tricky."

"I am not so sure," Herald said. "If you shifted . . ."

From there the conversation sort of devolved into increasingly ridiculous ways of bringing me into a prison in the heart of the city. It started with a large box and ended with a long, thin pipe carried on the shoulders of two people, with some ridiculous excuse about replacing part of the water drains. Val correctly pointed out that I could just shift and get in behind the others who'd go, but was booed down as a spoilsport. Sure, I could do that. And with Sempralia's permission I could probably even talk to the archer without being bothered by anyone who shouldn't know about my presence. But in the end I just didn't want to. Same as Zabra, I didn't entirely trust myself to see him again. Just because I felt better about my motives didn't make the frustration and the desire to destroy these people any weaker. Until I dealt with that, I didn't want to take any chances.

But it was nice. Talking about something silly was just what I needed, and Kira's idea of carrying me in a massively oversized backpack was pretty damn funny.

I sent them away after that, with the excuse that I wanted to sleep. I napped the rest of the day away, but I slept poorly.

Sometime in the evening there was a knock on the door. I could feel my sisters on the other side, and when I opened it they were dressed for sleep.

"We thought you could use some company tonight," Herald said as she settled in against me.

"I really do. And, Mak? Thanks for bringing everyone down today. I needed that."

"I know," Mak said, cozying up beside her sister. "I feel what you feel, remember? And there may be better cures for self-loathing than being surrounded by people who care for you, but I don't know one."

I ignored the fact that four out of the six had had their minds messed with to some degree. It was no time to let thoughts like that fester. And as long as I still had Tam and Val on my side, I *probably* hadn't turned into one of the dragon tyrants from their stories.

Probably.

Mak had sent a letter to Sempralia the same afternoon, never once mentioning me or anything else that might be considered incriminating but still making it clear that we would like to speak with the prisoner and have me on my way south as soon as possible. A reply came in the morning, though only to the first half. We were welcome to visit the prisoner the following day, with Sempralia asking to meet with Mak afterward. Kalder would be expecting Mak and whoever accompanied her two hours after dawn, on the steps of the Palace.

Besides Ardek, we decided that Val should go with Mak; that man seemed to know or know of every adventurer in the city. If anyone had any acquaintances in common with the archer, any common ground to build on if it became necessary, it would be him. Besides, where Mak had a naturally authoritative personality—somewhat damaged but healing nicely—and the benefit of my command and charisma advances, and Ardek had his likeability, Val had a solid, reliable and trustworthy air about him.

When I thought about it, it wasn't even the fact that this guy had been trying to kill me that had me so bothered. I hated it, sure, and I was glad to have put an end to it, and I looked forward to him getting some kind of punishment, even if it wouldn't be me doling it out. I was more bothered by the fact that the people around me had been in danger, but that wasn't the main issue, either. I'd expected to be hunted. I'd expected attempts on my life. And I'd known for a long time that being associated with me was dangerous. But the thing that truly, deeply bothered me about the whole situation with the archer was that he'd been able to find me.

If he could do it, others might be able to, as well. I had to know how. And between Mak, Val, and Ardek, I figured they shouldn't have any problems getting answers.

CHAPTER THIRTY-SIX

Reassurances

The rest of that day was uneventful. I thought about going to sleep on my hoard and trying to dreamwalk on Zabra, and then going to eat another Nest Heart with Herald, but I just didn't have it in me. I didn't want to deal with Zabra or her sister again, not yet. It felt too big.

The evening, on the other hand, was busy. The big thing was Herald insisting on going to see Maglan, but first Garal came by. We hadn't talked in a while; he'd come by to say hi a couple of times, with or without Lalia, but I hadn't had a real conversation with either of them for . . . I wasn't sure how long. Months? They'd been out on patrol almost constantly. I knew that they'd moved out of the inn a few weeks back, though Rib and Pot had stayed, but other than that I wasn't exactly up to date on anything to do with them.

"To what do I owe the pleasure?" I asked after letting him in. "Nowhere to rush off to?"

"Yeah. Lalia and I came in earlier today and were told that we're on leave for a few days. No idea why; the commander's being tight-lipped about it, which means something's going to happen. But no use worrying, right?"

"Right. How's the barracks coming along?"

"It keeps the rain off and the wind out, but that's about it. Still needs work. Get some dividing walls up, things like that. Honestly, as long as we have food in our bellies, there are more important things to spend the company's silver on. Like our horses."

"You've been working them hard, yeah?"

"We have. I've had to leave Melon in the city. She's a tough girl, but the way we've been abusing our poor mounts . . ." He frowned. "We've got some high-advancement tenders taking care of them. They deserve it. Anyway, those Tekereteki mercenaries are still out there. We guess they realized that we have that tracking medallion you gave us, because whatever it points toward hasn't moved for a while, and we have to spread out and move a lot to keep them in check."

I considered asking for the medallion back. It was a decent chunk of silver, after all. But then it occurred to me that the Silver Spurs might be able to track it just like we tracked the companion medallion that their commander held, and I was *not* going to just lead people to anything precious, whether that was my hoard or my family.

"That's too bad," I said, "but at least it did some good."

"Yeah." Garal was silent for a moment. "So are you going to tell me what you all have been so secretive about this last week?"

A tense silence settled in the small room as we watched each other. I was sure that he wasn't just baiting me. Everything I knew about him told me that if he asked, he knew that something was going on. And he was *Garal.* One of my family's oldest friends. Literally the first person I met here, and the first to defend me.

"Listen, I'm not asking to be let in on *everything*," he said when the silence stretched. "But when old friends start acting all anxious, having whispered conversations that stop when you get close, you wonder. I tried to see you a few days ago, and I knew you were here because I'd talked with Ardek, but they wouldn't let me into the cellar. I mean, Mak was embarrassed about it, but still. Then there were all the street toughs surrounding the place. And suddenly today it was fine, but there's a storm cloud above everything. So . . . anything you can tell me about?"

"Yeah. You should know about this, though I don't want it going beyond you, Lalia, and the cousins for now. Rib and Pot know some of it anyway."

"Ah. Something to do with what they've been helping you with, then?"

"Right. Long story short, we've dealt with the Night Blossom."

Garal's eyebrows slowly climbed toward his hairline, his lips parting silently. "That's . . ." He started, then tried again. "Shouldn't you be celebrating? Is she dead? Who was she? What happened?"

"Tespril Zabra. Do you know the name?"

"Never heard of her."

"Well, she's alive, and hopefully under control. Mak and her came to an agreement. Heavily in our favor, as you can probably guess. But the whole damn thing just . . . It feels like I've got a stain on my soul, if you'll forgive the drama. Herald and Mak aren't much better, and Kira just hated the whole situation. Tam and Val are a little more pragmatic, and Ardek doesn't seem to care much; I think he blames her more than me for his friends dying. But they weren't there at the end, so . . . We're glad to have won, but we're not proud of how we did it, all right? And I made some threats that I'd rather not have to carry out."

"But you will if you have to?"

"Yeah. If she goes back on the deal we made, I can't afford to let her live."

I didn't feel up to telling him about Kesra. Everything to do with her made me feel ashamed and confused, but I'd just have to live with myself and hopefully get over it.

"Do you regret anything? Is there something you could have done differently without changing the outcome for the worse?"

"If there was, I would have done it that way in the first place, wouldn't I? No, I don't see a better way to get the same result. If I had to do the whole thing over, I wouldn't change anything. But both what we did and the fact that I wouldn't change it forces me to ask myself some unpleasant questions about who I am."

"Well, that's good, isn't it?"

I looked at him silently until he continued.

"You're questioning yourself, and it seems like you don't like the answers. You probably already know this, but it can't hurt to hear it from someone else—that *is* a good thing. Perhaps there really was no other path to where we are now. Perhaps there was a better one, and you simply can't see it. But since you're questioning yourself, I'm sure that you'll look for a better way the next time you need to do something difficult. You may find it, and you may not. But as long as you don't stop looking, as long as you take the better path when it presents itself, I think you'll be fine. You may not be happy with yourself. It may take time to find peace. But you won't be a monster."

"But what if I can't do that? What if I can't take the better path, even if I find it? What if I stop caring?"

"Stop caring? I don't think that you could."

"What makes you so sure? I've changed. I'm still changing. And I've done just . . . awful things."

"But part of you is still the little dragon who hauled herself out of a lake, found me dying by a tree, and decided to help. Whatever you've had to do, I know that she's still in there, and I know that she's not going anywhere. And if I ever doubt that, I can always look in your eyes and see her looking back at me. I can see that you *care*. That's why I'm so sure. And if you're still worried that you're a monster, I can bring Lalia down here. If *she* says that you're not, you'll have to believe her, right?"

He grinned at me, full of mischief, and I couldn't help but laugh. "Monster this, monster that. You've been talking to the others haven't you?"

"Of course I have. They're my friends, and so are you. They may not have told me everything that's been going on here, but we talk about you. We worry. Surely you know that?"

"Yeah, I do. I guess I just need a lot of reassurance right now."

"But you don't know why? Or you don't want to tell me?"

I knew why, of course. It all came down to Kesra, hurting someone who I knew didn't deserve it, using her to get at her sister. But Garal was right, and so was Val. I cared. I felt regret. I wished I could have done things differently, and I would try to do so in the future. That would have to do for now.

"I know why," I told him with a sigh. "Perhaps someday I'll tell you, when I've had time to come to terms with it. But not today."

"That's fine. Whenever you're ready."

We spent another long while talking, just catching up and talking about little things until Herald came down looking so serious that Garal took it as his cue to leave.

"Don't be a stranger, all right?" I said as he got up. "I might be going away for a while, but let's not wait for weeks again before we really talk."

"I'll promise if you will," he told me.

"Deal."

Then he was gone, exchanging a few words with Herald on the way out, and she took his place in the room. She stayed on her feet, though.

"I'm going out," she declared.

I instantly felt worry boil up. I'd asked—though it was more like an order—that everybody stay at the inn to avoid possible reprisals from the Night Blossom's people. "Ah . . . are you sure?"

"Definitely. I have been cooped up here for days. Days! And I have no idea how much longer Mag will be in the city. They have been here for weeks now. Who knows when they will be sent back to the south? But you have been so worried these last few days—for good reasons!—so I thought . . ."

Ah. Her determination made a lot more sense now.

"So you wanted to see if it's okay with me?"

"Yeah." She sat back on her heels in front of me, losing some of the confident air she'd arrived with. "I know that I do not need your permission, but I did not want to surprise you." That was sweet of her. And prescient, too. I probably would have freaked out if she was just suddenly outside the inn. "And," she continued, "I thought I might ask you to come along."

"Oh!" Up until now she'd been keeping her meetings with her boyfriend secret from me, which had hurt. The last time we'd talked about Maglan she had promised to bring him to the inn and introduce us before he was sent back to the south, which was a step in the right direction. To be asked to come along when she went to meet him took me by surprise, to say the least. "Yeah, sure," I said. "I'll come along."

"Not to meet him, you understand," she said quickly. "I still think that it would be best to do that here. But you were right when you said that it would be safer to move through the city shifted, and even if the Night Blossom and her people are *hopefully* not a threat anymore, I would feel much safer with someone nearby. Just in case, you know?"

"So why not take Tam again? It's not like he needs to be able to see you to go to the same place as you."

"I just . . . I want it to be you." She wrapped her arms around her knees. "I love Tam, and I trust him, but nobody makes me feel safe like you do."

If I could have blushed I would have. "Aw, that's . . . Come here!" I sat up and moved a little closer to her. "Give me a hug, and let's go."

Since we knew that the inn might still be watched, Herald went upstairs and asked Mak to let us out the cellar door. Mak seemed more resigned than anything about Herald heading out to see her boyfriend. I even saw her silently slip her younger sister a small bag. Herald blushed furiously and not a word was spoken about it, which led me to believe that the bag must contain more of the contraceptive tea Herald had mentioned to me. Then Herald and I both shifted and left, moving quickly along the streets.

I knew where in the city the regiments were lodged. There was a fairly large military camp in the south of the city, and it was easy to find from above. From the sky I had become familiar with the city, and could find most of the important places easily. On street level, though, I still went by general direction, moving as straight as I could until I found the right area and then hunting around until I found what I needed. Herald, however, moved unerringly toward her goal along streets and alleys, never hesitating at a turn. I estimated it took us less than twenty minutes to reach the army camp, at which point she stepped into a dark archway and shifted back.

"Can you follow until I meet Mag?" She had her shadowsight on, and I gave a nod that only she could see. "Thank you," she said, then approached the guards at the gate.

Honestly, I would have expected some more suspicion or professionalism, but Herald got inside with barely a fuss. It didn't hurt that one of the two guards recognized her and called her by name, though the two weren't exactly subtle about why they thought she might be there. Sure, there were probably few reasons for a young woman to be visiting an army camp late in the evening, but still! There was no call for the crude, if friendly, innuendo they piled on her.

The encampment was surrounded by a wall about ten feet tall, which did as much to stop me as a line in the sand. I stretched and slipped over it easily. Inside was a parade ground, a fenced off area that I guessed to be a training yard, a large paddock next to a building that was unmistakably a place for stables, and numerous other buildings. There were a few people moving about, in or out of uniform, but no one questioned Herald. Some even gave her a friendly greeting. I was pretty sure that an unescorted civilian would have been stopped in about five seconds flat at an army base back on Earth, if they even somehow made it in, but things were clearly different here.

I followed Herald around in the shadows until she reached one of the buildings. She knocked on a door, which opened after a few seconds, and a cheerful voice greeted her by name. She spoke in an equally friendly tone, turned to smile in my general direction, and stepped inside. That was as far as I could follow without causing a commotion, and I didn't want to be around for what I assumed she had planned anyway, so I found a nearby roof to settle in and wait. It was a good night for it, cool and clear, like most nights on Mallin.

A few hours later Herald came back outside. She had a man with her, perhaps two inches shorter than she was, with wide shoulders, cropped hair, and a day's stubble on his round face. *So this*, I thought, *is Maglan*. He was handsome enough, but if I knew Herald, then the most important thing she saw in him was the genuine affection—adoration, really—with which he looked at her. The young man was, as far as I could tell, absolutely smitten.

They stopped outside the door for a while, whispering to each other, seeming reluctant to part. I couldn't see Herald's face, but Maglan looked sad. Then Herald wrapped one arm around his back, ran the other up his neck, and leaned in to kiss him passionately. Maglan looked strong, but there was something almost desperate in how he clung to her. Despite the jealousy that churned in my gut, I grinned. That felt right, somehow. This Maglan wouldn't be taking Herald from me. If anything, he belonged to her, not the other way around, and I could live with that.

Once they finally parted and Maglan went back inside the barracks, Herald turned and I could see her face. Tears streaked her cheeks, and she made no effort to hide them as she searched me out on the roof where I sat. She looked directly at me, then nodded in the direction of the gate she'd come through before heading toward it.

The same two guards were there. Poor bastards. I wondered how long their shifts were.

"Your soldier give you bad news, then?" One of the two looked with real sympathy at Herald as she approached. "Don't worry, Miss. He'll be fine. You'll see. Those Happarans make a lot of noise, but nothing will come of it."

Herald forced a smile. "Yeah. Thank you."

We met in the same archway where she'd shifted back. I was waiting for her in the flesh, but she didn't want to talk. "I'll tell you back at the inn," was all she said before shifting and taking off in the direction we'd come, back toward Her Grace's Favor.

Mak, ever reliable, sensed our approach and opened the cellar door for us, letting us enter without shifting back. "Now will you tell me what happened?" I asked Herald after thanking Mak. I could guess, but it felt important to let her tell us.

Herald sat down heavily on the bench that we kept there and looked up at Mak and I miserably. "Draka, you want to meet Mag before he goes back to the south, do you not?"

"That's what I said, yeah."

"Yeah. Well, he has been told to be ready to march within the week. I have invited him to come over. How do you feel about seeing him tomorrow?"

CHAPTER THIRTY-SEVEN

Maglan

Mak, Val, and Ardek left to question the archer early the next morning while Herald and I slept. It was close to noon when they came back and woke us.

"He wants to talk to you," Mak said as we gathered in the basement. "He hasn't even talked to the council's interrogators, though that might be because they've been unwilling to get rough with him until now. Kalder asked that we try, before they resort to harsher methods. I took the liberty of agreeing on your behalf."

"Sorry, boss," Ardek said. "Guy refused hard to talk. He's nowhere near as soft as he looks."

I groaned. "Why, though? Why couldn't he just talk to you? What the hell does he want?"

Mak shrugged. "To talk to you. He swears he'll tell us anything we want if he can meet you, and since his method of tracking you sounded so important to you . . . I didn't overstep, did I?"

I felt, more than saw, her anxiety when she feared that she'd displeased me, that my annoyance was directed at her, and I hurried to calm her. "No, you did good. If talking to him is what it takes, then I want to talk to him. Where and when?"

I knew she could feel that I meant what I said, and the tension left her as quickly as it had come. "Here, tonight. Mister Kalder will bring him."

"I assume that means that Kalder will be listening to the conversation as well?"

"Not if we don't want him to. He assured me so himself. We can leave him in the common room, but we'll have to promise not to hurt the prisoner."

"I mean . . . hurt? I can probably manage without hurting him, yeah. So, who is he? What do we know about him?"

"There is something of a mystery," Val said after Mak looked at him, inviting him to take over. "His name is Avjilan. He is no one I know, and no one I've spoken to knows him by description, though that description has been vague so far. Fairly new in the city, I believe. By his appearance and accent, I would think that he's from Faltha, far to the southeast. Nothing was forthcoming except that he's a monster hunter."

"Figures," I said, not trying to hide my disgust. "Do you think he's after the bounty, or just trying to kill me for killing's sake?"

"The bounty is still for a wyvern," Val said. "Even after the Adventurers' Guild matched the Alchemists' one dragon and twenty eagles, it's still for a wyvern. This man surely knows what you are."

"So he wants to be a big damn hero, or to sell me for parts, or to try to claim my hoard. Something like that." I felt the venom leak into my mouth as anger roiled inside me. "And you expect me not to kill this man when I see him?"

"Better not, boss," Ardek said. "This Kalder guy . . . Being around him is a little like being around you. You understand what I mean? Like you're only alive because he hasn't decided to kill you?"

I huffed. Ardek was right. The guy did have an aura of danger around him. Not like he gave off the impression of being violent, just extremely capable of violence. As you'd expect of someone guarding one of the most important people in the city.

"Yeah, fine," I said. "I get it. He, and by extension Sempralia, wants the archer alive, and getting on her bad side would be a huge pain. But I'll be relying on you all to shut him up and get between us in case he says something extraordinarily stupid. Or if I just really, really want to kill him for some reason, Mak."

"I'll make sure of it," she promised.

"Thank you. So. What did you agree with Sempralia? You were away for hours, but if the archer guy didn't talk, I can't imagine you spent long with him."

"I spoke with the lady justice, but not for long. I waited for hours before I actually met her. I don't think that was intentional, though. I wasn't the only person outside her office, not by far. Honestly, we didn't agree on much, other than another meeting in the near future."

"'Not much' isn't nothing, though."

"No. We did agree on this: If you help the forces in the south to the satisfaction of General Sarvalian, the lady justice will tell you what it is that the council needs your help with that they can't do on their own. We pretty much can't negotiate terms for that without us knowing what the issue is, so that will have to wait. But no matter what, if you fly south, she and some of her allies will start to work on public opinion in your favor. She wouldn't promise success, but she did promise her best efforts, and I believe her. She'll make sure that there are city guards, ones vetted by her own guard, Kalder, nearby the inn at all times as long as you're away. And I also got a promise out of her that the general will not ask you to put yourself at risk. That means reconnaissance only. You won't be expected to deal with any raiders or anything like that."

"What if I want to?"

She sighed. "Draka . . . Please be careful, all right? I know that you're you, and you have some aggression to let out, but don't take any unnecessary risks. Please?"

"Yeah, all right. But I'll decide what's unnecessary."

"That's the best we can hope for, I suppose. Ah, and I tried to get some gold out of her, but no luck, I'm afraid. I think she's worried how it would look for the city to be giving gold to a dragon. But I won't give up on that."

"I know you won't. Maybe see if you can get your taxes waived for the year or something?"

A grin split Mak's face at that. "I'm sure the lady justice could manage some tax relief for services rendered to the city. Great idea!"

"She's a clever one, our boss," Ardek opined from where he sat. The flatterer.

"So, there's one more thing," Mak continued, "and the lady justice was adamant about this. She wants you to travel south with a small group."

"What?" I asked flatly, my tone not at all betraying how annoyed I was.

"Sorry," Mak said. "She wouldn't budge on that. I know that it'll slow you down something awful, but she insisted. They'll all be mounted, and she believes that they can be trusted, but it's take it or leave it, I'm afraid."

"Yeah, it'll slow me down! And I'm guessing we'll be traveling during the day, too?"

"That was what she wanted, yes. She says that she wants you to be seen. Though maybe not together with the others."

"But why? If she wants me to be seen I could just fly long loops on my way down. Did she at least say why it's so important that I travel with these people? Who they are?"

"No. Only that if you agree, she'll inform us of a time and place to meet them. And I'm as confused as you are. This whole thing is supposed to show that you can trust each other, right? So if she doesn't already trust you, it's not likely that they're anyone important, or that they'll be carrying anything valuable. It smells of some kind of scheme, and she must know that we'll see that."

"Again, perhaps it is about trust?" Val suggested. "Do you trust her enough to do this despite knowing that there is a scheme behind it? Or perhaps she has decided to trust you already, based on what she knows. Your scouting for the army might be for the sake of the other council members. It could be that she simply wants to take the opportunity to use you to escort someone or something important. The mercenary raiders are still about, after all."

"Ugh, I don't like this," I complained. "I thought she was supposed to be straightforward."

"Fair and equitable in her rulings, and true to her word. That is her reputation. If she is a skilled enough schemer, there would be no rumors about her being underhanded."

"Fine. Tell her that I agree. I'm going to just hope that this is a sign of trust, and prepare myself emotionally for it to be some kind of scheme that makes me a new enemy," I sighed. "I'd hate for you all to get into trouble because I don't go along with her bullshit. Anything else?"

They all had things to take care of, so Mak and Val went upstairs. Ardek, to my surprise, stuck around, seemingly just to spend time. He told me a little about the people he'd recruited, mostly old friends or friends of friends, but other than that we didn't talk about anything serious. He taught me a dice game that was very similar to dice poker, except that you rolled six dice and got to keep one for your next hand. Ardek explained that there would usually be a lot of betting, and it wasn't unusual for a game to end in a fistfight, but that he'd appreciate it if we could not do that. That ate up a good hour. It was nice to have another game I could play. The others, Tam especially, had tried to teach me some local card games before, but I had trouble holding the cards. Ardek's large dice, though, were no problem.

It was pretty amusing, too, how Ardek had a dreamy, almost dazed look on his face half the time that we played. Rolling dice with a dragon had probably not been on his list of things he'd ever expected to do.

"Oh, before I forget!" Ardek said as he was leaving. He then cleared his throat, concentrated, and said, in Kira's dialect of Tekereteki, *"Hello dragon Draka! Name Ardek. Pleased!"*

"Ah . . . hello, Ardek. Very good!" I replied in the same language, nonplussed but amused. A little impressed, really. The grin that broke out across his face when I replied was irresistible, though, and I couldn't help but smile back at him. "Been spending time with Kira, have you?" I asked, switching back to Karakani.

"Yeah, been keeping an eye on her when she's healing and such. I've been helping her with the lingo, so she's been returning the favor. Didn't think I'd get along so well with someone I can't talk to, but she's easy to like, yeah?"

"She is that."

I let Ardek go without asking, but of course I immediately started speculating about if there was or might potentially be something going on between those two. They had something in common at least, me. Both of them had been forcibly brought under me through a combination of good and shit luck; they'd both been associated with groups I loathe, but I'd decided to spare them instead of slaughtering them, together with their companions. That and being put together in the relatively small confines of the inn—was that enough for a friendship or even romance to bloom? Time would tell.

Well into the afternoon there was a minor commotion upstairs, and I felt both Herald and Mak moving around, meeting up near the front door in the common room. Soon thereafter Tam popped down to let me know that Maglan had arrived, and that he'd be having a quick, late lunch before Herald brought him down. I thanked him, he left, and I commenced worrying.

I felt some guilt about forcing this meeting. Maglan had no idea that I existed; he would've probably heard the news about a dragon in the harbor, but that wasn't the same thing. But it wasn't him I was worried about, at least not directly. I was worried about Herald, and what would happen if Maglan freaked out.

Herald liked this guy. Liked him a lot. She had claimed not to be in love with him, months ago, but I couldn't help but think that had changed. She'd been so excited to go see him the previous night, and she'd left in tears after finding out that he was being sent south again. Now, if Maglan couldn't both accept and keep quiet about me, there was no telling what that would do to their relationship, and despite the jealousy I felt when I thought about her feelings for him, I didn't want to be responsible for ruining something good in her life.

I resolved to be on my best behavior, and only lightly terrify him if I absolutely had to.

I wouldn't let him run off into the night shouting about how the Tekereteki women at Her Grace's Favor were consorting with dragons, of course. I was hoping that his affection for Herald would translate into a willingness to keep a big, dragon-shaped secret, but if I couldn't trust him to stay quiet about me, I'd have to break him, one way or another. I couldn't kill him, for Herald's sake, but that was fine. I didn't want to do that anyway.

I didn't want to. I really didn't.

I'm going to kill him.

I squashed the thought ruthlessly, keeping myself still and ignoring Mak's worried looks.

Things had been going fine. I'd been perfectly polite, and Maglan had taken the whole thing well, once the shock wore off. He was visibly tipsy, which Herald had told me was intentional on her part. She'd also been preparing him to see something utterly, unbelievably amazing, so he'd properly steeled himself before I made my entrance. He'd prostrated himself, then stammered out an introduction once Herald got him back on his feet. I'd responded—very politely, I thought. I'd told him how much I'd been looking forward to meeting him. He flattered me outrageously. He made the connection between my eyes and the change in Herald's from a rich, deep brown to gold, and talked for a minute about how beautiful Herald's new eyes were and what an amazing gift I'd given her. Things were going just fine.

That was until Herald, sitting next to him, started unconsciously playing with his hand. He, equally oblivious, brought it up so he could kiss her fingers as we spoke.

Seeing them kiss at the army camp hadn't affected me a fraction as much as those small, affectionate gestures. Jealousy burned inside me. It was stupid and irrational, I knew that, but I wasn't sure how to deal with it. I loved Herald. She was my best friend and my sister. I was not *in love* with her. He was *not* a rival in that sense. But he was a rival for her attention, and her affection, and seeing them like that caused a cascade of what-ifs in my mind. What if she started spending more and more time away from me? What if they got married? What if they moved into a house somewhere I couldn't easily visit? What if they had *kids*?

It was the same ugly possessiveness that I'd been struggling with, and it was telling me, again, to hide Herald away so I could have her to myself. Only this time I felt like I should kill Maglan first, to remove that possible complication.

I even had to consciously keep my shadow from doing anything, which it most definitely would have if I'd let it.

Maglan, thankfully, was entirely unaware of the violence inside me. When he laughed nervously it had nothing to do with me wanting to tear him limb from limb. "You know," he said, "I was really nervous to meet Miss Makanna—ah, sorry. Lady Drakonum, I mean. And that never really went away. It was like meeting Herald's mother and older sister all at once, you know? But this, this is like— and I'm really sorry, Lady Drakonum, I know how wrong this is—this is like meeting the matriarch of the House. You have this air of authority about you, Lady Draka. It's—" He turned to Herald. "What was that word you taught me, love? When it's like you could touch it?"

Herald was rubbing his palm with her thumb, smiling softly. "Palpable."

"Right, yeah. Palpable! Like I could take one or two steps toward you, if you'd let me, but after that I'd really struggle."

"Unapproachable, am I?" I fixed him with a look that must have been much more like a glare than I'd intended, because the scent of fear in the cellar immediately grew stronger.

"Ah, not as such? Majestic, more like? Regal?"

"Like you do not feel worthy to be in her presence?" Herald suggested, openly trying to butter me up. She couldn't feel what I did the way Mak could, but she could read me like no one else. She knew how I felt about Maglan at that moment; the tension and worry in her eyes was obvious to anyone who knew to look for it.

Not that it stopped her from playing with his hand. Perhaps it was entirely unconscious.

While their words slid off me, that worry shamed me enough to make me behave.

"Herald told me that she learned archery from you," I said, changing the topic. I wasn't going anywhere with it; I just wanted to say something polite. "She's an excellent shot. You must have done a good job."

"Well, she's a quick study," he said, looking at her fondly. "And you liked it, didn't you, love?" He looked at Herald, who smiled back at him. "I could barely get her to go home from the range some days. Of course, we in the regiments mostly practice firing quickly at formations. The sniping, shooting birds in flight and all, that's Miss Lalia's doing."

"Right. You like being a soldier, Maglan?"

"I suppose. Pays well enough, and I've got my mates. Even got some pay when we weren't called up, just to come for training every morning. And now we're called up I don't spend much, so I can put most of my pay aside. But, ah . . . I haven't seen a battle yet, have I? So I don't know quite yet how I'll feel once I do."

That was honestly much more than I'd expected from him. I'd been prepared for him to try to impress us with bravado, and here he was giving a measured, thoughtful response.

"But you're going back to the border soon, aren't you?"

"Yeah. Tomorrow or the day after, I'd guess. Commanders won't say. Don't know what they're waiting for, but we all have to be ready to move every morning. I have a kid coming around the gate every morning in case I need to send a message to my Herald."

The two shared a sickeningly bittersweet look. Not in love, my scaly ass. And that whole "my Herald" thing didn't help with my jealousy at all, which made me want to do something unfortunate.

Mak probably felt the bitchiness rise in me, because she chose that moment to speak up. "So, Mag, you've met Draka. You know about our secret friend. Can you keep that knowledge to yourself?"

"Well, Lady Drakonum, I mean, it could put you all in trouble if I didn't, wouldn't it? I can't do that. And you, Lady Draka, you must be very important to Herald. She was so anxious about me meeting you, you know? And I haven't heard about you hurting anyone, excepting those pirates in the harbor, so I guess you can't be as bad as the stories. No, I'm not going to tell anyone."

I looked at Mak, who nodded at me. "All right," I told Maglan. "It was nice meeting you."

Herald took his hand and led him up the stairs, and I let him go, both frustrated and relieved that I didn't have an excuse to hurt him.

Late that afternoon there was a reply from the lady justice Sempralia. It came with a simple map. She respectfully requested that I prepare myself to meet my traveling companions at the specified location the next morning, two hours after sunrise, and then be ready to continue south. Everything was ready.

I had one last meeting to get through. One night with my sisters. And then, I was going to the front.

CHAPTER THIRTY-EIGHT

Avjilan

After Maglan, meeting the archer again was easy. All I had to do was not kill him.

Someone had healed his wrist. I hadn't expected that. Why make it easier for the prisoner to cause mischief? At the same time it was the humane thing to do, and while magical healers weren't exactly common, from what I knew— Kira did decent business upstairs—it only stood to reason that the prison would have at least one on hand. It was probably the whole ancient-medieval level of everything that threw me off and made me expect prisoners to be treated like dirt.

Kalder arrived with his prisoner through the cellar door. He made us promise not to kill or seriously harm the man, then left him with us, going around the outside to enter the inn through the front door. That left Mak, Val, Ardek, and myself facing the prisoner, whom we'd tied, seated, to one of the supports holding up the common room's floor.

I skipped the pleasantries. "So. You wanted to see me. Here I am. Talk."

"Would it help if I start with an apology?" he asked, in excellent, if heavily accented, Karakani, his vowels long and his consonants soft. And Mercies have mercy, the man's voice was captivating. It was in the higher range for a man, and clear and musical in a way that made me want to hear him sing. Nine words was all it took for some of my spite to give way to a soft whisper of a desire to make him mine.

"Unlikely, but you can always try," I managed. I hadn't been prepared for this. I'd only heard him scream before. Now . . . asking him to sing for me would be weird, but at least I could make him talk.

"Then I would like to do so. I, Avjilan of Faltha, ask your forgiveness for my repeated attempts on your life. Whether or not you can give it, my conscience demands that I express my regret and explain my actions."

Gods, he was so *earnest*. There was such contrition in his eyes that I couldn't help but believe him. I nodded, and settled in to listen. "Go on."

"I came to Karakan to hunt monsters—monstrous animals, trolls and the like. When the bounty for a single wyvern reached one and a half dragons, it was suggested to me that I try to claim it. When the Adventurers' Guild matched that bounty, I began to hunt. I should have stopped once it became clear that there was no wyvern, that you were a dragon and were in fact intelligent, but I convinced myself that I was too invested. For this, I offer my humble apologies. I have no excuse."

"The man is polite when he is not trying to kill me, I will give him that," I told Mak in Tekereteki.

"He also understands what you are saying," Mak said. I couldn't tell what she'd seen, but Avjilan nodded.

"I do understand some," he admitted in the same language. His pronunciation was careful. Considering how he rounded all the consonants in Karakani, his Tekereteki might have been completely incomprehensible otherwise. *"But do not speak much."*

"Well, shit," I muttered in English. "So much for our secret language."

Mak's face screwed up in concentration, and I could see her lips move, mouthing the words I'd just said. A grin flashed across her face, gone as soon as it had come as she schooled herself. "It doesn't matter. You said you'd tell us how you tracked Draka if we let you speak with her. Well?"

"I did say that. And I suppose it does no harm to tell you now, since I have neither opportunity nor intention to use it. It was magic, as you may have guessed, an advancement which has helped me immensely in my career. I had a piece of you, Lady Dragon. As long as I had that, I could find you. I quickly learned that you spent much time here, in this inn, and at a certain mountain. Then it was only a matter of following you, or moving fast enough to lie in wait between those places."

"You would have had to cover a lot of distance," I pointed out.

He shrugged. "I can move quickly. The magic also gives me some insight into how my prey might move. It made you fairly predictable. I only needed to keep in a general area and then adjust as you got closer."

"Wait, back up!" Mak's voice was full of outrage. "What do you mean you had a piece of her?"

I'd missed that, being too focused on the sound of Avjilan's voice, but when Mak pointed it out, a chill went up my spine. I remembered Herald's words back on the road, when we were going to clear out the trolls from Piter's Clearing. She'd kept the chunk of my scalp that I'd lost after nearly getting brained by a gremlin's axe. But she'd lost it.

"What exactly did you have?" I asked, and he answered, confirming my suspicion.

"Some dried skin, scale, and horn. I bought it cheap from a girl in a tavern. She had no idea what creature it came from, of course, but I thought it must be a fairly large one, with scale and horns, which pointed to a wyvern. And then the magic took hold, so I knew the creature it came from must still be alive. Of course—" He flared his elbows, indicating his bound arms. "It might have been better for me if I'd never bought the thing."

Of all the things that could have possibly come back to haunt me . . . "Where is it now?" I asked. I felt a powerful need to destroy it, or at least get it back. If this guy could use it to track me, so could someone else. Hell, he might even know where my hoard was! "Tell me!"

"I would happily return it to you, but you will have to ask the man who arrested me," he said with admirable calm. "I was stripped of all my possessions when we returned to the city. I imagine it's in the Palace, or somewhere similar."

"Mak," I said, turning to her, but she already knew what I wanted.

"I'm adding it as a non-negotiable part of what we want," she said. "Unless Kalder or the lady justice is willing to just give it to you in the name of goodwill. They might."

"Yeah." I was doubtful. Even if Sempralia wanted to trust me, she struck me as the kind of person who'd want as many fallbacks as possible. But it couldn't hurt to ask.

The archer waited in still silence while we spoke. I wished that I could tell what he was thinking. "Hey," I said. "Hunter. Avjilan. I still don't get it. Why was it so important for you to apologize? You must have known what I was after the first time you shot at me. You tried to kill me three times after that, and I doubt you would have given up if I hadn't stopped you. So why was it so important for you to apologize now?"

"I had some time to think," he said slowly. "First, you didn't kill me. Then, when I realized that my career and possibly my life were over, since the one you were meeting with was a lady justice, a councilwoman of the city, I examined what led me to that dark cell they kept me in when I was not being questioned. I was forced to admit that I had not acted righteously. It is as simple as what I said when I first apologized tonight—I have wronged you greatly. I understood that you were intelligent, and I still hunted you like a beast. And I did not wish to die without expressing my regrets and admitting my guilt."

"You expect to die, don't you? That's why you were comfortable making demands."

"Yes."

"And you don't seem worried or upset."

"I wish it were different. But I've already died once. I thank the Mercies for the years I've been allowed to truly live since then, but I've been prepared for my final death ever since. And now that I've apologized, I can die regretting only the things I did, and not what I didn't. It's a good time to die, I think. This way I won't have the chance to collect any new regrets."

I didn't know how to respond to that. He didn't want to die, he just didn't seem too concerned about it. That bastard Hardal had been the same when we fought him, but I didn't care one whit about him. This Avjilan guy, though? He'd tried to kill me four times, put my precious humans in danger, yet I didn't want him dead anymore. And while I couldn't rule out some "love me" advancement like Ardek had, I didn't think it was that. Nor was it his voice, though it would be a shame for that to be silenced forever. No, it was just that he seemed so . . . sad. Pitiful, even.

And what the hell was that about already having died once?

"Val, Ardek, stay here would you?" I said to the two men with us. "Mak, let's talk in private."

We went to the strongroom, and once inside with the door closed I turned to her in consternation. "I don't know what I want," I told her honestly.

"I can tell."

"Before he got here I wanted him dead. I wanted to know how he was tracking me, and then I wanted him to die. Now, I don't know. I feel kind of bad for him, I guess? I don't have a good reason for it, though. Do you think he's messing with my head?"

"If he is, I doubt it's an advancement doing it, if that's what you're worried about. But I know what you mean. He has a tragic air about him, doesn't he? For a moment there I almost wanted to give him a hug."

"Do you think that we could ask Kalder not to kill him?"

"Probably. I don't know if they'd do that, anyway. Normally only traitors and the worst criminals are killed. But this guy? I don't know. He might have seen you talking to Sempralia. They might not want that getting out just yet."

"But Sempralia's supposed to be fair, right?"

"Yeah, but we don't know how much discretion Kalder has. And I doubt he'd have his job if he wasn't exceedingly protective of the lady justice. But, ah, Draka? I'm getting some—I'm getting better at reading you, yeah? Do you want to keep this guy?"

"He's got a nice voice!" I sounded defensive even to myself.

Mak sighed. "Yeah. Sure. He does have a lovely voice. I'll see what I can do."

"Wait, what do you mean, 'you'll see what you can do'?"

"I don't know. If they let him live, I might be able to secure his indenture, or something. I don't know what he'd be good for around here, but—"

"Mak, that's like having a slave! I can't have a slave!"

The look that Mak gave me wasn't scathing. I quickly became convinced that was only because she *couldn't* give me scathing looks. Instead it was so very, very patient. She didn't even ask me the obvious question—when it came down to it, what was she? What was Ardek, or Kira? Instead, after a few beats she asked, "Do you want him to live?"

"Well, yeah. I suppose I do."

"He will be indentured if he lives. I can promise you that. Do you want someone else to have him?"

I sighed. "No."

"So, I can't promise you anything except my best efforts, but I'll see what I can do."

"Yeah. Thanks."

"Of course."

"By the way, Mak. What were you grinning about back there?"

"Hmm?"

"When I spoke in English, you grinned. Looked like you were repeating what I'd said, too."

"Oh." She got that same grin again. "I'm sure you can guess, but . . . I think I understood you. Not perfectly, but something about a secret?"

"Mate! That's absolutely brilliant!" I said happily. "We'll have to teach Herald, and then we'll really have a secret language!"

Mak laughed. "Not so fast! I *mostly* understand you. That's amazing as it is but, like I said, it's not perfect."

"We'll just have to practice, yeah?" I said. The idea of being able to speak English to someone who didn't live inside my head had me almost giddy. But I'd have to put that off for the future, and switched back to Karakani. "Come on, let's get back to the boys."

The boys had been getting along in our absence, as much as they could with one of them being bound. Avjilan had opened up completely once he'd been allowed to apologize to me, but there wasn't much we needed to know from him. He worked alone and hadn't told anyone anything he'd learned about me. It wouldn't have done him any good to help the competition, after all.

The biggest problem was that he did indeed suspect where my lair was, which Instinct told me meant that he needed to die. Conscience was on the fence, for practical reasons. She preferred not to kill anyone, but if he told anyone where my hoard was, I'd have to kill anyone who came looking, not just this one guy who'd already signed his own death warrant when he took a shot at me. That left whatever soup of the two I was, and I didn't want him dead.

The only alternative I could see was that I needed him to swear not to reveal anything. But in order for me to trust him with something like that, I needed to control him. And I only knew one way to possibly gain that control.

"Avjilan," I said after the questioning—more of a conversation, really—wound down. "For what it's worth, I do believe that you're sorry."

Then, as quickly as I could, I wrapped him in shadows and set them in place. He didn't even have time to scream.

"Mercies, Draka," Val said softly as the patch of shadow that was our archer thrashed weakly. "What is this?"

"This is how I make sure that I can allow him to walk out of here alive," I told him calmly. I didn't feel the slightest regret over what I was doing. I was doing this because I pitied him, and if it meant giving him a chance at life, redemption, and perhaps even happiness, I had no qualms about subjecting him to a few minutes of pants-shitting terror. Well, hopefully not literally. My nose was sharp.

"Avjilan," I said after removing the shadows, then again when his eyes didn't focus. He finally looked at me, his face slack, and I spoke to him without a hint of friendliness or mercy in my voice. "Before you leave, you will promise me one thing—that you will never tell another soul *anything* that might harm me. Do you understand?"

He only stared. He didn't smell right, either. "Answer me!" I commanded, and when that didn't get a response I wrapped him back up.

When I released him a minute later he smelled much more agreeable. When I asked him if he understood he immediately croaked "Yes! Yes, I understand! I swear!"

I believed him.

"Good." I put my hand on the side of his neck. "And you understand that if you should ever betray that promise, you should beg your jailors to execute you before I get to you?"

The look in his eyes was answer enough when his beautiful voice failed him.

I looked between the others. "I'd like to speak with Avjilan alone. Val, Ardek, Mak, please go tell Kalder that we're done here. Mak, keep him a while. I'd like a couple of minutes at least."

"Right." Ardek was already on his feet, Mak only just behind him. Val gave me a look, looked at Avjilan, then nodded at me, deciding to respect my privacy and trust that I wouldn't do anything worse than I already had.

"I'll knock before we come down," Mak told me. Then they left me alone with a defenseless man who'd tried to kill me on several occasions, and who'd put people I held dear in danger. Their faith in me was touching, really.

"There was one more thing I wanted to speak to you about. I thought you might want to keep it private, but you *will* tell me what I want to know, and you won't try to hold anything back or deceive me."

"All right, yes. Anything you want," Avjilan answered quickly. His composure was already recovering, but his voice was a little thick, his eyes a little wide. He clearly didn't want to feel the embrace of my shadows again if a few answers were all it took to avoid it.

"You said that you've already died once, and it didn't sound like you meant that metaphorically."

"I did say that."

"Well? What exactly do you mean?"

"I died. My life ended. My breath left me and my body failed. I mean no less than that."

"Yet here you are. What happened? Did someone save you?"

"In a way," he said slowly. He seemed reluctant now, despite everything.

"You're holding back," I warned him. "Go on. How were you saved? How are you still alive?"

"Magic." His answer was almost a whisper, like he was afraid to answer but feared the consequences of silence more. "Occult and forbidden. To prolong your life at the cost of another."

Disgust welled inside me. "You're going to have to explain that very carefully," I told him, making no secret of how I felt about what he'd told me. "Did someone else die to give you your life back?" I had seen enough to not doubt that such a thing might be possible. It might even be justifiable under the right circumstances. But if he told me that some poor innocent bastard had died so he could live . . .

His answer was emphatic. "No! He didn't die! He was supposed to, he *wanted to*, it was *his* idea, but . . . no. He's still alive, no less than I am. But I don't think you will believe me even when I tell you the truth."

"Try me."

"Mistress dragon, tell me, please. Do you believe that a soul might leave the flesh, and not be taken by the Traveler?" I tried to temper the excitement those words lit inside me. I failed when he continued, "Do you believe that that same soul might then take residence in another body?"

"Yes!" I hissed with the certainty of experience, and he smiled with relief.

CHAPTER THIRTY-NINE

Companions

The story that Avjilan told me, which I told to Mak after Kalder had left with his prisoner and to Herald once she returned, would have been entirely unbelievable if not for the circumstances surrounding my own existence. And the more he told me, the more excited I grew.

The most important thing, which anyone who did not know me would likely have rejected out of hand, was that Avjilan was not born as the man I met. Or he was, but the person I spoke to, who now lived in that body, was not. Mostly. It was a complicated situation, a kind with which I was intimately familiar. Because while the person I spoke to wasn't the original Avjilan, that man was still there, in the background.

The current Avjilan, the man who I didn't know but who had tried to kill me on no less than four occasions, had been born wrong. Those were his words. He didn't elaborate on whether that meant gender, some deformity, or anything else, and I didn't push. He had been born under another name that he never told me, and I didn't ask. He had lived like that, trapped, as he described it, for almost fifty years, hating himself and always searching for some way to "rectify the gods' mistake," as he put it. And then he found it. After a lifetime of searching around and beyond the Sareyan Sea, he found an enchanter who claimed to have rediscovered and mastered a method for transferring the soul of one being into another, based on ancient patterns from before the Collapse.

Avjilan had dismissed the enchanter as a charlatan or a madman. Who could believe such a thing? But then the enchanter had allowed him to watch as he performed the procedure, transferring the soul of an old man into the body of a young slave, and Avjilan couldn't deny the evidence of his own eyes.

He was only an exorbitant sum of money and a body away from realizing his wishes.

The money was the lesser problem. Whatever was wrong with him, it hadn't stopped Avjilan from amassing a small fortune as a monster hunter, and if he could make his dream come true, if he could finally truly live, as he put it, he would gladly spend every brass bit. No, the problem lay in procuring a body. And not just a body, but a living, *willing* person. Because if the target was not willing, the enchanter had explained, the procedure would fail, and the gods only knew what happened to the soul if the body rejected it.

Avjilan found his body in, well, Avjilan. The original. A singer from Faltha whom the current Avjilan had known for years, a close friend and confidant who loved him dearly and who, importantly, wanted to die.

"I tried to talk him out of it," Avjilan had said, his shame making it impossible for him to face me. "I swear that I did. But he had been weary of life for as long as I'd known him, and when I told him about what I'd found he begged me to use him. 'I could finally be happy, knowing that I died to let you live,' he told me. Gods help me, I was so weak. After only a few weeks I agreed. And while I can't say that I regret it, while it worked out better than I could have hoped and he is constantly trying to reassure me that he regrets nothing, I'm still ashamed that I told him in the first place, knowing him as well as I did."

"But he didn't die?" I'd asked. "He's still in there?"

"He is. And to our great surprise, since the day I took over he's been happier than I've ever known him. He lived in fear of death, you see, and wanted it over with, on his own terms. But in the moment that he was to die, he understood how much he still wanted to live." Avjilan stopped, then laughed. "He wants me to tell you that there is nothing better than realizing that you want to live, and then have that wish fulfilled while being completely freed from responsibility. The enchanter believes that wish was why he survived. Jil still welcomed me, but he wasn't ready to go." He chuckled without humor. "He'd never seen that before, the enchanter said, but he also admitted that I was only his fifth subject, so who knows?"

The last thing he told me, which he hadn't revealed to the enchanter and which he only told me when I pressed him on that point specifically, was that he'd gained the original Avjilan's advancements, up to the fourth minor. Most of which were related to song and music, but it was still a secret that he begged me to let him take to his grave. He didn't want to be responsible for what might happen if the wrong people found out, and I agreed wholeheartedly.

I would have liked to talk to him more, but at that point Mak knocked on the cellar door. I had to force myself not to tell them to fuck off as she came down with Kalder, who took his prisoner and left after promising to forward my wishes to his mistress. I didn't want to let him go; I just couldn't justify souring my relationship with Sempralia over him.

I didn't share his story with Val, or with Tam once he returned from wherever he'd been. But Mak understood and shared my interest. So did Herald, when she returned. Her eyes were swollen and her makeup a mess after a long evening of saying goodbye to Maglan, but despite her anxiety, she was pulled along at least a little in my excitement when I told her about the old enchanter and his rediscovered patterns, or formulae or whatever the preferred nomenclature was.

"You think there might be some connection to what happened to you?" she asked, already knowing my answer.

"Unless there's more than one way of putting a soul in a different body, yeah. I mean, my case was different in a lot of ways, but still! Do you think we could find the enchanter?"

"Perhaps. If he still lives, and if we can get this guy to help us. If he can be trusted, that is. Then perhaps we could find either the enchanter, or his notes. But, Draka . . . then what?"

"Well, then . . ."

I trailed off, my elation slowly draining. Then what? I had no idea.

"Do you want to be human again?" Mak asked gently.

"No." I answered instantly, completely sure about my answer. Half of me had never been human. The other half was getting used to being a dragon. It was a pretty damned fine thing, and all the problems I faced were because of humans being assholes. No, I definitely didn't want to be human again if I had a choice.

"What about . . . What if you could be separated again?" Herald asked, and the trepidation with which she asked made it clear that she feared I might say yes.

"No," I said again, more softly, a little less certain this time. "I'm happy with who I am. Mostly. I've got some issues that I need to work out, but the three of us in here—"

"Three?!" Mak exclaimed before lowering her voice. "What do you mean three? The human and the dragon—Who's the third?"

"Draka is a bit of a mix, I think," Herald answered for me. "But the human and the dragon are both still in there. Please do not ask her to explain it. She is more confused than I am."

"Honestly, she's right. I don't know what's going on in my head. Maybe I was always like this and the human part was silent, or maybe I was the human side which became more like the dragon and now a new human bit has budded off or . . . Don't think about it too hard, yeah? The important thing is that I don't want to mess with it."

"So what are you after?" Herald asked. "Is it just curiosity?"

"I suppose I want to know what happened to me. When Avjilan told me his story I got all excited, but now that you ask me . . . it wouldn't actually change anything. Maybe there's a way I could become human, or become two people again. Maybe I could go back to Earth, where my human side is from. But I don't want to. The more I think about it, the more certain I become. I just want to know."

"All right. There is nothing wrong with that," Herald said. "But let us make that a low priority, shall we? Getting you recognized as a person has to come first."

"I know that, yeah? I know. But this is the first real hint I've seen of a connection to what happened to me. It's . . ." I sighed. "What if they decide to get rid of Avjilan before I can learn anything else? It wouldn't change anything, but I'd always wonder."

"I don't think they will," Mak said soothingly. "I didn't get that feeling from Kalder at all. If anything, I think they'll want to hold onto him, or control him, as leverage against you in case they need it. Which they won't, so that's all fine, right?"

"Right." If my tone didn't convey how unconvinced I was, Mak would have felt it directly anyway. "Just see what you can do, all right, Mak? I'm not asking for any miracles, or for you to make any concessions for his sake. Just see what you can do."

"I will." She scratched the base of my neck lightly, and the pleasant feeling soothed me a little despite myself. "Do you want some company tonight? It's been an emotional day for all of us, and you're going in the morning."

"Yeah, I'd like that." I wasn't going to pass up a chance to get some extra physical contact in before I left. I looked at Herald, who smiled and nodded at my unspoken question. "All right, then. Let's get some sleep."

My internal clock woke me well before sunrise. I tried to move as little as possible, simply enjoying the feeling and the gentle sounds of Herald and Mak sleeping snuggled together under my wing. Soon enough, though, I had to wake them. Not that I had much in the way of preparations to take care of, but I needed to both get out of the city and to the meeting place unseen. For all that we'd talked about trust, I wanted to get a good look at these companions that were being foisted onto me before I approached them, and that meant I needed time to take things slowly.

We said our goodbyes. I was probably more worried than they were. Even with Sempralia providing some guards around the inn, it was still too early to be confident that the Tesprils wouldn't try anything desperately stupid, especially if they found out that I was away. My sisters' greatest concern was that I'd see something I couldn't abide and get myself into trouble, and they made me promise to be careful. And yeah, fair enough. That was how we'd ended up with Kira, after all.

I made my way to the garden quickly, taking off and heading south. I was somewhat familiar with where the meeting place was, having seen it from above, but I'd never taken a close look at it.

The actual meeting was to take place in a small wood that sat among the fields. Whether it was decorative or there for some productive purpose was a mystery to me, but it fit our needs for a sheltered place to meet nicely. Sempralia's message had described a path that entered the woods from the west, leading to a small clearing at its center, and I found that center from the air. Instead of landing there, I got close to the treetops, shifted, and drifted the last dozen feet until I caught hold of a tree that I could use to descend.

I found the clearing easily, but I had arrived early and there was no one there. The sun rose as I waited among the trees. It took another hour before three riders came down the path. They were all hooded, but two of them looked familiar by their builds, posture, and equipment, and as I looked closer I realized that I knew their horses!

What the hell is going on, I asked myself as I watched Garal and Lalia dismount, leaving Melon and Windfall free to graze. The third rider, a tall, broad-shouldered man, got off his horse with little grace, then threw off his hood to reveal someone I'd met only the day before.

Gods damn you, Sempralia, I cursed. *What's Maglan doing here?*

I didn't believe for a second that this was some bizarre coincidence, that these three just happened to be here only an hour before I was supposed to meet some supposedly trustworthy traveling companions, or that they'd been chosen by some chance unrelated to me. No wonder Sempralia thought that I could trust these people! She probably knew everything about my relationships with Garal and Lalia at this point, however she'd gone about it. Maglan was perhaps a gamble, but a clever one. I'd never met him before the previous day, but she must have done her homework on Herald, and she likely assumed that I wouldn't do anything to harm Herald's—and I hated that this was the only appropriate word—lover.

I just didn't know *why*. *Why* did she want me to travel with, or escort, these three at all?

I was about to approach them when Lalia's voice rang out across the clearing. "Hey, Mag?"

"Yes, Miss Lalia?"

"I don't suppose your commander told you who we're supposed to be meeting, and you just weren't allowed to tell us until we got here?"

"Afraid not, Miss Lalia."

"Well, shit. Rallon didn't tell us anything, which usually means that he doesn't know, either. Bullshit, if you ask me. Why are they sending a single archer south, anyway?"

"Sorry, Miss Lalia. Wish I could tell you. All I know is the others are marching later today, but I'm being sent ahead with a message." He held up a leather tube that hung by a strap around his neck. "Though why they sent it with me instead of a messenger, and why you two are here, the gods only know."

That, I decided, was my cue. "Probably because you're all connected to me," I declared. I walked out of the trees, all three of them whirling to face me as I entered the clearing.

"Lady Draka!" Maglan was the first to speak, stammering as he saw me approaching.

Garal just grinned and waved. I'd expected Lalia to say something snarky or rude, but perhaps she was too stunned by the turn of events. "Oh," she said, then, "Morning, Draka. This just raises more questions."

"Morning, all. Didn't expect to be seeing you again so soon, Maglan. And yeah, Sempralia's going to have some explaining to do once we get back."

"Sempralia?" Garal asked. "The lady justice Sempralia? She's behind this?"

"That's the one. We're supposed to be 'building trust.'"

"Damn weird way to go about that," Lalia muttered.

I nodded. "Right? None of us could figure out what her plan was when she demanded I travel with a group. And I don't know what kind of statement this is supposed to be." I gestured to the three of them. "Better than a bunch of strangers, though."

"What, even me?"

Lalia's mocking tone drew a snort from me, and a shocked stare from Maglan. "Yeah, even you. I haven't wanted to hurt you for ages, now. We're practically friends!"

She gave a single, barking laugh. "Sure, yeah. So—" She looked between myself and Garal, only sparing Maglan a glance. "How do we do this? We can't exactly ride down the southern road with a dragon in tow, no matter how merciful and magnificent she may be."

Everything she said was correct, no matter how insincere her flattery was. "I've been thinking about it since Mak told me," I said. "The best I've come up with is that I keep an eye on you from the sky, and when you make camp you do it somewhere I can hide within earshot. It won't exactly be the most companionable way of traveling, and now that I know it's you I'll be escorting, I wish that there was a better way, but it is what it is."

They thought for a moment, but all three agreed that my plan made sense. "We'll just have to look extra hard for places to camp," Garal said, forcing some cheer into his voice. "That way we can talk a little, at least."

"So, ah . . ." Maglan broke the short silence that followed. "You all know each other from before?"

"Oh, yeah," I said. "Garal and Lalia and me, we go way back. Since before I met Herald, even! I saved Garal's life, and then Lalia tried to chop my head off for my trouble." I grinned as Lalia just rolled her eyes. "But we get along better now."

"Since you didn't run for your life, I guess you've met Draka, too," Garal said.

"Ah, yes. I have. Only yesterday."

"Herald promised to introduce us before he went back to the border," I said.

Lalia snorted. "Poor girl's been so nervous. 'What if my boyfriend doesn't like my dragon friend? What if she tries to eat him?' I told her that's just the risk you take when you introduce your friends to each other, but she didn't seem to like that."

"She did *not* suggest that I might eat Maglan!" I protested.

"Not in so many words. But you know what I mean."

"I mean, I wouldn't have *eaten* him . . ."

"Ah, excuse me?" Maglan looked a little pale. "You're joking, right?"

Lalia didn't miss a beat. "No, she's serious. She's promised not to eat anyone."

"I promised not to eat *you*," I corrected. "Right, Garal?"

Garal sighed and went to bring back the horses, which had wandered a bit.

The early morning light revealed a thin sheen of sweat on Maglan's brow. "So, to be clear, yesterday—"

"Ah, don't worry, Mag," Lalia said, dropping her teasing and becoming serious. "Herald would have never introduced you two if she wasn't entirely sure. Besides, I'm pretty sure that Draka is entirely unable to do *anything* that might hurt that girl, and that includes harming you."

"I did promise Herald that I wouldn't hurt you, no matter what," I confirmed. "The worst I would have done if I didn't feel like I could trust you would have been to make sure that you'd never talk about me to anyone."

Maglan didn't look reassured. "Ah . . . how?"

"Oh, I have ways. Believe me, you'd be happier not knowing if you can help it. But don't worry about that. For now, just think of me as a second older sister—"

"Third," Lalia butted in. "I'm an honorary big sister already."

"A third older sister, then. Just with sharper teeth and a warmer personality than the first two."

"Oh, come off it! Mak's a perfectly lovely woman!" Lalia said, then stuck her tongue out at me and went to join Garal. When we were alone I approached Maglan, who stood his ground admirably. In a low voice I said, "For real, though. Herald loves you, yeah? I don't know if you've had that talk, but she does. So you have nothing to fear from me, as long as you don't do anything to hurt her."

I walked away without waiting for a reply, leaving him to think about what exactly I meant by that.

Five minutes later we were on our way, me five thousand feet up and them riding along a narrow lane that would take them to the main southern road. I had to fly in long, sweeping circles so I wouldn't pull too far ahead. It was a good thing that the weather was fine and the view great, because it was going to be a *long* trip to the border.

CHAPTER FORTY

Suicide by Dragon

According to the humans we had about a hundred and thirty miles to cover. It would take them about four or five days, and that was with them mounted and riding along a good, gravel-covered road, not the churned up mess that was the northern road through the forest.

I could have been there in less than three hours. Sempralia and I were going to have a conversation when we got back.

I flew endless circles above the humans, barely aware of time passing. I soared and I kept an eye on them, but nothing happened. I couldn't even join them on their breaks, since the landscape was so open. I probably got spotted a hundred times in the air, and I wondered if that was part of why Sempralia had anchored me to the trio of humans. But while an unknown flying creature circling a mile up was a cause for concern, that same creature being seen sitting around near the road would probably trigger either a panic or a mob, and I didn't want either.

I spent some of the time feeling for the little threads that connected me to Nest Hearts. They'd been getting easier to find the last few days, and a faint but growing need told me that the power of the one I'd last eaten was running out, wearing off, being consumed, or something else. Most of the threads pointed back north, or west to the mountains and beyond, but more and more led south. I tried to keep track of those, in case we got close enough to one of them for a detour.

As night drew close on the first day I flew ahead and landed as covertly as I could, hiding in a dense field along the road.

"It looks like there's an inn in the next town," I told them. "You should just stay there for the night."

"What about you?" Garal asked.

"As long as I know where you are, I can just head over to the mountains and find somewhere to hole up there, then come back in the morning. Just keep an eye on the sky, and I'll recognize you once you're on the road again."

Lalia spoke up, with a surprising amount of concern in her voice. "What about food? You haven't eaten all day, have you?"

I threw an exaggerated glance at Maglan, who gave me the most forced grin I'd ever seen. "Don't worry. I promised Herald, remember? But I haven't eaten, no, and flying all day's hungry work! No worries, though. I'll hunt something up in the mountains tomorrow night or the night after. I don't need to eat too often."

Lalia didn't let it go, though. "Are you sure? We're getting our expenses covered, and hunting takes time, doesn't it? I'm sure we could figure something out."

I looked at her skeptically, but she looked entirely serious. "I mean, yeah. If you could buy me one of those big birds or something—nothing too big, five or ten pounds of meat, counting the insides—that'd be great. I'm sure we could figure out a handover."

"That's settled, then. We'll figure something out, and if we can't, we'll try along the road or in the next village tomorrow."

"Sure, yeah. Thanks!"

"Don't mention it."

Garal grinned at the two of us. "Look at you two, getting along," he said, and Lalia gave him a playful smack on the arm. "We should get into town and arrange rooms, then. Draka, we'll see you tomorrow."

"Yeah, see you," I said. I made my way deeper into the field before taking off and climbing as fast as I could. If the locals saw me, they saw me; they could damn well get used to it. The town ahead of the trio was a place with no walls but about two hundred buildings, which seemed to have sprung up around a bridge where the road crossed a large canal. I circled above them until they got into the town proper, then turned west to the mountains to find a place to sleep.

I returned to the skies above the town shortly after sunrise to find the three humans already waiting on the road at the southern outskirts. When we managed to meet up they had a whole leg of lamb for me. It had been sitting wrapped up for a good few hours by then, but I didn't mind.

"Hope it's enough," Maglan said as they handed it over. "The innkeeper arranged it for us. We couldn't get anything live, but he had a boy run over to the butcher. It's not a problem with the bone, is it?"

"Not at all! Here, you'll want to see this." I grinned at him, then broke the leg in half at the knee. Then I tossed the thigh up in front of me, snatching it out of the air in my jaws. With a few deft movements I turned it around so that it was aligned with my gullet, and then I simply swallowed it. It took some work, and I'd never been sure if I actually unhinged my jaw when I did that, but it wasn't at all uncomfortable. And the look on Maglan's face, somewhere between fascination and horror, was priceless.

"You're quite the topic of conversation," Garal said after I'd swallowed the rest of the leg.

"Oh, yeah?"

"Yeah. A few people saw you land in that field and take off again. They asked us about it, since we'd stopped along the road. We told them that we'd been trying to spot you, but that we weren't going to be trampling someone's field, especially if there was some big, flying creature in it. They seemed to accept that."

Lalia snorted. "Accept it? There was a chorus of 'Ayes' and 'Yeaps' from all the brave men who insisted that they'd have gone after you if they could have seen you. As if a single one of them could have done more than amuse you."

They slept in a smaller village that night, and on the morning of the third day the trouble began. Clouds had rolled in during the night, and at the altitude I kept to, even I was feeling the chill. The humans had been on the road for about two hours, moving into a more hilly landscape where plowed fields gave way to pasture, when I noticed a pair of riders following them. They were moving parallel to the road, perhaps a mile to the east, and cutting through the various plots without a care for whose crops they trampled or whose sheep they frightened. I didn't like that, but I also didn't want to make myself too obvious by swooping in for a closer look. For all I knew they weren't the least bit interested in my group, and since they neither approached nor left, I chose patience, keeping an eye on them as they kept pace and distance with my three companions.

Two hours later Garal and the others stopped for a break, and one of the two took off to the northeast while the other stopped, moving into a position where the hills wouldn't block their sight of the trio. That started all kinds of alarm bells ringing in my head, and I made a snap decision. I could have followed the rider that left, or I could have gone for the one that remained. Instead, I chose to stay and warn the three I was supposed to be accompanying.

Ignoring anyone who might see me, I passed low over the small camp the trio had set up, then landed in a pasture behind a hill where the rider wouldn't be able to see me. A flock of sheep scattered as I came down, and with my blood up as it was, I had to consciously rein myself in from going after them. A large, shaggy dog—the kind that I could never quite understand how they see anything past their fur—calmly took a position between me and the flock. We looked at each other. It was a bloody big dog, standing as tall as I did at the shoulder, but it didn't bark or make any aggressive moves. I felt like it was telling me that as long as I didn't start anything, it wouldn't, either, and after a few seconds I ducked my head, turned around, and took a few steps away. When I looked back over my shoulder it had laid itself down, though it was still watching me keenly.

It didn't take long for Garal to appear around the hill, riding Melon at a trot. "Mercies, that's a big dog," he said when we were close enough that he didn't have to shout. "I'm guessing that with the way you came in, whatever it is, it's urgent?"

"Yeah. You're being watched. Two riders followed you for a couple of hours, then as soon as you stopped here one took off. The other is still watching the camp. I'm sure they saw me coming down, too. What do you want to do?"

"Well . . ." Garal thought about it. "You suspect that they're with the Tekereteki raiders? The Silver Spurs, was it?"

"I don't know why they'd be interested in three travelers, but yeah. Them, or the council's keeping an eye on us. Or the Cranes. Or someone else, for all I know. This whole setup stinks."

"It does. All right. The horses need rest, but we'll just have to push them a little farther. According to the map there should be another village five miles up the road. We'll stop there and hope that deters whoever's following us, and you can get a better idea of who they are in the meantime."

"Right."

Garal headed back. I decided to put some distance between us before taking off again, to make it a little less obvious that we were together. The dog had been relaxing a bit, but sat up attentively when I moved, so I made sure to keep my distance from it and the sheep until I was far enough away that running shouldn't spook it. I liked dogs and always had, and I didn't want to give it any grief.

Once I was back up, it took a moment to find the rider. They'd dismounted and put their horse under a tree, and it was a damn sight harder to spot a person crouching on the ground. But there they were, still where I'd last seen them, presumably still watching my three companions.

Screw it. I'd give them something else to focus on for a minute.

"Just destroy them and be done with it!" Instinct insisted. I could see where she was coming from. No matter who they belonged to they shouldn't be stalking my humans, and they should suffer the consequences. And, as so often I had to force myself to disregard Instinct's advice, because if it *was* someone from the council, or the army, or some local militia, or anyone except the Tekereteki mercs, then killing them would be a terrible look.

Warning them off, also known as scaring them shitless, though? Swooping at them, going a hundred miles per hour ten feet off the ground and roaring at them? That was fine. They shouldn't be in whatever line of work they were if they couldn't handle being swooped at now and then.

I passed above them so quickly that on the first pass all I had time to see clearly was a bearded man staring at me in absolute horror as he threw himself to the ground. By the time I came back around he was on his feet, dashing for his horse. I came in slower the second time. I got a better look at him, but it didn't help. He didn't look like he was in uniform, but that didn't rule much out. I guessed that the regular cavalry wore uniforms, but I wouldn't expect them to wear them if they were out spying on someone. Nor did I recognize him as one of the Tekereteki mercs. But there was one easy way to check if he was one of them.

Well, in for a penny and all that. After I made my second pass I turned and braked hard, setting down a hopefully non-threatening distance from him as he was getting on his horse.

"Hey, you! Beardy!" I shouted at him in Kira's vulgar Tekereteki. He turned in the saddle to stare at me, slack-jawed, as his horse snorted and pranced beneath him. And the predator in me saw just what it wanted—recognition.

"*Yeah, I'm talking to you!*" I said, trying to soothe Conscience by confirming what I already knew. We wouldn't want to make a terrible mistake, after all. But I hadn't needed to worry.

"*You speak!*" the man answered me in that same vulgar Tekereteki, and that was all I needed. I was forty feet away, but what was forty feet to me? I pushed off hard, claws gouging the earth as my wings tore the air, and I bowled that murdering bastard out of the saddle before he had a chance to spur his horse into motion. I didn't smash him into a sack of broken bones the way I would have if I'd been diving on him, but I still carried him a good distance before he hit the ground, hard. I stepped off, watching him, letting him slowly catch his breath and get to his feet if he could. I hadn't been sure if he'd broken anything, but when he got to his hands and knees I was somewhat impressed. The bastard was tough.

I told myself that I was giving him a chance to surrender or say something to save himself, but I knew, deep down, that I was just playing with him. He was one of the raiders, I was sure of it, and they murdered villagers and captured magic users to send them into slavery. There was little he could do to save himself at this point.

Perhaps I should have tried to interrogate him, but his reply to what I said next nipped any chance of that in the bud.

As he rose unsteadily to his feet, looking half out of it and having trouble grabbing his sword, I told him, "*Bekiratag is alive and well in Karakan, by the way. If you all were wondering.*"

When he spoke his voice was slurred, but it dripped with contempt. "Beki," he grunted, and spat a red glob into the short grass. "*That traitorous whore.*"

And then he died. One moment he was standing there, swaying on his feet. The next he was a red mess beneath me.

It was his tone more than anything that made me snap. Merely saying her name with that kind of contempt was enough for me to throw myself at him in a fury, and in his state it wasn't like he could either escape or fight. If circumstances had been different, I might have overlooked it; it was such an incredibly stupid thing for him to say. He'd probably hit his head and wasn't thinking properly. But I'd been lethally frustrated for days at that point, and then this murdering bastard spat after saying *my* Kira's name. My kind, sensitive Kira, who just wanted a chance to be happy. When he spoke her name the way he did, when he insulted her with such contempt, all that frustration suddenly had a deserving outlet. Here I had someone in front of me who, in my eyes, very much deserved to die, and there was absolutely nothing holding me back.

If he wanted to make sure that I didn't get anything useful out of him, well, bloody great success!

Before the bearded mercenary decided to commit suicide by dragon, I'd been thinking about what to do if I had to take him prisoner. Now I had to decide what to do with the body. Even Conscience had no regrets about what we'd done, but I couldn't very well leave the guy there. I was pretty sure that I was in some kind of shared pasture, and I'd come down enough from my murderous rage that I didn't want to leave a shredded corpse for some shepherd to find.

I looked at the body. I considered the direction his companion had ridden off in. His horse had run the same way.

I felt a nasty grin creep up my face. I had an idea.

Reconnaissance only. No one would ask me to put myself at risk if I agreed to go south. That had been the agreement. But then, when had anyone needed to *ask* me to get violent? Holding myself back was my natural state at this point, and once I relaxed that control it was easy to let it slip further and further. Reining myself in again—that was the hard part. Despite my frustration, despite the need that was nagging at me again, I'd been all right as long as there was nothing to provoke me. Now the bearded Silver Spur had given me the perfect excuse to drop that control almost entirely. I had three humans in my care. They were in danger. And I had begun to destroy those that threatened them, but this one man was not nearly enough. He'd had a companion, who had surely gone back to report to the main group.

I had killed one of my enemies, but it was not enough. Beyond the fact that my companions were not safe yet, I was not satisfied. Not by far. It was probably a stupid idea to leave my companions behind just to go off and be spiteful, but as it happened I was glad that I did, or they wouldn't have had the warning they had.

I'd stuffed what I could back inside the dead mercenary scout before I took off with him gripped in my feet. It only took about five minutes before I could see something whipping up a lot of dust in the distance, and a few minutes later I confirmed what I suspected; it was a band of horsemen, and they were coming my way fast.

Once I got a little closer it became clear that there were too many of them for me to take on by myself. When I'd wiped out the small group that Kira was with, I had taken them by surprise. They'd been resting, not ready for a fight. The ones ahead of me now would see me coming, and there were about a dozen of them. Probably not close to all of the remaining Spurs, but too many for me to take on alone in the open on the best of days. It was another frustration, but one that I would need to bear for now. I'd promised Herald and Mak not to take any more risks than I had to.

I considered my options and decided that there was realistically only one thing I could do. Something that I'd wanted to try for a long time.

My human side had an older brother, David. When we were growing up he'd been obsessed with the second world war, and despite my own complete lack of interest, a few things here and there had stuck with me. One thing that he'd shown me about a million times was how small airplanes carrying bombs would dive on ships and tanks and other things, lining themselves up and going almost into free fall before releasing their bombs and turning up again. It was a tricky maneuver to replicate, but I gave it a shot.

I started from about a mile up and dove on the riders at an angle. I got the free fall part right, but perhaps I should have waited before I released my payload. Since I wanted to be able to see what happened, I dropped the remains of the bearded merc from about a thousand feet up, but unfortunately he lost all of his forward momentum and hit the ground a few dozen feet in front of them instead of smashing into the lead rider, as I'd hoped. The panic it caused among the riders was bloody funny, though.

I was sure that they must have gotten a good look at me as I came in, but I didn't care. Let them see what they were dealing with. Maybe that would make them think twice about being such utter bastards.

CHAPTER FORTY-ONE

Outnumbered

I'd hoped that the riders would be deterred when I dropped the shredded corpse of their fellow mercenary on them, but no such luck. They recovered in moments. I could see them coming in the distance when I looked back, though that distance stretched rapidly as I approached the road where I'd left Garal, Lalia, and Maglan; no horse in any world could keep up with me. But they were still only a few miles away when I reached my companions, and I threw caution to the wind, setting down beside them.

"The mercs are coming!" I told them. "A dozen, riding hard. Go! Go!"

They didn't waste a moment hesitating or questioning me. Garal took the lead and Lalia the rear. It was miles to the next village. From the air, it didn't look large enough to have much of a militia, if any, but it would have to do. What that meant for the villagers . . . I didn't want to think too hard about it.

The hilly terrain made it impossible for the two groups to see each other, but I had no such problems. Best I could tell, the Silver Spurs were about four miles from the road, and my companions had about the same distance to go before they got to the village. I didn't need to be good at geometry to know that we should leave them in the dust, but the mercenaries were coming in at an angle. They didn't aim for where their scouts had split up or for the village, but some point between it and the trio, and I wondered how the hell they knew where to go. I made sure not to fly directly above Garal and the others, but that made no difference. From where I was I could see them turn slightly as they got closer, seeming to adjust for the trio's movement. They were still far out, and the terrain should have blocked their line of sight. It was a disturbing thing to witness.

At the point where my group would reach the village in two minutes, maybe a little more, the Spurs would be a minute behind them at most. It was getting late in the morning, and most of the villagers would be at work tending their flocks or fields or whatever else needed to be done. There was no way that there'd be enough time to call anyone to arms, if they'd even be willing; we'd either need to keep going, or fight alone. Four against twelve were terrible odds in a straight fight, even if one of the four was a dragon.

Whatever Garal and Lalia intended to do, I needed to even those odds a little. I dove hard toward the incoming riders, not relying on gravity but actively driving myself downward with powerful beats of my wings to the point where the air was roaring past me as I broke it with my face. Beneath me flocks of sheep scattered in every direction as I got closer to the ground, but I was only barely aware of them. I was now directly in the path of the riders, they were close enough to make out individual people, and we were approaching each other at a combined speed well over a hundred miles per hour. An arrow cracked past me, moving so fast that it didn't even register until the second and third passed over and under me; they were shooting from the saddle, but I was not a stationary target, and neither was I easy to see, thanks to my stealth advancement helping me blend in with the cloudy sky.

They had time for a fourth and fifth arrow, both of which were close but not close enough, and then I passed above them. I stayed just high enough that they shouldn't be able to reach me with their lances, and sprayed a concentrated stream of venom below me. I didn't bother trying to hit many of them; I doubted that would have done anything. Instead I went for the densest grouping, hoping to do some damage to a few.

I was passed before my venom hit them, and when it took effect I was hundreds of feet away and turning. What I saw when I came around was heartbreaking, and viciously, viscerally satisfying.

Two of the horses were down in a writhing, screaming pile. One of the riders had been thrown far ahead, while the other was nowhere to be seen, probably somewhere under the horses. I felt only a vicious glee about the Spurs, but terrible for the horses. I knew how fragile horses could be. Going down the way they had at a full gallop, there was no way they didn't have broken bones.

The remaining Spurs seemed split on what to do. Some peeled off to aid their fallen comrades, but unfortunately, some did the smart thing and joined back up, riding in a looser formation this time. Even with two of their number down and a gods-damned dragon at their back, if they even knew what I was, they still stayed on target, riding hard directly for the small village that was now only scant minutes ahead.

There was no way for me to coordinate with the others, so the most productive thing I could do was harass the Spurs. I did so gladly. First, though, I climbed high enough to get a look at the road ahead and the village. I couldn't see my companions—they must have been among the houses, either passing through or waiting to make some kind of stand—but I hoped they saw me.

Harassing the riders was easy, in the sense that they couldn't ignore me. Doing any damage with my venom glands empty, though, was tricky. I tried a couple of swoops, but these were skilled riders on agile horses, and some of them were comfortable with shooting their bows from the saddle, so I had to dodge arrows while trying to hit moving targets. Those that didn't have bows had lances, and they did their best to jab at me while still controlling their horses. In the end, all I managed was to scatter them as I forced the ones I targeted to dodge and slow down. For my trouble, I got another hole through the wing, and one arrow struck my belly at an angle where it slipped under my scales and penetrated, though thankfully not deeply. The fact that they made me bleed, though, pissed me right off.

That's not to say that I didn't help. For one, between every swoop I rose so that I'd be in sight of the village, showing the others where their pursuers were. For another, the fact that the riders had to pay attention to me if they didn't want to be bitten, clawed, or dragged off their horses meant that they weren't paying attention straight ahead.

That mistake was punished harshly as they crested the final hill before the village. From there they had to ride down the side of the hill into a gully, and then back up to the village. This left them fully open.

The first incoming arrow struck one of the lead riders on the right flank, but she stayed in the saddle. The next one that I saw missed, but the third took one of the horses high in the neck, and while it didn't go down, it turned sharply, forcing others to slow or stop or turn themselves. This split the group up further, with the left flank continuing at full speed while the center and the right were slowed. Some of the Spurs returned fire, but sporadically. Arrows continued to come in at an impressive rate, and I remembered Herald telling me that Lalia was almost as good a shot as herself, without any supporting advancements. And Maglan, of course, was an archer through and through.

I didn't waste the opportunity. I hit the center group, not caring who I went for. I just grabbed one of them that wasn't looking my way and took off, then dropped him, kicking and screaming, onto the rearmost of the four on the left flank, who were now nearly in the village. Aiming was much easier at such a low altitude, and my payload struck his companion hard. The two hit the ground at speed, in a tangle of limbs that wasn't likely to get up soon. Instinct screamed for me to fall on them and finish them off, but there were still three from that flank entering the village, with another five staggered behind them. I tried to strike the next in line, but they stuck close to the buildings, and I had to abort or risk smacking my wing against a tile roof or brick wall. Instead I climbed, continuing forward over the roof in time to see Garal and Melon crash through their line between the second and third riders, taking them by surprise.

As cheerful and kind as he could be, Garal was not soft. His sword flashed low as he passed, hamstringing the second rider's horse, which crashed screaming to the ground. His readied shield skillfully lifted the point of the third rider's lance, guiding it over and behind him. It happened so quickly that the third rider didn't respond until Garal was through and away, though she turned to follow him. I let her, and went after the lead rider, who was now turning to strike Lalia and Maglan from behind. Garal could handle himself against a single mounted opponent, or at least I hoped so. Maglan and Lalia, however, were now trapped between the rider behind them and the five in front.

Or so I thought. I climbed to get into a better position to strike and took the opportunity to get an idea of where everyone was. Windfall and Maglan's mare stood at a corner of the village's small square, moving nervously but too well trained to run. Lalia and Maglan themselves had both turned to face the Spur coming at them from behind, which confused me until I threw a look at where the rest of the riders should be coming from and saw five mounted horses making their way back up the hill, heading back the way they'd come. Whatever the Spurs' goal had been, it must not have been worth losing their entire group.

My first thought was that they were *escaping*, and a sense of great indignation welled up inside me. How dare they run? I almost gave chase; they had no right to get away when they'd attacked *my* companions. But those same companions were still fighting, and their safety had to come first.

I needn't have worried. Among the houses, and against two archers, the mounted Spur was at a severe disadvantage. He tried, but he couldn't run them down since they could just pop around a corner, and when they separated he couldn't follow one without risking an arrow in the back from the other. And that was without taking me into account. The houses made striking from above difficult but not impossible, but he had to keep checking where I was to keep as much brick between us as possible. It only took half a minute before he gave up. Garal returning was the final straw. He turned for the open hills to follow the others who had already retreated. I set after him, and while I could hear Lalia shouting, I was too focused on bringing down my prey to make out what she was saying.

Alone and in the open he didn't stand a chance. He rode well, but he was scared, and his horse was tired. They made mistakes, and before he reached the top of the hill I bodily tackled him out of the saddle. I fell on him, pinning his arms, and my blood sang with the joy of a successful hunt. I was about to tear his throat out when the roar in my ears died down enough that I could hear both Lalia and Conscience shouting, "Alive! Alive, dammit!"

I hissed my annoyance, and the man beneath me blanched. "*Do you surrender?*" I spat at him, hoping that he would refuse or try to fight me, and feeling disgusted with myself for my own bloodlust. When did I become so blasé about killing? What happened to not killing for convenience? Hell, I'd been about to kill him for—what? Fun? Predatory pride? Because I could, and I had an excuse? That was far worse. Fortunately, he robbed me of any excuse I might have had when he choked out a "*Yes!*" between clenched teeth. Not even a "You speak?" or "Oh, gods!" Just "Yes!"

"*Fine*," I said, releasing his sword arm. I didn't bother telling him to get rid of his weapons. I simply tore through his belt with my claws and pulled it off him, sword and dagger and all. That tore a scream from him, and I wondered what the hell that was about until I told him to stand and he choked out, "*Can't. Leg's broken.*"

I backed off, and his left leg was indeed bent at the thigh. Not much, but thighs aren't meant to bend. I snorted and paced a while, wondering if I could use this as an excuse to kill my *helpless, unarmed* prisoner. *Obviously not, you bloodthirsty psycho bitch*, I told myself, and grabbed his chain mail shirt with both hands. "*Right*," I told him. "*You're going to hate this.*"

He screamed when I took off. He screamed for the few seconds it took to fly him back to the village. And he screamed when I put him down in the square. I thought that shock would normally deal with at least some of the pain of a broken bone, but apparently it wasn't enough for a broken femur being jostled about with absolutely no care at all.

To my surprise he wasn't the only prisoner. My three companions were guarding two others that sat on the ground, though I wasn't sure how long either of them would survive. A woman who I recognized as the third rider—the one who'd gone after Garal—was supporting a short man, presumably either the one I'd dropped or the one I'd dropped a man at. I hadn't gotten a good look at either. The woman was missing her right hand, and the tourniquet didn't seem to have stopped the bleeding completely. The man, meanwhile, was pale and sweating, barely conscious and badly hurt in some way I couldn't see.

I left my prisoner with the two others and turned to Lalia. "There. Alive, just like you asked," I told her petulantly. "Now what? What do we do with three dying prisoners?"

"First of all, we stop them from dying. We've made the first two drink healing potions already. They look bad now but should be better in an hour or three. Did you disarm this one?"

"I took his sword belt," I told her, and she had the audacity to roll her eyes at me.

"Fine, I'll do it properly." She drew her sword and approached the prisoner. "Don't so much as twitch or I'll stick this in your gut, hear me?" she told him. He probably didn't understand a word she said, but he did understand the universal language of "angry woman I just tried to kill has a sword pointed at me," and he stayed very still. With the point of her sword in his belly button, she removed a five-inch dagger from his boot and threw it to Maglan, who caught it by the hilt. She then gestured for the prisoner to take off his coat, and when he'd done that she relieved him of another two blades, a wicked-looking curved thing that he had in a sheath at his waist and a short, triangular punch dagger at his left wrist.

"What do you think, Garal?" she asked. "Do you want his trousers off?"

"Too tight," Garal said. He was nursing a long, diagonal cut high on his shield arm. "You should be fine."

"All right."

I gaped at her. "Wait, how'd you know, though?"

"Draka, how many blades do you think I have on me right now? How many do you think Garal has? Hell, how many do you think Mak or Herald carry when they're out on business?"

"I mean . . ." I trailed off. I had no idea.

"I can tell you that Herald has one on the inside of one of the skirt plates on that fancy new armor of hers, and that's not the most easily accessible one. I like to think I taught them well, her and Mak both. You never know when you'll need a dagger, or which parts of your body you'll be able to reach. I'm pretty sure Mak carried her shark tooth when they went to meet the lady justice. She's usually got it in her sash when she wears a wrap like that. Be just like her to put it in by habit. Now, Maglan. Potion, please."

Maglan took out a bottle, the little glowing flecks in the liquid inside marking it as a healing potion, and uncorked it. With the bottle in one hand and a dagger in the other, he knelt by the prisoner, who drank it down without a fuss, and even some gratitude.

I was still sulking about the whole thing. For all that I'd berated myself for being bloodthirsty, I didn't like that I'd been told not to kill this enemy that I'd taken down fair and square. "And *now* what? What are we supposed to do with three prisoners?"

"We were hoping that you might question them," Garal said. And knowing me, he went straight for flattery. "We need to know why they targeted us, how many of them there are, and if they're still attacking villages. With your amazing, unheard-of skill with languages, you're the only one who can talk to them."

"You're an unrepentant flatterer," I told him, and he just grinned at me.

"Is it working?"

"Of course it's working! Ask your questions, and I'll translate."

The prisoners, the two who were mostly conscious, at least, talked quite freely once the questioning began. They'd been looking at us, and me especially, with confusion and fear, but had wisely stayed quiet. Once I spoke directly to them they were eager to please, and after I told them that I had questioned Bekiratag thoroughly they mostly stopped trying to lie or deflect, at least according to Garal who was apparently good at reading such things. The woman was Leretem, the man with the broken leg Kordon and the by then unconscious man was Sergen. Their detachment had indeed been following us. The Spurs had been waiting for us to come south—they didn't know how the commander had known—and had sent out about a quarter of their remaining number to attack us on the road. Yes, they were still attacking villages, trying to round up magic users, but it was getting harder as their numbers shrank. Their commander had been trying to get permission to pull back for weeks now.

The only thing they both clammed up about was why and how they'd been tracking us. Anger and threats didn't help. Threatening to bite off the Leretem's other hand only got me begging from Kordon and a very brave, eyes closed tight, "Do it!" from the woman herself.

Lalia and Garal didn't much like it when I stopped translating and went off on my own, but neither tried to stop me. Maiming Leretem had been an empty threat, of course. I could have, but I wasn't going to. Kill her? Maybe. Torture?

Maybe someone I hated. Tarkarran, if I hadn't promised him to the girls. The Night Blossom, before I started to pity her. Some random mercenary raider who hadn't done anything to me personally, no matter how much of a murdering shithead she was? No.

Not physically. I had no qualms about making her absolutely piss herself until she talked.

CHAPTER FORTY-TWO

One Minute

For all that I liked Garal, and even Lalia in many ways, I didn't want them to see what I could do. All they needed to know was that I could get results, and when the dragon wants to have a private chat with a prisoner, the dragon gets to have a private chat with said prisoner. My companions protested loudly, making all kinds of concerned noises when I grabbed Leretem by the neck and dragged her away from the others, but they didn't try to stop me. Hell, the protests may have been theatrics for the benefit of the prisoners, for all I knew. The prisoner herself stank of fear, and that was before I spread my wings wide and covered her with them, creating a nice little bubble where there were only the two of us.

I got my face right up in hers before I spoke, so she could feel my breath on her skin and really think about how many sharp teeth I had. *"It's time to talk, Tammy,"* I crooned. *"Last chance before I make you. And I will make you. How were you tracking us?"*

She didn't cry. Nor did she beg. For all her faults she was brave, I suppose, though she started hyperventilating a little. *"Company secret,"* she told me between breaths. *"I'll die before I tell you, dragon or not."*

"No, you won't. You'll tell me anything I want when I'm done with you."

I didn't give her a chance to respond. I just took the darkness surrounding her, and squeezed. I'd had quite a lot of practice by then, and I hadn't used my magic much lately. I could keep it up for hours if I had to.

"Listen, Tammy," I whispered to her when she gasped, then choked. *"I'd tell you that I'll stop if you talk, but people usually can't speak while I do this. But I'm going to release you at some point, and then you'll have an opportunity to tell me how you were tracking us. What you do with that is up to you."*

I left her like that for a good thirty seconds before I drew the shadows back. Then she cried. The silent, teeth gritting, heaving sobs of someone who was too proud to cry openly but just couldn't hold it back.

I gave her a few seconds before saying, "*You're not talking,*" and putting on the pressure again. And this time she begged, though her pleas were quickly cut off.

The next time I released her she took a single breath and started babbling. "*The medallion! Someone in your group has a tracking medallion, the one we lost when Marg and the others disappeared with Bekiratag. That's how we followed you, someone has a medallion and we have the other one. Captain Selim has it, he's—I don't know, I think he got away, so he should still have it. Please, that's the truth! By the Warrior and the stars and the City of Rains, I swear that's the truth! Please don't— don't put me in the dark again!*" She began sobbing openly at that point, not even trying to hold back. "*Gods, the old folks told me but I never listened to them. I never should have—! Please, Great One! Please!*"

Just over a minute. That's how long it had taken me to break a hardened mercenary. I was both pleased and just a little bit disgusted with myself. She'd deserved it. I had no doubt about that. She deserved far worse, honestly. But that didn't stop me from feeling dirty about how eager I'd been, and how satisfied I was about how quickly and effectively I'd done it.

When I dragged her back she collapsed and curled up weeping on the ground. Kordon stared at me with renewed horror. Understandably so; two minutes ago the woman had been willing to let me take her remaining hand, and now she was a blubbering wreck.

"*Tammy. Look at me, Tammy,*" I said, and she did, forcing herself up into a sitting position, her stump giving her some difficulty. "*Cooperate, and keep your friends from doing anything stupid.*"

She sniffled and gave me one sharp nod. "*I will.*"

"All right," I said to the others. "One of you has a tracking medallion on you. The same one I gave to Lalia, so I doubt it's her. Garal? Maglan? Are either of you carrying a silver medallion?"

Garal and Lalia looked at each other, then turned as one toward Maglan.

"You pack your own gear, Mag?" Lalia asked.

"I mean, yeah. Who else?"

"Could anyone have put anything in it without you noticing?"

"Doubt it. I've been through it since we started out—bags, clothes and all. I would have noticed by now. All I have that I didn't pack myself is the message. I'm sure of it."

The two Wolves shared another look, then looked at me. I nodded.

"Maglan, get the message case out, if you would."

"Aw, shit, Mister Garal, you don't think—?"

"Just get it out."

Maglan opened his jacket, showing the leather tube with the message inside. It was about a foot long and an inch and a half wide.

"What do you think, Lalia?" I said. "Wide enough for the medallion, yeah?"

"Yeah," she agreed sourly. "But we can't open it. Tampering with military communications—They'll throw us from the rock for that. Or just cut our heads off."

"Yeah, bloody tough situation." I looked at the case. It had a lid at one end, knotted shut with a leather cord, which was covered with a wax seal that had to be broken to undo the knots. "You'll just have to blame the dragon."

Before anyone could respond, I unceremoniously relieved Maglan of first his jacket, then the case. The strap caught on his neck, pulling him off-balance, and he sat down hard in the dirt. "Maglan resisted. You both saw it," I told the other two. "Lalia, hit me. If you can knock me out, I'll give the case back."

I didn't need to tell her twice. Lalia hauled back and punched me right in the jaw, hard enough to snap my head to the side. It actually hurt! Lalia, for her part, was shaking her hand. "Mercies and fucking Sorrows, Draka," she hissed. "What are you made of?"

"She tried to fight me for it," I told them after working out the ache in my jaw. "I think that about covers your asses."

I tore through the leather cord with my claws and opened the case, shaking it into my hand. First came a scroll, but it stuck halfway and from its center a cloth-wrapped package fell into my open palm. I pushed the scroll back into the tube and handed it back to Maglan, who looked at me with open dismay.

I unfolded the cloth. In my palm lay that same damn medallion that Kira had taken off her dead leader when I captured her.

"I don't know what the *fuck* Sempralia is playing at," I growled at the others, "but we're going to have a long, serious conversation when I get back. 'Building trust,' my scaly ass."

"At least now we know," Garal said. "And if we get rid of that medallion they won't be able to track us as easily."

"It'll slow them down a little at best," Lalia said. "There are only so many ways for us to move if we want to keep going south, with all the rivers. And I'd bet that they'll be back in force. We'll need to try and outrun them."

"Or," I said, "you three take care of these prisoners you wanted so badly, and I go and deal with this right now."

I channeled some magic into the medallion, and felt it stir. It twitched and jumped in my hand, seemingly in one specific direction, and I got the idea to hold it by the necklace. When I did that and channeled more magic it swayed in the rough direction of where the Spurs had come from.

"Draka, please," Garal said, coming up and laying his hand on my back. "Don't do anything hasty."

"I won't. I'm just going to talk to them. If they don't want to talk I'll bail out."

"You're going to confront an entire mercenary company? What do you think you could possibly accomplish doing that?"

"Won't know until I try it, will I? But I see two things happening in the next few hours. This village will be razed to the ground, and anyone living here will be lucky to survive. And you will be fleeing down the road with four dozen experienced, mounted mercenaries after you, and I don't know how that'll end. So I'm going to go talk to them, and I suggest that you get going. Take the prisoners with you, or leave them. It doesn't matter much to me. Leretem at least won't give you any trouble."

Garal gave me a searching look, then an exasperated sigh. "Right. Love, Maglan, let's get the men on horseback. The unconscious one can go on Melon; she's a steady girl. We're moving in five minutes and no longer!"

I gave Tammy a baleful glare, and she ducked her head obsequiously. "*You'll be moving out*," I told her. "*Behave.*"

I didn't need to make any threats. "*I will,*" she told me, and I believed her.

"I won't be long," I told the others. "I'll see you on the road." Then I took off, the medallion clutched in my hand.

It took about half an hour to reach the Silver Spurs' camp. Since I didn't know where it was, I had to rely on the retreating survivors to lead me there, and I deliberately stayed low and kept my speed down to make sure they wouldn't spot me, landing every so often to make sure I was heading in the right direction. Along the way I found the spot where I'd first hit them. Two horses lay dead on the ground, their throats cut, but there were no bodies; I guessed the mercs must have collected their dead or wounded as they passed.

The camp I found sat beside a shallow stream which ran south to north between two wooded hills, only easily approached from up- or downstream. It was much simpler than when I'd found them in the western hills, and looked like it was set up to be quickly broken down if needed. This time, when I approached the camp, I didn't sneak. Darkness and shadow were my allies, but this was no time for stealth. Instead I flew a couple of lazy circles around them to let them get a good look at me, riling up the horses and making soldiers stop to look up, before landing a few hundred feet upstream and striding confidently toward them.

A few of the Spurs shouted orders. Others readied bows or lances or mounted their horses. Most of them just stared.

"*I will speak with your commander!*" I roared as loud as I could, and the volume of my own voice caught me off guard. I had no idea I could be so loud. I used Tekereteki, my family's Tekereteki, what Kira called classical; I'd been told that I had a noble accent. I relied on that and my command and charisma advancements to keep the nervous soldiers from starting anything. Even if the individual mercenaries didn't understand me, I hoped that their officers would.

It worked beautifully.

Soldiers lowered their weapons, not sure what to do, as a few of them ran to the tent I recognized as belonging to their commander. I wasn't arrogant enough to march into the middle of the camp where I'd be surrounded. I sat down tall and proud outside the perimeter and let them come to me; it felt like the more regal choice.

It took a few minutes for the commander to appear, flanked by four older-looking mercs. When she did she was fully armored, except that she left her close-cropped head bare. She was a woman in her late forties to middle fifties. While she had the same general features as any Karakani, she would have stood out anywhere by her eyes, which were hard and nearly black, and by her height—she was only an inch or two shorter than Herald.

She showed some impressive survival instincts by stopping well out of spitting range. "*You asked to speak with me?*" she said. Her voice was strong and steady and her shoulders low and relaxed, but she stood upwind of me, and she couldn't mask her fear entirely. The camp reeked of it, but every person was subtly different. I could always tell.

The fact that she didn't introduce herself annoyed me a little. I already knew from Kira that the commander's name was Sarahem, but it was the principle of the thing.

"*Do they not teach basic manners in Tekeretek? Or are you making some pointless attempt at hiding who you are? Let me make it easy for you: You are the Silver Spurs, a mercenary company out of Tekeretek in the pay of Happar. You have been raiding the Karakani countryside, and on the side you've been abducting magic users and sending them back south. Do you wish to deny anything so far?*"

"*I deny everything,*" she said. I thought she was trying to be flippant, but she only came across as uncertain and bitter.

I snorted at her. "*It does not matter. Whoever you pretend to be, I am fed up with you, and I am here to make you an offer. Leave. Release any prisoners you may have, ride south across the border, and do not return. If you agree, I will return Leretem, Kordon, and Sergen to you.*"

I gathered the shadows around me. In the light of midday it was a pain, but I didn't gather so much as to make it obvious, only to give off a sense of wrongness and make myself more menacing. As if sensing the mood, my own shadow began to subtly twist and squirm. "*Refuse, and I will destroy every soldier in this camp, except for you, Commander. By ones and twos, everyone around you will disappear, until there is only you left.*"

"*You think a single creature, no matter what you are, can frighten us?*" I wasn't sure if the words were for my benefit, for her soldiers', or for her own. But for all that I despised her for what she'd done, I admired her self-control. Her voice, her expression, and her posture all shone with confidence. It didn't matter, though. No matter what she said, the cloud of fear that hung over the camp grew thicker, her own included. She took my threat as deadly serious, and she was terrified.

"*I do. Look around you. Your soldiers believe me. They may be ready to die in battle, but they do not want to be swallowed by the night. They don't want to turn their backs on a friend for a second, only for that friend to vanish with no trace but a few spatters of blood. They would much rather just go home. Don't you want to go home, Commander? Wouldn't that be much better than seeing everyone around you disappear, one by one?"*

This time I didn't need to rely on scent. I could see her falter; the way she tensed subtly, the uncertain set of her eyes. My audience of four dozen stood spellbound, and I gambled. I took a lazy step forward, then another, gathering more shadows as I went. I stopped ten feet ahead of the commander, close enough that when I raised my head high my shadow fell on her. I let it wrap around her, and as her eyes widened and her breath grew shallow I said, low enough for only her and her escorts to hear, *"And if you do not believe me, Commander, you should know that this is not the first time I have seen you, though there were a lot more of you in that wooded gorge in the hills. Remember? Before Bekiratag disappeared? Do you need me to tell you what the inside of your tent looks like, Sarahem? Which books you keep by your bedside? Do you need me to map your scars for you?"*

The commander's breath hitched, and she took a step back from me.

"There is no need to answer. You have until sunset to act. All you need to do is release your prisoners, leave, and not harm anyone else. Do that, and I will return my captives to you. Fail, and your people start dying tonight. I'll be watching."

With that I leaped into the air and climbed as fast as I could, before someone grew a pair and took a shot at me.

I hurried back to the others. They'd made it a few miles down the road, most of them walking while the still unconscious Sergen and Kordon with his healing leg were tied to the backs of Melon and Maglan's mare. I quickly informed my companions of what was happening, then left again to watch the Spurs.

By the time I returned to the mercenaries the camp was already half struck. Half an hour later they were moving south, leaving a small group of prisoners behind with some clothes and a small package of food. I decided not to approach the released prisoners; I didn't want them to scatter and lose track of each other, leaving only one of them with anything to eat.

After sunset I brought the mercenaries Sergen. He'd come to during the afternoon, but even with a healing potion in him and a day's rest he was still a mess. It turned out he was the one I'd used to knock one of his companions out of the saddle; the target had taken most of the force and died on impact. Tammy had explained things to him, and he'd behaved himself well enough, riding Melon in sullen silence.

Sergen did not like me, and he did not like flying, but it wasn't like he'd have been able to resist me even at perfect health.

I spent the night watching the mercenaries' new camp, about ten miles south of where I'd originally found them. I'd nap, then move somewhere else, and nap again; if they were using the tracking medallion, I didn't want them to ever be sure of where I was.

In the morning, as they were breaking camp, I brought them Kordon. He was less wriggly than Sergen in the air. More like Kira, in that he was first rigidly terrified, then went entirely limp once he accepted that he had no control over the situation.

The Spurs made it about twenty miles that day, an impressive distance considering most of it was through fields and pastures rather than on roads. As the sun was setting I brought them Tammy.

Tammy hadn't wanted to go.

"*Please*," she said, on her knees before me. "*Can't I stay with you?*"

"*I have no time or place for you,*" I told her. "*Now stand and get ready to fly.*"

She did as I ordered. Of course she did. She'd broken faster and more completely than anyone except possibly Mak, and I'd been far harsher, less controlled, with Mak. She stood and faced me, her arms out the way I'd instructed Sergen and Kordon before her, and she asked me again, with tears in her eyes. "*Please. I never belonged with the Spurs, not really. Please let me serve you!*"

I considered it. I couldn't deny that I wanted to keep her. She was mine, after all. I didn't like to part with anything that was mine. The fact that I despised her as a murdering sack of crap didn't even figure into it. But this was a time to be reasonable and responsible; not only would she be a burden, but I'd told Sarahem that I'd return her soldiers. If I went back on even part of my word, she and the Spurs might become a problem again, and that would be a pain in the ass.

But perhaps Tammy could be useful after all? "*If you want to serve me,*" I told her, "*return to your company, if they'll still have you. See what you can find out about all those prisoners you've been sending south, and if you can learn anything about the prisoners someone called the 'Night Blossom', or possibly Parvion Tarkarran, has been selling to Commander Lakatekete.*" I looked at the stump where her forearm ended halfway. It had scabbed over and was healing closed, but was still wrapped in bandages. "*And see if you can find a healer who can regenerate your lost limb.*"

"*As you wish, great dragon,*" she said, smiling through her tears, eyes shining with purpose.

"*Draka,*" I told her. "*My name is Draka.*"

One minute, I thought. *One damn minute to reduce a hardened soldier to this.*

CHAPTER FORTY-THREE

I Wanna Be in the Cavalry

A *ll right, Tammy. Remember what I want you to do?"*

I'd brought Tammy to within half a mile of the Spurs' camp. While she didn't try to hide how unhappy she was about leaving me, she wanted to disappoint me even less.

"Stay with the company, if they'll have me. Learn all I can about the slaves taken or bought from Karakan. Get my hand restored," she recited obediently, then turned hopeful. *"Return to you?"*

I snorted. *"No. I'll tell you when I want you back."*

She looked absolutely crestfallen at my casual rejection. *"But—But my lady, how will I tell you what I've learned?"*

"Don't worry about that. I'll come to you, wherever you are. Just make sure that you get a proper night's sleep whenever your duties allow."

She, of course, took that as a religious commandment. *"I will, my lady!"*

I watched her go with mixed feelings. She was a murderer and a slaver, or at the very least a repeat accessory to both. She didn't have a shred of remorse that I'd seen, and I was glad to see the back of her. At the same time, she was mine now. Letting her go took some genuine effort, and despite everything, I worried for her. She'd lost her sword hand. Without it, how could she remain with the Spurs? How would she make a living? I'd been told that it was possible to have lost limbs restored, but would she be able to afford it? Did she have any skills that would let her work without it? Would she end up a cripple on a corner somewhere, begging passersby for bits?

I shouldn't have told her to go. Surely Sarahem and the Spurs wouldn't miss her? And if they made a fuss, I'd deal with them. I should just call her back, take her back to the inn where I could keep an eye on her. Or maybe she could guard my hoard? I should—

You should let her go, just like we decided, Conscience told me sternly. *She's a bad person. We don't like her. We don't want her around our family or anyone else important to us. Especially not around Kira! She's made it clear that the only person in that company she could stand is already dead.*

"Yeah," I whispered to the still air. Conscience was right. She usually was. Besides, I'd made a deal with the Spurs, and the idea of going back on it didn't sit well with me. Tammy was on her own.

Well, unless things got really bad. Then we'd have to see.

I watched from a distance as three riders met her. One of them got off their horse and wrapped her in a blanket, turning the action into a hug that lingered for a few seconds before whoever it was helped Tammy onto their horse. I thought I saw her look back my way, and then the horses turned and rode for their camp.

"So, Draka," Lalia said once I was back with the others, "what the fuck was that?"

"I have no idea what you mean," I lied. I didn't even try to do a good job, either.

"Ler—Lat—whatever her name was. Tami. You wrapped her up in your wings and said a few words. Ever since, she's—and I do not use this word lightly—worshiped you. That little display before you flew her away, that wasn't just fear of you carrying her. I don't know what you both said, but I know what adoration looks like. What. Did. You. Do?"

"My waves and stars," Garal murmured, leaning in close and putting his hands gently on her shoulders. "Perhaps we should not—"

I cut him off. "I am a *dragon*, Lalia. I am a creature of *magic*. I showed her what that means. I showed her the living hell I can reduce a human's life to without ever touching them. And I would show you what I mean by that, but honestly, I like you too much." *And not nearly enough to have you hanging off my tail for the rest of your life,* I added silently to myself. "Though I was surprised at how effective it was. Maybe she's one of those hidden dragon worshipers Kira told me about."

"She looked happy at the end," Maglan said from where he sat, poking at the fire with a long stick.

"Yeah. I told her what to do to make me happy with her. She liked that. Now drop it."

Lalia had a sook after that, going off to "look for firewood" among the sparse trees near the little campsite they'd found. I could hear her swearing and the snapping of wood for a good, long while, before she returned with a few sticks. "You 'like' me now? Not just 'tolerate?'" she asked, putting the sticks on the already entirely sufficient pile near the fire.

"I guess, yeah. You haven't been nearly as much of a bitch to me these last few months, and you're a decent person from what I've seen. Damning with faint praise and all, but yeah."

"You're all right, too," she admitted sourly. "You can be infuriating and scary and creepy as the Sorrows themselves, but at least you look after the people close to you. And you care about innocent people. So keep your secrets for now. I'll just have to trust you not to do anything terrible to anyone who doesn't deserve it."

"I'll try not to disappoint."

The next two days passed without incident, but not uneventfully. The others, my friends—though Lalia, and especially Maglan, were still on probation— continued along the road, and I stayed in the air, flying long back-and-forths between them and the Spurs. The mercenaries kept moving south, and I made sure that they saw me behind them to keep them motivated.

From the air it was easy enough to follow them, but they must have been good at what they did, because more than once I saw smaller groups of horsemen pass within a few hundred yards of their column; cavalry patrols from the Karakani army, no doubt. Sometimes the Spurs would change direction, sometimes they'd speed up, other times they'd do nothing. They made their camps in hidden places, ready to move at a moment's notice, and not once were they caught.

As I circled one of those camps I imagined Tammy looking up at me, and I wondered how she was doing. *My* Tammy.

I'd made a not entirely welcome discovery about myself since I returned her to the Silver Spurs. It had happened before, but I'd written it off. Quite simply, I found myself worrying about the people I'd . . . what? Touched, subjugated, dom- inated, broken? And, I realized that my concern for them was no more natural than their adoration for me. I just hadn't noticed it until recently.

There had been reasons for me to think a lot about all these people. Herald needed no explanation. With Mak and Ardek, I'd thought that it was simply because they could be useful. Then it had felt natural since I was around them all the time. The same with Kira, once she joined us. Jekrie had a whole little tribe that I'd promised to protect, and they were mostly an extension of him in my mind, so he was the one I focused on. And of course I'd thought a lot about Zabra and Kesra, both before and after we worked out our differences. Avjilan . . . well. Even before I broke him I'd wanted to keep Avjilan for myself for entirely different reasons.

I'd wondered about Barro and the scholars as well, but I'd gotten to know Barro, and the scholars might still be useful to me. It was harder to explain why I should sometimes wonder about what had happened to some random mugger that I'd seen for all of two minutes in an alley.

With Tammy it became impossible to miss. The transition was simply too sharp. Until I broke her, I'd wanted her dead. I hated what she represented, and I despised her for what she'd allowed herself to be a part of. It didn't make much difference to me if she'd done it due to cowardice, indifference, or malice; she'd taken part in the murders of innocent people to cover up that they were enslaving others. Defenseless or not, I would have gladly killed her myself in that village if Lalia hadn't been so insistent on keeping our prisoners alive.

That had changed once I broke her, and because I'd already had my suspi- cions, I knew what to look for. For all that I'd thought and said, for all that she still genuinely disgusted me, I cared about her. Not in the way I cared about people I liked—nowhere close—but I wanted her to live and grow and remain useful to me. To be happy, even. As the Spurs crossed the river, forcing their way across an ancient stone bridge into what must be Happar, judging by the unfamiliar standards on the southern bank, I worried about her; there had been a small Karakani force guarding the northern end, and the mercenaries eschewed diplomacy and simply charged across. Once they were over the bridge I wondered if I'd ever see her again. If she'd get her hand back and be able to make a living. Try as I might, I couldn't make myself indifferent to her future hardships.

She was *my* Tammy. Of course I worried.

I couldn't help but think about how this was only a small part of what everyone I'd touched must be going through, and I didn't like it. It was disturbing to have my head messed with like that, even when it was me doing it.

Not that Conscience cared about my discomfort. *Don't be so bloody pissy about it*, she told me. *Empathy is a good thing.*

Prior to my revelation, I'd been thinking about how much easier things would be if I just started subjugating everyone who didn't need to die immediately. Sempralia, for one. I couldn't think about her without tasting venom. I didn't know what game she was playing—Lalia had read her letter, but there were no clues there, only instructions from the council to Sarvalian, the general in command. But she would tell me. I was going to finish this little mission of hers, and then we were going to have a long talk. And, if she didn't want to be open and honest with me, well . . . I had ways of making people talk. I'd just have to deal with Kalder first. And wouldn't he be useful, if I could take him, too?

Thoughts like that had made Conscience decidedly uncomfortable. Violating someone's free will was no better than any other kind of violence, as far as she was concerned. So, for us to be able to feel even a little of what that meant, to not have it just be something abstract that was easily disregarded at my convenience, was entirely positive in her eyes. Or her perspective, rather, since her eyes were mine and Instinct's, too. Now that I knew for sure that claiming someone as my own meant that I would feel responsible for them, whether I wanted it or not, that should make me a little more careful about whose head I messed with.

Or I'd just go all out, create a cult of worshipful former enemies, and set myself up as queen somewhere. That was Instinct's suggestion, anyway.

On a completely different subject, at some point in our trip, the nagging desire to consume Nest Hearts stopped trying to pull me north and turned south instead. The need had been getting stronger as time passed, especially after I broke Tammy and intimidated the Spurs' commander, and my guess was that I'd used some of the power I'd devoured. It fit; all my magic became easier as long as I was "charged," so to speak. Instinct agreed, though she didn't go so far as to explicitly confirm it. I wished that she would; she'd been a lot more helpful back before our merger, when I still thought of her as the dragon.

When I watched the Spurs thunder across that bridge into Happar some of the threads had been so thick and bright that I considered going after them. A dozen or two miles, at most, and I'd have a Nest Heart to feast on. I knew it in my bones. But, I'd also be in what was not officially, but was actually, enemy territory, and I couldn't risk passing out once I finished absorbing a Nest Heart. They would just have to remain there, achingly, tantalizingly close.

Perhaps I'd have a look when I did my scouting flights. Just a peek.

It was weird, though, how there were any Nest Hearts here at all. On the Karakani side there was maybe one, and that was somewhere toward the coast. So why were there so many on the Happaran side? Did no one live there? Did no one clear them out when the monsters became a problem? Maybe they just didn't have any of those nest killing crystals?

There had to be a reason for it; I just wasn't seeing it. Another reason to look for them when I went out scouting. Perhaps take a closer look, just in case. This was important, after all.

When I thought that I'd be heading south on my own I'd figured that I would just take things as they'd come. There was no way that Sempralia would send me there without warning the general ahead of time, and their patrols must have seen and reported on my approach. I'd just find whatever looked like the main encampment, circle it for a while, and then land in the open some distance away and namedrop General Sarvalian when someone came to talk to me. If things turned sour, I'd just bug out. With three companions by my side, things went even smoother.

The army camp I found was a small town. I had vague ideas from modern media about army sizes in different time periods and about camp followers and all, but that didn't help all that much with guessing how many people there might be. There certainly were a lot of tents. Hundreds of them for sure. Probably not more than a thousand, but most of them were big. I found it a full day before Garal and the others reached it; it was near the bridge that the Spurs used to cross back into Happar. Since we moved along a major road, it was inevitable that one of the cavalry patrols would find them and move in to investigate. Once that happened I gave my companions five minutes to explain the shadow circling them before I landed and approached.

I walked as casually as I could, trying to imitate the relaxed saunter of a friendly cat. The six horses of the patrol snorted and stamped nervously. "Are they ready for me?" I called ahead, and the mounted soldiers, who'd been keeping themselves so cool and collected, startled at my words.

Lalia burst into laughter. "Weren't sure if she was real until she spoke, were you?" she asked. "Don't worry. She's harmless."

The man I'd pegged as the leader of the group, judging by the fancy crest on his helmet, looked at her incredulously.

"Well, I say 'harmless' . . . She will absolutely destroy you if you give her a reason. But it needs to be a good reason, like killing kids or trying to pick up a silver eagle she had her eyes on. For a terrifying monster out of legend, she's nice, really."

"My love, *please* . . ." Garal drew his hand over his face.

At the same time I said, "Nah, yeah, don't leave any valuables out. That'll trigger a negative dragon interaction."

"*Draka! Please!*" Garal turned to the leader. "Captain Vestem, please allow me to introduce the dragon, Lady Draka. I ask that you try to put aside any prejudices you may have from stories and myths, ignore her unfortunate sense of humor, and judge her on her own merits. She is *not* a threat to your men or to any other soldier of Karakan."

"I'm here to help," I confirmed, getting as close as I could before their horses started acting too uncomfortable. "And I should hope that General Sarvalian is expecting me."

"Mercies preserve us," the captain whispered low enough that I barely heard him, as he did his best to calm his horse without taking his attention off me. This close I could see how young he was, about Maglan's or Ardek's age, and I figured they must assign ranks based on wealth here, like in the dumb old times back home. For all his shiny armor and his very impressive horse, it was almost cute how nervous he was. "Well met, ah, L-Lady Draka? I'm Captain Vestem, ah, captain of the second group, fifth wing of the Karakani cavalry. Well met? No, I said that. A plea—We will be escorting you!"

I sat down. "Thank you, Captain. Lead the way! I'll stay back here with my friends, yeah? Give your horses a little time to get used to me."

I couldn't smell relief, but with Vestem I didn't need to. "That's, ah—Yes! Splendid idea, Lady Draka! If you would all please follow, then. Horsemen, with me!"

With that, Vestem took his fearfully whispering soldiers, turned them around, and started down the road. We followed. I trotted along next to Melon, who had been used to me for ages, while Lalia and Maglan stayed a short distance behind. Windfall could tolerate me, but I doubted that the gelding would ever be as comfortable as Melon, but Maglan's mare still needed time.

"Look at that little pay-to-lead run," Lalia chuckled behind me. "Too bad his House couldn't buy him a stiffer spine!"

"Please, Miss Lalia," Maglan said. There was laughter in his voice, too. "They're not all bad."

"You have a rivalry with the army, or something?" I asked, bending my neck so that I was looking right behind me.

Lalia threw me an exaggerated grimace. "Remember what I told you about being creepy?"

"Not my fault you've got a short neck. So, rivalry?"

"The army tends to look down on us mercenaries," Garal answered from beside me. "The cavalry more so than others."

"Rich boys and girls, all of them," Lalia said. "And the officers are the worst. They elect their officers, right? But there's nothing that says you can't bribe your wingmates, so the richest bastard usually ends up as the captain."

She snorted. "'Captain.' A captain in command of eleven wingmates. And look at that kid. He's not half the leader Garal is and not a third the soldier that I am. And even if he's the type that actually takes his position seriously, and not just as a way to get impressionable girls to spread their legs, I doubt he's even got his first major advancement yet! And they have him leading eleven other boys and girls around like he knows what he's doing. It's got to be funny, or it'd be sad, wouldn't it?"

I imagined what would have happened if Vestem and his group had run into the Silver Spurs. I couldn't imagine it would've been pretty. "Why would they do it like that?" I asked.

Lalia snorted. "Got to be able to afford the horses and the arms to be a horseman, don't you? City doesn't want to pay for a standing force of cavalry, so they raise them from whoever wants to and can afford to join when they're needed. And the cavalry's a bit of a social club for rich kids, so there's no will in the council to change it. A stupid relic of the past, really. Look at Maglan, here! He's got a salary, the army pays for all his gear, and his officers usually know what they're doing." She looked quizzically at Maglan. "Or so I hope."

"Assholes, the lot of them, but they know what they're about, yeah." He lowered his voice. "Until you get to the regimental commanders. Luck of the draw there. Political appointments, you know?"

Lalia spat, making her opinion of that perfectly clear even before she spoke. "We're lucky Karakan hasn't had a land war for decades. The Happarans may be poorer, have a smaller population, and be ruled by absolute scum, but at least they have competent officers on every level. They don't just let anyone who wants to, and has the clout to, make others vote their way lead a regiment, or worse, an army. The Wolves worked for them a decade ago, expanding around the south end of the island, and as Rallon told it, they have the best land commanders around the Sarey, infantry and cavalry. And their navy is no joke, either. Without the league I'd be really worried if it came to a fight for this island."

Neither Garal nor Maglan argued with that. Those were the last words said on the topic. It was difficult to ignore the fact that there was likely a war brewing, one that might be hard fought. The rest of the walk was spent in thoughtful silence.

General Sarvalian

After the reaction I got from Vestem and his troop, walking through the gate into the army camp about two hours later was just as much fun as I'd hoped. I'd primed the assembled soldiers when I flew over the place, and the patrols I'd seen had every chance to see me right back. Word must have gotten around. Add to that Vestem sending one of his horsemen ahead when we got close, and there was a crowd waiting when we arrived. They were packed tight. Everyone wanted to get a look, and they only parted to let us pass under the batons and furious curses of the officers—once they got their own eyeful, of course.

Being treated like something between a movie star and a poorly caged Bengal tiger would have been terrifying to me as a human. My three companions and their horses were visibly nervous. But, while Tark had given me a valuable lesson in my lack of invulnerability, I knew that, if I wanted to, I could just leave. With that in mind, I allowed myself to relax and enjoy their amazement. It was only right; I was amazing, after all.

The entire camp was surrounded by a palisade, tall and strong enough to keep anyone out who couldn't fly or make themselves an entrance. Inside and surrounding the center was another, lower wall. It looked more like a privacy fence than anything, and I suspected that it served the same purpose. We were led past this second wall into an open area, which might be some kind of assembly or training ground, and there Vestem stopped and asked us to wait.

"I will go," he told us, bristling with importance. "I must inform my commander that you have arrived, with a message and a visitor for the general." He turned to the others. "Make sure that our guests are not bothered!"

The four remaining horsemen answered as one. "Yes, Captain!"

No matter what the others may have said about the cavalry being a glorified social club for rich boys and girls, these four at least took their role as escort seriously. While there wasn't a mob like there had been at the entrance, they still had to fend off a curious aide-de-camp or two and, at one point, explain, extremely politely, to a woman of indeterminate rank that we were guests of the general.

That turned out not to be entirely true, though. At first someone arrived to take Maglan's message, but he refused, saying that he had strict orders from the council, via his regimental commander, to put it directly into the hand of General Sarvalian. The way his voice trembled when he did so suggested that the person he was refusing was several ranks above him, but he didn't give in. My approval of him went up a little. The officer finally relented and instructed Maglan to come with him, but I interrupted.

"I'll be coming with him," I said, stepping closer. "The message case has been opened, and I'm the one who did it. I won't have Mag getting in trouble for something I did."

The officer had steadfastly ignored me, and when I came near it became clear why. By his smell, the man was terrified. I couldn't tell if he used his best judgment to get the message delivered or if he just didn't dare to contradict me, but he "invited" me to come along almost instantly, only glancing at me for a second before looking away again. "Great!" I said, and decided to push it. I turned to my remaining two companions. "No point in you two sitting around in the sun all day. Let's all go!"

"Draka, I'm not sure—" Garal said, but the officer spoke over him after a half-second of hesitation.

"I'm sure that can be accommodated! Come, all of you, then! Captain Vestem told us that you fought some mercenaries on your way. I'm sure the general will want you all to report in person!"

The unnamed officer, whose name or rank I never learned, still didn't look at me. The man who I knew in my bones must be General Sarvalian, however, looked at me like he was evaluating a new piece of equipment. It was unnerving. I'd gotten used to being looked at with various levels of fear, curiosity, and adoration. Being coldly evaluated was not entirely new—Zabra's man Hardal had been the same—but it still made me uncertain. What I was sure of was that no matter what the others had told me about political appointments and rot in the army's command structure, this man was not just some rich guy here to pad his résumé. The three men and two women in the large tent with him looked to him for how to react when we were brought in, and he had an undeniable air of authority that even I felt. On top of that, the man looked more like a soldier or a farmer than a politician, in his late middle years but still with some considerable muscle on him, with large hands and thick forearms.

Instinct was *furious*. I could see my shadow ahead of me, straining to get at the man. No matter who or what he was, he was human, and she wanted one of two things from humans—fear or adoration. Being treated as an equal, like with Sempralia or Zabra, had been bad enough. Being treated as something below or even outside of the hierarchy? That made her want to put this man in his place.

Even trying to do something like that would have been an absolute disaster. I couldn't tell if the man himself had a hope in hell against me, but two of the people with him, a man and a woman, both had that same air of sudden, terrible violence as Sempralia's bodyguard Kalder. If Tark had been able to injure me, these two may actually be able to disable or even kill me. I could still shift, of course—

I forced myself to leave that line of thinking. Instinct was a part of me, and her anger was hot enough that it was making me think of ways to get out *if* I turned this into a fight. I need not even consider that option, if for no other reason than I had three people with me. I coaxed my shadow back to stillness, mollifying Instinct with silent promises that Sarvalian would understand the pecking order soon enough.

Sarvalian almost ruined it by addressing Maglan first. His voice was richer and warmer than I would have expected, but still clipped and to the point. "My tribune tells me you refuse to give your message to anyone but the general in command. Well, soldier, I'm General Sarvalian. Hand it over!"

"Yes, General!" Maglan snapped to obey. In two seconds flat he had the strap of the message case over his head and was holding the leather cylinder out for the general to take.

"This seal has been broken. I've been told that there is an explanation. Speak!"

"I opened it," I told him. "Maglan tried to stop me. Lalia tried to take it back." I indicated her with a sweep of my head. "They failed."

"Of course they damn well did." The general was already scanning the message. "And why, Lady Draka, did you open the message?"

"I thought there might be a tracking medallion inside that the Silver Spurs mercenary company was using to follow us." I fished it out from under my tongue, where I'd been keeping it, and held it out for him to see. "There was."

There was absolutely no difference in the way he looked at the piece of enchanted jewelry and how he'd looked at me. "This would be the same medallion that Commander Terriallon recovered from the mercenary raiders some time ago?"

"One and the same, yeah."

"And I assume that you are not willing to part with it."

"Right again."

"Enjoy, then. The mercenaries have crossed into Happar anyway, as I suspect you know." He turned to my companions. "I will speak to Lady Draka alone. One of my tribunes will show you where to go. Verlan, see to it. Parvion, Veretil, you can return to your other duties."

There was a flurry of salutes and bows and "Yes, Generals." Then it was just me, Sarvalian, and his two bodyguards.

The general looked around the large tent. It wasn't circus sized, but it must have been forty or fifty feet on a side, with large screens dividing it into two uneven sections. "Wait here, would you?" he said, his speech much more relaxed than it had been. He disappeared into the smaller section, returning moments later with two large, flat pillows which he put next to each other on the floor. He then set up a tent chair about five feet away from them and sat. "I'd offer you a chair, but our carpenters are busy as is. This work for you?"

"Sure, yeah." Sarvalian's bodyguards eyed me warily, taking positions next to and slightly in front of him as I padded over and rearranged the pillows a little, then lay down. His change in attitude had caught me off guard. I'd been prepared for a surly bastard, whom I'd just have to tolerate until I fulfilled my end of the bargain, but the general suddenly seemed, if not friendly, then at least approachable.

"You hungry? Thirsty? Never played host to anyone who's not human before, but I'm sure we could rustle up something."

"Ah, nah, that's all right. Later. Thanks."

"Well then, Lady Draka, how do you think that we should proceed here? That letter you four brought me is officially from the council, but really it's from Sempralia. There's no mention of any tracking medallion. Mostly it just asks me to make good use of you and not to piss you off, with some suggestions of things to avoid and ways to keep you happy. But as for how to best employ you . . . honestly, I'm going to pretend that I don't know anything at all about your kind. The fact that you are here, talking, making agreements, that's pretty damned crazy, and goes against everything I've ever read or been told. So, Lady Draka, I'll defer to you. How can I use you?"

How could he use me? Not how could I help him, or what could I do for him, but how could he use me. He may have been acting more amiable, but he still clearly saw me as a tool. Instinct didn't like it, but I found it hard to hold against him. He had no problem treating me as a person; I suspected that he saw everyone in terms of how useful they could be. Perhaps that wasn't a terrible trait in an army commander; perhaps it made everyone hate him. I had no idea.

So, how could he use me? That should be easy enough. "My deal with lady justice Sempralia was that I'd scout for you. I can fly, I can see perfectly in the dark, and against a night sky I'm as good as invisible. Just tell me where you want me to look and send me out at night, and I'll be back by morning."

"How are you with maps, recognizing and recording troop types and numbers, and things like that?"

"Ah . . ."

Honesty felt like the best policy, but I didn't want to tell him that I only had the barest idea. Admitting ignorance stung my pride. He seemed to pick up on it from my hesitation, though.

"Would you like to speak with one of my aides, perhaps, to make sure that we don't misunderstand each other?" His meaning was clear: Do you need to be taught all of this stuff?

"Nah, yeah, that would be for the best," I said. I knew that I was being handled, but I was grateful for the consideration nonetheless.

"Then I'll have Tribune Veretil take care of it once we're done here. Can you go out tonight?"

"If I can have a snack and a nap, sure, yeah."

"That's set, then. I'll have some—" He paused and looked at me. "I'll have a couple pounds of meat and a barrel of water brought to you once you finish with Veretil. Unless you'd prefer something else?"

"That's perfect."

He nodded. "Guards, leave us and inform tribune Veretil that I will need him earlier than expected."

The female bodyguard saluted with a "Yes, General," but the male hesitated. "General, with all—" he said, looking at me.

The general cut him off. "Your concern is appreciated, soldier, but unnecessary. Get to it!"

". . . Yes, general." He followed his fellow guard out, but he didn't look happy about it.

"You're not the least bit scared of me, are you, General?" I asked when we were alone. "Most people stink of fear when they first meet me. Those that don't are usually at least nervous. You're so calm that it's almost insulting."

"Am I? Perhaps I've overcorrected, then. Sempralia suggested you'd appreciate being treated like just any other important person."

"I mean, yeah, I do. I'm just not used to being disregarded like this."

"Well, let me put you at ease. There's no disrespect intended. I simply don't fear you. It has nothing to do with underestimating your capability. I have no doubt that you could kill me, should you wish to. I simply trust Sempralia's evaluation of your temperament. Is she wrong when she tells me that you're unlikely to resort to violence without provocation?"

"Nah, she's right enough. So, what did you want to talk about that you don't want your bodyguards hearing?"

"Tell me, Lady Draka, what is your opinion of lady justice Sempralia? Your honest opinion, right now?"

His question caught me off guard. My first thought was, what did it matter? My opinion of the woman wouldn't make any difference as to whether I'd do my best to do a good job here. But by the calculating look he was giving me, I figured that he'd asked for a good reason. And I didn't see how it could hurt to be honest; even if he sent off a message to Sempralia, that only meant that she'd be forewarned that I was not pleased with her.

"I thought that she was honest and direct when I met her, " I told him. "Now, though, I'm rather pissed at her. I'm going to have some questions for her next time I see her, and she'd better have some good answers for me if this cooperation is to go anywhere."

The general nodded without taking his eyes off me. "The medallion?"

"That, and why she'd have me babysitting three messengers for five days in the first place, when I could have been here in a few hours at my own pace. Why are they all three people I know? Why is she sending a message to you on paper at all? Don't you have some way of communicating by magic? It doesn't sound like there was anything secret in there except that she mentioned me. In that case, why not just have me carry the message alone? All of those things together with the medallion being in the message case makes it look like she was endangering people important to me on purpose, and if her judgment is as good as you seem to think it is, then she should know very well how I'd react to that."

"Which is?"

"If she was anyone else, I'd tear her to pieces. As it is, I'm restraining myself, and hoping that there are good reasons for everything."

Again, Sarvalian nodded. "That is about what I expected you to say, considering you're still here. For the sake of Lady Sempralia and the relationship between you and the council, I'm going to tell you a few things that I do not want to leave this tent. Can you promise me that?"

"Well . . . I can't promise that I won't tell my most trusted friends. Those would be Lady Drakonum and her sister. I rely on their advice. If that's all right with you . . . ?"

"Can you vouch for their discretion?"

"Absolutely. If I tell them that I want something kept secret, they won't tell a soul, not even their brother."

"That's acceptable. Lady Draka, I believe that you've been caught up in some political game, colored by some possible treason. Am I right if I say that you escorting the messengers was a last-minute thing?"

"Right, yeah."

"Sempralia says in her letter that she was refused permission to send it through the communications circle, on the excuse that it was not an official council communication but a personal one from her to me. It's a shit-poor excuse, but she was told to send it by messenger instead. She doesn't say so in the message, but knowing her she would have become suspicious that someone might try to intercept the message, and I agree. As for her choice of messenger and escort, that was most likely a direct and transparent manipulation by her. She paints you as deeply loyal to your friends. By what Captain Vestem said, and how you four held yourselves earlier, I'd guess you're friendly with the mercenaries at least, correct?"

"Garal for sure, yeah. And Lalia, too, these days, I suppose. And Maglan— that's the soldier—he's not so bad, either."

"She would have chosen them to make sure that you would be compelled to protect them. It would have been easy enough. I'm sure the poor archer's commander was confused, but he wouldn't have refused a direct request from Lady Sempralia to borrow one of his soldiers. Nor would Commander Terriallon, though I suspect he's being well paid for the use of those two."

"She could have bloody told me!"

"I agree. But what difference would it have made? In the best case, you would have known slightly earlier who your companions would be. Worst case, her message to you could have been intercepted and some political enemy of hers would know exactly who would be carrying her message." He shrugged. "She would have known that this would annoy you. She simply calculated that it wouldn't annoy you too much to be worth it."

"Yeah, but this damned thing!" I brandished the medallion. "She could have told me about this!"

He shrugged again. "I truly don't think she knew about it. She didn't mention it in her letter, and there has been no word that something like it would be sent to us. I think someone planted it in the message case."

"Aw, fuck. Who? And why? To make it easier to intercept the message?"

"Probably. Or to get the medallion back to the Silver Spurs. As for who, we'll need to investigate who had access to the message case before it was given to—Maglan, was it? That's not something you need to worry about. My point here was that I don't see any reason Sempralia should be the one responsible, and I hope that you won't hold it against her."

"She's still going to have to explain herself. But yeah, sure. I'll give her the benefit of the doubt. For now."

"Thank you." He stood from his chair. "And now, I hear Tribune Veretil outside. Lady Draka, I look forward to working with you. It's not often one meets a living legend, after all."

After some hesitation he offered his hand, and I shook it by reflex more than anything. I held back my strength, but I got the impression that he did, too; his forearm barely tensed, but his grip was like a vice. We could have each squeezed as hard as we could, but all that would've accomplished was making us look like a pair of wankers.

"Same to you, General Sarvalian. I'll enjoy making you glad that I'm on your side."

"I'll look forward to it," he said, and the smile that accompanied his words was honest, friendly, and full of anticipation.

CHAPTER FORTY-FIVE

Scouts and Sentries

Tribune Veretil was a tall, thin man, somewhere in his forties, clean shaven but with eyebrows that looked like two mustaches attached to his forehead, the hairs curling every which way. I wondered if they got in the way of his eyesight when they moved. I got to see those eyebrows move around *a lot*; the man's face was as expressive as his eyebrows were bushy.

While he was nowhere near as terrified of me as the first unnamed officer had been, he still had a healthy dose of respect. He was also careful not to say or do anything that might possibly wound my pride. As he went through the different things that a scout should take note of, I asked a lot of questions, usually because there was something I didn't understand or needed clarification on. Without fail he blamed himself, being careful to phrase everything in such a way that it couldn't possibly be my fault that I hadn't understood. That grew old quickly, but I put up with it; the man was a fount of information and seemed to know everything there was to know about maps, geography, troop types and armaments, and military logistics. If I came across a camp, he even wanted me to count the number of each type of livestock, which he could apparently use to estimate something or other. When he tried to explain anything beyond what to look for, it quickly went over my head, but the important parts stuck pretty well. He even copied the key points down on a scroll for me to take with me.

After class I was shown to a small part of the inner camp where two large tents had been set up. Garal and Lalia lay on the grass, holding hands and basking in the last rays of the sun as a nervous-looking soldier stood guard nearby—a tall, square faced woman. The soldier's eyes nearly popped out of her head as we approached. It took Tribune Veretil clearing his throat for her to notice him, at which point she quickly snapped to attention and saluted.

Garal and Lalia got to their feet. They didn't salute the tribune, since they weren't part of the army, but they did give him one of those hand-on-chest half bows that I saw every so often. I could only assume that they had orders to be on their best behavior and make nice with the officers.

"Thank you, Tribune," I said. "I won't take any more of your time."

The man's face was all over the place as he answered, his eyebrows seeming to move by an inch or more as it stretched and contorted. It was a little disturbing, like some kind of early Jim Carrey character. "Oh, no trouble at all, Lady Draka! None of my other duties this afternoon were nearly as important or urgent. Call on me any time if you have further questions. Sentry—" He peered at the guard. "Your name is . . . Darim, soldier. Is that correct?"

"Yes, Tribune!"

"Sentry Darim here will see to your needs. If you need something or wish to speak with someone, tell her and she will take care of it. Mister Garal and Miss Lalia, an evening meal will be served in the command mess, the tent over there with the green flag, in about an hour. We'd be delighted for you to join us. Lady Draka, the general has instructed me to arrange some meat and water for you, but if you'd rather . . ."

He looked doubtfully toward the mess tent. I took pity on him. "A few pounds of meat and a small barrel or large bucket of water will do nicely, Tribune."

The relief radiated off him. Feeding two extra mouths was surely no trouble, but accommodating me might have been difficult. And that was without taking into account the commotion I'd cause just by being in the mess tent. "I will take care of that immediately, then. Good evening!" he said, then turned and walked quickly away.

"So. Good evening, Garal. Lalia. Sentry Darim?"

The soldier looked back to me, her eyes bugging out again. She swallowed and licked her lips, and I got the impression that her mouth was very dry. "Ah—Ah—Yeah?" she managed, then jerked to attention, looking horrified. "I mean, yes, Lady Draka. What can I do for you?"

"Are you going to be hanging around the whole time we're here, or are you just here for the evening?"

I couldn't decide if she looked relieved or crestfallen at my question. "I, ah, I was assigned to look after yourself and your two companions for the duration of your stay, but if you're not satisfied, I'm sure I could—"

"Yeah, nah, that's not it. No worries, all right? But if you're going to be with us for a few days, I can't have you looking like you're about to piss yourself the whole time. Come on. Have a sit, chat a little, get used to me."

"I, ah, I'm supposed to—"

"Come on! Think of it as a request from an important guest. And whatever you're supposed to do, guard us or keep an eye on us, you can do it better from right next to me. Here, now." I lay down on the grass between the two tents. "Sit down, and let's talk a bit."

"I—Yes, ma'am."

Garal and Lalia had both watched the exchange with open amusement, plopping down next to each other to my left. "Go on, then!" Lalia said, leaning over and patting the ground in a spot that would make a triangle with myself and her and Garal. "Sit, sit!"

Darim approached us cautiously, as though she feared walking into an ambush. With clear reluctance she adjusted the sheathed sword on her belt, then sat smoothly on the grass with both legs beneath her. She looked ready to bolt at any moment, but with how skittish she was around me, I counted her taking a seat at all as a victory.

Maglan, it turned out, had been sent away to join the rest of his regiment. Only half of them had been sent back to Karakan for rest and relaxation; they were currently marching south to join us, but the other half were still here, eagerly waiting for their turn.

"Oh, yeah, I can take you to him. Now, or later, after we eat. No problem," Darim told Garal when he asked. The contrast between how she treated the Wolves and me was ridiculous. With them she was easygoing and something of a chatterbox, but whenever I spoke up her whole posture changed. She went stiff and silent, and she kept her eyes on my chest, as though trying to predict how I might move in case I decided to—I wasn't sure. Eat her? She was slow to ease up, too, and I was starting to regret asking her to sit down. What was the point if she was just going to make it awkward?

"So, Darim," Lalia said, glancing between the two of us. "You mentioned siblings?"

"Oh, yeah! A sister and a brother, both younger than me. My sister just married out, but my brother's a real little prince. A bit of a surprise blessing, you know? He's only eight, and gets whatever he wants." She rolled her eyes, but with a smile on her face. "We couldn't afford nice things like what he gets when I was growing up. That's why I joined up, you know? Army feeds you, clothes you, and pays you. Left the folks more money for my siblings. But Papa picked up a new advancement two years back that lets him sew the finest, surest seams in minutes—he's a tailor, you see—and now business is better than we ever dreamed. He offered to buy me out of my contract, but I like it here. Stable, orderly, good friends, handsome men—what's not to like?"

"I did something similar," Lalia said. "Though not wanting to be a wood carver was a big part of it, too. And I joined the Wolves instead of the army, of course, though that's mostly this one's fault." She ruffled Garal's hair affectionately. "I've got a little sister, Lahnie. Draka loves her. Don't you, Draka?"

"Yeah, she's a sweet kid. Loves to ride around on my back. A bit reckless, but she's what, six?"

"Six, yeah. About to turn seven, though, and won't let anyone forget it. She was born about four weeks after the solstice, so it's not far off now. Close to Herald, actually."

"Wait!" Darim turned large, astonished eyes on me. "You let a little girl *ride* you?"

"I mean, yeah?" I said. "Like I said, she's a sweet kid. I don't take her up, though; I don't know if she could hang on. Don't know if I could hold her tight enough without hurting her, either."

"Up?"

"Yeah, you know." I looked skyward. "Up."

Darim followed my gaze upward, then back down. For the first time, instead of apprehension, I saw wonder and maybe something like longing on her face.

"Do you want to try it?" I asked carefully. It was a total impulse. I hadn't planned to try to win her over. I didn't need her to like me; it had just bothered me that she looked so damned uncomfortable. But there was something about the look in her eyes that made me think I could literally make a dream of hers come true, and it would cost me nothing. "I fly regularly with a friend of mine. It's safe and all."

"I have duties to attend to," she said, and when she did, when she looked away from me, it was with such clear reluctance and regret that my heart hurt a little.

"Well, find me when you're off duty, then. As long as I'm here, you have an open invitation. I don't need any preparation. Just say the word and I can have you a thousand feet in the air in two minutes."

Her head snapped to me, and all her fear was gone. All I saw was hope. "You mean that? You're not just saying that?"

"Yeah! Just say the word! I'll be out tonight, but just catch me between naps during the day and we'll get you up there." I turned to Garal and Lalia. "What about you two? You wanna fly?"

"No, thank you!" Garal said quickly. "Your offer is appreciated, but I love the land and want to stay on it."

"Lalia?"

Lalia looked nonplussed. "I—Maybe? Someday? Don't think I'm ready yet, but yeah. Someday. I think."

"All right. The offer stands."

Soon after that my dinner arrived—about ten pounds of raw, fresh meat, along with a small barrel of cold, clear water. The others left for the mess tent. The sun had descended behind the distant mountains, and as the light slowly faded a buzzing excitement filled me. In my mind these reconnaissance flights had just been a formality, a means to an end, but since arriving at the army camp, since talking to General Sarvalian and Tribune Veretil, I'd become invested. I wanted to do well, not because I wanted to impress anyone, but because I wanted them to do well in turn, thanks to the information I might be able to give them. If there was a war brewing—and it looked like there might be, no matter if they rotated companies or not—I wanted Karakan to win. Not because I owed the city anything, but because everyone I knew and liked called it or its territories home. So I was going to do my best, and I was going to take the experience and whatever feedback I got, and the next night I was going to do better, and better, and better.

The draw of the nearby Nest Hearts, their threads bright and strong, added to my motivation. I wanted to know what was going on with that, why there were so many near the border. And to be perfectly honest with myself, I was hoping to find one unguarded, so I could eat it. I knew that I shouldn't. I knew that it was dangerous, and that I would probably pass out again. But the temptation was strong, and I wanted to know if I'd at least have the option. Maybe if I found one, I could take Lalia out with me for a quick flight, and she could guard me. Maybe "someday" could come quickly. Maybe.

I gave the meat and water a good sniff, then tasted a little bit of each and gave it a few minutes. I didn't expect anyone to try to poison me, but whoever had prepared and handled my food and drink, they weren't my friends. When nothing happened it took me only minutes to go through the rest; ten pounds of meat was nothing unusual for me, and it wasn't like I needed to chew. It wasn't nearly enough to send me into a torpor, but I lay down for a quick nap anyway. I ignored the large tent that was intended for me and simply lay down on the grass, trusting that no one would be stupid enough to bother me.

I woke to the sound of Lalia singing "The Wrong Scabbard," a raunchy song that I'd once heard from Pot, about a drunken soldier who had trouble sheathing his sword where it belonged. From her volume and the way she slurred her words she was nearly as drunk as the soldier in the song, and Garal kept trying to shush her. When I looked up Darim was walking behind them, grinning like a damn fool and joining in on the refrain, though she seemed sober herself.

"Did you have a good dinner?" I asked as they got close, and the song finished with a ringing crescendo. Lalia had a surprisingly good singing voice, even when drunk.

"Excellent!" Lalia replied, enunciating carefully. "Good food, and damned good wine!"

"Though a little stronger than my waves and stars is used to," Garal said, smiling patiently. "No quarter wine in the officer's mess here. They like it strong in the army!"

"Oh, they water it to a quarter for us soldiers!" Darim said. As they got closer I could see that I'd been wrong—she was a little more relaxed than she'd been, a little looser in her gait. Not leggy, but definitely riding the upper edge of tipsy. "How long are you staying? I could get used to this!"

"A couple of days," I told her. "I can try to drag it out a bit. Anyway, I was just waiting for you guys to get back, so I could tell you I'm heading out."

"Just. Reconnaissance!" Lalia said, still speaking slowly and carefully and punctuating her words with a finger that she poked toward me. "Kira's nice and all but you can't be dragging back any Happarans, right?"

"Yeah, yeah. I promise. I'll only look and not touch, all right?"

"I'm serious, Draka! We're not at war with 'em yet!"

"I promise!"

Veretil had suggested that I stay in the air the entire first night. I did, but it was a struggle.

I flew along the Happaran side of the border in long, overlapping circles, starting from the coast in the east and working my way west, covering about a fifteen-mile strip on the southern side of the Divide, the river that separated Karakan from the duchy. The terrain below me was less hilly than on the northern side—more suitable for farming—but there were few villages and no towns at all. Despite the favorable terrain, the area was as sparsely populated as the northern reaches of the forest. The emptiness looked somewhat recent, too; I could see the remains of abandoned villages and a few small towns, their fields, streets, and squares overgrown but the buildings still whole. I flew low over some of them, and the small trees growing there; they couldn't be more than two years old at most.

The reason was simple—monsters. I didn't know how it had happened or why they were allowed to persist, but that strip of land had a shockingly high density of Nest Hearts, rivaling the far northern forest. They weren't everywhere, but there were enough of them that anyone living there would be continuously at risk. They were only on the southern side of the river; I checked. Nor were there any within a few miles of the large road that continued south from the bridge the Spurs had crossed; I assumed that those Nest Hearts, at least, must have been cleared out. But everywhere else there would be one every few miles, dotting the landscape. Tempting me, drawing me in and forcing me to use all my willpower to not land for a taste.

None of them were out in the open; I noticed that immediately. They were hidden away in woods or gullies, or even beneath hills. I flew low over those that weren't well covered, and I saw lots of goblins, but also valkin, which I'd hoped never to see again. Both types of creatures liked to build their small villages around Nest Hearts, and a few of them had grown into proper settlements. I even saw rough fields and pens of animals in some of them, something I'd never expected, but which shouldn't come as such a surprise. The valkin in the mountains had kept humans and taken their draft animals and livestock; why couldn't they keep sheep and poultry, or farm the land? The goblins seemed less inclined toward keeping livestock, but even they had some small garden patches. They traded for things, so why couldn't they produce? It made it hard to think of them as monsters, and I wondered if the Happarans had reached some kind of agreement with them.

Other Nest Hearts were unattended. For those, I had no good explanation at all. Nor did I have any way to decipher what kind of creature they might spawn. Those were the most tempting, and I almost talked myself into going for one of them. It was nighttime, after all. Surely most creatures would be asleep? But my encounter with a monstrous bear one night some months ago, while I was traveling in the mountains with Lalia, had taught me that I was not the only enormously dangerous creature that hunted at night. The thought of a three-ton bear coming across me while I lay unconscious and using my head as a chew toy was enough to put me off the idea, but not by much.

Not tonight, I told myself and flew on. I had army encampments to scout.

CHAPTER FORTY-SIX

The Golden Hour

Compared to finding a bunch of Nest Hearts all along the border, the Happaran military camps were boring. They were easy enough to find, since they each had multiple fires going and were ringed by torches. A few closer looks revealed that they were all set up according to some common plan similar to that of the Karakani camp, surrounded by palisades and with the largest, most important-looking tents at the center. I didn't get too close; I didn't want the Happarans to spot me, and Veretil had asked me to only get a general idea of how many, where, and how large their camps were. My report would be far from perfect, but I did my best.

Their organization was clearly different from that of the Karakani army. "Our" side had its troops concentrated in a single, sprawling camp town a few miles from the large bridge, with only some small outposts along the rest of the border. In contrast, the Happarans had a fair number of camps of roughly equal size. Another difference was that, judging by the herds of horses I saw surrounding each camp, they must have had far more cavalry. Just two of those camps together had as many horses as the entire Karakani army, from what I could see. I thought about Captain Vestem and his eleven subordinates, and I wondered what the hell they expected to do if they had to face the Happaran cavalry. What little I'd learned about the ancient history of war back in school told me that when it came to cavalry, the general idea was "more is better." I thought about Genghis Khan and the Mongols steamrolling the world and hoped to God that the Karakani were prepared. Surely they'd be prepared, right? They wouldn't just think, "there's more of us and we're richer, so we'll win."

Right?

Instinct gave her opinion: *"The only thing humans do better than arrogance is overconfidence."* And while she was one to talk, she did have a point. Another thing I remembered was that history was full of overconfident armies getting stomped.

I forced down my worries. General Sarvalian didn't give me the impression of an arrogant or overconfident man, and I knew nothing about how either army fought. I'd have to ask Darim about it; she should have at least a general idea of how they expected to beat the Happarans if it came to it.

As a light blush touched the eastern sky I circled back toward the Karakani camp. The night had been clear, but morning brought gray clouds from the north, promising rain. I flew high, following the river, and again wondered how all those Nest Hearts could exist on the south side—and only the south side—of the river. The Happarans had to know about them; I'd seen lots of mounted patrols on their side, even at night. And they definitely had the troops to clear the nests out. Why didn't they? Were they part of some plan? Why were most of the settlements here abandoned in the last few years? I knew that there must be a connection, and it felt important, but so far it was a complete mystery to me.

I caused quite a commotion when I flew into the central, fenced-off area of the camp. The sun had just come up when I arrived, but the place was already bustling with activity. Soldiers doing morning exercises stopped and looked up, and horses whinnied and pulled on their tethers as I passed above them, and in the central section aides scurried away and sentries came to meet me as I landed. The sentries weren't threatening or anything. They were just there, making themselves known and getting in the way.

Looking around, I saw Darim hurrying from the corner where our tents were pitched. "Sentry Darim!" I called to her. "Get me a map of the borderlands, one I can draw on. And some writing materials. And tell Tribune Veretil that I'm back!"

She took it literally in stride. She didn't even slow down; she just gave me a crisp, "Yes, ma'am!" in passing on her way to the tribune's tent.

"And someone get me a couple gallons of water," I said to the gathered sentries. I put all the authority that I could muster into my voice, and started toward our tents without waiting for a response. The two sentries in my way stood staring until I got within ten feet. When I gave them a questioning look and showed no sign of stopping, though, one said to the other, "You heard her! Let's get a barrel of water!"

They both got out of my way, hurrying off somewhere.

Darim's small, single-person tent stood open, but the Wolves' was closed and gave off the soft sounds of sleep. I let my friends rest, settling down on the grass to wait for Darim. She arrived a few minutes later, carrying a rolled up map and a box with brushes, quills, and ink. A second sentry carried a small writing table, a smoothly polished, inclined surface on a stand about a foot high. I had them set them up, then asked Darim to do the actual marking on the map as I pointed with a claw; I didn't want to risk making a mess of it and having to start over.

It took some time. Despite Veretil's lessons, Darim had to help me read the map, but I got the locations of all the Happaran camps I'd seen, or at least close enough. The scale of the map, which covered about seventy miles from the mountains to the sea, made any exact locations pretty much impossible anyway. We also marked any towns and villages on there that had been abandoned. At some point my water barrel showed up, but I barely noticed.

"Great," I told her as we were finishing up. "Now for the Nest Hearts."

"Nest Hearts?" she asked with some confusion.

"Yeah! There's heaps of 'em on the Happaran side. Now let's do this before I forget, yeah?"

There were too many Nest Hearts, and they were too densely packed, to put all of them on the map. I focused on the goblin and valkin settlements, trying to get their locations as accurate as I could and give a relative size for each.

"I don't understand how you found them," Darim said as she worked. "Aren't Nest Hearts made of darkness? And you say they're all hidden."

"I mean, yeah. But do you know how at least some magic users can sense the things when they get close?"

"I've heard something like that, I think. But I've never seen it."

"Well, that's how it is. And I can do the same thing. Just at a much longer distance than your average magic user."

"Oh." She looked at me with wonder. "Can you use magic, then?"

I gave her my best enigmatic smile which, by her reaction, must have been terrifying. "I'm a dragon," I told her. "I *am* magic."

I didn't tell her I could eat the things. I'd keep that in reserve.

Garal and Lalia awoke at some point. We were waiting for the ink to dry when Garal came out, half dressed, to say good morning before hurrying off to the latrine. Lalia followed him a few minutes later, looking like hell hung over. When they got back we all talked a little as they dressed properly, and then they took Darim with them to get some breakfast—the three of them carrying off the table, map, and writing materials. By that point the long night and lack of proper sleep was catching up to me, and I got into the tent that had been provided for me. It was a little cramped but shielded me from the morning sun, which was all I needed.

I didn't sleep for long. Darim woke me up about an hour later, telling me that Tribune Veretil would like to see me at my earliest convenience. I stretched, almost knocking the tent down; it was big enough for me to curl up in comfortably, but it wasn't made for someone as big as I was to spread their wings. One of the poles came out, and one of the corners fell in on me. With some annoyance I pushed my way out and stretched there instead, as Darim hurried to right the tent.

Nobody got in my way as I casually retraced my steps from the previous day to Veretil's tent. I was followed or watched by about a dozen sentries and aides at all times, but nobody tried to stop or slow me. It was a strange but pleasant feeling to just walk around, out in the open and surrounded by strangers. They were freaked out by my presence, and probably my very existence, but the fact that no one made a fuss was good enough for me.

I found Veretil's tent and stuck my head in. He must have been expecting me; he was sitting at a desk with a scroll in front of him, but his pen was safely stowed and he had his hands in his lap, facing the opening of the tent. I wondered if he had been a scout, and had some advancements improving his hearing or other senses; he did seem to know just about everything about maps and recognizance.

"Ah, Lady Draka!" he said with a false cheerfulness that was betrayed by the way his eyebrows seemed to be trying to eat his eyes. "Good morning!"

"Morning, Tribune." I entered the tent and tried to sit down in front of him, but I'd forgotten how low the top was and my horn caught on the canvas, even though I was bending forward. I carefully got my horn loose and lay down instead while Veretil sat stock still, a wan smile plastered on his face. The wide-eyed sentry next to him, a tall, skinny kid who couldn't have been older than eighteen, licked his lips nervously. He twitched when I rustled my wings to settle them.

"You wanted to see me?" I said once I'd gotten comfortable.

"Ah, yes! I've been looking over the map you made—excellent work, wonderful really—and I had some questions. Hoping you could add some detail and such. Do you have time now?"

"As long as I get to sleep properly afterward, I have all the time you want."

"Of course! Of course! Now, these camps, here and here . . ."

That night Veretil had me looking closer at the Happaran camps, starting with those closest to the large road and working my way east toward the coast. It wasn't that he was uninterested in the Nest Hearts, but he was a military man, not an adventurer, and it was the enemy he was most interested in. The tribune wanted my best estimates of the number of soldiers and how heavily they were equipped, as well as the number and types of horses. That required me to land, shift, and get into the camps, but I wasn't bothered. It was slow going, but fun.

The night after that I did the same thing, working my way west. I also had Veretil's feedback on what I should focus on, which I'd apparently only had half right.

During the days I mostly slept or spent time with Darim. Garal and Lalia were doing their best to make nice with the army, joining in on physical training, weapons practice, and even patrols with the army cavalry. And Maglan had precious little time. He'd been returned to his regiment as soon as he'd handed over the message he carried to General Sarvalian, and now the rest of that regiment had returned from their R & R, turning that whole part of the camp into an overpopulated mess. Getting to talk to him was easy enough; I only needed to find where he was, and then I'd interrupt whatever was going on by simply existing. But after the first time, a junior officer, trembling either with fear or impotent rage, asked me to please not do it again, and to send for Mag if I wanted to speak with him. Apparently my presence was disruptive. The guy seemed caught between a need to continue whatever they'd been doing and absolute despair at trying to make me do anything, and I felt bad enough for him that I stayed away after that.

Darim was a pleasant surprise, relaxing and opening up once she got used to me. She was a tailor's daughter from Parkon, a large-ish coastal town about fifty miles south of Karakan. She loved birds. She was only twenty, and had been assigned to us because she was being considered for a promotion to something called a watch officer.

"As long as I don't mess this up—prevent you all from getting robbed or hurt—I'll have eleven men under me by this time next month," she told me, then froze and blushed when I snorted and grinned at her. "I'll have command of eleven sentries," she corrected herself carefully.

We'd just had our evening meal on my third day in the camp. Garal and Lalia were out with Vestem's wing, and Darim had brought her food to our tents to eat with me. The sky was clear, and there was still a little sunlight left—a beautiful early evening for flying.

"All you need to do is keep us and our stuff safe?"

"And make sure you get whatever you need, that messages get to and from you, get rid of gawkers so you're not disturbed; things like that, yeah. Basically make sure that you have a pleasant, productive stay here." She paused, leaned in, and lowered her voice. "Honestly, I'm only responsible for you, but I figured you'd be less than happy if your friends weren't taken care of. Besides, I like 'em."

"Yeah, Garal's easy to like. And Lalia grows on you when she's not trying to kill you, I guess." Darim's eyebrows shot up in an obvious question, and I obliged. "We didn't exactly start off as friends, me and Lalia. Let's leave it at that."

Darim didn't leave it. "But you two get along now?"

"Nah, yeah. Lalia's all right. She's just *really* protective. But, hey, Darim? If you just need to look after me, does that mean that you're free to go with me if I go somewhere? While you're on duty, I mean."

"I think I'm technically always on duty. But I don't see why not."

"Well, we've got a good sky right now. How about it?"

"Hmm? What do you mean?"

"I thought I'd go up for a while. Take a turn around the camp in the golden hour and see everything in sunset colors. Want to come up with me?"

Darim looked at me, then took a sharp breath. "Really? Flying? Right now? I can go flying *right now*?"

I grinned at her. "I don't see why not."

Darim was a different kind of companion than anyone I'd taken flying before. She held on tight, but not with Mak's half-panicked death grip. She was completely quiet to the point that it made me worried, but when I called back to check on her she just answered, "I'm great! This is great!" her voice bubbling with laughter, and then went silent again. That was how she'd been with whatever we were doing, and whoever was around. She'd been happy enough to join in on conversation when appropriate, but she wasn't one to break the silence. I could only assume that she was enjoying the sights and sensations of flying.

"How's your night vision?" I asked her as the last sliver of sun disappeared behind the mountains.

"As long as there's moon or starlight I see normally!"

"Color and all?"

"Yeah!"

Well, damn. That filled me with envy. I told her so and she laughed at me. "I don't know anyone else who can see color, but we can't have night-blind sentries! People don't sneak around with torches, you know!"

I stayed up until the light failed and the stars were out. With what she'd just told me, it probably didn't make much difference to her, but I wanted to get a view of the world at night before I returned her to camp.

"Thank you," she told me after sliding off my back and getting the wobbles out of her legs. She was flushed and smiling hugely. With how large her mouth was, it was a huge smile indeed. "Truly, from the brightest spark of my soul, thank you, Lady Draka. That was the most wonderful experience of my life."

"Yeah, no worries," I told her, a little abashed. "Glad you enjoyed it. Some people don't like the height and all."

"I used to stand on the cliffs above the sea north of my home, and watch the gulls sail on the wind. I always wondered what that would be like, but I never imagined I might do the same. You've made a life-long dream come true, Lady Draka. I can't thank you enough—is there anything I can do for you?"

"Nah, I'm—" I stopped as something occurred to me. "Actually, there is something. Do you know who Maglan is? The archer who arrived here with us?"

"I saw him, yes. I think I could find him if I need to."

"He's the lover of someone very important to me. Now, I know he's part of a regular regiment or company or whatever, but I think he's gotten mixed up in something political, together with the rest of us. If you could try to keep an eye on him, I'd consider it a personal favor."

She looked thoughtful. "I'll do what I can," she said after a moment.

"That's all I ask. I know that you have your regular duties and all."

She nodded, then said, a little hesitantly, "My lady, I'm sure that you have plans for your mission tonight, but may I make a suggestion?"

"Sure, yeah!" I was going to be looking closer at some of the Nest Hearts that didn't have settlements around them, to see if I could figure out what kinds of creatures they were connected to, but I was open to suggestions.

"I saw a lot more activity near the river than normal as we flew, and I thought I might have seen some hidden camps as well. It looked suspicious. I'll be reporting it to Tribune Veretil, even if I have to ask his sentries to wake him, but would you take a closer look along the river specifically?"

"Sounds important. Yeah, I'll do that. You've got good eyes on you!"

She smiled at my praise, and lowered her voice conspiratorially. "It's my major. I could have spotted a rabbit in the grass at night from as high as we were. That's part of why they want to promote me."

Well, damn, I thought for the second time. So that was what the major version of what Herald's minor did. Herald had sharp eyes and saw well in the dark, but Darim was an order of magnitude beyond that from what she'd told me. Eagle eyes with full color at night? Anyone would be jealous of that!

"All right. You go tell the tribune. I'm heading back out. No point in hanging around here, yeah? Good night, Darim."

Still smiling, she gave me a fist-over-heart bow. "Good night, Lady Draka. Good hunting to you."

CHAPTER FORTY-SEVEN

Building Bridges

There were indeed people at the river, and they were up to no good. I couldn't see what exactly they were doing, since I was staying high, but there were enough of them at the river, at night, that there was no way in the world they weren't doing something sneaky. And it wasn't just in one place, either. I covered a lot of miles quickly, just scanning the riverside, and for every single Happaran camp, there was a group doing something by the river.

While I couldn't tell what exactly they were doing, I had a pretty strong suspicion about what they were trying to achieve. Once I'd covered forty or fifty miles westward, I'd seen enough and decided to take a closer look at one of the groups and then head back early.

I landed about a mile away to make sure they didn't see me, then trotted along the river until I got close enough to hear them. I'd noted a small copse of trees as I flew over, and there I shifted before continuing. Moving while shifted had been slow the last few nights; I'd gotten used to the speed and ease with which I moved while I was pumped full of Nest Heart, and going back was a pain.

At least I still had the improved sight and hearing from my second major. At first I only heard the sounds of people working, splashes, and low thumps that I couldn't identify, but once I got close enough I also heard the soldiers. I'd heard a little bit of Happaran before, when I was checking out their camps, but those had been mostly single words or short phrases. It was just like one of the prisoners I'd rescued from the Silver Spurs had said months ago when I captured Kira—very similar to Karakani, but some of the words and a lot of the pronunciations were different. A little harder on the consonants, perhaps.

"It's damned bullshit, is what it is," one said, speaking in a low voice that wasn't quite a whisper. "Sending us out to do this in the middle of the night, in the dark, with no sleep."

"You're right, but what good does it do to complain?" another replied. "Something spooked the high-ups, and you know they're at their worst when they're spooked. I heard some mercenary group crossed over from the north. Maybe they had something to report that pushed up the time table?"

"Brother, I don't care why. I know it does no good. I just want the damn world to know that I'm pissed they woke us at sunrise this morning, and that I'm still awake at midnight driving poles into the riverbed."

"Would you rather have done it during the day, when one of the lemon bastards' patrols could see us? The whole point of this is for them to not know about it. If not tonight, it would have been some other night, and you know the rain is coming."

They went on like that, the other ten soldiers weighing in or telling them to shut the hell up every so often, but nothing they said was particularly interesting. What they were doing, however, was. They were, like the first soldier had said, driving long, sharpened poles tip first into the riverbed, a few feet between each. They were driving the things in deep; I didn't know how deep the quickly flowing river was, but the poles they'd already placed were sturdy enough that they could use them to anchor a platform, from which they drove in the next pole using a big, metal tube thing with handles. I had to imagine that the post driver was heavy, with the man handling it being damned strong; it drove the posts in half a foot at a go, and they were making good time. The Divide was a fast river, but not wide. If everything continued as it was, I could see them crossing the hundred and twenty or so feet before sunrise.

And I had no doubt that was what they were trying to do. A few things had come together, making a fairly clear picture. The poles, the fact that they were doing this under cover of darkness, the talk about moving things up ahead of schedule; the Happarans were going to cross the river. They were doing it in numerous places, and the Karakani had their forces mostly concentrated near the bridge, to prevent a crossing there. This was happening.

I only withdrew a hundred feet at most before shifting and taking to the air. Secrecy be damned; the shit was about to hit the fan, and General Sarvalian needed to start organizing his forces right the hell now! As I flew along the river I could see more of the little platforms in the water, and it spurred me to fly faster. I almost hoped that I was seen; maybe that would cause some confusion among the crews and slow them down in their work, buying us some time.

When did Karakan become "us," I wondered. I knew a small handful of people in the army, and a few more in the city itself. Many of them feared me. Was that truly enough?

Yes, I decided. I may not be a citizen, or even an official resident. The council may fear me or try to use me in their games. But, it came back to the same simple reasons as before—as long as my family considered themselves Karakani, as long as the people I cared for identified with and lived in the city, I was on Karakan's side. And so long as Maglan was in the army, and Herald cared for him, I would help that army.

I entered the Karakani camp at speed, braking at the last second and landing heavily in the command section. The sentries did *not* appreciate me landing in front of and heading for the general's tent. That wasn't a problem; there wasn't much they could do to me. But neither did his personal guards, and when one of them burst out and put himself between me and the tent, sword drawn and ready to fight and die if necessary, I paused. Instinct didn't like to be challenged, but when that challenger might actually have a good shot at winning, even she stopped to consider the situation.

I decided not to be coy about why I was there. The guy was *intense*, and they'd all need to know anyway. "All right," I said in my most calming voice. "We're all friends here, so let's calm down, yeah? I may have come in a little hot, but the Happarans are preparing to cross the river, and the general needs to know right bloody now!"

The bodyguard didn't relax one bit, but neither did he move to do anything. In the darkness behind him I saw the tent flap move. A woman's face peeked out, and I recognized her as one of the tribunes who'd been in the tent with the general when I first met him; I was pretty sure her name was Verlan. We locked eyes, and hers widened before she disappeared back into the tent. A minute later the general emerged, wearing only sandals and a robe but looking entirely unbothered by the hour or the situation.

"Thank you, Mersil," he said, putting his hand on the bodyguard's shoulder and pushing him gently to the side. "You may stand down."

The bodyguard gave me another long look, then sheathed his sword and took a step to the side, staying close to the general.

"Good night to you, Lady Draka," the general said. "What is this I hear about the Happarans being up to some mischief?"

"Not mischief, General. They're preparing to cross the river, in multiple places. This is an invasion. I'd stake my horn on it."

It is hard to describe exactly what happened to the general when I said that. It was like he snapped into focus—he became entirely present in a way that the others around him weren't. When he spoke, his voice was loud and clear, and demanded an immediate, clear, and concise answer. "You've seen this yourself? Tonight?"

"Right before I returned," I confirmed. "All along the river westward, and I assume east as well. It looks like every camp is preparing their own crossing. I'm not sure how they're planning to do it, but they're driving poles into the riverbed. I don't see what else they could be for."

"Veretil!" the general snapped, looking past me. "Scouts up and down the river to verify, now! Parvion, rouse the cavalry and send messengers to the bridge and the outposts! They are to fall back if attacked! Verlan!" He turned toward his own tent. The tribune I'd seen peeking out of the general's tent stepped out. She was wearing a simple cinched soldier's tunic and looked quite embarrassed. The general continued as though the situation was entirely normal. "I want the infantry ready to move in one hour. First through twelfth cohorts to the east, thirteenth through thirty-sixth to the west. Hastel! Where's—"

"General! General!" An elderly man I hadn't seen before came running as fast as his old legs could carry him. He gave me only a quick glance before continuing. "An emergency sending, general! Disaster in the city! Fighting in the streets! Betrayal! The White Cranes have turned!"

Sarvalian didn't lose a moment, whirling on the old man. "Details! What have they done?"

He stepped back, stammering. "They—The Cranes, they're attacking the Palace, as well as the homes of several councilors and commander Terriallon's estate. The city guard and the Grey Wolves are fighting back, but with so many of the Wolves out patrolling the countryside—"

My gut twisted at his words. "General!" I said, turning. "I'm going back to Karakan. The two mercenaries who were with me, they're out with that cavalry captain, Vestem. They need to know what's happening. I'd consider it a favor if you'd send them north as soon as possible . . . and maybe keep Maglan, the archer who carried the message, in reserve. If that's possible," I added with some hesitation.

"You're sure? We could use you," Sarvalian said.

"My humans are in danger," I growled. "I will not tolerate any threat to those who belong to me."

He considered me, then nodded, once. "In that case, would you take a message?"

"If you're quick."

The general didn't even need to signal. A small writing desk with parchment, pen, ink, a message case, wax, and a seal appeared almost as if by magic, and he quickly wrote and sealed a short message.

"Thank you for your aid, Lady Draka. Please, get this to Sempralia," he said, holding the case out. I simply lowered my head, and he hung the shoulder strap around my neck without hesitation. "I consider your side of this bargain fulfilled and more, and I will make sure that the soldiers know who warned us. Mercies watch over you, and may we meet again."

"Same to you, General." I bowed my head, then turned to go. As I did I spotted Darim standing at the edge of the circle surrounding us. I made my way quickly to her, aides and sentries getting out of my way.

"Darim," I said. "Looks like those eyes of yours are even more valuable than I thought."

"Lady Draka," she said, but anxiety choked off her voice.

"You can drop the 'lady,'" I told her. "Stay safe, yeah?"

"Yeah," she said, in almost a whisper. "I'll—I'll try to look after the archer. If I can. I promise I'll do what I can."

"I know you will. If you see Garal and Lalia, tell them that I've gone to look after the others. And, ah . . . Mercies watch over you, Darim."

"And you, Draka."

I left the camp surrounded by as much commotion as when I'd arrived, although I was only indirectly the cause this time. The medallion nestled under my tongue nudged southward, and dozens of threads tried to lure me in the same direction with the promise of all the Nest Hearts I could eat, but I raced north. I had a hundred and thirty miles to cover, and even at the best pace I could maintain over that kind of distance, it would take me hours. Hours where everyone I loved and treasured in the city was at risk.

The Wolves were fighting the Cranes in the city, and I didn't see any reality in which Rib and Pot would sit that out. And if Rib and Pot were fighting, if Wolves were dying, my family would be getting involved in some way. I was sure of it. Tam and Val especially had too many friends and acquaintances among the Wolves to stay neutral, and the sisters would do anything to support them. *Fucking hell*, I thought. *They may even be getting involved in the fighting. Or the Cranes may have attacked the inn. They went after Rallon, and if they knew that his cousins might be at the Favor . . .*

The thought spurred me to increase my speed and force myself to keep it up. I could still feel Mak and Herald there, far in the distance, but I didn't know if they had to be alive for that ability to work, and I didn't have anything similar for any of the others. *Gods, Mercies, and Sorrows*, I prayed. *Don't let them get hurt. We've only been family for such a short time. Don't let me lose any of them.*

I didn't give a damn about secrecy when I arrived at the city. I landed in the bloodstained square in front of Her Grace's Favor. The door stood broken, smashed in and off its hinges, but to my relief I could feel Herald moving around inside.

Mak was in there as well, but hadn't moved since I got in range.

"*Sisters!*" I roared, and Herald stopped, then rushed to the door. I felt equal parts rage and relief when she exited the inn and ran to me. Her face was bruised, one lip and eyebrow split, and her armor was spattered with blood. By the way she moved, though, she wasn't badly hurt, and when she threw her arms around my neck she felt as strong as ever.

"Draka!" she sighed, before releasing me and speaking rapidly in Tekereteki. "*I am so glad to have you here. They withdrew half an hour ago, but we do not know if they are coming back! It is a sick house in there, Draka! So many injured . . . The yard is full of bodies, both ours and theirs. It is—*" she took a deep breath and let it out slowly.

"*The Cranes?*" I asked.

"*Yes. It is horrible! They attacked the Wolves, and the Wolves only had a small force in the city, with most on patrol. It was a bloodbath. Those who could withdrew to here, since we had a force of guards around the inn, and . . .*" She gestured helplessly to the square. "*We had to barricade ourselves inside. They broke in the door, but that is as far as they made it. At that point the adventurers in the inn got involved, and we drove them out and held them there. But there are so many injured. Rallon survived, but there are probably less than a dozen Wolves alive in the city. Boot is dead. Arlal lost an arm. Everyone else has cuts and bruises or worse, and Mak and Kira are both exhausted. Ardek is trying to get potions from the alchemists, and Barro went to find a healer he knows—"*

She wobbled suddenly, and sat down on the bloody cobbles. I started toward her, but she held up a hand. *"I am fine. Just . . . tired. So very tired. How are you here?"*

"I was with the general when the message came that the Palace was under attack, and that there was fighting in the streets. I had to come!"

"The Palace? They attacked the Palace? I thought this was something between the companies!"

"They did. The Palace and many, maybe all of the councilors. And the Happarans are crossing the river. I will eat my own tail if that is a coincidence."

"Bastards!" Herald hissed. *"Damned turncoats!"*

"Yeah." I nuzzled her hair carefully. *"Is everyone else going to live?"*

"Of ours? Yes. Cuts and bruises, some worse than others, but we will all live."

Like Herald, I was tired. So damned tired. I'd pushed myself to the limit getting back to the city, and now that I knew my humans were safe, at least for the moment, I needed to get back up there. *"I am going to search the streets from above,"* I told Herald, nuzzling her hair. *"See what the situation is, in case they have gathered for another attack or anything like that. Barricade yourselves again. Stay safe, and tell the others I am so relieved to hear that they are going to be okay."*

Herald got to her feet heavily, using my neck to pull herself up. *"I will."* Then she looked at me with worry. *"Lalia and Garal, how are they? How is Maglan?"*

I didn't question how she knew that they'd been with me. It must have been obvious after we left. *"I do not know for sure, but I assume that they are fine. Our Wolves were out with a patrol when everything happened. I asked the general to put Maglan with the reserves, and a very competent sentry to look after him, but . . ."* I shook my head uncertainly.

She blinked rapidly, and a few tears cut through the blood on her face, but she nodded. *"All right. He will be all right. Thank you for trying. Going so far as to ask the general . . . he will be all right."*

"Yeah. Of course. Now, take this tube. It needs to get to Sempralia as soon as it is safe."

She did as I asked, taking the leather case from off my neck, and I nodded toward the inn. *"Get back in there, okay? Try to get some rest. I will be back as soon as I can."*

"Okay. And Draka?"

"Yeah?"

"I love you, big sister."

"I love you, too, little dragon."

CHAPTER FORTY-EIGHT

Pursuit

The city was desolate, even for an early, overcast morning. At least the part between the mercantile quarter, where the inn was, and the Palace. Those few desperate souls who scurried along the streets moved cautiously, looking around corners and crossing intersections quickly. No one looked up. They were too focused on avoiding any possible fighting.

I didn't see any sign of active combat, but as I got to the Forum it was clear that this was where the most blood had been shed. The stone was stained dark, as were the steps of the Palace itself, and dozens of bodies had been laid out in rows on the great square. I couldn't tell which way the fighting had gone; the bodies were in two distinct groups, but I had no way of telling which group was which. Either way the Cranes were gone, and that meant one of two things—they had either succeeded in whatever they were trying to do and had left, or they'd failed and been driven off.

People slowly began huddling together, looking up and pointing as I circled low above them. I tried to make up my mind as to what to do. Herald and the others were safe for the moment, which was my biggest concern, but that wasn't the only reason I wanted to find the Cranes. I wanted vengeance. The Cranes couldn't get away with this. They had killed and maimed people I knew. They had wounded *my* humans, *my* family, and damaged our property. There was no question as to *if* I was going after them; Instinct screamed for vengeance, and Conscience wanted us to find the Cranes to track them, to make sure that they weren't coming back to attack again—maybe even to help bring them to justice. The only question was if I'd involve the humans on the ground or not.

I searched the upturned faces for any that I recognized. Despite the hour it didn't feel unreasonable that Rallon or Sempralia might be there, if they were still alive. I didn't find them. There were some people who were clearly in charge based on how they were dressed and how others were gathered around them, but no one I knew. In theory, the entire council should know about my deal with Sempralia and what I'd been doing in the south. Despite what Sarvalian had told me about the lady justice's possible reasons for keeping me in the dark, I didn't have a whole lot of trust for the woman at the moment. For all I knew she'd been running the whole show on her own, with her colleagues none the wiser.

Ah, fuck it. I didn't know which way the Cranes had gone, and I didn't want to waste time flying off in the wrong direction. I picked the one guy with the most orbiters. He was standing next to some other man who had a few followers of his own, looking up at me, and I landed fifteen feet from them, to gasps and screams and awed whispers of "The dragon! The dragon!" Half of the people around them scattered but were replaced by a number of loyal, if nervous, guards who cautiously moved in to surround me.

"Councilors!" I said, addressing them both with all the arrogance and imperiousness I could muster. "Which way did the turncoats go?"

When I addressed them, the more important-looking man, a thin, old fellow, rediscovered his wits and shuffled back a few steps, putting the other man half between us. "Dragon!" he breathed. "Apologies, 'Lady Dragon'! Why are you—"

"The Cranes!" I demanded. "Where did they go?"

"They—" He turned to the man between us, who was regarding me with hard, narrowed eyes. This man looked to be about the same age as the presumed councilor and was just as thin, but where the councilor looked almost frail, this man was made of tanned leather and steel wire. "Lord Commander, if you would, tell the lady dragon where they went!"

The commander chewed it over for a second. He didn't look surprised to see me, but neither was he pleased about it. For a moment it looked like he might refuse to tell me anything, but then he gave me a snort and a nod. "South," he said gruffly. "They left through the south gate, then turned east."

"All of them?" I asked.

"Sorrows take me if I know, but I hope so. Enough of them."

South and east. That would do. "Thank you, Lord Commander," I said, and turned. The guards around me, and the crowd gathering beyond them, surged back when I moved. I leaped into the air, and the people now behind and below me rumbled with surprise, fear, and wonder.

I turned generally southeast, cutting across the harbor, and followed the coast out. I didn't bother with the gate. I'd passed above it when I came in and hadn't seen anything. That had been ten or fifteen minutes earlier; if the Cranes had all left the city when they withdrew from the Favor, they had at least a forty minute head start. If they were all mounted, which I had to assume, they could have made it seven or eight miles from the city, farther if they didn't care much about their horses. I climbed rapidly until I was high enough that I'd blend in with the dark clouds; I still didn't know what I was going to do once I found them, but I wanted the option of following them without being spotted, and I shouldn't have any trouble seeing a large group of riders even from a mile up.

Perhaps I should have asked why the Cranes had attacked the Palace in the middle of the night. I understood going after the councilors, but if they'd attacked the Palace in the middle of the day, they might have been able to kill most of the council anyway. What was the point of doing it at night? There had to be one.

It did occur to me that their attack in the city had been timed to coincide with the Happarans crossing the river. A little before, even. Perhaps the only goal had been to distract the Karakani commanders and delay their response to the invasion?

It took me fifteen minutes to find the Cranes, following the coast south. They were pushing their horses hard, and without my worry to drive me, I couldn't keep my speed up the way I had on my way north. My flight muscles burned, and when I could finally switch to a lazy glide, which was still more than fast enough to catch up to them, I groaned with relief. Locking my wings like that was practically effortless, and I held my position above and slightly behind them, invisible against the thick clouds that were rolling in, circling occasionally so I wouldn't overtake them.

Following them passively like that gave me time to think. Now that I'd found them I wasn't sure what I was going to do. There were too many of them to try to stop; I didn't know how many they'd been originally, but it looked like they numbered well over a hundred now. I didn't know where they were going, either. Happar seemed like a safe bet, but the border was more than a hundred miles away. At the pace they were going they'd have to stop and rest their horses long before then. I'd picked up enough from Garal and Lalia to know that even a strong, healthy horse couldn't keep going at a trot or a canter for more than six or seven hours, and then only if you planned to let it eat and rest properly the next day. We'd taken several days from the city to the border because we didn't want to risk the horses' health.

The Cranes' pace bothered me. It was unnecessary. They were miles from the city, and there was no one chasing them. There was no one who *could* chase them—the Karakani cavalry were all in the south; the Wolves in the city were all dead, injured, or trying to help their comrades; and the rest of the Wolves were on patrol and wouldn't know about the Cranes' betrayal for hours. So why the rush? Why push their horses so hard instead of saving their strength? They'd need their horses to be in peak condition once they got close to the border, to avoid the army. It didn't make any sense.

I soon realized their goal was much closer than that.

A little more than twenty miles south of Karakan the cliffs opened to a bay, and in that bay ten ships lay at anchor. They were large enough that I spotted them easily from a mile up, and all my intuition told me that there was no way in hell this was a coincidence. I flew ahead to check them out. They all lay close to the shore, their sides facing land and with long, wooden ramps extending into the surf from openings in the upper hull. In the sea outside the bay three sleeker ships waited, as a fourth burned on the rocks.

The Cranes didn't need to worry about joining up with the Happarans or crossing the border. They'd done their job, and now they were leaving.

I was furious. I had a deep-seated need to hurt them for what they'd done, and now they were getting on a bunch of boats and sailing out of my reach? It was absolutely unacceptable. I wouldn't allow it. In a moment of absolute insanity I considered trying to destroy the ships, and began to descend to look for rocks to drop on them. It must have been Instinct's influence, but thankfully I snapped out of it quickly. Not only was there no way I could do any meaningful damage to these things, but they were also something like two-hundred feet long, with massive masts and dozens upon dozens of oars each, and they were well defended. Besides their large crews, the ships had massive crossbows at the fore and aft, with stacks of bolts like small spears next to them. I imagined trying to swoop in on the ships and getting shot at by twenty of those things.

Nah, fuck that! I'd watched *Game of Thrones!* I knew what those things could do! Sure, my ex, Alex, had to pause the show to rant about how ridiculous it was when one of Dany's dragons got shot down, but I wasn't going to risk it. If I wanted to do something, I would have to hit the Cranes *now*, while they were still miles away from the ships. And I *was* going to do something.

I approached the column of fleeing turncoats with a smug sense of anticipation. I could see them ahead of me, the distance shrinking rapidly as we approached each other, and my focus narrowed until they were all I could see. I'd only get one shot at a first impression, and I wanted to put in my best effort.

I was going bowling.

My plan was to dive and pick up some ridiculous speed, then level out and turn all of that into horizontal momentum. In my arms—with some help from my legs; it was awkward, but it worked—was a large, jagged rock. I'd found it below the cliffs by the water, and it was the largest thing I'd been able to find that I could grab and fly with. Getting back in the air had been a bitch, but I'd done it, and now I was lining myself up to strike.

Let's see how they like a big bloody boulder moving at a hundred miles per hour, I thought viciously as I readied myself.

There was a small wrinkle as I began my descent. From the west I could see another group of riders, about two dozen strong, moving in to meet the Cranes. I couldn't be sure, but my guess was that they were a Grey Wolves patrol that had spotted the cloud of dust the Cranes were kicking up. If they were Wolves, they'd be completely ignorant of what had happened in the city, and I wasn't going to let them get ridden down by an overwhelming force if I could help it. Hopefully, though, that wouldn't be a problem.

I turned my descent into a steep, controlled dive, not quite a freefall but picking up speed rapidly. The ones I thought to be Wolves were still a few minutes out, but they were also on a hill, so they'd have a front-row seat to what was about to happen.

I knew from experience that simply diving from a mile up took around twenty seconds, but it would take a little longer this time since I needed to control my dive carefully with the extra weight. I wanted to do as much damage as I could, so I timed my dive to put me just in front of the Cranes when I released my payload. That way me and my rock wouldn't lose much speed, and the thing should plow through them like a cannonball. I targeted the lead guy. I had no idea if their commander would be at the front or not, but I couldn't be picky.

By the time I started leveling out I was sure they'd seen me. I'd gotten to a size where, with my wings spread wide against the cloudy morning sky, I should be visible from the few hundreds of feet that remained between us. To my absolute joy, they responded to the threat by bunching up, instinct and training telling them to close ranks against an approaching threat.

I went horizontal twenty feet above the ground, barely a hundred feet in front of the Cranes. I let go immediately. The rock dropped straight down and we shot forward, crossing those hundred feet in a flash. We were close enough that I could see their astonished faces, raised to watch me as I came.

For a heartbeat all I could hear was the air tearing around me. Then there was a mass of wet, splintering noise, and the sweet sound of screaming pandemonium erupted behind me as the Cranes and I passed each other and two hundred pounds of rock plowed through them. God, I loved being a flying creature in a world with no concept of aerial attacks!

Their close ranks had made sure that my rock did more damage than I possibly could have hoped. I wondered, distantly, how many people I'd just killed. But thinking about it was pointless. In the seconds it took to have that thought, I was far past their column and starting the turn for my second run. I'd get a good idea in a moment.

The Wolves were thundering down the hill. I didn't know their intentions. Perhaps they knew of me, and were coming to join in on my side. Perhaps they had never heard of me, or thought that I'd gone rogue, and were coming to try to help the Cranes. It didn't matter.

I came around. The Cranes had stopped, and were forming a large circle studded with spears and a few bows, all pointing in my direction. In the center of the circle was carnage.

When I'd attacked a small contingent of Silver Spurs, I'd felled the two lead horses with my venom, probably by blinding them and making them stumble. This time it was hard to make out how many horses and humans lay in the squirming pile that the Cranes had gathered around. While I hadn't seen it, I could easily guess what had happened. The rock I'd dropped, weighing about two hundred pounds and traveling at something like a hundred miles per hour—not counting my targets' speed—had hit the first horse or rider and just kept going. It must have taken out dozens of them in a fraction of a second, and in their close ranks those who were hit would have knocked into the horses beside them, taking them down as well. As I approached I could see dismounted people trying to get to any survivors, probably to try to heal them with magic or give them healing potions.

I decided to avoid the helpers. Killing their healers, magic users or not, would have weakened the Cranes considerably, but I chose not to. Perhaps I'd spent too much time with Kira, but it felt like anyone who chose to be a healer must be worthy of some mercy. Besides, there were plenty of targets around them.

I flew fast and erratically, closing the distance in heartbeats. Arrows zipped past me, but none were magically empowered, and those that hit only grazed along my scales. Archery was clearly not the Cranes' strong suit. I'd been planning to turn left and spray that side, but my mind was changed when a goddamn *javelin* flew at me and I had to jink to the right instead. I saw it pass as if in slow motion; three feet of dark wood, tipped with ten inches of barbed metal, perhaps bronze by its color. As if arrows weren't enough, now I had to worry about javelins! I was reminded of the harpoons the Barlean fishermen had thrown at me. Those had drawn blood. At our combined speeds, and with the mass that thing must have had, I wouldn't have been surprised if it skewered me!

I emptied my venom glands at the nearest Cranes and turned up and out, quickly putting distance between us. I didn't know if it would be enough to kill any of them, but the point was to cause fear and confusion. I didn't have a plan anymore; I'd dropped my rock. That was as far ahead as I'd thought. From here on out, I was making things up as I went.

We were only hundreds of feet from the cliffs, so I dipped over the edge, landing among the stones. I didn't waste time searching; I simply grabbed something big, a hunk of stone that I needed both hands to hold, and went back up. I didn't bother with anything fancy, and I didn't get close. I just climbed to a thousand feet, dove at the mass of circled riders at a sharp angle, and dropped my rock from high above them, well out of javelin range. This time I went into a long turn immediately, so I could keep my eyes on them, and grinned with satisfaction as they meandered, getting in each other's way as they tried to get out of the path of the falling stone. Two of them were smashed out of their saddles.

The Cranes milled around. The Wolves grew closer. I returned to the cliffs to rearm.

CHAPTER FORTY-NINE

Rain

I got another run in before the Wolves were close enough that I had to intervene. The west side of the Cranes' circle was forming up like they were going to meet the incoming Grey Wolves with violence, and I had no reason to believe that the Wolves had any idea of the danger they were in.

There were many things I could have said. I could have told them that the Cranes had turned traitor, or that they'd attacked the Palace. I could have said that they tried to kill Commander Rallon or attacked the Wolves' barracks.

What actually came out of my mouth as I braked and hung in the air above them was, "They killed Boot! These fuckers murdered Boot! Turn back!"

Being told by a dive-bombing dragon that the people ahead of them had murdered a beloved weirdo of the company was clearly not something the oncoming Wolves had expected. They split and circled, milling about and babbling in confusion before coming to a stop. I quickly turned to look behind me, then turned back, satisfied that the Cranes were right where I'd left them.

"You—You're the dragon from the bandit camp, aren't you?" One of the Wolves approached, struggling to control her horse as I hung in the air before her. "And from the harbor?"

"See a lot of dragons around here?" Hanging in the air the way I was, everything had to come out in short bursts. I couldn't just glide and speak the way I did when flying properly. "Yeah, I'm that dragon! Go! Turn back! The Cranes turned traitor! They tried to kill Rallon! They'll kill you!"

The mercenary, who I figured must be the captain of this group, stared at me, mouth half open, then just said, "What?"

"Oh, just fuck off!"

I angled my wings, and the mercs' horses shied as I shot above her, turning sharply to return to the Cranes. I heard "Wait, what?" from behind me, but I'd done my part in protecting them.

The Cranes had decided that getting rocks dropped on them while they couldn't fight back wasn't to their liking. They were moving south again, taking parting shots at me that missed horribly. They left a mess of dead horses behind, but no bodies that I could see. They'd also left me a gift, in the form of a certain two-hundred-pound rock. I pounced on it, intending to drop the same damn rock on them again, but as I did, two things stopped me from leaving immediately. The rock was now slick with blood and other substances, making it difficult to grip—the first time I tried to take off I dropped it. I wasn't about to give up, though, and when I dropped back down to try again, a scent caught my nose, above the blood and spilled insides of the men and horses I'd smashed.

The smell was unmistakable, and I left the rock where it lay as I hunted in the long grass, letting my nose guide me until I found it—a single gold dragon. With a grin I grabbed it, wiping the blood off with my thumb before popping it in my mouth with the medallion I still carried. *Should probably leave that somewhere rather than drag a beacon around*, I thought for a moment, but I quickly got distracted. I could still smell gold! I sucked on the coin like a lollipop as I hunted around, finding four more. They joined the first in my mouth. Then, close to the front of the mess, on the saddle of a horse with its chest smashed in, a torn pouch of dark brown leather stuck out. It had the smell of gold on it, and without pause I heaved the carcass up and whipped the pouch out with my tail.

Inside the part that had been pinned under the horse were another five dragons.

I looked at the torn pouch. I thought about the coins I'd found—ten dragons in total, left behind by the Cranes in their hurry—and my mind took some logical steps.

The Cranes had brought at least one pouch of gold coins with them. It was much too big for just ten coins; it could have held a hundred. Hundreds, even. They'd spilled, and the Cranes had collected most of them.

The Cranes had a bloody ton of gold with them. Probably everything they'd had in the city. And they were getting away.

I spat my coins into the pouch. The tear was long but just under the cord, and I could easily hold the pouch in my mouth so the coins were in the whole section on one side of my teeth. I galloped over to my trusty rock, really digging my fingers in under it and pressing it hard to my chest, then used my legs and wings together to get into the air. This time I maintained my grip on the rock, and once I was up, I brought my knees up to help keep it in place.

The Wolves had closed in. They'd been looking at me curiously from a hundred feet away, and when I looked back as I was leaving, they were by the horses the Cranes had left behind. They gave them only a cursory onceover before following me.

The Cranes only had a few minutes' head start, but now they were driving their horses into the ground. When I caught up to them they were in sight of the bay and the ships at anchor there, so I had to hurry if I didn't want to be in range of those big crossbow-things. For my first attack, I'd simply hit the front of the formation, in the hope I'd get Larryman or whatever their commander's name was. This time I looked carefully, and I got to enjoy the alarmed cries of the traitors as I passed over them, identifying two riders. Most of the Cranes had large packs behind them. These two only had large leather bags, and I couldn't see what else they'd be carrying if not a bunch of heavy metals.

I felt the paper-cut stings of arrows passing through my wing membranes. Others bounced off my scales, some leaving little pinpricks of pain, telling me that I'd flown too close and too slow for too long. I pulled up. I'd seen enough, and I had my targets. Now I just needed to get them before they reached the ships.

I turned my climb into a clumsy wingover, then did a half corkscrew so I was diving on them from behind. This time they knew what to expect. Pretty much all of them turned their faces skyward off and on, and they were spreading out, riding in erratic patterns to avoid getting splatted. On some level I was impressed. They'd learned admirably fast, and if my goal was to get as many of them as I could, I would have been very frustrated just about then. Unfortunately for two of them, I had specific targets in mind, and all their fancy riding only made it that much harder for any of them to get a good shot at me.

My two targets were well apart, so I picked the one whose horse seemed a little less nimble—and who just happened to have three sacks instead of two. Arrows zipped past me as I closed in, missing me by yards. I paid them no mind.

I got close enough that I could see the terror on the man's face when he looked over his shoulder. I'd already released and pulled up. He didn't even have time to scream before the rock hit him high, obliterating him and knocking his horse to the ground, then continuing on to bounce once off the ground, spinning and wiping out another two horses before coming to rest.

I looped and rolled, coming back down toward the felled horse. It was trying to get back up, but it was having serious trouble. Other riders had closed in, but they scattered when they saw me coming. Others gave me a wide berth, two of them picking up the riders of the horses I'd felled, as I settled on the ground by the smashed sack of meat that was what remained of the unfortunate man I'd hit. I barely noticed them. I was laser focused on the bags, which were still tied securely to the saddle. All I could think about was the gold that was surely inside, and that I'd need to deal with the horse so I didn't get bitten or kicked while I got them loose.

I was trying to figure out which cords I needed to cut, cursing myself for not just putting the horse out of its misery while trying to stop it from rolling over and kicking me, when a thunder of hooves made me look up. I'd thought that any remaining Cranes had passed and moved on to the ships. Perhaps they had, but this guy had turned back, and was out for blood, his long, thick lance aimed at the base of my throat.

I threw myself backward. I barely avoided getting skewered, but in doing so, I put myself directly in the way of his horse.

The mad-eyed animal didn't have time to dodge or jump. It kicked and then slammed into me, chest first, taking me full in the side. I'd been hit by a charging horse once before. I was bigger now, but so was this horse. To put it simply, it sucked. I'd been pummeled by monster bears and smacked around by trolls, and getting T-boned by a charging warhorse was right up there, if not worse.

The force of the impact wasn't enough to truly send me flying. I was too heavy for that, but I skidded and rolled quite a few yards, getting to my feet in time to see the man's stunned horse stumble away. The Crane himself, a wide-shouldered man with a smoothly shaved head and a full beard, was somehow on his feet. He lunged at me with his lance and I jerked back, swatting at it as I tried to get my bearings and my breath back. The guy was relentless, pursuing me with jabs and thrusts as he screamed wordlessly.

He was between me and my prize, and every step I took backward stung my pride. He was both challenging me and keeping me from a treasure I had already mentally claimed as my own, and backing up felt like a betrayal of everything I stood for. Whether he was trying to drive me off from the gold in those bags or kill me, he had to go. It was as simple as that.

There were a few problems with that, though. I was in a lot of pain, and my head was swimming from the impact with his horse. Avoiding his attacks was hard enough, never mind counterattacking. I also had the pouch of gold in my mouth, all ten dragons of it. With my mouth full I could neither bite nor spit at him, but I couldn't bring myself to drop it. I could have taken it in my hand instead, but then I'd be down one limb, and I needed those so I wouldn't get skewered. And I was reasonably sure that I *would* get skewered. There was a speed, a force, and a directness to his thrusts that left me with no doubt he could penetrate my scales with a well-aimed thrust.

So I found myself already on the back foot, snarling through the leather in my mouth, trying to grab the lance out of the air as the bastard danced and flicked it around like a goddamn kung-fu monk, when two more horses came charging back from the south. Loyalty to one's companions is admirable and all, but I was properly pissed off. Not only was this one guy giving me trouble, but here came two more traitors to keep me from my well-deserved gold. Worse, the horse with the bags was getting to its feet! Blood ran down its side in a wide sheet and one of its legs seemed to be injured, if not broken, but fear or sheer grit was driving it to get away from me.

That was the push I'd needed. I couldn't allow my treasure to ride away. The Crane was still between me and the horse, and I surprised him with a headlong rush. Quite literally. With my mouth full, I used my head as a club. He thrust at my neck, but I deflected the lance, and as he leaped to the side I clipped him on the shoulder with my horn. He rolled in the dirt before landing in a crouch, the lance still trained on me, but I was already sprinting past him for the horse.

The injured animal stumbled away from me, heavily favoring its left rear leg. I leaped the last few feet, intending to pull it down by the flanks, but overshot as it stopped suddenly. Instead my claws lodged in the thick saddle. The horse jerked forward; I pulled back. Between my weight and the horse finding a new burst of strength, the saddle slipped backward. The horse then tried to kick me, but I was too close, and its bad leg buckled, bringing it down. I jerked; the horse again pulled forward, and the saddle slipped all the way back to tangle around its legs.

The two mounted Cranes coming in were only seconds away. If I could only get the saddle off I could—

A sharp pain stabbed my lower back and slid up my side. I whirled, a feral snarl tearing from my throat as I batted the lance away. I cursed myself. I couldn't believe it. I'd been so focused on getting those bags, on doing the first thing that came to mind to get them off the horse so I could grab them and fly off, that *the man who was trying to kill me* slipped my mind!

Fuck you, Instinct! I screamed into my own head. *You'll get us killed!*

All I got back was an overwhelming, incoherent rage.

I had to think, goddamnit! I was not an animal. I was not a monster. I was an intelligent, thinking being! I'd been imitating World War 2 air-to-ground attacks only minutes ago, but one damn whiff of gold and I became completely single-minded, thinking with my greed and unable to see more than a few seconds ahead. No more! I had to think if I wanted to get out of here alive *and* with those bags!

Leaving without the gold presumably within them didn't even register as an option.

I swallowed my pride and leaped into the air to survey the scene. The horse was kicking itself loose from the saddle. Good; I didn't have to worry about my gold disappearing. The two new riders, a big, scarred woman and a short, stocky man, both with lances, arrived and joined up with the bald guy I'd been fighting.

"The bags! Grab the damn bags!" the bald man roared as he kept his lance trained on me. The two newcomers, who'd already shown that they were made of sterner stuff than most by coming back, threw fearful glances at me as they slid off their horses. They closed in on the saddle, which now lay discarded as the horse that used to carry it slowly made its way south, and started undoing the ties that held the bags in place.

Mindless rage flared again. *No*, I told myself. *Think. Be smart.*

I needed to prevent them from leaving with the bags. That was the first thing. Fine. I could do that, or at least make it difficult for them.

I dove on the two messing with the saddle. The bald man reacted immediately, throwing himself between me and them with the lance braced against the ground. If I'd kept coming, I'd have impaled myself. But by moving he put some distance between himself and the horses—big mistake. With a flick of my wings I changed direction, faster than he could react, and got in the horses' faces. I didn't even need to touch them; they screamed and reared and took off at a gallop as I climbed back out of reach of the now cursing man's lance. Then, to add insult to injury, I flitted over to the man's own horse, which had so recently rammed me. I was starting to really feel it, too, and the impulse to get my own back was strong, but I'd killed enough innocent horses. I scared it off simply with my presence, and that was that. Let the bastards run with the bags if they wanted to. I'd pick them off one by one and get my prize.

The three Cranes were properly pissed off now. They screamed after me, calling me variations on every filthy thing under heaven. I ignored them and climbed again. The Grey Wolves looked to still be a few minutes out, having taken their time. In the direction of the ships was a confusion of White Cranes, spread out along the way. Some were gathered in groups, seemingly unsure what to do as others milled about on the beach, preparing to board. Discipline seemed to have broken down, but some of the groups gathering were looking my way, and I suspected that they were gathering courage to come and help their comrades. Gods only knew if they'd manage that, but I didn't want to take the chance. I needed to get those bags!

I considered my options. Wearing them out felt like it would take too long, but I could charge in, or grab things to drop on them. The rock lay nearby, and I might be able to get it in the air before I got stabbed. Or there was the smashed body of the man who'd been carrying the bags on his saddle. Then it occurred to me that there was one obvious thing I hadn't tried. There hadn't really been an opportunity, but here we were. Three human turncoats with one lance and a couple of swords between them, carrying three heavy bags, and one pissed off dragon between them and freedom.

I landed fifty feet away from them. The cut on my back stung as I put weight back on my legs, but it was only a minor distraction. I stood between the Cranes and the ships. They stood between me and my prize. A breeze rippled through the tall grass. No one moved.

Rain began to fall, light at first but growing heavier by the second. It was perfect.

I took the leather pouch from my mouth. My jaw was stiff from holding it firmly shut, and I worked it a little as the Cranes watched me intently, weapons ready. I looked across the short distance separating us, considering them each in turn and watching them fidget and squirm.

"I'm going to give you a chance," I told them. They did the customary "It talks!" double take, but I didn't pay it any mind. "One chance, yeah? One. Leave the bags, and shove off. I'll let you go in peace. I can't speak for the Grey Wolves' patrol that was following me, and they could be here any moment, but I won't go after you. That, or die, here and now. Your choice."

To make my point I started slowly walking toward them. One step at a time, relaxed and unhurried, only made a little awkward by the pouch clutched in one hand. At the same time I sent my shadow snaking toward them through the grass. The thick clouds cut the morning light to a minimum, and manipulating my own shadow took barely any effort.

Thunder rumbled in the distance, a neat little nudge from Mother Nature in my favor.

"I expect an answer," I growled. I'd covered half the distance, and they were looking decidedly uncomfortable, the woman and the stocky man's courage flagging when faced with the reality of my presence.

I chose to focus on them, ignoring the bald man who'd already shown a degree of fearlessness. My shadow merged with theirs, flowing up their legs, and I could see the moment that cold terror gripped them. They weren't quite paralyzed, and the woman backed away, stammering, "We—We should—At the harbor! It killed all those people, we shouldn't—"

The man followed. Then he stumbled backward over one of the bags, crashing to the ground, and that was the trigger. The woman took off toward the coast, turning south in a big arc, and the stocky man scrambled to his feet and went after her, his eyes locked on the bald man, screaming, "It's not worth it, Jel! It's not worth it!"

The bald man, Jel, looked after his fleeing companions, his expression more shocked and betrayed than angry. "Well, Jel," I said, taking a few more steps toward him. I left my shadows as they were. "It's just us again. What's your answer?"

He gripped his lance tighter. He glanced down at the bags, then at the dead man, and back at me. His face split in a furious scowl, teeth bared, and I thought that he'd decided to fight it out. Then he began slowly sidestepping away, the lance still pointed at me as he made his way around me. "You killed the commander, dragon," he said, his voice tight. "Him and so many others. The White Cranes will not forgive this. We will not forget."

I leaned in, close enough that he might have been able to reach me with a lunge, and hissed, "You should. This is the last time I offer a White Crane mercy. Stay off my island!"

Jel kept circling until he had his back to the sea and a clear way to the safety of the ships. His eyes flicked between the bags, the dead man on the ground, and back to the place where I'd killed dozens of his comrades. Then, when the sound of hooves from the north became audible, even over the rain, he looked at me with a final impotent grimace, turned, and ran. He didn't look back.

CHAPTER FIFTY

Remuneration

I watched the Crane run until I was sure that he'd keep going. The rain came down in sheets, but I didn't care. I made a canopy of my wings to keep the worst off as I approached the bags, circling them, sniffing them, savoring the moment. I had a flash of disappointment when I smelled silver. How insane was that? I was disappointed to smell silver! But the gold was there as well. I'd just have to be content with what I had. For the moment, at least.

I took one of the bags and hefted it. The leather was thick, but I could feel the shape of the contents. All coins. Forty pounds or thereabouts. Even if it was *all* silver, it was a tidy fortune. With gold mixed in it could be comparable to, or even more than, what Tam and Val had brought back from Tavvanar. And now it was mine. If not for the fact that I would have a hard time closing them back up, I would have opened one of the bags right there.

The patrol of Wolves reached me while I was listening to the coins jingle, but I didn't pay them much mind until the woman I'd tagged as their captain cleared her throat. She'd approached as her soldiers held back, and spoke loudly above the rain, with a tremble to her voice and a Tavvanarian accent that I hadn't noticed before. "Ahem. My, ah . . . My good dragon? I'm sorry, I don't know how to address you. I am with the Grey Wolves mercenary company, currently in the service of the city of Karakan, and I would like to ask you some questions. If I may."

"Draka," I said absentmindedly. "Or Lady Dragon. Madam would do, too."

"Ah. Lady Dragon, then. May I ask you what just happened here?"

I put the bag I was holding on top of the others and looked up for the first time since she'd spoken to me. She'd left her horse with the patrol and stood fifteen feet away, wearing a heavy raincoat, for all the good it did her. The wind drove rain into her face, and she had hair plastered across her forehead as water dripped from her nose. She must have been miserable.

Seeing her made me aware of how awful it would be to fly back to my hoard if it didn't let up. It was enough to make me stay and talk to this captain instead of just going home.

"I already told you. The White Cranes turned traitor." I gestured to the dead man and the horses with my head. "I've punished them. Their commander is dead."

Her face went slack. "Commander Larrallan's dead?!"

"So they said."

She swallowed and nodded. "I—I see, but why? Are the rumors true? Have you been working with Commander Rallon this whole time?"

"If I have been, and the commander hasn't told everyone, don't you think that there's a good reason for that? And come here if we're going to talk, would you?" I rustled my wings, sending water spraying every which way. "It's not perfect, but it'll keep you from having to wipe your face all the time."

She looked at me hesitantly, then took one slow step toward me, then another and another until she stood barely two feet away, trembling with cold and fear as I looked down on her. This close, standing still and without the veil of rain between us, I finally got a good look at her. She must have had some Barlean blood in her, or some other culture with similar features. She wore her fear openly on a heart-shaped face with wide green eyes, the light brown hair that stuck out from under her helmet still plastered to her forehead.

My opinion of the Grey Wolves had always been fairly high, but she raised it another small notch. She was as afraid of me as anyone. She didn't even pretend otherwise, but she'd approached me to speak anyway, and came closer when I invited her. She wasn't fearless by any means, but she controlled it well. I respected that.

"Listen, Captain. Is that right? Captain?"

This close to me, her voice had a slight squeak to it. "Yeah!"

"What's your name?"

"My name?"

"Your name. I'd like to know who I'm talking to."

"My name. I'm, ah—My name is Meletti, Lady Dragon. A pleasure to meet you?" Her voice creaked at the end, turning the statement into a question, to which she desperately hoped that the answer was "Yes."

"Same. Listen, Captain Meletti. I have some human friends who are very, very important to me. And through them, I have some friends among the Wolves. I want my friends to be safe, and I also don't want to see the good people of Karakan suffer unnecessarily. So, sometimes, my interests and those of the Wolves have been the same, and I've cooperated with Commander Rallon. We've done some good together. Does that answer your question?"

"Uh, yeah. I mean yes, Lady Dragon! Thank you. And the White Cranes? Did they really . . . ?"

"They attacked the Palace. Tried to kill Rallon and the council in their homes. Rallon's alive, but I don't know about the others. They did kill and maim who knows how many Wolves and city guards. They hurt my friends." The last came out as a growl.

Meletti took a half-step backward, but recovered. Her face was stricken. "You're sure you don't know how many Wolves were killed? Can you guess?"

I shook my head. "My friend said that she didn't think there were more than a dozen Wolves alive in the city. Most of them were at Her Grace's Favor when I left. Do you know where that is?"

"It's that inn Lalia and Garal like, yeah," she half-whispered. "Mercies be kind. Only a dozen . . . And you killed Young Lord Larrallan?"

"That's what they said." I looked at the bag of meat and bone that lay only a few feet away. The rock had torn out or flattened most of the grass, and the dirt and blood were turning into a dark red mud in the rain. "'Young Lord,' huh? That's not him, then?"

"'Young Lord' doesn't indicate age, it's just . . ." She trailed off as she followed my gaze. After a second she retched a little. She quickly looked away and swallowed hard, then spat on the ground. "No, that's not him. Larrallan was taller. More hair."

"Less flat?"

"Less flat," she confirmed with a shudder. She looked again, then past the corpse. "So that's what the rock was for. We wondered."

"Yeah. Worked wonders. I really should have tried it earlier. Damn bears . . ." I looked at her. Her eyes had frozen on the body, and I waved a hand in front of her face to get her attention. "You should get back to the city, Captain Meletti. I've no doubt that your company needs you. And if you see any other patrols on the way I suggest you tell them the same."

"Yeah." Her eyes strayed down to the bags piled in front of me. "And those? What are those?"

"Mine!" I snapped, stepping over the bags so they were safe beneath me. The pains in my back and side spiked, making me grimace. It happened without a moment's thought, and this time Meletti jerked back from me. Beyond her I saw her patrol loosen their swords and ready their bows and lances, then relax when nothing else happened. I adjusted my wings to keep her sheltered, and forced myself to release the sudden burst of jealousy and suspicion that her innocent question had set off. "I took them from the Cranes," I said, more calmly, "and I'm keeping them as compensation for my trouble."

"All right, yeah, yeah, no problem," she agreed quickly, backing into the rain. "That's all, Lady Dragon. Draka, was it? Lady Draka? Thank you for your time, and for the information, and it was a pleasure meeting you! Good day!"

"Good day, Captain Meletti," I said, as she speed-walked away from me. I decided I should put in a good word for her the next time I saw Rallon; the amount of fear that she'd fought through to speak to me had been truly impressive.

The Wolves went south. I couldn't fault them for not doing what I'd suggested. It was obvious where the Cranes had gone, and it made sense to verify what I'd said. For all I knew Meletti hadn't believed a word I'd said, and just agreed with everything in case I turned murderous if she didn't.

With the little pouch in my mouth, and the three larger ones gathered in my arms, I looked up at the pouring rain and sighed. I opened up the canopy I'd made of my wings and immediately regretted it, then took to the sky. I took a long, low turn to the south; the Wolves were still on the move, and other than a few stragglers, the Cranes were all on or near the ships. No one was running, which was vaguely disappointing; I'd wondered if the Wolves would catch up to Jel and the other two, but the other Cranes must have picked up the stragglers.

The bags I carried presented a problem. I wanted to get back to Herald and the others, to convince myself that everyone was okay and to be there for emotional support. But the bags were full of coins, and I needed them to be safe. They'd be safe at the inn, but the inn wasn't my hoard, and the sheer *mass* of what I was carrying made me desperate to bring them home. And my hoard had been calling to me as it was, that itch to get back and check on it that I always felt when I was away for too long.

In the end my family won out. My hoard would be fine for a few hours longer. And as long as I kept the bags with me, they'd be as safe as they possibly could.

The flight back to the city was as miserable as I'd expected. My whole left side was a mess of aches and pains. Every beat of my wings brought with it a little stab that then bloomed across my side, making me wonder if I had a busted rib. On top of that the rain didn't let up, getting in my nose, blurring my sight as it ran over the protective membranes covering my eyes, and finding its way under my scales with no chance of drying out.

I considered just going above the clouds. It would have been so nice to get out of the rain for a while, and I was confident that I'd be able to stay on course despite the clouds reaching from horizon to horizon in every direction. But I felt a vague sense of responsibility to the Wolves, and I wanted to keep my eyes open for patrols so that I could tell them about what had happened during the night. And so I flew in the rain.

I stayed low—the rain cut the visibility to almost nothing anyway—and I followed small country roads back to the large southern road that ran from Karakan all the way to the bridge into Happar. It didn't do me any good. There were some few unfortunate souls out, but no large groups of horsemen.

It's the thought that counts, I told myself, over and over. *It's the thought that counts.*

I passed over the gate, the guards on the walls ducking as I came in, even though I was a hundred feet above them. I landed in the yard behind the Favor and shifted, the bags hitting the ground with a heavy, metallic rustle. It was the best I'd been able to think of. I couldn't leave my new treasure somewhere while I made my way carefully to the inn, but I didn't want to sit there, fully visible, while I waited. In my shadow form I wasn't holding the bags, but good luck to anyone who tried to take them from me.

On the opposite side of the yard near the street bodies lay in rows. It seemed no one had the time to take them away, or even cover them. They lay bare to the sky, the rain washing away the blood from waxen faces and glassy eyes. I had a powerful urge to look closer, but that would have meant leaving the bags unattended, and so I stayed where I was.

Sitting in the heavy rain like that was even worse than flying in it. Mercifully, I didn't have to wait long before the cellar door opened and Mak stuck her head out. She quickly found me in the corner where I sat, and must have understood the problem perfectly. She sprinted to my side, the mud splattering under her feet. "It's clear!" she whispered. "Come on, get inside!"

She grabbed the pouch and the bags, gathering them in her arms, and to my relief I didn't feel the least bit of anger or possessiveness when she ran back toward the inn. It reminded me of the first time I showed Herald my shadow magic. We'd been traveling through the hills in the south, on our way to find her—now our—family. I'd shifted and dropped a pouch full of silver eagles, and when she'd picked it up for me I hadn't been worried at all. Instinct, or "the dragon" as I'd thought of her then, hadn't objected, either. Herald was safe. She could be trusted. And now, here, so could Mak. Forget her mistakes; they were in the past. She was my sister, and we were bound together, and I knew in my bones that I would trust her with anything precious to me. Nothing could prove that so effectively as the fact that I was calmly following her as she ran away from me with over a hundred pounds of my gold and silver in her arms.

When I entered the cellar Herald stood at the foot of the stairs. "Oh, thank the Mercies," she said, crashing into me and wrapping her arms around my neck when I materialized. "Where did you go? Why were you gone so long? Mak thought that you were fighting!"

"Yeah, I was. I went after the Cranes." I felt bad about making her worry, but I wasn't going to hide anything from her. "Which reminds me. Mak, could you take a look at my wing, and the cut on my back? And also, like, my whole left side. I got rammed by a horse."

I stretched my wing so they could see where an arrow had pierced it. They fussed over me for a bit, with Mak healing my cuts first, then spending whatever she had left on my side, soothing my pains. Her healing me seemed to soothe Herald, too. Maybe seeing me go from hurt to whole helped, after the awful night she and everyone else just had.

And it had been awful. Truly awful. I understood that fully as they told me what had happened. The first they'd heard of it had been Med practically kicking the door down and shouting for Rib and Pot, telling anyone who'd listen that the Cranes had tried to storm Rallon's estate in the city. They'd failed, barely, but only because Med and Boot and some others had gone there to plan patrol routes, and ended up staying in the guest rooms.

"Boot did not make it out." Herald sighed and sank down the wall onto the bench beneath her. "He died holding a hallway while the others formed up. They lost a couple more that I did not know, but they fought their way out and made it to the city guard's headquarters. And about when Med finished telling us, that was when the others arrived."

Med had arrived breathless and absolutely livid, barely able to get his story out as he waited for the Terriallons to get their gear on. The other Wolves had arrived in the middle of a running battle. The clatter of hooves and the screams of men and women fighting and dying as they rode down the streets had brought some of Ardek's minions running, and it was a good thing they did. Thanks to them, my family, the Terriallons, and half their guests had been armed and ready when the fighting reached them.

"The wounded came first," Mak said. "Some of them were barely in their saddles. Really woke the guards that the lady justice sent. So we started getting the wounded inside, but then the rest charged into the square, and we were in the middle of a small battle. It was a fucking mess, honestly. It's lucky most of the people who stay here know a Wolf or two, and the Cranes never had the best reputation, so at least we didn't have to fight our own damn guests. Hell, Yana and her group even joined in the fighting once the Cranes bashed the door in. Turned the fight in our favor."

The name sounded familiar. "That's the woman with the hair, yeah?" I interrupted.

"Right. Anyway, Jor—that's the big guy with the beard and the bow—he took a spear in the gut. Kira got to him almost immediately, though. He's gonna be fine. But the Wolves who didn't make it inside didn't stand a chance, and a bunch of the guards got killed once they got involved." Mak had sat down next to Herald. Now she slowly pitched over until her head was in her sister's lap. Her eyes fluttered close, and she whispered, "A gods-damned mess."

"And you?"

"Cuts and bruises," Herald said when Mak didn't answer. "Some pretty bad cuts and bruises, to be honest, but nothing potions and magic cannot fix. Just . . . tired. So damned tired. And I was not even healing."

She gestured down with her head and stroked Mak's hair. Our sister was already asleep on her lap.

"She woke when we felt you coming," Herald whispered. "I told her not to get up, but she insisted."

"I wish she wouldn't. She needs more rest."

"She does. But . . . you know. You are important to her."

"Yeah. What about Kira?"

"Sleeping. She has been wringing herself out healing all night, but Barro found that healer I mentioned, and he has taken over caring for the few people who were not already stable when Kira collapsed. He may ask for some kind of payment, but I have no doubt the guard will take care of it. Most of the wounded are guards, after all." She paused for a second, then asked, almost coyly, "So, what is in those bags? Something important, I assume, with the way you are brooding over them."

The wet leather bags lay on the floor where Mak had left them, and I had, without thinking of it, moved so that I lay with my arms around them. I grinned at her. She kept a straight face for a few seconds, before a smile of pure, unguarded avarice slowly split her face. She knew very well what was in the bags, and she didn't ask where they came from. All she said was, "Can we open them?"

I thought about it. I'd intended to just take everything back to my hoard and tear the bags open there, but the idea of seeing it all now was tempting. A carpet of coins, clinking and tinkling as they spread out on the floor, glimmering in the light of the lamp that hung from the ceiling . . .

"Aren't you tired?" I said, swallowing thickly.

Herald turned her grin on me. She knew that she had me. "Not too tired for this! Come on. I need something to cheer me up after the night I have had."

I took one of the bags. With hands shaking from excitement I carefully fiddled with the knot on the cord. The wet leather resisted me for five seconds more than my patience lasted. Having tried and failed, I simply tore the cord with a claw, and upended the bag on the floor.

CHAPTER FIFTY-ONE

Fortitude

I emptied the bag slowly, mesmerized by what I saw. Forty pounds of metal made a lot of coins, and they rained down onto the stone floor, ringing and tinkling, the light flashing off them as they spun. Most settled into a fair-sized pile. A few bounced and rolled, but the floor was too uneven for any to get far.

All too soon the bag was empty. In vain hope I shook the bag, but nothing more came out. Silence settled over the cellar, only to be broken by a voice whispering, "Again? There's two more bags. Can you do that again?"

Mak still lay on the bench, but sideways now, looking intently at me and the pile. The falling coins must have awoken her.

"Can you?" Herald seconded the request, and in the moment, drunk on the sight before me, I saw no reason not to. I grabbed another bag. This time I didn't even try to open the knot, and the coins rained down just as prettily as they had moments before.

When that was empty they didn't need to ask. I poured the third bag out as well.

With careful steps, Mak made her way to the pile. She ran her hands through the coins, grabbing handfuls and letting them rain back down. She looked half out of it with fatigue.

"Where'd this all come from?" she asked between handfuls.

"I took them from the Cranes," I told them with great satisfaction. "Killed that Larrallan guy, whoever he was, along with, I dunno . . . two dozen others, maybe three? I'd guess this is their company treasury or something."

"Their operating funds, perhaps," Herald said, joining us by the pile. "Most of their money will be with a treasure house somewhere, or held directly by House Larrallan. But this . . ." She dug her hand into the pile and raised it, palm up, tipping the coins back out, "this is still a fantastic haul."

That was a hell of an understatement. With forty eagles or eighty dragons to a pound, basic math told me that there must be about five thousand coins in that pile. Granted, most of them were silver, with a much smaller part than I'd hoped being gold. Something like one in five was even brass or bronze, which was a real disappointment. And despite that, it was, as Herald said, a fantastic haul.

Once the initial excitement wore off Mak fell asleep again, curled up right there on the floor. This time Herald decided that enough was enough, lifting our unprotesting sister and carrying her up the stairs. She returned sometime later, having put Mak properly to bed and collected a few pouches.

"What's it like up there?" I asked her.

She shook her head. "I am trying to escape from the reality of what the common room looks like. There is not much I can do anyway. Please, let us just focus on this."

Together we separated the pile by value. I grabbed large handfuls of coins, and Herald deftly picked out the dragons and the peacocks before I dumped the eagles into the leather bags I'd brought them in. When we were done she brought down a set of scales. Rather than counting the peacocks and eagles she simply weighed them. We ended up with just under twenty pounds of peacocks, worth anywhere between fifteen and twenty-five eagles depending on the mintage, and about a hundred pounds of eagles, which would have bought half of Her Grace's Favor.

The dragons she counted by hand. There were eighty-eight of them, just over a pound of gold, and they all went in one of the leather pouches she'd brought. It was more than I'd received as my share for the old book we'd sold, and the single largest amount of gold I'd ever held.

"Draka," Herald said in her most serious voice as I shook the pouch. "You know that I love you."

"I do. Though I appreciate the reminder."

"And I am so glad to have you back after your trip south. I missed you."

"Me, too."

"With that in mind, I think that you should go, and take all this to your hoard as soon as possible."

"Yeah? What about you? Why not come along?"

"Normally I would love to, but in this rain? No. I would rather not die of the shivers or consumption before we even reach the mountain. Besides, I need to stay here. I need sleep, and there is so much to take care of. But can I ask something of you?"

"Of course. Anything."

"This is an utterly unreasonable thing to ask of anyone," she cautioned me.

"Herald. Anything I can do, anything I can give, just ask."

She pursed her lips and took a deep breath. "When you pass your next threshold—and if my estimations are anywhere close to correct, I think that you will—please take something to keep yourself safe. You keep getting hurt. Mak almost got killed when we took Tarkarran, and again tonight."

"Wait, what—" I tried to interrupt, but she kept going, taking my head in both hands.

"I *cannot* lose either of you. Please, Draka. You told me once that you had an option to choose a more powerful version of the advancement that lets you shrug off most arrows, swords, and other attacks. I beg you. Take it."

"Is that all?" I said it flippantly, but I knew what a huge request it was. It was like asking someone back home to get a full back tattoo, or to change their career or move countries for you.

In this case, though, I was all too happy to oblige.

"Don't worry. If I pass a threshold, I'll take greater fortitude. I promise."

"Thank you. Now, let us get some new cords on those bags so you can—"

"Actually," I said, cutting her off, "I think I'll only take the gold."

"What?" Herald's relieved tone shifted into a nervous laughter, as though I'd just told her, out of the blue, that I was applying for a spot on the council or something similarly insane.

"Yeah. I'll take the gold, and leave the rest here. My contribution to the family funds."

"But your hoard—" Herald protested.

"No worries, yeah? It's fine. Let's put the eagles and the peacocks in the strongroom, and I'll be off."

I'd been rolling the thought around my mind for the last few minutes, and found that it didn't bother me at all. It was the old idea of, "What's theirs is ours." I could leave some of my treasure here. They could even spend some of it if they had to, and it wouldn't bother me as long as it wasn't frivolous. It would all go to keeping my family comfortable, safe, and happy, and to keeping the inn running, making more money in the long run.

Herald protested weakly a few more times, but I was determined, and she couldn't convince me otherwise. Finally, we did what I wanted. The eagles and peacocks went into the magical lockbox in the strongroom. Then Herald opened the cellar door for me. She offered to bring the pouch to an alley for me, but she was right about the weather. Once I'd thought about it, I didn't want to drag her outside, and I wasn't worried about being spotted leaving the inn. Visibility was near enough to zero, and anyone watching the inn already knew I was there, or should know so that they didn't get any stupid ideas.

"Go on, then!" Herald shouted over the roaring rain as I did my best cat impression, standing before the open door but not making any move to actually leave. "But please! Be back soon!"

"I will!" I promised. "Oh, yeah, before I forget—" I dug the medallion out from where it still sat between my jawbone and my tongue, and held it out to her. "Take this." I didn't want the homing medallion anywhere near my hoard.

"Draka! Ew!" Herald's face twisted as she gave me her best "Are you serious?" look. She patted herself, looking for something like a napkin, but lacking pouches and pockets, she finally had to just take the thing. "Ech, it's all slimy!"

"It's a homing medallion," I told her. "It has a twin somewhere. Possibly still with the Silver Spurs. They can always find each other. Keep it safe . . . Maybe give it to Kira. She'll recognize it."

"Are you not worried that they might follow it here?"

I thought about it, then shook my head. "Nah. They're not stupid enough for that. Me and their commander, we came to an understanding."

I looked out into the water thundering down and then, not wanting to look like a wuss, I was off. I climbed as fast as I could to get out of the damned rain, entering the heavy clouds in minutes and breaking through into the morning sun shortly thereafter. The water streamed off of me as I cruised toward home. The peak of my mountain was too low to be visible, but that made no difference. My hoard was a beacon, and it didn't matter how many miles separated me from it. It was already beneath hundreds or maybe thousands of feet of stone; what difference could a bit of cloud make?

I practically skidded to a stop when I reached the ledge outside my cave. I splashed through the puddles that had formed there, getting my belly wet as I hurried into the shelter of the mountain. I paused only to quickly shift in and out, water falling onto the floor before I descended.

My hoard was waiting for me, safe and beautiful and, almost as important in the moment, dry. I took a round of the small side chamber where I'd made my nest, Instinct reassuring me that everything was in order, not a single eagle missing. Avjilan's bow leaned against the pillar where I'd left it. The small box with its handful of golden dragons that I'd taken from a dead healer at the lake camp when I first met Garal stood in its place, slightly higher than everything else; the box itself was worthless and broken, but it was my first treasure, the seed of my hoard, and held a lot of sentimental value for me.

With little ceremony I opened the bag around my neck and poured its contents onto the carpet of coins. Eighty-eight dragons wasn't a lot of volume, but they made a beautiful addition to the silver that dominated my hoard.

Herald had been right. I wasn't sure how she'd known, but I shivered with delight as I felt the tingle of a threshold crossed. My choices lay before me, inserted directly into my memory by the magic of this world—greater fortitude, to weather all but the mightiest blows; physical greatness, to increase the power of my body in all ways, at the cost of needing more food and drifting more toward a draconic way of thinking; cunning, to plot and see through the schemes of others; grace, for peerless ease of movement in any element, which I assumed meant that I'd be able to swim like a croc; and a new one, of course, acid spit, for foes who resisted or knew to avoid our venom.

They were all interesting. I'd especially been considering grace for my next minor. It might help with both attacking and defending in a fight. Being able to swim properly could potentially be very useful, and anything that let me do some fancy flying sounded like a lot of fun. At the same time, being able to spit acid would have been useful in a lot of fights I'd been in, and it might have uses outside of fighting as well, which my venom didn't.

"*Physical Greatness!*" Instinct hissed in my ear. "*We must become what we were always meant to!*" Because of course she did. Becoming bigger, stronger, and scarier was everything that she desired. But I felt her satisfaction with the one we did take, and which I'd promised Herald.

"Greater fortitude," I whispered into the silence, and the changes washed over me.

I was instantly wracked with pain, crashing to the bed of coins as my whole body spasmed. Gods and Mercies, it hurt! My only consolation was that after the initial shock, the burst of fear and adrenaline, I knew what was happening and why.

It wasn't the effects of the advancement itself; I could feel it doing something to my skin and muscles and a host of other parts of me, and a fine black dust rained from me as scales shifted and changed. It was an odd sensation to be sure, itchy and uncomfortable, like every inch of me was peeling after a bad sunburn. But it wasn't painful. No, what hurt was the growth. I'd figured out months ago, and Herald had confirmed with her own eyes, that adding to my hoard made me grow in leaps and bounds. Eighty-eight dragons was not a lot of coins, but over a pound of gold was a hell of a lot of value, and value was what counted. A young laborer in Karakan could retire to raise a family and live the rest of their life in reasonable comfort on that kind of money. And so, as the advancement took hold, I felt every bone in my body stretch and widen and whatever else bones did when they grew, forcing all my other tissues to grow with them.

The pain when I'd added my share of the book money had been bad. This was hell. Sheer bloody torture. Worse than a sword through the lung, and I would know. I whined, then groaned, then roared and hissed as I writhed on the carpet of coins, trying to find a position that offered any kind of relief. There was none. What relief can you find when the problem is that your body is temporarily too small for your bones? All I could do was wait and suffer through it, and wonder why the hell my upgraded fortitude didn't help.

A horrible thought came to me. Maybe greater fortitude *was* helping. Maybe this was only a fraction of the pain I'd have felt if I'd chosen something else. I would have shuddered if I wasn't already shaking.

And then it passed, fading out as quickly as it had come on, leaving me panting and hungry on a scattered carpet of gold and silver.

I took some time to gather everything. It was slow going; I was mildly dazed after my ordeal, and I'd already been so damn tired.

Once I finished and my head cleared somewhat, I made my way back to the cave's entrance. I was returning to the city immediately. I would have liked to stay with my hoard, to just sleep for a day or two and to check on Jekrie and the others, but things were too unstable in Karakan. I needed to be there. I'd landed in the Forum, for Christ's sake!

I stood looking out at the rain for some time. It hadn't let up one bit since it started. If anything, it was heavier; fat drops leaping high into the air where they splashed into puddles, water making a partial curtain in front of the cave as it poured down from the mountainside above.

This was going to suck. Again.

Half an hour later I was back in the cellar. This time it was Tam who let me in. He'd been waiting, watching the yard with the cellar door open just a crack. "Herald said you were coming," he said, massaging his eyes and breaking into a huge yawn. "Begged me to let you in before I tucked myself into bed."

"You're a legend, Tam. Thanks." I shifted rapidly to get dry, and he blinked up at me.

"Neat trick. Maybe next time you could not bring the water inside in the first place, eh? But, uh, is the ceiling caving in, or are you bigger?"

"I should hope so. Best not have gone through all that pain for nothing."

He stepped up and took a closer look at me, then reached out, stopping just short of touching me. "Do you mind?"

"Nah, go ahead."

He ran his fingers over my scales, then tapped or flicked some. "Your scales are different," he declared. "Not by much, and it's hard to see with the color, but they are. Did you pass a threshold?"

"I did!" I admitted smugly. "But I'll tell you about it later. We both need sleep. Do you have people guarding the upstairs?"

"Yeah. Most of Ardek's people are still around and awake, and some of the guests who already got some sleep have volunteered to stand watch. I guess Herald must have told you already, but it's a damned sick house up there."

"She said, yeah. So don't worry about me. Get some sleep and take care of everything, and I'll be here when you can spare some time. Though, if you can somehow get hold of a couple pounds of fish or meat sometime soon, that would be brilliant. I'm starving."

"I'll see what I can do." He handed me the strongroom key and turned to go, then turned back and gave me a tired smile. "It's good to have you back, sister. It was strange, not having you around."

"Sleep well, bro." I bopped him lightly on top of the head with my chin.

He left, and I made my way into the strongroom, where I finally passed out after one of the longest nights and mornings of my life.

The day passed slowly. The highlight of my afternoon was when Tam came downstairs with a large box, the wood stained dark by rain.

"Thank Ardek's little minions," he told me when I thanked him. "They're the ones willing to run down to the docks in this deluge."

"What did that cost us?" I asked, cracking the box open and gazing greedily at the long, thin fishes inside.

"We already give them three meals a day and a warm place to sleep," Tam grumbled. "But three peacocks each. And I'm pretty sure that they pocketed most of the change on top of that, the thieving bastards. I mean, that's what I would have done."

All through the day the rain kept falling. It didn't matter where I was in the cellar; it was a constant presence, impossible to ignore. Even in the strongroom I could hear it hammering down. I could have sworn that I even heard the storm drains below us, a rushing sound that was almost a rumble.

That's not to say that it was unpleasant. There's something comforting about knowing that the world outside is drowning, while you yourself are warm and dry.

I mostly stayed in the strongroom, reading or napping. Herald and Mak ran around upstairs all day, rarely stopping in one place for more than a few minutes at a time. Every so often someone would come down and exchange a few words, letting me know what was going on. With the help of the city guard's healers the wounded had all recovered enough to be able to move, or at least to be moved. The wounded guards and mercenaries had all been removed, along with the bodies outside. The wounded guests all had their own rooms, and by evening the common room was in a state where food and drinks could be served again.

They tried, and failed, to get any news about Sempralia and the other councilors. That, we decided, was bad. If the councilors had all survived, surely that fact would be announced loudly. Instead there was only silence.

Sometime after sunset the family plus Kira and Ardek gathered in the main cellar. My humans were all tired—Mak, to my satisfaction, was visibly less so than the others. Some of them had new scars. Some of them had lost friends. All of them had been through something terrible, and the atmosphere reflected that. But they had all fought successfully to protect what they could, and they were all alive and whole. And that, in the end, was all that mattered.

CHAPTER FIFTY-TWO

A Hole in the Ground

All right," I said, opening our family meeting. "It's been one hell of a day. Let's talk."

Val didn't hesitate to speak. "There is much confusion about what is happening in the south," he said. "Herald says that there has been an invasion by the Happarans. Is this true? There have been no announcements, and the Wolves don't know anything."

"They were preparing to cross the river when we heard that the White Cranes were attacking the Palace. All along the river as far as I could tell. General Sarvalian was mobilizing when I left, but I imagine they must have crossed by now."

"So it is war," Herald said. The others looked at her with sympathy. Maglan was down there, his life at risk, but Herald was taking it well. She'd had months to get used to the idea in general, and all day to accept that it was happening. "Happar alone against the entire Sareyan League."

"I don't get it." Ardek stretched his arms high over his head, and something popped in his shoulders, making him grunt with satisfaction. Kira, sitting beside him, gave him an exasperated look and rubbed his back. "They're proper fucked, aren't they? I've heard some grumbling about the state of our army, but if the Happarans manage to push north, there's thousands of people to levy. And it's not like Happar could take the city before the rest of the League gets here, anyway. Once that happens, they're done. There's not even going to be a city of Happar by next summer."

"They appear mad or desperate," Val agreed. "But we must assume that they are not fools. This was planned. A river is not crossed on a whim. They may have some secret strength that they are relying on. But that is for the council—those who remain—and of the League to worry about."

"Mag will be fine," I told Herald gently.

"I know." Her tone said that he'd better be, or she'd find someone to take the blame.

There was a soft babble as everyone agreed with various levels of conviction, which sputtered into an awkward silence. Into that silence Kira spoke, suddenly and in halting Karakani. She looked around the room. "Draka, ah . . . more big?"

The babble came back, stronger now that everyone was relieved to have a less depressing topic to talk about. Over the course of the day I'd already received plenty of looks telling me that they'd all noticed, but Kira was the first since Tam to bring it up. "Thank you!" I told her, speaking clearly. "Yes, I am *bigger*."

"And that's not all, is it?" Mak said. She grinned, a mad gleam in her eye, and looked at Herald who gave her the barest hint of a nod. That was all the warning we had before she drew a knife from her belt and slashed it across her own arm. It was fast enough that no one could move to stop her, but slow enough that we could all see the skin crease around the edge. It left behind an indentation and a line of fine, cut hair, and that was all.

The room exploded with noise. Tam and Val protesting and grabbing the knife from Mak. Kira leaping forward to make sure that Mak wasn't hurt, cursing at her in Tekereteki as she did so. Ardek kept exclaiming, "What the hell? What the hell?!" And Mak and Herald broke out into a shared fit of laughter.

I was as surprised as the rest of them, though not for the same reason. When we'd grabbed Tark I'd seen Mak take a cut along the neck, leaving only a shallow scratch behind. I knew that my own upgrade to greater fortitude would make her more impervious to harm as well. I just hadn't expected her and Herald to have planned something like this, nor the delight they clearly took in having freaked the hell out of everyone present. It was a side of them that I'd rarely seen before. It was fun, and nice to see them laughing, especially since everyone else joined in when it was clear that Mak wasn't at all hurt.

"So, I passed a threshold this morning," I told them. "And I think you all know by now that Mak inherits my own minor advancements. We're both a good bit tougher now, as she so kindly demonstrated."

Mak grinned impishly and Tam flicked her on the forehead, sparking some half-hearted protests. "If no one else has any pranks planned," he said, pausing to look around before turning to me, "would you tell us about your trip? From what Mak's been telling us, it sounds like you had an exciting time."

"Yeah, you could say that," I agreed, and went into the tale of my journey to the border, starting from when I'd discovered who my traveling companions were.

"We figured that out easy enough," Mak said, "since all three disappeared the same day you did. But even if we hadn't, the lady justice sent a message two days after you left. Not *quite* apologizing, but asking me to contact her to arrange a meeting between the two of you once you got back. Which I'll do tomorrow, if that's all right with you? With any luck she's still alive to reply."

I agreed, then got back to the story. I hoped that Sempralia had made it. I really wanted her to explain herself.

Herald translated for Kira, as usual, and when I got to the part with the Silver Spurs, our healer's eyes slowly fixed themselves on the floor. She'd told me once that there was no one alive in the mercenary company that she cared about, but I'd never really believed her. They'd abused her, forcing her to be part of things that went completely against her nature, but she wasn't the type to hold grudges. And she'd been with them for years. She knew everyone in that company to some degree, and if she'd taken the death of a number of them with anything other than sadness, I would have been much more shocked than I'd been at Mak's bit of fun.

When I told them how I'd returned the captured mercenaries, and convinced their commander, Sarahem, to take her remaining troops back to Happar without further bloodshed, Kira released a shuddering breath and looked up again, eyes full of gratitude. Ardek put his arm around her, and she leaned into him. I blinked a few times, as though that might change what I was seeing, then just accepted it. No one else batted an eye, so I figured it must have been going on for a while. I'd just missed it.

Ah, well, I thought. *Good for them.*

"Leretem was always an outsider," Kira told me. She spoke in her own dialect, and my sisters listened intently, trying to understand. Tam paid polite attention, but he was still struggling with relearning classical Tekereteki. *"She was as bad as the rest of them, doing what she was told without complaint, but she never fit in with the rest. We talked a little. She was from some little village up in the mountains of my province. I wonder . . . You remember how I told you that there are still some that hold to the old ways?"*

"Dragon worshippers?"

"Yeah." She didn't elaborate. She didn't need to.

They were all shocked and angry about the homing medallion, of course. But they also agreed with General Sarvalian that it probably wasn't Sempralia who'd had it put in the message case. Both because it didn't make any sense, and because she hadn't mentioned it in her letter. She'd apologized, sort of, for surprising me with Garal, Lalia, and Maglan. So why, they reasoned, wouldn't she have done the same for inviting an attack?

Why, indeed? All I knew was that she'd better have a good excuse ready for me if I saw her again.

I skipped ahead quickly after that, only touching on talking to Herald and then going to the Forum once I returned to the city.

"I can't believe you did that," Tam said, shaking his head with a smile. "What happened to the secretive dragon we met just a few months ago?"

"I'd already shown myself to every officer in the army," I said with a shrug. "Secrecy and hiding is not a thing anymore, though I'd prefer not to pull too much attention to you all. Anyway . . ."

Of all that came after that, up until the part where I returned to the inn, it was my tactics against the White Cranes that got the biggest response. "The possibilities!" Val said, alight with enthusiasm. "A catapult may be able to throw larger stones, but the precision! One large stone was effective, clearly, but consider a net with many fist-sized ones. You could disrupt a whole section of a line! Or a bag full of even smaller stones, dropped on a camp at night. They wouldn't cause much harm, but they'd damage equipment, crack storage pots, make holes in tents, frighten animals . . . That's not even mentioning what you could do with alchemical concoctions . . ."

He went on like that for a while. I wasn't entirely sure about his background—he didn't like to talk about it—but strategy and tactics were apparently interests of his.

As for their side of the story, I'd already learned everything I needed to know about the previous night from Herald and Mak. That left the previous ten days.

"I got your horn back from Kalder," Herald told me. She could barely look at me, she was so embarrassed. "I burned it in the fireplace."

"And thanks for that, by the way, Kitten. Made the whole common room stink like burned hair the whole afternoon," Tam complained with a disgusted face. "Hope we never have to do that again."

"Good," I laughed with relief. "Glad to know that's out of the way. What else?"

"Kesra came by on the same day we got the lady justice's letter. She wanted to talk to you," Mak said. "She seemed disappointed when I told her you didn't want anything to do with them."

"Kesra? Not Zabra?"

"Yeah, Kesra apologized on her sister's behalf. Apparently the older sister is unwell."

"She hasn't left that house in the high city since you let her out," Ardek added. "She goes out into the sun, sometimes. Or, well, she did until the rains started. But . . . yeah."

"Still?"

"Ten days now, and I've always got someone watching the house. Unless they have a secret tunnel or something, she's been in there since you left."

"Huh." I could only suppose that I'd shaken her even more than I'd intended to. And I didn't feel a shred of guilt over it. "All right, what did Kesra have to say?"

"Nothing new," Mak said. "They're getting their books in order, it might take a while to gather the money without looking suspicious, things like that. I got the impression that she just wanted to show that they're cooperating."

"And how did she seem to be doing?"

"Not great. She's not happy with her sister. That's obvious whenever Zabra comes up. And she looked beyond tired, like she hasn't been sleeping much. Almost like she just found out that her sister's a crime lord, and now she has to deal with everything on her own after said sister had a mental breakdown. Like that."

"Right." I felt a little worse about that, but it was impossible to tell if it was because I still genuinely believed that Kesra was mostly innocent in all this, or if it was a lingering effect of her advancement making me want her to be happy. "I'm going to need to talk to them both," I decided. "I don't care if Zabra never steps outside again, but I don't want her organization collapsing if you all think it can make us some money."

Mak nodded. "I do think so, but the way Kesra looked . . . Yeah, I think it would be best if Zabra were back in charge, or if they could at least share the load. Of course, if they do lose everything . . ." She shrugged.

"Unfortunate, but good riddance," Herald agreed.

"Ah, I don't know." Ardek spoke up, less confidently than before now that he was contradicting Mak on . . . well, anything. "I know we talked about this before, yeah? If the Night Blossom disappears, if her organization goes to shit, things are gonna be bad while her territory and her property get carved up. Like, lots-of-people-ending-up-in-the-river bad. And a lot of those people won't have had anything to do with it."

"I'll talk to them," I reassured him. "I'm sure I can get Zabra back to doing her job."

Not much else had happened until the previous night. Kesra had come one more time, three days earlier, again asking for me, and again just to show that they were complying with our conditions. Other than that, there had only been one other thing of note, and they'd been saving it for when we were finishing up.

"So, we've spent a bit of money on the inn," Mak began, and her face was strained that way some people get when they're trying not to smile and losing. "And a bit extra to get it done quickly, to be honest. We wanted it done before you got back, and since we had no idea when—"

"It was Tam's idea!" Herald burst out, beaming at her brother. "The weather made a mess of things, but we can still show you and you can try it later!"

"Show me what?" Their excitement was getting me worked up, and curiosity had always been one of my vices. I couldn't help but laugh. "You're going to have to let me in on the secret right now!"

"Come on, Tam. You do the honors," Mak told her brother, and he happily complied, getting to his feet.

"This way, then," he said, waving his hand at the small doorway which led to the strongroom and the smaller storage room which was our improvised cell.

As he led the way, I thought that he must be leading us to the strongroom, and I wondered what I could have possibly missed. I'd spent most of the day there, after all. It was a surprise when he instead opened the other door, the one to the cell.

The sound of rushing water, the constant noise that I'd long since filtered out, became louder.

A heavy wooden hatch, banded with what might be bronze, sat in the middle of the floor, the stone around it still bearing chisel marks.

"No!" I exclaimed happily. It was all I could think to say.

"Oh, yes!" Tam replied, opening the heavy hatch. The sound of rushing water became a roar. Underneath the hatch was a set of bars, spaced wide enough for me to get through when I was shifted. "It goes into the storm drains, as you can probably guess. Stonework the whole way. Now, it's not a smuggler's tunnel. Not like the ones you found. The bars are intended to be permanent, so no one can get through except you. And snakes and rats and such, which is why we have the hatch. But this way, if we expect you to be coming, we can just leave the hatch open and you can come and go this way. Even if you go fully public, you can use this way for privacy. No more waiting around in the yard, no worrying about being watched. If you're carrying something big you'll still have to come through the door, I guess, but—"

"I love it! How did you get it done so fast?"

"Ardek knows a guy who knows a guy. And it's not illegal to put a drain in your cellar, especially not when you block it off properly so that it's definitely not a smuggler's tunnel . . . not that we intend to report its existence."

"Nah, yeah, I get that." I looked around the small group. They'd clearly all known, and were just as clearly delighted with how much I liked the surprise. "Thank you all. It's lovely."

It was a literal hole in the ground, but as always it was the thought and the message that counted. I'd always had to wait for someone to let me in. This way I could come and go mostly as I pleased, and it was at once a small but significant step toward making me truly feel at home at the Favor. A little like being given a key to someone's apartment when you've been staying with them for a while; a move from just being a guest to someone who lives there.

"You all are the best humans, the best family, that a dragon could wish for," I told them, meaning every word. They had given me a hole in the ground, and it meant the world to me.

CHAPTER FIFTY-THREE

Heart to Heart

I took a quick look down the new drain in our cellar before they left, confirming that I could fit between the bars with ease. It was stonework all the way down as far as I could tell, and I wondered again just how they'd gotten it done so quickly. The obvious answer was "magic craftsmen," but still!

I also deliberately avoided wondering what they'd paid for it.

The drain slanted down to the storm drains, which were, of course, half full of water. The city was several square miles, and while much of it drained into the river, most went into the drains. There were only a few, three or possibly four, outlets, and being in the mercantile district, near the harbor, we were near one.

I decided to turn back. I couldn't go onto or into the water; it played all kinds of havoc with my magic, exhausting me quickly and forcing me to shift back. The newly built drain that I was in was at most a foot and a half wide, and I had no interest in finally finding out what would happen if I shifted back in a space where I couldn't physically fit. I'd done it under a bed once, and it had been knocked into the air with some force. With only stone and packed earth around me, though, I suspected that my body would yield before the walls did. And while I could have gone into the water and shifted back there, that would have forced me to go through an outlet and then back to the inn. Fine if I was leaving, but for now I wanted to get back inside as fast as possible.

After again telling them all how happy their gift made me, my humans returned upstairs. All except for Herald and Mak, whom I asked to stay behind.

"Right, so, let's start with the most important thing," I told them. "Kira and Ardek? Am I reading that right?"

"Ah . . . we think so?" Herald said tentatively, turning to Mak, who nodded. "I do not think that anyone has asked them outright—"

"Yeah. Not even Tam," Mak added.

"Right. Not even Tam. We are all curious but do not want to . . . somehow spoil it, I suppose. They are so cute together!"

"Yeah. Don't want to make them self-conscious, but they've been spending a lot of time together. All the time they can, really," Mak said, turning to Herald. "And they've been very touchy for the last, what? Two weeks? Three? Since before Draka left."

"About that, yes," Herald confirmed.

"And they really like each other?" I asked. "Kira really likes him? It's not just his advancement?"

"Nah," she said confidently. "Lots of people like Ardek. Kira is the only one making moon eyes at him."

"I'm pretty sure I caught them kissing in the kitchen a few days ago," Mak said, "but I don't think it's gone any further than that. Kira hasn't asked me or anyone else about . . . you know. At least as far as I know." She mimed drinking something and looked at Herald, who blushed.

"The maiden's friend?"

"That, yes. And I know that she has a background as a midwife's apprentice, so she should know better."

"Ah. About that," I said. There must have been something in my tone, because they both suddenly looked at me very intently. "Kira may have told me that she really, really wants to have kids. A lot of them. And I told her that I won't get in the way of her being happy."

"Oh." Mak's voice was flat as she looked in the direction of the stairs. "Perhaps I should have a word with her? Just in case? Make sure that she's sure?"

"Ardek, too," Herald said. "*If* something is going on, he should know."

"Yeah," Mak sighed. "Tomorrow?"

"Tomorrow," Herald agreed.

"Tomorrow," I echoed. "If that's what they want, though . . . don't pressure them, all right? Just make sure they've thought it through and talked about it. Which, I mean . . . can they really talk to each other?"

Mak shook her head. "Gods only know. Kira's Karakani is getting better, but she's like a four-year-old on her best days. And Ardek's Tekereteki is . . . Well, I'm impressed he's learned any at all in the time since he started."

We looked at each other. "Ah," Herald said. "Maybe you should talk to them sooner. Like right now. Just in case."

The next day I awoke with the need really starting to make itself known, the threads that would lead me to distant Nest Hearts strong in my awareness. I forced it down; it was an annoyance, nothing more.

That day we sent a reply to Sempralia's letter. It was just me and Mak in the cellar, with everyone else keeping busy despite the rain that just kept falling—Herald was out, following Kesra around. I didn't like it, and she didn't like being out in the rain, but she was also pretty damn well suited for the job, and she had insisted. She wanted the practice, she said.

We planned a simple message, saying that I would be more than happy to meet with the lady justice, and that there were things I wanted to discuss with her. Things that had come to light after I departed, and which I would very much have preferred to know about beforehand.

"Tell her that we can meet in the same place as our first meeting," I told Mak. My handwriting was atrocious, despite my practice, while hers was practically a work of art. "And that we can decide on a time once the rain lets up."

Mak's pen stopped, and she looked up from the small writing desk she'd brought into the cellar. "Are you sure that you want to put it off for that long?" she asked. "Or do you mean that we should try to arrange it for a lull?"

"What?"

"You know, the . . ." She trailed off. "Oh, right. You don't know, do you? Draka, the rains won't stop for some time. We hadn't expected them for a while yet, but now that they've started, it could be weeks!"

"Weeks? It's going to keep raining for weeks?!"

"Well, yes. It's like this every year. Isn't that true where you're from?"

"Nah! I mean, there are months that are wetter than others, and sometimes you'll have four or five days in a row and catch a couple of inches, but not like this! Fuck me dead, Mak, this is some Darwin shit!"

Mak blinked at me rapidly. The corners of her mouth spasmed, her face contorting as she fought to keep herself from grinning. I got the distinct impression that she wanted to say something heinous, but she got herself under control, barely. "I'm going to assume that you don't mean that literally. And I have no idea what a 'Darwin' is."

"I'm not sure I want to know where your mind just went, Mak." I looked at her impassively, doing my best not to give anything away. Not that it mattered when she could feel what I did. Every so often she would jerk, little hiccups of suppressed laughter that got closer and closer until she was practically vibrating, her eyes shut tightly so that she couldn't see the oh-so-serious face I was making. "You're thinking something dirty, aren't you?"

"Yes!" she tittered, clamping down hard to keep from breaking down.

"We're writing a serious letter here, you know? Important stuff. Official correspondence or whatever with a lady justice."

"Mmm-hm! Sorry!"

There were tears at the corners of her eyes, and I decided that this had gone on for long enough. "It's fine if you laugh at me, you know that, right?" I told her. "And you know better than anyone that I'm not thin-skinned. I don't need to know what's going through your head, but Mercies' sake, let it out before you kill yourself!"

That finally broke the dam, and she broke into hiccupping laughter. Kneeling as she was, she first folded forward, then lay down sideways on the floor, whining and yelping with laughter over some joke only she understood. Every so often she'd squeak "Fuck me—!" or open her eyes and catch a glimpse of me, and she'd break into renewed laughter.

I both wished that I knew what she was laughing about, and was glad that I didn't. I suspected that the fact that what I'd said could be interpreted as an order had something to do with it, but from her reaction I was almost afraid to ask.

Once she'd calmed down I lay down, resting my head on the stones in front of her. "You all right there, Mak?"

"I'm—I'm fine," she huffed, still grinning.

I couldn't help but smile back. "You've gotten a lot more relaxed since I've known you, you know that? Ever since you took that advancement, really. You never used to joke much while I was around. You certainly never would have laughed at me like you did just now. And there was that prank last night with the knife. Where's this all coming from?"

She casually reached out and rubbed the nub where my left horn was growing back in. "Should I not?" she asked. Not nervously, just asking for instructions.

"I don't mind at all. The knife thing freaked some of the others out, but c'mon, it was funny! Though I suppose it was mostly funny at their expense, so maybe not too much of that. But, yeah. I like this side of you. I just never expected it."

She hummed happily. "I suppose that I *am* more relaxed. Especially lately. You telling me to get more sleep did wonders for me. I didn't sleep well for years, you know that? Always too much to do, too much to worry about. Now things still get done, but I somehow get a couple of hours of extra sleep each night. I'll think, *Oh, I should go to bed*, and I just do it. And then, miracle of miracles, I *fall asleep*! Even these last two days, with all the chaos. Perhaps I leave some of the worrying to you. I may be the head of the family, officially, but we both know how things stand, and so do the others. So I just . . . I let you be the responsible one. Even if I'm the one making the decisions and giving the orders, I know that if anything goes wrong I can rely on you to fix it."

Her smile turned a little guilty. "Sorry. Perhaps that makes me a bad . . . whatever I am to you. Expecting you to clean up any mess I make that's too big for me to handle. But I feel safe. Knowing that you're out there, feeling your satisfaction, your happiness, even your annoyance and your rage; it gives me a sense of calm and security that I haven't felt since before my father died." There was a long pause, and she asked, "Did we ever tell you about him?"

"No."

"I think you would have liked him. He was so kind and gentle, but he was a big man. He was tall—Herald had to get it from somewhere—and he was so strong. Even as a foreigner from a hated enemy nation, nobody dared anger him. I always thought that he was invincible."

She sighed. "Then he got sick, and he died. Things were bad for so many years, and I was so afraid. All the time, you know? Keeping a roof over our heads, keeping everyone fed and clothed, I was so afraid that I'd fail them and . . . Well, you heard Tark. I did things I'm not proud of, for a meal or a gift or just for money, so that Tam and Herald could have just a little bit more. I'd like to say that I'm not ashamed of anything I did, but I've been lying to Herald about it for years, so . . . yeah. And then there was Val, and Lalia and Garal, and things got better. We had enough money for three meals a day and all for a while, but that brought a different fear, you know? A fear that we'd lose it all, or that someone would get hurt so bad that I couldn't help them. And then Tam got into trouble. I could see everything crashing down . . . and you saved us. I couldn't admit it to myself at the start. I only saw another new fear, of losing Herald to something I didn't understand. But all you did was save us. You saved our lives, and Tam's freedom, and you brought us wealth and social standing and . . ."

She was smiling again by that point, and sniffling. The stone her cheek rested on was wet. "I know that my thoughts and feelings are not my own when it comes to you, and I don't care. I don't care, because I'm not afraid any more. Even while the Cranes were breaking down our door I wasn't afraid. I knew that you'd come. I could feel your worry, and I could feel you getting closer, and I knew that we only needed to hold on until you got here. Even if we had to fall back to the cellar, you'd come, and we'd be fine. And, I know they left before you arrived. It doesn't matter. If I hadn't known that you were coming, if the others hadn't known that help was on its way, we might have despaired and given in. But we didn't. Because we have you, and fear . . . It's not an enemy. Fear belongs to you, just like we do. It doesn't touch us anymore."

She sniffled loudly, then let out a shuddering breath. "I'm sorry. I'm rambling, and I'm being melodramatic. I've *been afraid*. Of course I have. I've been terrified. In the beginning, and when you took me flying, and when you got hurt . . . but I haven't *lived in fear*. I haven't had that weight crushing me for months now, and it's thanks to you. Understand?"

I'd laid there, silently listening as she bared her heart, and I didn't know what to say. So instead I shuffled up closer and cocooned us both inside my wings, wrapping myself around her. If someone had come down the stairs while we lay there, I wouldn't have cared. They'd find out about the dragon in the cellar sooner or later. It may as well be today. The letter lay half-finished on the writing desk. It could wait.

I don't know how long we lay there. Not too long. But we lay in silence long enough for me to gather my thoughts and put them in order, and to make peace with how I felt. And finally, after searching my heart to make sure that I was being honest with myself and with her, I found the right words.

"I forgive you, Mak."

She didn't go stiff with surprise. She didn't ask me if I was serious, or if I was joking. She didn't say anything. There was no need; she could feel what I felt. All she did was bury her face in the scales of my long neck and cry, with great, heaving, silent sobs.

"I love you, little dragon, and I forgive you."

We managed to finish up the letter and send it out. We left it to Sempralia to suggest a location which, by her judgment, should be acceptable to both parties, and at her earliest convenience. Ardek volunteered as messenger, running up to the Palace and delivering our letter himself, along with the one Sarvalian sent with me. He had firm instructions not to hand over either unless it was to the lady justice personally. He told us later that he'd waited there for over an hour, until finally Kalder, Sempralia's personal guard, came to escort him.

Ardek happily admitted that he'd been utterly terrified. The lady justice had, apparently, been amused.

Her reply came early the next day. She offered to meet the day after that, on the roof of the tallest building—not counting towers—in the upper city. After my visit to the Forum, as she put it, there was little need to leave the city for our meeting.

I didn't really know the building. I'd seen it from the air, of course. It was a large, imposing building, which reminded me of a cathedral from back on Earth, with a high wall separating it from the rest of the city. Val told me that it was ancient, nearly untouched by the cataclysm and thought to once have been a palace. Now it belonged to the city, and no one knew much beyond that. It was strictly off limits. But since we'd be on the roof, no one had any objections to it as a meeting place.

I didn't distrust Sempralia anymore, as such. I'd cooled down. I needed some answers from her, but I didn't think that she'd do anything stupid. I still took a quick, miserable recon flight the night before the meeting, circling the fortress on the hill a few times. The roof space we'd use belonged to the central building, about a hundred yards long and thirty wide. It was wide open, with two cupolas as wide as the building at each end of the long, rectangular space. No place for anyone to hide except for behind those cupolas. It would do.

When I arrived for the meeting, eight or nine hours later, they'd set up an open-sided pavilion made of what looked like sail cloth to keep the rain off. It only covered about a quarter of the roof, leaving most of it wide open for an easy landing. I appreciated that; the rain, as always, had me in a bit of a mood, and I didn't want to stay in it for longer than necessary.

The pavilion turned out to be tall enough that I could sit up straight and even spread my wings comfortably. I came in fast, landing hard and making half the poor humans there jump when I skidded the last few yards into the shelter. It probably didn't help that I came in with my body low, ready to continue right through them if I didn't like what I saw. That was the problem with the pavilion; I hadn't been able to see who or how many of them there were.

Fortunately for all of us, the first two people I saw were the lady justice and her bodyguard, Kalder. They were not, of course, alone. Besides a handful of people who were obviously just guards or scribes, I recognized three others. The first was the same secretary Sempralia had brought with her to our first meeting, whose name I didn't quite remember. The remaining two were the commander of the city guard and the councilor I'd spoken to in the Forum.

The rain and the nagging need already had me irritable, and I felt a rush of intense annoyance at the uninvited participants, to the point where I considered just leaving. This was supposed to be a meeting between myself and Sempralia, to discuss things that were just between us. What the hell was the point of meeting on a damn rooftop if she was going to bring along whoever she felt like?

But I wanted this meeting. I wanted to know what she had to say for herself, and I wanted to know what it was they needed my help with. And, in fairness, it wasn't as though I was alone, myself.

There was a tension in the air. I couldn't tell if it had already been there or if I'd caused it with my landing. Maybe they picked up on my annoyance. It certainly wasn't helped by Mak, who'd been half choking the life out of me as she held on, sliding off my back.

Whatever the cause of the tension, I didn't let it rattle me. I'd been advised to always be honest with the lady justice. She was about to get a heaping pile of honesty.

CHAPTER FIFTY-FOUR

A Small Surprise.
A Minor Revelation, Perhaps

Lady justice," I said, looking from Sempralia to the two uninvited guests. "I don't appreciate surprises."

She had the good manners to look chagrined, at least. "Nor do I, Lady Dragon, but I'm afraid that my two colleagues wouldn't take no for an answer. Though I can't help but notice that you yourself have brought someone with you. My lords, may I introduce Lady Drakonum Makanna?"

Mak stood next to me, her heavy leather raincoat dripping onto the stones. She looked momentarily stunned, then quickly swept into a bow, saying, "My apologies, my lady justice. My Lords, it is an honor to meet you."

She stayed bowed like that for a long while. I was about to tell her to get up when the lord commander grunted. "Mercies' sake, is no one going to—Lady Drakonum, please rise. You're embarrassing everyone involved."

Mak quickly unfolded. "I'm sorry, my Lord Commander, I—"

"Yes, yes, no worries. It's not every day you meet three lords and ladies of the council. I get it. Hells, I've been there. For the future, no matter how many of us you meet, a quick bow is enough. Please."

"Of course, my Lord Commander."

"*For Lady Draka's benefit*," Sempralia cut in sharply, "these gentlemen are Lord Commander Barvon and Lord Exchequer Soandel."

I ducked my head. I didn't want them there, but they *were* on the council, and it couldn't hurt to be minimally polite.

"They were *not* invited to this meeting, but it seems some of my staff need a lesson in discretion. They more or less ambushed me this morning."

"Please, Sempralia," the lord commander scoffed. "Lady Draka here came to the Forum, and then a few days later you start arranging for a pavilion on the roof of the citadel. Were we supposed to just sit idle? We didn't even have a chance to introduce ourselves last we met, much less to get to know each other."

"You were *supposed* to let me handle any business between the city and Lady Draka, lest our new dragon ally become irate at any unwelcome participants in our *private* meeting, and unwilling to help us any further!"

The lord exchequer looked at me anxiously. "Ah, forgive us, Lady Draka, for imposing. We mean no insult. We only feel that the stakes are now too high to be handled by a single councilor. Lady Sempralia, as you can imagine, disagreed. We would have put it to a vote, but with sessions temporarily suspended . . ."

"We decided that ambushing her on her way up was the way to go," the lord commander concluded for him.

Sempralia looked at them both sourly. "Again, Lady Draka, I apologize. Can I ask that the meeting proceed despite the intrusion of these tactless old goats?"

"Fine. There were two things we were supposed to talk about, yeah? One, what the hell you were thinking when you sent me south—" Sempralia winced almost imperceptibly at that. "And two, what it was that you were so keen on me helping you with, and if I'm still interested. Anything else?"

"I'd like to talk about why two dozen of my guards have been on rotation watching, and dying to defend, a certain inn," the lord commander said, "but that can wait, I suppose. It's the second of the two issues you mentioned that I'm most interested in, so if we could get the first out of the way . . . ?"

"It's the first that interests me most," I snapped back, "so we can damn well take our time. Sempralia, my traveling companions—why them, and why not just tell me from the start?"

She sighed. "Because for various reasons I expected someone to attempt to intercept my message, and I did not want anyone to know who exactly would be carrying it. Your companions themselves did not know until the morning they left. I especially did not want anyone to know who would be protecting them. As for you, Lady Draka . . . I simply do not know you well enough to be certain that you would be discreet. And I judged that if you were the type to take such offense that you would refuse to work with us afterward, then we would be better off without you."

I sputtered a little at that, but she pressed on. "As for why I chose those particular individuals, it's quite simple. Again, I do not know you well. Beyond a single, admittedly friendly meeting, I've had only the opinions of your close friends and confidants to go on, and I am not well acquainted with them, either. I needed to be sure that you'd stay close and protect the messengers. My people have connected you to the two Wolves. As I understand it you've saved both of their lives, on different occasions. And the young archer has been involved for some time with Lady Drakonum's younger sister, who I know for sure is quite taken with you. I admit that he was something of a gamble, but I needed someone from the army to carry the actual message. It was him or an infantry tribune who was once involved with Mister Valmik."

"And where does the damn tracking medallion come in?"

"Nowhere. You have my word as a lady of the council and a woman of honor that I knew nothing about, and had nothing to do with, that. When General Sarvalian reported that you had been attacked by the same mercenaries that have 'eluded' Commander Rallon and his Wolves so long—"

"'Eluded,' my ass," the lord commander grumbled. "We all know that Rallon would have wiped them out weeks ago if he hadn't been hobbled. Our thanks for dealing with them, by the way."

"On that, we're in full agreement," Sempralia said with a nod to her colleague. "That tracking medallion was handed over to the White Cranes, since they patrolled much farther south than the Wolves, albeit only along the coast. We hoped that they might be able to keep track of these mercenary raiders. How the thing found its way into the message case, which I sealed myself . . . I simply don't know. Kalder handed it directly to your young archer friend's commander, who passed it on directly. I trust Kalder implicitly. The commander has been questioned at length by our finest interrogators and found entirely innocent of both wrongdoing and carelessness. I don't suppose that the young archer in question could have the skills to recreate an official seal?"

Mak laughed, a short, musical burst before she covered her mouth and looked down in embarrassment.

"Lady Drakonum? Anything you wish to share?"

"No, no. Mag?" Mak cleared her throat and tried to be serious, but her mirth still tugged at the corners of her mouth. "It just seems unlikely, that's all."

"Quite. With all that said, Lady Draka, despite this slight, you still chose to fulfill your side of the agreement. General Sarvalian was quite clear about his satisfaction, both in his regular reports and in the message that I understand you brought north. I believe that we can work together, and so, I hope, do my colleagues." Sempralia looked at the two lords, who both nodded. "The question is, are you willing?"

That was the question, wasn't it? Was I satisfied with her excuses? I wasn't sure. But the whole mess had left me in a stronger position. That tension that I'd felt at the beginning of the meeting, which had broken once we started talking, was back. They were anxious. Nervous. They wanted my cooperation, and they were worried that I'd refuse. They weren't even pretending to negotiate. They were in a bad position, and they didn't care if I knew it.

Sempralia had told me that there was something I was uniquely suited to helping with, but now I got a feel for just how important it was to them.

I looked down at Mak, who nodded and gave me a small, predatory grin. The message was clear: "Squeeze them."

"Very well," I told the three councilors. "Tell me what the problem is and what you want me to do about it, and I'll tell you what I want in return."

"Ah, well, Lady Draka, you see, it's quite simple." I turned my head from Sempralia as the lord exchequer, who had mostly stood silent, spoke. His voice was shaky and he looked almost sick, but neither of the others interrupted him. "The problem is that there is a dragon heading our way. And we want you to help us."

For a long while the only sound was the rapid drumming of rain on the taut cloth above us.

"You're serious?" I asked hoarsely. "And you're sure?"

"Serious as the pox, and sure as death, Lady Draka."

Another dragon. My mind went momentarily blank as I tried to decide how I felt about it. As I aimlessly scanned the assembled staff, I became aware of how none of the guards, scribes, nor anyone else accompanying the councilors seemed at all surprised. Sempralia and her colleagues must trust these people implicitly, I decided. They probably knew all kinds of things. Like how there was another dragon on its way here.

I was elated and terrified and curious and outraged. There hadn't been a dragon on Mallin for centuries, or so I'd been told. Not since my father died, was my guess. I hadn't actually expected to ever meet one, and that had been a source of both relief and disappointment. Now the council wanted me to help them deal with one. Somehow.

What did they expect me to do? Talk to them? Was that even possible? I'd been told that I was much more intelligent than anyone expected, and I was pretty average. I could admit that much. Could a normal dragon be reasoned with?

Or were they expecting me to fight them? Surely not. They knew as well as I did that I was bloody tiny compared to an adult dragon. I remembered how big my father had been in my memories, and the size of his teeth. He must have stood ten feet tall at the shoulder and weighed literal tons! I couldn't fight something like that, advancements be damned. An adult dragon would rip me to shreds without even slowing down, and that was assuming they didn't roast me in the air.

But would I even have a choice? Why were they coming here? Did they want to carve out a territory? This was my island. Instinct and everything else in me that was draconic recoiled at the idea of sharing it with another of my kind, especially one I didn't know. I wouldn't have it. No dragon would; I knew that in my bones.

If anyone, *anything* tried to take this island from me, I'd fight. I'd have to. My hoard was here. My humans, too.

I'd fight. I just prayed it wouldn't come to that, because I didn't see how I could possibly win.

Everyone was looking at me. I'd been silent for too long, and now the humans were nervous. They couldn't read me, I realized. They didn't know if I was scared or shocked or offended, and they were all braced for how I might respond to the lord exchequer's request.

A small, firm hand on my neck snapped me out of it. Mak looked up at me, and all I saw on her face was her faith in me. She didn't say a word. She just smiled and nodded, then lifted her hand and patted me twice, hard, as if to say, "You've got this. You'll figure it out." And I'd better, hadn't I? It wasn't like I could run.

I gave her the slightest nod back and turned to the councilors. They were waiting patiently, Sempralia calm and collected, Lord Commander Barvon full of anxious energy, and Lord Exchequer Soandel looking like he was on the verge of a panic attack.

"Yeah, all right," I said, relaxing onto the stone roof. The tension melted away as I settled in. "Tell me everything you know."

Two hours later, my humans and I sat silent in the cellar. I'd just finished telling them about the meeting, with Mak's help to fill in details that I'd missed, forgotten, or hadn't understood the significance of.

The mood was tense and uncertain, and there was quite a bit of wine being knocked back by everyone except Mak.

There was another dragon coming to Mallin. There was no doubt about it. No room for any kind of misunderstanding.

"The world is vast," Sempralia had begun. "So large that if you tried to explain it to the average citizen, they wouldn't believe you. The mind boggles at the scale. There exist people and nations in places so far away, that to travel there even by the fastest ships would take months. The city of Karakan, even the entire League, and those nations have little real interest in each other. We are each aware that the other exists, but our people do not mingle. There is no trade, except by fourth, fifth, or sixth hand. Yet we stay in contact, because some events are too big not to warn each other about.

"A few days before I contacted you, Lady Drakonum, asking for a meeting with you, Draka, a dragon was seen several thousands of miles to the northeast. That itself is nothing terribly unusual, since dragons are more common in some areas than in others. But this one was a true monster, massive in size and with fiery brass scales, and so far as anyone knew, it belongs hundreds of miles north of where it was seen. As you may imagine, those who live in areas where dragons are prolific keep quite meticulous records of such things, and the news went out via sending circle to anyone who would listen. Then, the day before I sent that message the same dragon was reported a few hundred miles southwest of the first location, on a line that, if it continued, would bring it close to us and not much else. And so, I penned that letter."

"That early?" I'd asked. "Wasn't that risky, getting involved with me just in case this dragon kept moving? What if they stopped somewhere, or turned back?"

"Lady Draka, the moment you revealed yourself the council began discussing what should be done with you. Based on the testimony of your friends we decided that you should be explored as an opportunity rather than a threat, and that it was better to try and make you an ally than attempt to dispose of you. In any case, the dragon did not turn around, though it appears to stop for several days for every few hundred miles it travels. It kept moving along that same line, and while you were on your way south with my messengers it became all but certain that it was heading here.

"The last report we had was two days before the Cranes' treachery. It placed the dragon some two thousand miles away. And at the pace it's been going, we have two weeks before it arrives, give or take a day or three."

There had been no more reports of the dragon since, for one simple, devastating reason—the Cranes' attack on the Palace had been successful. I'd wondered why they attacked the place at night, when only the night guards were there, and now I knew. Their goal had not been the council, but the magical sending circle that allowed the city's leaders to communicate instantly with others around the world. The large, complex enchantment had been smashed beyond repair, and they couldn't tell me how long it might take to replace. Herald, when I asked her, guessed months, and that was once they brought together a group of enchanters capable of performing the work.

All in all, Karakan was in a tough spot. The city was cut off, forced to rely on messages sent by ship to communicate with its allies. It was under attack by an enemy that was in theory weaker, but which was now confident enough to go on the offensive. And, on top of that, there was a dragon coming, one that was seemingly on a mission, traveling thousands of miles across the world to come here. One which was, by all accounts, a giant among our kind. The kind of creature that, if the histories were to be believed, could destroy cities and bring down nations.

The dragon even had a name. None of the councilors knew if it was their real name, or just what they were called, but it didn't matter much.

The dragon was known as Reaper.

It was no wonder that the council was so anxious for my help. Could they fight a dragon? Perhaps, but the price of failure was too high to bear thinking about. Instead they hoped to negotiate, to find out what Reaper wanted and possibly buy them off. And they wanted me to be their representative.

I'd told them that I'd think about it. We were meeting again at the same place in two days. Two days to decide if I was going up against another dragon.

"So," Herald said, "how much are you going to demand?"

"Hmm?" I was so lost in my own thoughts that her question didn't register.

"They want you to put your life on the line for the sake of a city that does not officially recognize you as a person. In the best case, you successfully see this other dragon, Reaper, off. How you accomplish that does not matter. In the worst case . . . Let us not dwell on that. No matter what, you will have risked everything and inconvenienced yourself significantly. So how much are you going to demand?"

"Oh, right. I hadn't thought much about it."

That was a bit of a lie. I'd thought about it a lot. I just hadn't tried to figure out what I could reasonably get away with.

"You should let them make the first offer," Tam said. "Or open with something obscene, like fifty pounds of gold."

Next to me Herald snorted, sputtered, then began coughing in earnest as she choked on her wine. Her golden eyes were ringed with pink and had the most avaricious gleam in them I'd ever seen as she wiped her mouth and looked at me. "Do it!" she said hoarsely. "Ask them for fifty pounds of gold! Let them negotiate you down to ten if you have to, but do it!"

"I thought you were a patriot," I said, chuckling. "That you were grateful to this city for giving your family a chance. You want me to rob your city blind?"

"What else is our tax money supposed to go to, if not to assure the security of the city?" Val asked, to a chorus of agreement from the others.

"They already owe you for warning them that the Happarans were crossing the river," Mak said. "Did I tell you what they offered us for your help in the south? One year of tax exemption. It's ridiculous! Skin them!"

"Hear, hear!" Tam toasted from where he sat, nestled in Val's arms. Wine sloshed onto the floor from his full cup. "Get our damn hundred-and-twenty eagles back, too, while you're at it!"

Outside, winter crept closer as the rain continued to hammer down. In the city people stayed inside as much as they could, as the council dealt with the damage wrought by the betrayal of the Cranes. Meanwhile, Tespril Kesra, the sister of the Night Blossom, struggled to keep her sister's organization under control and to comply with our demands. In the north, nearly forgotten as the southern border heated up and ignited, communities were devastated and evacuated as monsters pushed the frontier back into settled lands. In the south, soldiers died in the first open movements of a war whose purpose we didn't know, and which on paper the invaders were doomed to lose.

Somewhere in the northeast a dragon, a *real* dragon, not whatever I was, came closer every few days. I was going to have to face them. I could only pray that this Reaper could be reasoned or bargained with, or my time in this place might be cut short.

But that day—and it was a long day, which extended into the evening as Garal and Lalia joined us, dripping wet, fresh from reporting to Rallon, and bringing Rib and Pot with them—we did our best to forget our worries and the struggles to come. We talked, and joked, and laughed, and we played stupid games and ate and drank too much and were generally irresponsible.

If we were lucky, there would be time enough to worry in the future, once we were out of the shadow of the dragon.

EPILOGUE

Sower of Embers, Reaper of Flame

Sower of Embers, Reaper of Flame awoke in a cavern she'd carved for herself. It was a slow, ponderous thing, waking up. Awareness came in a multitude of trickles; an ache here, a bothersome noise there, and the pleasant scent of cooling stone all around her. Then the many different connections, pulling her every which way—her hoard, of course, safe deep beneath a mountain some few hundreds of miles to the north; the rifts, wellsprings of life and power, in every direction but nowhere as concentrated as where she was going; and her offspring, spread across the world and decreasing in number between every period of wakefulness.

It occurred to her that it had been a long time, too long, since she'd laid a clutch of eggs. Unconsciously and by old habit she felt around her, finding two males within the thousand miles or so that her senses reached. It was a somewhat embarrassing advancement that she'd taken in her younger, wilder days. It was not one that she'd readily admit to another dragon, but neither did she regret it. Life was for living, after all.

Ah, but she didn't have time for that. Later, on the return trip, perhaps, but not now.

She stretched and found the space too small to spread her wings. She'd carved it too quickly. With a rumble of displeasure she turned around, stepping out onto the mountainside and into the autumn sun. It was a beautifully clear day, and free of the cramped hole she spread her wings wide, basking there for a few long, glorious moments. She'd chosen the southern side of the mountain for just this reason; there was nothing to wake you up after a few days' sleep like a good bask. She would like to have slept outside in the first place—nothing would have dared bother her, and sleeping in the sun and under the stars always brought such pleasant dreams. But it had been raining when she decided to rest, and she could abide neither flying nor sleeping in the rain.

Once she'd had her fill of the calm of the mountain and the morning sun she continued her journey. Embers rarely left her territory anymore, but this trip was special.

Months ago, in late spring, as her rivers ran wide and fast with melting snow and green filled her valleys, she'd felt something stir in the southwest. At first it had been so strange and so faint that she'd ignored it, and it had blinked out as quickly as it had appeared. But as the weeks and months passed it had come back, again and again, for minutes or hours at a time, becoming stronger and more unmistakably familiar until she could ignore it no longer.

Embers knew where all her offspring were at all times. It wasn't particularly useful now, but when you had a nest full of yearling whelps, crawling everywhere they could reach, getting into every crack and crevice and eager to take to the air, it was indispensable. She'd had the same sense for a few favored members of her flock, too, though it had been some time now since she'd felt that connection with a human. What she had felt, far to the southwest, was unmistakably one of her children. But all of her surviving children were accounted for, and none of them had their territories in that direction. This one was new, and had come from nowhere. And it kept fading in and out. It made no sense, and Embers was going to investigate.

If her destination was the island she thought it was, then it was a place she remembered well. She had spent some time there, long ago in her more adventurous days, cavorting with a delightful male. He Who Darkens the Night had been a bit small, perhaps, and not very strong of body, but he'd made up for it in cunning, interesting magical talents, and the size of the flock he'd gathered. His form and coloration had been particularly pleasing as well—lithe and black as the deepest night. None of that speckled stone gray that was so common these days. He'd been beautiful.

Their time together had resulted in a clutch of eggs, as such things were wont to do. She'd left them with him; she laid them in his territory, after all, and they'd both known that he'd be getting bitey soon. Never mind that she'd laid the things; old, stupid instincts die hard. She'd accidentally maimed a male or two herself when she was broody. So, she'd returned to her hoard to rest and tend her flock for a few years, with a promise to return when the whelps had hatched.

She'd never seen them again. Over the centuries since, Embers had often wondered what happened to that male, and their clutch. Perhaps he'd perished in the cataclysm that had awoken her, and which had scoured the island, but she doubted it. Humans and other low creatures, certainly; there was only so much wild magic they could survive, after all, the poor things. But a dragon? A dragon, so close, would have feasted. Even if the whelps had not yet learned to feed on magic when it happened, they should have felt only a comforting warmth. Night would have glutted himself, and been all the stronger for it.

No, something else must have happened. When Embers had reached the island to investigate why she couldn't feel any connection to either Night or their brood, her suspicion naturally fell on the multitude of humans who had populated the place. Only humans or another dragon could have killed Night, small though he was, and she doubted any dragon strong enough to defeat him would have been able to catch him or pursue him into the narrow tunnels of his mountain lair.

That left the humans.

The human population had been absolutely devastated. Even so, she'd considered venting her displeasure on the survivors. It was not the first clutch she'd lost, but it stung nonetheless, and it was an insult that demanded retribution. Worse, she'd *liked* Night, and had hoped to have a few more clutches with him, perhaps settling their young in territories that linked their own, like some other dragons did. It would have been a pleasant arrangement. Comfortable. She'd daydreamed about it, and now it was not to be. Someone needed to pay for taking her dreams away.

When she'd passed over the ruins that had been mighty cities, though, she'd changed her mind. The humans had been in such a pitiful state that she instead chose to leave them to their struggles. Their ships were all gone, either sunk or fled. They were beset by monsters, spawned from the bounty of rifts that had opened all over the island. Their fields and orchards were wilted and overgrown, their herds gone feral and ravaged by animals that had not only survived, but absorbed the unleashed magic, and had grown to impressive sizes and levels of power. She could have reduced their ruins to slag and their remaining crops to ash, but there was no point. They were already dying.

She'd eaten well of the empowered wildlife, glutted herself on rifts, and then abandoned the island and its inhabitants to the worst punishment she could imagine—life in a place they no longer ruled.

Centuries later, she was now returning. She flew high above the clouds, where the air was so delightfully cool and the sun bright, keeping at a leisurely pace. She felt no rush, which was fortunate. She was large, even among others of her kind of similar age, and flying so far was strenuous. Flying quickly when she didn't have to simply wasn't worth it. She would save a day or three of flying, perhaps, but then she would need to choose between spending hours upon hours hunting or consuming rifts, possibly in another dragon's territory, or spending those saved days and more resting, absorbing the ambient magic to restore herself. No, it was better to take it easy. She'd become a bit lazy over the centuries, and she was comfortable with that.

Still, it was good to feel that the concentration of rifts at her destination was as dense as it had been just after the cataclysm. In her own territory she could only take one every so often, lest she ruin the delicate balance of the monster population. Fewer rifts led to fewer monsters, which led to fewer new rifts, and so on. Normally she only consumed the ones that caused her flock trouble, or if a petitioner came from farther afield, which didn't add up to many in a year. Soon she would be able to truly have her fill of rifts for the first time in many years, and enjoy the strength and boundless energy that came with it. It would be fun, something that she'd lacked lately, and she looked forward to it.

But it was the presence of her offspring that drew her. A mystery child whose thread she did not recognize, which flared and faded, on an island she hadn't visited in centuries. She could only presume that an egg of hers had somehow been stolen by some intrepid human from a clutch she'd left with a male somewhere.

Possibly even the one she'd had with Night. Preserved, timeless, it had now hatched. Stranger things had happened, and through magic many things were possible. That might also explain why the thread didn't feel quite right.

However it had happened, she was going to find her child. She was going to take care of it until it could manage the journey home, and then she was going to raise it properly in her own territory until it could claim and hold a territory of its own. She only hoped that being alone without its parents hadn't been too hard on the poor thing. The fact that the whelp had survived these past months without either her or its father to look after it meant that it must be in the clutches of one group of humans or another, and the appropriate response to that would have to be decided once she knew more. She might reduce their cities to ashes and flowing stone, or grant them a boon, or anything in between. It depended entirely on how her child had been treated and how respectful the humans in question were.

She flew until the sun approached the western sea. At that point she descended beneath the lowest clouds. She remembered there being a chain of islands . . . Ah, there! On the horizon was a large island, the volcano that made up much of its bulk still giving off a thin plume of smoke, just as it had the last time she'd come this way, several decades before. She made her way over, and noted with some interest that a sizable human settlement had sprung up on its southern shore. Boats dotted the water and ships sat at anchor, and Embers imagined with amusement how the little creatures must be looking up, gazing with amazement and terror at her magnificence.

Do not worry, little ones, she thought. *You have nothing to fear.* Even if she weren't already on an errand, all the gold and silver and gems on this island couldn't possibly make a difference to her hoard, and then there was the issue of transporting it. It wasn't worth the bother.

She would rest here for a few days. Perhaps she'd find something to eat in the temperate forest that ran from the mountainside to the beaches—she remembered there being some colonies of seals last she'd been here, though the humans might have overhunted them, as they were known to do. And then she would move on, and the humans would be left with a new appreciation for life and tales to tell their young.

Embers circled the fiery mountain slowly until she spotted what she was looking for. Far above the highest trees was an opening in the stone that shouldn't be there, and she praised her own foresight. She'd made it intentionally large when she carved it, in case she returned later and larger. She settled, her talons gripping the ledge she'd made for just that purpose, and folded her wings. Ducking inside, she blew a small flame to light the space. Birds and bats had used it over the centuries, and the floor was thick with their droppings, but that was easily dealt with. She was about to blow a stronger, hotter flame to cleanse the place when she saw something at the back.

Stepping inside to get a better look, she was delighted with what she found. The humans, in their courage and ingenuity, had made it to this cave, and for one purpose. At the back of the cave was a shrine—an effigy of a dragon, possibly herself, standing upon a pedestal with a stone bowl before it. And in the bowl, covered with bat shit and dust and tarnished by time, was a large number of silver coins. An offering to the rulers of the skies, the mightiest creatures of this world, bringers of flame and death and terror, or of peace and prosperity, dependent upon if one showed proper deference or not.

Embers cleansed the place. She was not going to sleep in a cave full of guano. But she was careful to keep her flames cool enough so she wouldn't damage the stone. The silver coins ran together a little, but that was fine. The little altar was undamaged, and that was what mattered.

After appreciating the humans' offering for a while longer, she turned around and settled, her face resting on the ledge. She watched the little ships drift slowly across the water as the sun dipped beneath the horizon, and she enjoyed the scents of the forest below as she drank in the ambient mana. It was strong here, as it always was near volcanoes. It was an altogether pleasant resting place, and she again praised her younger self for making it.

In the direction of the setting sun her child's thread flared. She noted with satisfaction that it was still in exactly the direction she expected, before it faded again.

She would sleep here for a few days. Embers would awaken refreshed and sated, and then she would continue her journey, covering another few hundred miles of the vast sea that separated her from that island of her past. She would continue like this, one day traveling, a few days resting and consuming ambient mana, until she reached the island, a few thousand miles to the southwest.

She would be reunited with her unexpected child. She would find why its thread was so strange. And if any human had harmed so much as a scale on her baby's tail, that island would burn.

Embers liked humans, but sometimes they needed to be reminded of the natural order and their place in it.

About the Author

AvaritiaBona is a proud nerd whose biggest joy in life is to turn tea into words. His stories are about friendship and not being quite right. He lives in Sweden with his wonderful wife, surrounded by supportive friends.

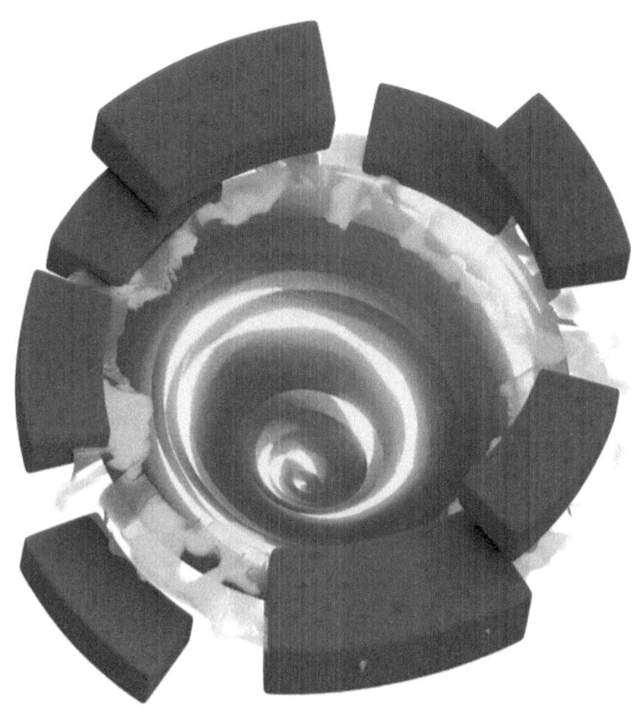

RESPAWN YOUR CURIOSITY

follow us on our socials

podiumentertainment.com

@podiumentertainment

/podiumentertainment

@podium_ent

@podiumentertainment